COMPLINE

Gladys Pagendam

ALSO BY GLADYS PAGENDAM

for children:
Frizzy's Rainbow
Maggo Ribbo
B Bopp Goes Bim Bam Boom
Sit Beside the Gnomon

www.gladys.pagendam.com

First published August 2012 as
an Amazon.com Kindle ebook.

This edition published November 2012.
ISBN 978 0 9874166 0 5

Acknowledgements

This book is dedicated to my family and in particular to my husband, David, who has encouraged me since I first mentioned the idea, many years ago. His belief in my ability to achieve this dream gave me the courage to attempt it. His laughter and tears and enthusiastic feedback, while reading it, helped me go on to refine it. His rigorous editing, demanded my very best, and the delight he has always found in *Compline*, even after multiple readings, gave me hope that others might find it worth the read. David, for all these things, and for designing the front cover, I thank you.

For my children, whose ideas, creativity, passion, and sense of fun was so inspiring it made me want to find my own. *Compline* is an expression of what you ignited in me. You are always in my heart.

For my granddaughters, whose visits brought me out of my solitude and into an awesome, love filled world.

For my readers, Annette and Karen, who bravely gave me honest feedback, *Compline* has benefitted from your input and I from your friendship.

For Jen, who proofread my manuscript and offered many helpful comments. You are phenomenal and your input has been invaluable.

For Maria, Elizabeth and Laura for allowing me to use your names. The characters in this story in no way bear any other resemblance to you three gorgeous women.

And for those who bore with me when I could talk of nothing else but *Compline,* you are legends! Thank you for your patience and for seeing it through to completion with me.

I thank the Emmaus Community for my 'first stone'.

I asked myself
what right have I
to write this book?

It is a medium.

We either do it well
or badly.

All you can do
In the end
is to keep on doing
the best you can
for yourself

and try to keep

unattached

George Harrison, I, Me, Mine: (1980)

Unlikely friends

Kate spat into George Harrison's eye and gave his face a vigorous rub with her hanky.

"We don't want you looking like a scruff now do we, George? You might've died, but down here in the land of the living, you've still got an image to maintain."

She moved on to a framed poster, announcing that Eddie Cochrane would top the bill at the Liverpool Stadium, and ran her finger over the newspaper clipping she had stuck to it, reporting his death a couple of days before the show.

"You topped the bill instead," she said, turning to a photograph of Gene Vincent.

Most of Kate's Mersey Beat memorabilia was arranged around a very large framed black and white poster of The Beatles. "You lot hadn't even found each other yet. You were there, though, Ringo. You played with Rory Storm and the Hurricanes - with their fancy suits and impressive dance moves. Very snazzy!"

"You were still the Silver Beatles," she said, looking first at John Lennon, then at George Harrison and Paul McCartney. "You were still trying to make a name for yourselves. I loved going to the Cavern to see you."

Kate still had her old gramophone and record collection. She put on *Please Please Me*, the Beatles first album, turning it low, then climbed into bed sinking down into her soft downy pillows. Somewhere between the beginning and end of *Love Me Do*, she drifted away to a place where George Harrison was, unexpectedly, waiting for her.

"Is that you, George?" She said hopefully.

"Hya girl."

"Hya!"

"Any idea where we are this time?"

"Probably Australia."

"Australia! Bloody Nora. We don't 'alf get around, don't we. Why Australia?"

"I live in Brisbane now."

"An' I 'ad a place just up the road on Hamilton Island. If I'd known I would've asked yer over."

"I know. I read about it. In fact I followed your life very closely, George."

"Why didn't you get in touch?"

"It would've spoiled things… and when you died… well… anyway, just recently I've thought a lot about you and I was longing to see you and talk to you again."

"Were yer?"

"It's been such a long time, hasn't it? I'm surprised you recognised me, I've grown old."

"Yer still look the same te me, girl."

"And you're still a smooth bugger George." They laughed, becoming comfortable again with each other.

"So! What de yer wanna talk about?"

"Well, I wanted to… you know… get your perspective on things. You always had good things to say in difficult situations."

"Did I? I'm glad I was able to 'elp! So how can I 'elp now?"

"Tell me about dying."

"Arh 'ey girl. That's a bit morbid, isn't it?" They both fell silent before George asked.

"Why?"

"Because I've got cancer and I know you've been through it. I want to know how you coped."

"Oh!" It was a good half-minute before George spoke again. "Well, as I see it, there's death and there's dying. Which one de yer wanna know about?"

"Both."

"Okay. Well - and I can only tell it as I see it. Yer get that don't yer?"

"Of course."

"Well let's take dying then. I coped with that one day at a time just like you're probably doin'. I was lucky 'cos I 'ad a good family who made it easier. As for death, well that's different. It's just a crossin' over really. Part of me looked forward to it. I saw it as a time when all me questions would be answered."

"And were they?"

"Yeah! Sort of!" His face became sad. "Leavin' family was the hardest bit, but by the time yer that sick yer just want it to end… and surprisin'ly, the actual bit where yer die is over before yer know it." George fell silent again before his eyes began to twinkle in that old familiar way, animating his entire face. Kate was aware that he didn't look dead. In fact he looked very much alive. His voice broke into her thoughts. "It's a bit like going te sleep and waking up with a new family. Ye'd be surprised who's here!"

"Is the King there?" Kate's wide-eyed anticipation amused George, and his eyes twinkled even more.

"There's two kings here, girl - one who sings and one who rocks." Ablaze with curiosity at this unexpected answer, Kate would have questioned George further but she felt something clawing at her. It was something far greater than herself and it was snatching her away from George.

"Ooah!" She cried unsuccessfully trying to grab hold of her old friend, who had no substance. She began to lose sight of him. He was fading into nothingness, while she…well, she was falling back down…down…down… into her wrecked body.

"Mum," Emily was saying. "Are you awake?"

"I am now," Kate was disorientated and disappointed, and her head was still elsewhere… with George. She complained grumpily. "What did you wake me up for?"

"You told me to. Anyway you looked weird. Your eyes were wide open and you were saying things. It freaked me out. Are you okay?"

3

"Of course I am. Stop being a fusspot. Go away and shut the door!"

"You said to wake you up. You said you wanted to shop before the girls arrive."

"What time is it?"

"Two o'clock."

"They're not coming until four. Wake me up at three." Emily shut the door, shaking her head at her mother's crossness. Kate waited a few seconds and then whispered. "Are you still there, George?"

Three Sisters

"I can get some," Maria shouted so as to be heard above the thrum of traffic through the open car window. Beth took her ear-buds out in the middle of a Madonna song and, holding down bobbed hair that was whipping in the wind, asked:

"What sort?"

"Skunk. He says it's one of the better strains. I can get enough to last a couple of weeks. I could have got a plant but it's too risky."

"I could keep it at my place," Beth volunteered.

"No!" There was no hesitation in Maria's response. The three students Beth shared a house with may well be trustworthy, but was Beth? Besides, their place was a thoroughfare with all the comings and goings, and partying that went on there. Someone might find it and blow the whistle, or even worse, want some. "We agreed the fewer people involved the better."

"Did you get any?" Beth shouted over her shoulder to Laura who was still in uniform.

"What? Sorry! Can't hear!"

"Dope!" Beth repeated. "Did you get any?" She had turned her head as far round as possible so Laura could lip read.

"No! I told you how I feel about that."

"Phf! You're becoming so…blah, Laura." Laura didn't hear what Beth said but her body language was loud and clear.

"I'm a police-officer. I've got my job to think about. You shouldn't even be talking to me about acquiring it. Maria, can we have the window shut? I can't hear myself think back here."

"The air con isn't working. We'll all suffocate."

"What?"

"How about I close it for a minute?" Maria pressed the button and the window slid up. "So you still think it's a bad idea, do you?"

"When you have to hide what you do, you can usually guarantee it's a bad idea." Laura's conscience-pricking logic did not go down well with Beth, who argued the point.

"But it's for a good cause. I think it's okay to want to minimise Nan's pain. That's humane!"

"It doesn't matter what you think. The law's the law and using drugs for any reason is illegal."

"And that's exactly why people break the law. It's complex and your argument is simplistic. It's not that black and white, Laura."

"I'm not getting into colour coding right and wrong because no matter what you say, the law's still the law. Anyway, if you've got some you'll have to stash it somewhere Mum and Uncle Matt won't think of looking."

"Where?" Maria asked. Nobody answered. Beth swung her head around so Laura could lip read.

"Come on, Laura! At least tell us where not to hide it. Where do cops always look?"

"It's not the cops you need to worry about. It's Mum and Uncle Matt."

"We could hide it in Nan's copy of your PhD," Beth suggested, turning to Maria. "Nobody reads that because they can't understand it."

Maria, used to Beth's lack of tact, let her sister's bluntness slide right over her head. Besides, it was true. Scientific academic parlance, of the kind she used, was way beyond the comprehension of most people.

"We could hide it in the Beatles Anthology." Maria and Laura laughed, but Maria became thoughtful, then said.

"You know, that's not a bad idea."

"Oh...you're kidding, right? I was kidding," said Beth.

"No! Think about it! Mum and Uncle Matt would never look there. You know how they feel about Nan and the Beatles."

"I don't know why they're like that. I wish I'd been young in the sixties." Beth had read Nan's Beatles Anthology recently and a retro wardrobe was gradually replacing her usual clothes.

"Me too!" Maria agreed. "I can't understand why Mum and Matthew cringe at the mention of the sixties. I think Nan must have adopted them!"

"I bet they were born straight, not all curled up in a foetal position, like proper babies." said Beth. Her sisters laughed.

"Are we agreed then?" Asked Maria. "Shall we hide it in the Beatles Anthology?"

"No, Nan opens it too often. I reckon we should divvy it up, when we get it, and stash it in several different places. That way, if Mum or Uncle Matt find any of it, they won't find all of it."

"Beth, you do realise we don't actually have any yet, so it's all hypothetical?" Beth ignored Laura. Suddenly her face lit up.

"The Liverpool wall," she blurted. "We could tape small packets of it to the back of Nan's Beatles memorabilia."

"If we ever get any," interrupted Laura, "which is highly unlikely because we've been talking about it ever since Nan first got diagnosed."

"Yes, but it was never intended for the early days. It was always going to be for when she's in unbearable pain," said Beth.

"Which she isn't, is she? And, anyway, isn't that what doctors are for?"

"We know that." Hostility was creeping into Beth's voice. "We're not stupid, Laura. You know as well as I do it's just for towards the end… in case she wants to be at home."

"Which we all know she does," said Maria. "The Liverpool wall's a great idea. I'll only be getting a small amount to start off with. Just to see how things go."

Tea Ceremony

Maria, Beth and Laura were approaching the T-junction at the top of Nan's street when they caught sight of her coming out of the corner store.

"Stop!" Beth cried. Maria hit the brake. Nan was leaning on her walking stick with one hand and carrying a green recycling bag in the other. She was clearly labouring.

"We should pick her up," Maria said, pulling into the kerb.

"She'll say no," Beth said. "Independent old bugger."

"Beth!" Maria protested.

"What? It's a term of endearment."

"Hi Nan," Laura shouted, hopping out. "Want a lift?"

"Oh! There you are!" Nan always greeted you as if she had been looking out for you. "I'm just on my way home. Your Mum's there and I won't be far behind you, only I need the exercise."

"She probably needed to get away from Mum," Beth said.

"I'll walk with you Nan," Laura said slamming the car door. As Maria edged away from the kerb she saw in the mirror that Nan was waving the car away with her handkerchief just like she used to wave them off to school. Oh Nan, she thought as tears blurred her vision. It's not fair.

Maria swung the car into Nan's driveway and found Emily, their mother, in the garden with a small spade. This was a new experience for her daughters. Emily was a senior administrator at the local university, which was a job that was more academic than practical. It was true that she must have looked after her daughters in early childhood, so she must have had to get to grips with nappies and school lunches, but the girls could not remember much about those years. Once they had all moved in with their grandmother, Nan had attended to all the practical needs of the family.

As for their father, well, the girls had a minimal relationship with him. In fact he had almost become a virtual presence in their lives, keeping in touch mostly on Facebook. They saw him at the odd wedding or funeral, but Skype was the nearest they usually got to seeing him in the flesh. This left them with rather pixelated memories of him.

"What are you doing Mum?" Beth asked getting out of Maria's metallic pink Hyundai.

"I'm pretending to garden but really I'm just checking to see if your Nan's on her way back. She insists on going out each day. I don't think she should. It's too much for her."

"She's not the type to sit at home knitting like a good little granny, Mum."

"I know that Beth. It doesn't stop me worrying, though."

"I suppose not. But you know she'd die of boredom sitting in an armchair all day, so stop worrying about her and let's go in and have a cup of tea."

"Oh look, there she is now! Bugger! It's the police again."

"What do you mean, again?"

"She walked too far the other day and ended up too tired to walk back. A police car was passing and she flagged it down. She told them about Laura being in the police force and they gave her a lift home."

"Chill Mum! It's Laura. We picked her up from work on the way here, so she's still in uniform."

Diminutive Beth stepped across the threshold and breathed deeply of the house she and her sisters had called home during their growing years. Furniture polish... and mint, she thought. Nan always kept a vase of mint in the living room and kitchen because it was supposed to keep ants away. It didn't work. In fact they came in droves because of all the baking she did – or used to do when she looked after them all.

"Mm! Something smells good!"

"Leg of lamb! Nan left me looking after it." Emily saw the looks that passed between her daughters. "I can cook," she said indignantly.

Nan tended to cook roasts when they all congregated. She was a Scouser at heart and to a Scouser, a roast dinner was the most welcoming meal you could offer, if it were affordable. Otherwise you got Scouse, the dish of beef, carrots, potatoes and onion, so popular in Liverpool that it had provided the good citizens of the city with a nickname. Nan was proud of being a Scouser because The Beatles were Scousers too.

While Beth savoured the smells that, to her grandmother, symbolised loving hugely, Maria, being the more visual one, looked for what was new in Nan's home. Since childhood she had a way of zooming in on anything that had not been there when she went to school that morning – like the bright red wooden clogs she had once found on the bedside table she shared with Beth. How Maria had loved them and tried to squash her feet into them. Beth had been the one to acquire them though, because she was the only one with feet dainty enough to fit into them. Nan would put on an old Heidi movie starring Shirley Temple, and Beth would clog dance with the child star as they both sang, *Have you seen my new shoes, they are made out of wood*, which was all she could now remember of the song.

Maria put the kettle on and got out a variety of 'tiny tea-pots'. These were a good example of the kind of whimsical bric-a-brac Nan filled her home with. She put a variety of herbal teabags in a bowl and picked a handful of fresh mint leaves for her own special china teapot and just as the kettle boiled, Laura and Nan arrived home. Maria added two more tiny teapots to the tray. Each teapot was different and pretty and had been fought over when Nan first brought it home years ago. Once, there had been tiny teacups to go with the teapots but they all liked a good-sized cup of tea these days. One of these pots would provide one perfect cup of tea with that special taste of childhood. Even though the teapots were made of fragile china, they had been allowed to use them from the time they were small, learning not to bash them down on the table, but to set them down gently so they would not break. A few of them had, of course.

"Don't worry," Nan would say. "I'll buy a new one," and, true to her word, a few days or weeks later, there it would be. Nan always said, "If you've got something nice, use it and feel the joy. If it gets broken, well, it's time to buy something else nice."

"So! What's going on?" Beth asked now they were sipping. No one would mention the reason they were all there. Over the course of the weekend they would talk about that behind closed doors, in various permutations of twos and threes.

"I'm officially on long service leave," Emily announced. "So I'm going to stay with Nan for a while." There was a communal gasp and everyone looked at Nan for evidence of how *she* felt about this. She avoided their eyes. To cover the uncomfortable silence Beth gave her 'diplomatic' opinion on the matter.

"Well that'll last all of five minutes!" She was the only one who could get away with stating the obvious and her forthrightness always provided a forum for the truth to be acknowledged and discussed.

"I know," said their mother. "But Nan and I have talked about it. We're going to give it a try until... well, we'll see how it goes. We're going to try to make it work. I won't be stressed with work, so it will be good for us to have some quality mother/daughter time together." Quality mother/daughter time was a concept not much experienced amongst the women of their family.

"It's great Mum," Maria smiled. "Isn't it Nan?" Each of them wondered whether that flicker of doubt in Maria's eyes was something they had imagined. Nan adeptly shifted their focus to the cooking.

"Has anyone checked the lamb?"

"It was alright a quarter of an hour ago. It's browning nicely," said Emily.

"Can I help with dinner, Nan?" Laura offered.

"Ask your Mother! She's cooking."

"Am I? I thought you were."

"You're here to help, aren't you, so you might as well get stuck in." Nan didn't wait for Emily to reply. "Well now, that cuppa was just the thing." Turning to the girls she patted the nearest of them, Beth, on the shoulder. "Why don't you all go and settle in? If anyone has time, the table needs setting."

"Okay. Mum, sing out if you want help," said Beth, who picked up her small rucksack, and went off, chattering to Maria, down the hall to her room.

"You look tall in your uniform," Emily said to her youngest daughter. "I can't quite get used to you being in the police-force."

"I know - you tell me that every time you see me wearing it," Laura replied, a little caustically. Laura was the youngest of the sisters and, a year ago, at the age of twenty-four, she had dumped her loser partner of three years. Soon after, she left her job as a kindergarten assistant to join the police academy. One day she hoped to be a detective.

The family had been unprepared for how much Laura would change as she settled into her new profession. She had always been compliant so they were surprised when she began to show signs of a mettle they never knew she had, evidenced by her resistance to family pressures. She had, overnight, it seemed to her family, become the most hard to read of them all. Her sisters would have been astonished, for example, to know that she had gone further than making initial enquiries about acquiring cannabis. An opportunity had presented itself and she had taken it, though she was still struggling with whether she should hand it over. On the one hand, she told herself, Sherlock had been a bit partial to opium and it didn't seem to cloud his judgement, so where was the harm? On the other hand, she reasoned, the law is the law and you just don't take it into your own hands.

"Oh come on here and give me a hug," Emily said, attempting to embrace her daughter. "You're my baby. Nothing changes that." Laura's body language remained unresponsive, and Emily's words scratched at existing wounds.

"I haven't been your baby for a long time. I'm grown up Mum. I deal with more real life in one week than some people experience in their entire lifetime."

"I know and it's precisely what I can't get used to," responded Emily, feeling the ice In Laura's tone and putting some distance between them.

Emily noticed Nan was back in the kitchen, despite having handed over the cook's apron to her, and she acknowledged that her mother would find it hard to relinquish the running of her home to her. Nan had thought long and hard about it herself and knew she would have to - she even wanted to, but it was hard breaking the habits of a lifetime, and when she was busy she wasn't thinking about what lay before her. Nevertheless, it had become blatantly obvious to her that it was time the relationships in her family were set right. So, when Emily asked what she was doing, Nan said she had only been putting the cups in the dishwasher, and went in search of her granddaughters again.

Mothers and Daughters

"Have you got everything you need?"

"We're fine Nan," Laura said. "If not, we'll help ourselves."

Of course they will, Nan thought. *Stupid question! They've explored the contents of every cupboard, drawer, nook and cranny of the entire house many times over.*

Laura and Beth shared a bedroom that had been theirs since Nan separated Beth and Maria, aged twelve and eight, because they had begun to bicker a lot. Maria's bedroom was further down the corridor at the back of the house, overlooking the garden.

Nan had put Emily in the downstairs room, usually referred to as 'the crypt', because it put distance between mother and daughter, acknowledging, if she were honest, that she, and probably Emily too, would prefer this. Anyway, downstairs had been Emily's 'pad' since she had been in her teens, because her mother thought having her own room might help her feel a bit more independent. It had worked then, so how was she to know it would not work now? But earlier, Emily had been shocked by the intensity of her own feelings as she sadly made her way downstairs. Dormant pain came flooding back and sat heavy in her chest like a great crushing knot where her heart usually was.

Beth and Laura had managed to turn their bedroom upside down in the two minutes it took Emily and Nan to sort out who was wearing the apron. Nan, hovering on the threshold, thought of the happiness these two darlings had brought her over the years, and hoped that their current disagreements would never become so great that they would forget the love they had shared in the past, when they had been the best of friends. But now, compliant Laura was learning to think for herself, and headstrong Beth, who had always managed to bend Laura to her will, was struggling to adjust to the change. As a police cadet, Laura was learning alternative ways of evaluating and responding to others. She had become assertive, and even if Beth was finding this hard, her grandmother was glad to see it. *If only Doug could see them*, Nan thought. *He'd be so proud.*

Grandpa Doug had always said their home was built like a ship - long and narrow with all rooms branching off the central corridor that stretched from the front, to the back of the house. When they had arrived in Brisbane as Ten Pound Poms, Nan and Grandpa Doug had bought the house because of its proximity to transport and good schools for Emily and Matthew. It had once been a small house, but Doug had extended it three times so it served not only their living needs, but also their hobbies. Beside the living/dining room there were five bedrooms upstairs, two of which used to be a veranda overlooking the garden. Matt used to sleep in one of these back rooms at the far end of the house. His room was now Maria's. The other room was identical and had become Grandpa Doug's art studio.

Nan liked to sew in Grandpa Doug's studio because the walls were crammed with his paintings. She said it helped her remember him because, at times, the memories grew dim, and most of the paintings were of places they had visited together. It had been difficult for Nan to accept his death because he had been drowned and there had been no body and so no closure. He just sailed out into Moreton Bay, one day, in the wooden boat he had lovingly designed and crafted, and never came back. Only the upturned boat had been found.

Nan found Maria unpacking.

"How are you doing, love?" She asked.

"I'm okay Nan. More to the point how are you?"

"Not too bad, love" she said. It was the standard Scouser's reply. It was a reply that warned of a subject off limits. It was the liar's reply. "I'm all the better for seeing you girls," she said brightening. "It's lovely of you to come and see your old Nan."

"Well it's not often we can all get here together, Nan. But it just seemed to work out this time. How did the radiation go?" Maria asked.

"Oh alright. I feel as if I've got sunstroke and I get these funny pains that take me by surprise. They come and go! I don't have them all the time. You haven't brought much."

"No, well I thought I wouldn't bother bringing my entire wardrobe since we're just here for the weekend." Nan laughed at Maria's attempt at humour but she knew Maria was checking her out as she chatted. Maria did not fail to notice Nan's huge green eyes had sunk into purple, puffy rings. The skin that had always been so flawless and soft seemed bloated, and yet still managed to hang loose on her gaunt face, around which, wispy strands of salt and pepper hair fell. Before Nan could notice the tears that welled up into her eyes, Maria turned to fluff up a pillow, sniffing and blinking fiercely. Then she turned to her again and asked.

"Are you taking care of yourself, Nan?"

"Of course I am. What a question? Don't you worry about me, luv. You worry about yourself. You've got all your life ahead of you. So, tell me, how's the job?"

"Oh you know. Busy."

"How's the love life then?" This was asked with a smile full of anticipation.

"Oh you know! I've got my whole life ahead of me. You don't need to worry about me. You just worry about yourself." It was perfect mimicry and Nan rippled with laughter. She gripped Maria's chin just as she used to when Maria was little, and looked her in the eye.

"You're getting too clever by far, my girl, but just because you're a Doctor of Science doesn't mean you can fool me. Now tell your old Nan about him?"

"There's nothing to tell, Nan," she replied truthfully. "Women have more options these days… and more purpose.

My research is valuable and I feel fulfilled. I'm independent and I like it that way. Relationships can ruin women's lives."

"But, what about children?"

"I'm not the type to have children and then dump them in a day care centre. Nor am I the type to give up my work to look after them."

"But you could hire a nanny. Your job pays well."

"Like I said, Nan. There's no one, so it's not an issue. If it ever becomes an issue you'll be the first to know, I promise. Anyway, the world's not like it used to be when you were young. Girls don't marry the boy next door. They marry their colleagues or someone from another country, or even one of their girl-friends."

"I didn't marry the boy next door," Nan objected. "I nearly married a boy a few streets away though." Maria had touched on a memory that had triggered one of Nan's stories. However, Maria had never been able to pin her down to a detailed account, so she was keen with interest.

"Who was he? Tell me about him, Nan."

"I wrote it down like you asked me to." Maria managed to look both astonished and thrilled at the same time.

"I didn't think you would," she confessed.

"A few people have suggested that I should write my stories down, but I never took them seriously. To be honest, I couldn't imagine who on earth would want to read them. But I can understand why *you* would. It's part of your history, after all."

"I think your life's fascinating, Nan – Beth and Laura do too. I can't believe you wrote it down. Where is it?"

"I'll give it to you later." Nan lifted her hand to pat her granddaughter's face. For a moment she glimpsed the sweet child with the radiant, enthusiastic eyes that had glittered with interest when Nan told her stories in the past. Her granddaughters had filled her life with so much love. It was true that she and Emily might not have an ideal relationship, but she was grateful to her daughter for having shared these three incredible girls with her. "You know, I'm surprised how much I'm enjoying writing it down. It was a very good idea of yours - and very therapeutic. It's helping me come to terms with the here-and-now. When you look back, you think times were hard, but one day, you realise those hard times were the best times of your life."

"I'm so glad, Nan," Maria said, fighting back tears again.

"Can someone set the table?" Emily called.

"What time's Uncle Matt coming, Nan?"

"Soon." Matthew was Nan's only son, a pretty cool uncle, and a hardworking eligible bachelor. He had worked his way up the corporate ladder quickly, because he was not fixated on girls, booze, or drugs but, rather, on his plan to become an actuary, with his own consultancy. He was, at heart, a mathematician. He did a PhD in some sort of incomprehensible specialty, and his office was decorated with impossible calculations that spilled off white-boards, onto walls, across doors and around corners, ending somewhere that undoubtedly got him into trouble with cleaners. But Matthew had a charismatic smile that could probably bewitch Satan and, at such times, he used it to his advantage. After his post-doc year he joined a multi-national insurance company and was now managing an entire floor of their eleven-story office block. He wasn't far from going solo. Matthew's voice broke into Nan's thoughts.

"Come on and kiss me Kate!" Matt's arms were stretched wide, ready to embrace his mother. He began making this theatrical entrance after his father went missing because he overheard someone who had recently been bereaved, telling a friend that nobody hugged her any more. Also, one of Matthew's female colleagues confided in him at a Christmas party, that her husband had left her after thirty years of marriage, and that sometimes she would go for a massage just so she could feel someone touch her. Matt thought that was the saddest thing he had ever heard, and he began the 'come-on-and-kiss-me-Kate' ritual so his mother would sometimes feel someone's arms around her. Not that she was really short of hugs. Not with her three grand daughters coming and going.

Matt used to pick up Nan and swing her around when he hugged her, much to everyone's delight and Nan's consternation. She would turn puce, and even though she protested vehemently, everyone knew Nan loved the fuss. That had stopped, though, when, one day, Matthew had hurt her ribs and he realised that his mother was not indestructible.

"Nice timing." Nan said, leaving Maria so as not to miss the warmth of Matthew's embrace. She heard Nan say as she went down the hall: "Isn't it great. We're all together again."

Break Up

Emily's leg of lamb was a triumph, and the appreciation she received did much to chase away the cloud that had settled on her earlier. Nan suggested a game of charades afterwards, but she soon grew tired and toddled off to bed. Maria excused herself soon after, when Nan had returned from the bathroom and had said goodnight. She wanted to catch her before she went to asleep.

"Where's your story? I'd like to read it tonight."

"It's there on my desk. The blue folder."

"Thanks." Maria kissed her grandmother's cheek, which, despite her age, was still soft. Returning to the kitchen she made herself a hot chocolate, deciding to make an early night of it, since Emily was clearing the table and Matthew was stacking the dishwasher before going home. Laura and Beth were just beginning a game of Scrabble.

"Goodnight night owls." Maria said. Beth quickly responded with a smirk.

"Goodnight morning person."

"Goodnight." Maria gave Matthew a brief hug.

"Night night," he replied, kissing her cheek.

"Night Mum," she said, giving her mother a smile, though her mother would have preferred a hug. Emily was aware that she and her girls had never been demonstrative and, on impulse, decided to change that. She strode forward and gave her daughter a kiss.

"Good night love. Sleep well."

Maria quickly got into her pyjamas and without brushing her long dark glossy hair, or cleaning her teeth for the usual three minutes, quickly climbed into bed. She loved this room where nothing had changed since she was a child, and where her bed was still draped with the Holly Hobbie quilt Nan had made for her when she had started school.

Pulling the two pillows from behind her, and plumping them up, Maria repositioned them until she was comfortable. Then she did a little wriggle squirming down the bed a bit, and finally smiled.

Maria hoped Nan's writing would fill out some of the mysterious gaps in her grandmother's stories, as well as clarify which of her stories about the Beatles, and her life as a nun, were true, and which were not. She could scarcely believe Nan had written so much. She would add the pages to her own, for Maria liked to write herself and had quite a sizeable chunk of Nan's life already down on paper. She didn't really know why. It just seemed important because somehow, Nan's story overlapped her own. Without Nan's story, her own story was incomplete. She opened the folder and began to read.

Ridiculous as it may sound, the thing that most bothered me, the night I broke up with Andy, was the awful sucking noise my legs made every time I got up off the vinyl couch. I was wearing a mini skirt, which meant there was nothing between my legs and the couch, so somehow they became glued together. Perhaps I wouldn't have noticed it only I got up and sat down so many times. I suppose that was nerves. In the end I decided to stand. That way I could make it short and sweet and then get away quickly.

"Hello luv." Andy's Mum always showed me into the parlour with a smile, which was reassuring, because she was very hard to read. I noticed her giving my skirt the once over and I tried to pull it down. Mum had already had a go at me about it saying:

"It barely covers yer arse!"

Andy's family was a bit of a mystery to me. Even though Andy often talked about us getting married, I'd never been invited into their kitchen, not even for a cup of tea. With my Mum it was: 'You bring yer mates 'ome here, so I can 'ave a look at who yer knockin' 'round with.' Once a friend had passed muster, they were in, and when I say in, I meant allowed into the kitchen... and if they happened to be there at mealtimes, they were just treated like one of the family and expected to sit down to dinner, then lick the plate clean like the rest of us. I'd been visiting Andy's almost every week for a year and I hadn't a clue what Andy's family was like at home! I never got beyond the parlour. That would be the first room on the right as you went through the front door into the lobby.

I supposed the rest of the house wasn't much different from all the other houses in the Liverpool suburb of Everton. They probably had a back yard like ours, where a metal bath hung against a whitewashed brick wall. The lavatory would almost certainly be at the bottom of the yard near the wooden door to the back jigger, but I bet Andy's Mum never had to scarper into the jigger when the rent-man knocked, like my Mum did. This only happened when my mother had spent the rent on other more urgent necessities like food, which happened occasionally, mostly in the winter when Dad was snowed off work and Mum had to lay out extra on coal to keep us from freezing to death.

In Flint Street, Mum and Dad used the parlour as a bedroom because, with six kids and only three bedrooms, we were overcrowded. I could never imagine Andy's Mum sleeping in the parlour where I was waiting. It was a lovely room with its turquoise blue patterned carpet that was gaudy with golden swirls. One really nice feature of the room was the cream coloured tiled fireplace that was always set but never lit. Andy's Mum had lovely china ornaments arranged on top of it. My Mum used to put her false teeth on top of ours.

Andy took so long that I ended up sitting down again and I thought, damn you Andy for not putting a bloody move on. I fiddled so much with the ends of my nails that I broke a couple of them, so then I fiddled with my bracelet instead. Eventually there was movement outside the parlour, but it was only Colin, Andy's brother.

'He's not keepin' yer waitin' again is he Kate? He's got no idea how to treat a girl. I'm goin' dancin' at the Locarno. Bugger 'im! Come with us!'

'Get lost, Casanova!' I said, throwing a cushion at him while trying to keep my face straight. 'You're too young for me.' He caught the cushion with graceful ease and sent it speeding back.

23

'You're the same age as me,' he argued.

'Yes, but I like me men shavin'.'

Arh 'ay! I've got a few whiskers,' he protested, closing the door behind him. I heard his voice at the foot of the stairs.

'Hey Andy! Kate said to tell yer she's fed up waitin' and she's cumin' te the dance with me.' The front door slammed behind him. By the sound of it Andy came down the stairs two at a time and, within seconds, he was in the street, and I was looking out of the window, startled to see him half shaved and wielding a razor. He was looking up and down the street for me. Finally he noticed me in the parlour window, but I'd had enough time to observe him with his feathers ruffled. He was barefoot, had shaving cream down the left side of his face, and his shirt wasn't tucked in. I'd never seen this Andy before. This Andy was extremely appealing, homely and… well, sexy. Spotting me in the window, Andy looked relieved and leapt over the doorstep into the lobby where I met him.

'Did you really think I'd go off in a huff with your brother?' He didn't answer. It struck me that Andy often didn't answer my questions.

'I'm sorry to drop in without warning, Andy, but I've got something important to tell you. Go and finish getting ready. I'll tell you then.' I could see he was wondering what the matter was but it didn't stop him from gripping my upper arm with the hand that wasn't holding a razor, and stooping to kiss me. I struggled to resist, blocking him with my hand.

'Hey! I'm not letting a half-shaved nutcase with a razor kiss me.' I smiled.

'Okay.' He paused for a moment and then turned to leave. 'I won't be a tick.' He halted at the door turning to me again. 'What did you want to talk to me about?'

'I'm not telling the nutcase with the razor anything. I'll tell Andy when he gets here.'

Maria closed the folder. She lay back on her pillow feeling disappointed. Nan had revealed a lot but she still had not written about the actual break up with Andy and that was the bit she really wanted to know about. *Oh well,* Maria thought. *Nan didn't really tell the story I expected, but the background stuff, about when she was a teenager, does bring it all alive.* Maria had often wondered what 1960s Liverpool was like and had sourced photos on-line in order to better understand her grandmother and the part her roots had played in forging Maria's own identity. The photos were great, but they only revealed so much.

Maria put the writing on her bedside table and padded along to Nan's room. She heard noises coming from inside and, realising Nan was not sleeping, knocked on the door. That brought Nan to see who it was.

"I'm looking for something," she explained, going back to the task of searching through the contents of a trunk full of junk that she kept at the bottom of her bed.

"Can't you sleep?" Maria asked.

"I'm too excited to sleep." Nan's eyes were brilliant.

"Why? What's happened?"

"I'm trying to find one of my old diaries."

"Why?" Maria asked.

"Because I wrote in it about meeting George Harrison on a bus. He sat next to me and we had a good old gab."

"You should be resting. Why don't I help you to look for it tomorrow? Shall I make you some hot chocolate?" She felt Nan's forehead, but it felt normal – a little cool if anything. "Here put this shawl around you. You don't want to catch a chill."

"Hot chocolate would be lovely, dear. The thing is, I want to find the diary now. Only memory's so fleeting, and I'm afraid I won't be able to remember what I was looking for tomorrow. The annoying thing is I remember things I'd rather forget. Don't you think it's funny the way we can't control what we remember? I'm talking about the way a treasured memory can be gone for years, lost in a fog, or in a whirlwind of busyness and then, one day, there it is at the forefront of your mind. Tonight, I remembered meeting George on the bus. I especially remembered why I wrote it down all those

25

years ago - it was to capture it forever, because I wanted to think about it every single day. But after I wrote it down I forgot about it anyway. I want to find it for you because I think you'd be interested."

"Go for it, then, Nan. I won't be long." Maria closed the door and left Nan to her search.

Vocation

Nan was sitting up in bed when Maria returned with hot drinks.

"I found it. It's in that diary on my desk."

"Move over," Maria said. "I'll have my cuppa with you, and I'll leave the diary for another day." Nan fluffed up the pillows and Maria climbed in. "I've been reading about Andy and where you lived when you were growing up. You write well, Nan."

"In our day, schools prepared you for very ordinary jobs. We got a good grounding in reading, writing and arithmetic and that was about it because, let's face it, most of us were factory fodder. But I was lucky because my teacher encouraged me to go to commercial college so I could become a secretary. That diary over there was written not long before I went into the convent while I was still working as a shorthand typist."

"And you've still got it?"

"Yes. I'm surprised my mother didn't chuck it out, but I found it again when I left the convent. It was a good idea of yours to get me writing again because it makes me feel happy, and it takes my mind off the fact that I'm..." Nan fell silent. Maria guessed Nan didn't want to talk about her illness, so she moved the conversation forward in another direction.

"Do you mind me asking what happened with Andy when you told him you were going into a convent?"

"He was terribly shocked."

"He must have had an idea you were thinking about it, though."

"No, he didn't. I'd never mentioned it. I wasn't sure I would definitely become a nun. I honestly never believed they would take me, and even if they did decide I could enter the Novitiate, I thought there was plenty of time because you couldn't become a novice until you were eighteen. I did love Andy very much, in my immature way, but then, out of the blue, the nuns told me they'd applied for a special dispensation so I could enter the novitiate before I was eighteen and a whole new world of possibilities opened up to me. They applied for my early entry to the Novitiate because they thought I was so much more mature than their usual novices. The nuns considered me street-wise and old for my age. I suppose it would be true to say that I more or less went from the Cavern to the convent."

"How did they come to the conclusion that you were mature?"

"Well, I'd had a couple of jobs you see. Also, I used to tell them about going to dances to see all the new groups that were becoming famous around that time: Gerry and the Pacemakers, Screaming Lord Sutch – bands like that. I used to tell them all about my friends and about Andy and I suppose they thought I was very grown up compared to most novices. Maybe they thought if they brought it to a head it would force a choice… and it did. When it came to the crunch, I chose the convent."

"Did the nuns teach at your school?" Asked Maria, wanting to know where the idea of becoming a nun had come from since nobody she knew had ever considered it.

"Good Lord, no. There was only one nun in my school. She was the headmistress and she was horrible. I'd never have gone into her convent."

"So what made you want to be a nun if the only nun you knew was horrible?"

"I read stories about saints who were nuns, and…well, I loved God very much. One day, I ran all the way down to our local church just to get away from the bickering at home. Mum was on the warpath and I used to go to church just to get some peace and quiet and to hear myself think. There was a community of Jesuits at our church, so priests were always around. One of them stopped to talk to me that day and asked me what was up. Well what could I say? I mean I couldn't tell him about Mum because one of the Ten Commandments is honour your father and your mother. I knew I wouldn't come out of it well. Priests had a way of turning things around so that kids ended up in the wrong, and then you'd just go away swamped with guilt. So I told him I wanted to be a nun. It just came out. I was as surprised as the priest. It wasn't that I hadn't thought of it before. I had – lots of times, but it was just a daydream until then. That day, it was as if the thought made a gigantic leap from the back of my mind to the front, and the next obvious step was to make it happen.

I think that priest must have had a job in the Gestapo during the war, because he interrogated me rigorously for quite a while. He was probably trying to understand my motives because he kept asking me why?

'I just do.' I said. 'I've been thinkin' about it for a while.' It mustn't've been the right answer because then he said:

'Lots of people think about it. What's so special about you?'

'I dunno. I luv God.'

'So do lots of people.'

'Well I luv 'im more.' He gave me a dubious look.

'How on earth could you possibly know that? You've got no idea how much others love Him.'

'Yer, but I know 'ow much I luv 'im...' I said, '...an' I don't see anyone else queuing up to enter a convent so they can devote their lives to 'im.' He looked at me for a long time with a bit of a smirk on his face. In the end he broke the silence and I was glad because I really needed to blink. Then he said.

'What about a vocation? People in the religious life are usually called to it. Do you have a calling?'

'Well, God never shouted down my ear, if that's what you mean. I never 'ad a midnight visitation or saw a burnin' bush or anythin' dramatic like that. It's 'ard to explain. I've just sort of 'ad a sense that it was an option for me.' I must

29

have said something right because after that he stopped interrogating me. The next time I saw him he told me he'd set up a meeting with some nuns and that's how I started visiting them. The priest took me the first time. I went to see them often, on my own, after that.

You would have thought I was royalty the way they treated me, giving me tea in the parlour in bone china cups that were so fine you could nearly see through them. In our house you were lucky to get a chipped mug with a handle on. The milk and sugar were in genuine silverware. The only place I had ever seen the likes was in the Kardomah Cafe's ground floor tearooms, where they had silver service waitresses all dressed in black with lovely starched white aprons and hats. I'd had a three-week holiday job clearing tables in their serve-yourself café in the basement, where they only had muggen cups for those who were not so flush.

I liked going to see the nuns because they would ask what I'd been up to and I would tell them which Liverpool pop idol had a record in the charts that week, or which dance I'd been to that weekend, or whether I'd seen Andy. What was nice about the nuns was they actually wanted to know about me, unlike most of the adults I knew, who just assumed you were always up to no good when you went out dancing.

All the nuns in the Liverpool convent were Irish and some of them would wander into the parlour when I visited. They showed me a postcard of the boarding school the nuns owned in Ireland, with the Novitiate built alongside it. To me it was as posh as Buckingham Palace and when they told me that they had convents in France, Spain, Italy, Malaya, Singapore and elsewhere – places that all seemed very remote, romantic and exotic to me - well it was enticing. If I became a nun I could end up anywhere. If I stayed in Liverpool I would end up being Andy's wife, with only the odd fishing day to look forward to. Well, you can see the appeal, can't you?

I was only the second English girl to enter the order's Novitiate. The other one was already there, but then she made her vows and moved off into a proper community. We did have two months together, though. We both left eventually.

The nuns thought it strange that I would go to the Cavern in my lunch-hour from work, in order to get warm in the winter. I didn't realise how unusual I must have seemed to them, until I entered the Novitiate and saw how removed convent life was from what nun's used to call 'the world outside'. I must have been such a curiosity, with my bucket-bag covered in graffiti bearing the names of John, Paul, George and Ringo. I know stories about me must have reached the Irish convents because, when I did enter the Novitiate, the girls in the boarding school used to call me Sister Beatle, probably because I used to have my hair in a Beatles cut.

One November day when I had been seventeen for three months, Reverend Mother told me I could enter the convent in February."

"So what did Andy say?" Interrupted Maria

He asked me not to. When I crossed his path one day after I had left the convent, he was happily married and I was glad for him. Maria glanced at her watch.

"It's half past eleven." She hopped out of bed to retrieve Nan's glasses from the floor. "We'd better get some sleep. You might manage sleep deprivation well, but I need the full eight hours."

Generations Collide

"Morning Nan," Maria said as she entered the kitchen late the following morning.

"Morning."

Maria put the kettle on for tea and popped some bread in the toaster. Carrying her breakfast to the table she sat down near Nan, who was doing a crossword.

"What was it like in the convent, Nan?" Nan looked up, her eyes narrowing for a moment with the concentration of trying to see into the distant past.

"It was amazing. Some things took me by surprise. For example, I remember being astonished by the rule of silence. I didn't expect that - especially the Grand Silence."

"What's that...?"

"The rule says sisters are not allowed to speak from when the bell rings for Compline - that's evening prayers - until after Matins, Matins being the first prayers of the morning. There was a rule of silence during the day, too, but it was not so rigorously enforced as the Grand Silence. If you broke the rule of silence you had to confess it at Chapter."

"What's Chapter?"

"It's where you kneel before the whole community and confess the rules you've broken during the course of the week."

"That sounds positively medieval." "Well that's when the practice probably started. You have to be immersed in convent life to appreciate it. It sounds all very legalistic but it isn't intended to be. You are there to cultivate a desire to live a God-centred life and all the rules are reminders of what a nun's whole day should be about."

"And that is..."

"God."

"So how does a rule telling you not to speak, for example, make your life God-centred?"

"Well, you don't speak to others so you can speak to God. Silence encourages an inner life."

"I see."

"What do you see?" Beth asked, entering the room at that moment.

"I'm trying to understand what convent life is all about," Maria replied.

"I want to understand all that stuff too." Said Beth, sitting down on the other side of Nan.

"Nan's written it down. I've got the bit about Nan telling Andy she's going to be a nun. It's in my room, and Nan told me lots more last night. Come on! I'll show you." Nan returned to her crossword.

As it drew closer to lunchtime, Emily was pegging out washing and that's where Laura found her. Trying to be helpful she picked up a t-shirt from the basket and began to peg it out.

"Laura, please don't hang my t-shirt like that! It'll go baggy."

"Muuum!" There was frustration in Laura's voice. "I've told you. If you hang them this way the wind blows through them and dries them quicker."

"Yes, and I've told you that I hate it when t-shirts are pulled out of shape at the bottom because of the way you hang them," Emily said. As she was protesting she took the badly hung t-shirt and repositioned it on the washing line.

"Now you'll have peg marks on your boobs," Laura said in annoyance.

"My t-shirt, my choice," Emily said, not meaning to be provocative.

"Pfh!" snapped Laura. "Whatever!"

"What?" Said her mother, not understanding why her choice should exasperate her daughter so much that she would storm off upstairs. Laura found Maria had begun putting together pieces of a jigsaw.

"I have no idea where you get the patience to do those things," said Laura, petulantly. "It'd drive me nuts. You'll rip it apart the moment you've finished it. What's the point?"

"It's Liverpool. I thought Nan might enjoy it." Laura's impatience subsided as quickly as it had erupted.

"You're so kind Maria. You're always thinking of others."

"What's bugging you?"

"Emily is." Laura sometimes used her mother's name when she was annoyed with her. This was a throwback to her childhood when she might have heard Nan using the same tone.

"What's she done now?"

"She picks on everything I do. She's so anal the way she hangs out washing. I was just trying to help."

"Are you still upset about that? I can't see why. You can hang your own washing any way you like, but it's up to me how I hang mine." Emily had entered the room with an empty washing basket and the reprimand was enough to take Laura off to her room with a loud slam of the door. It was a few minutes before she came along the hallway again. She ignored her mother, who was now stacking the dishwasher. The kitchen and dining room were open plan so the snub to her mother, as she spoke only to Maria, was noticeable.

"What's Beth reading Maria? She just told me to bugger off and she won't talk to me," Laura complained. "I don't know what can be so gripping."

"Nan's memoirs!" Maria answered distractedly trying to find a Liver Bird's eye.

"What?" Asked Emily.

"Just something about her early life in Liverpool that I was curious about."

"Oh not all that rubbish," Emily grumbled.

34

"Oh for goodness sake, get a grip you two!" Maria was not quick to anger, in fact she smiled as she chastised. Let's all try to have a nice weekend? Anyway, I beg to differ, Mum. Nan's writing's not all rubbish. She paints a very vivid picture when she writes. It's good to know your roots. It helps you know who you are, after all, Nan's history is our history too." Beth reappeared having finished reading about Nan and Andy.

"What do you want me to do with this now?"

"Give it to me. I'll make sure Nan gets it back."

"She told me once that she had written her life in poetry." You should ask her for it if you're that interested." Emily said.

"Poetry?" Beth was genuinely surprised. "Where is it?"

"I've no idea."

Nan wandered out of her bedroom just as Maria was clicking several jigsaw pieces into place at once, and Nan stood over her gazing at the picture of Liverpool that was emerging.

"I used to work there," she said, pointing. "In that very building! Behind that very window, actually! It's near the Pier Head." Maria pulled out the chair next to her.

"Why don't you sit down and help me?" Nan sat down, but she only watched as Maria slotted in new pieces. After a while, Nan broke the silence pointing at the jigsaw and tracing a route.

"You know only a short walk from where I worked, up this way, and down a laneway behind that building, is where the Cavern was. That's the route I walked when I went to dance there in my lunchtime." There was a short pause while other recollections surfaced. "One day, when I was there, a man came into The Cavern and put a white package onto the stage and I noticed that Paul McCartney nodded at him and picked it up when he'd finished singing. I found out later the man was his Dad and the package was a pound of sausages for their tea. Paul used to do some of the cooking because his mother was dead, and he was usually first home."

"Here we go again!" Emily muttered under her breath.

"That's such a good story, Nan. Let's put some Beatles music on?" Laura suggested. Emily wasn't sure if her daughter was deliberately trying to provoke her, but Nan brightened up and began to sing.

"Get back. Get Back. Get back to where you once came from." Seeing Nan and her daughters so happy, Emily began laughing too, and she began to sing along. Maria joined her mother in the kitchen.

"I'll get Nan a cold drink," Maria said. "I've noticed she doesn't drink much water."

Nan took a long drink from the glass Maria offered, then, putting it down, grabbed Maria's hand.

"Come and have a dance," she said, taking up the next song. *"She Loves You Yeah, Yeah, Yeah!"* Nan sang the first line and then danced through a couple of verses, but soon grew tired, retreating to her rocking chair. Beth knelt beside her to ask about her poetry.

"Can I read it? Where is it?"

"I've forgotten; probably somewhere in my room. I'll try to find it for you. Give me a minute. I've run out of puff."

A little later, Emily put the kettle on and, as it boiled, she watched Nan rocking to and fro. *I remember sitting with her in that rocking chair – usually for a story and never hearing the end of it because I always fell asleep. Now it's her turn to be comforted in it.*

Maria was curious about the memory Nan had recorded in her teenage diary and so she went in search of it, finding it open on Nan's writing bureau where she had left it for her. Taking it, she went to sit comfortably on her bed at the end of the house, where nobody could distract her. Once Maria had started reading, she couldn't stop.

A Chance Encounter

23ʳᵈ November 1963

Dear Diary

I'm still pinching myself. George Harrison sat next to me on the bus today! He's really nice. I didn't know who he was till he was getting off the bus. He's dead ordinary really. A bit thin faced but his smile makes up for that.

I didn't notice him coming upstairs. I was probably preoccupied about just telling Andy about me going into the convent. George said Hiya and sat down next to me. I moved over to give him a bit more room and he took the Mersey Beat out of his pocket and started reading. After a while we got talking about how so many Liverpool groups were really going places. I told him that what I liked about Liverpool's music was the way it seemed to bridge the gap between the sexes and between rich and poor. He smiled when I said Liverpool's throbbing music was like the heartbeat of Liverpool and he gave me a funny look – as if he was studying me. It embarrassed me, so I gabbed on saying that The Beatles were the best thing that had ever happened to Liverpool. I told him I loved going to the Cavern when they were on, but that I missed them now that they were becoming famous and didn't play there much any more. He agreed it was a pity, but said one good thing about it was it did give other Liverpool bands a chance to shine.

He went back to reading his Mersey Beat and after a while started going on about a poll the newspaper had done to find out which groups were the most popular. The Beatles came first and Gerry and the Pacemakers came second. I said how all the best musicians seemed to come from Liverpool, and it was great that they were getting billed with big names like Lonnie Donegan, Guy Mitchell, Johnny Ray and Frankie Vaughan, and how it made me really proud to be a Scouser. The only problem, I said, is trying to decide which bands you want to go to see at the weekend, because they're all so great. I asked him where **he** went, and he said he went all over the place, but he liked Litherland Town Hall best. I told him how much I'd like to go there, but couldn't, because it was too far away. I asked him how he got there, and he said one of his mates took him because he's got wheels.

I told him I usually went to the Grafton, or the Locarno, with my cousin because you can rely on the buses from there, and how I sometimes slept at my cousin's because then my Mum didn't know what time I came home, and Aunty Bea didn't seem to mind us coming home late.

Then he stood up saying it was his stop. I noticed we were at Allerton and I said do you live here? It's dead posh! But he said he lived in Macketts Lane. He was just going for a jam session with his mate John. Then he gave me his Mersey Beat and said 'Terah then Kate.' As he was moving down the bus I asked him how he knew my name? He laughed and said 'from the graffiti plastered all over yer handbag.' As he reached the top of the stairs I shouted 'what's your name?' He said his name was George. You can call me a gormless cow if you like, but I still didn't realise it was him. I just had time to shout Terah to him before he disappeared down the stairs.

I started to read the Mersey Beat. The Big Three were featured on the front, alongside a small picture of people dancing in the Cavern. I looked for myself but I wasn't there. What I did find, though, was a name, written at the top of the page in biro. I was absolutely gob-smacked. I looked up just as George stepped off the bus, and that's when I noticed his guitar case. Bloody Hell, I thought. That was George Harrison! I wondered if the newsagent had written George's name on The Mersey Beat or whether George had written it himself. I hoped George had because, if he had, it would mean I had his autograph. The bus was pulling away from the kerb so, holding the front cover of the Mersey Beat against the window, I tried to ask him if it was his writing, but he just smiled up at me and waved.

For the rest of the bus journey I was on Cloud Nine. I hugged the Mersey Beat to me, hardly able to believe it. I couldn't get over

38

how modest he was. I mean, he didn't even tell me who he was. I was kicking myself because, while I had been talking to him, at the back of my mind I'd been asking myself where I'd seen him before.

I searched through the Mersey Beat's headlines for news of The Beatles. There was an advertisement on the back page saying they were coming to the Empire in February. It was a couple of months away yet and I had already promised my cousin I'd go. I decided to get tickets before they all sold out. It could be a going away present to myself because I'd probably never see the Beatles again – unless I got sent to a leper colony where they were doing a charity gig. Famous people did that sort of thing.

When I got home, I exploded into the living room saying 'Guess who I've been talking to on the bus?' There wasn't even a flicker of interest. 'George Harrison, I said. Guess where he lives?' Now I had their attention. However nobody was answering, so I answered myself. 'Around the corner in Macketts Lane!' That got everyone's attention. Rita, Mike and Joe spoke at once. 'You're Kidding!' 'Honest to God?' 'You mean George Harrison the Beatle?'

*'Yes, George Harrison **the** Beatle,' I said. 'He's dead nice! Look, he gave me his copy of the Mersey Beat. It's got his name written on it but I don't know if it's his writing or the newsagent's.' They all wanted to see. 'He's not big headed or anything.' I told them about the lovely chat we'd had about all the new bands in Liverpool, and how great The Beatles are, and he never let on he was George Harrison and I never realised until it was too late. If he lives in Macketts Lane, close to our church, we've probably waited for the same bus as him hundreds of times without realising it.*

Rita wanted to know what number Macketts Lane George lived at. She was as disappointed as me when I said I didn't know. Then the cheeky bugger asked me if she could have George's Mersey Beat when I went into the convent. I told her that made me feel like she can't wait to get rid of me, so she snatched the Mersey Beat out of my hand and I had to fight her to get it back. She's older than me, but I can clobber her.

Maria had come to the end of the diary entry but Nan had attached a page that she must have written some time later – maybe even last night when she found the diary.

That Mersey Beat was nearly worn out before I went into the convent. Every time I read it I was struck by how impressive the Liverpool club scene was. It had launched lots of Mersey Beat musos into a stellar world and Liverpool teenagers were bursting with pride in their hometown's talent. We would talk about them as if they were family or as if they were best friends with our brothers, or lived next door (well one of them nearly did). I knew I would miss it all when I went to Ireland to enter the Novitiate but, despite the fact that I loved dancing at the clubs, the truth was that there were times when, in the middle of the dance-floor, I would feel myself disappear and sometimes, even worse, feel as if I was looking down on everyone, and all I could see was a writhing monster rather than separate individuals; and I wasn't even on drugs.

Just then Beth knocked and opened the door.

"Have you finished with the diary, Maria?"

"Yes. Why? Do you want it?"

"Not yet. I'll read it later. You said you'd asked Nan lots of questions. Did she tell you what happened when she and Andy broke up?"

"Apparently it was like a bolt from the blue. He asked her not to go. Poor Andy! Can you believe she'd never mentioned it to him, even though she had been visiting the convent? I got the distinct impression, from what she told me, that Nan never really thought she would ever actually go."

On the River

"Does anyone want to go for an afternoon row on the river?" Matthew was smacking his lips over a bowl of pea and ham soup Beth had made. "I've checked the tides and we can catch the incoming tide to travel upstream. Then we can travel back downstream with the outgoing tide. It'll be about a three hour trip, I think."

"Me, me, me, me," Beth said in the same child-like voice she had used when she was small and going out in Grandpa Doug's boat was a frequent treat.

"I would," said Nan with surprising enthusiasm. Matthew studied her with raised eyebrows, surprised that she wanted to go. He glanced at Emily who said.

"If you go, Mum, do make sure you drink a lot. The doctor said it's important."

"Do you think she's well enough to go, Em?" Matthew asked.

"It's up to the two of you. Only you know if you're up to it. For what it's worth, I think, bearing in mind how much Mum loves the Brisbane River, it might do her the world of good. Do you feel up to it Mum?"

"I wouldn't have put my hand up if I didn't."

"Beth, you can come too, but you'll have to sit in the bow if Nan's coming."

Nan was reminded of Doug as Matthew organised them for the excursion with his no-nonsense instructions.

"And make sure both of you go to the toilet before you leave. There are no toilets in the middle of the river."

"Cool," said Beth. "I'll help you get the boat down. Do you think it's safe after all these years?"

"Let's go and check it out."

Grandpa Doug had kept the boat in the carport, where he had built it. It was strung up so that it sat on ropes about a

41

metre above where Nan's car would have been, if she had not sold it a couple of years ago.

"The public transport's so good here," Nan had explained, when Emily and Matthew had asked why she was selling it. "And it's cheaper. I want to do my bit for the environment. I don't go far these days."

"I'll need to put Dad's roof rack on my car before we can lower the boat," Matthew said. Emily moved her car out of the carport so the boat could be lowered directly onto Matthew's by way of an ingeniously simple rope pulley system Doug had rigged up. It told you a lot about the man Nan had loved, as did the boat. As Matthew lowered the boat, Nan told Beth,

"Every time we went on holiday, Grandpa Doug would build toy boats. First he built them out of paper, then cardboard and eventually he made some out of balsa wood. When he made a new one, or altered an old one, we would all go down to the beach to test it in the puddles left by the retreating tide. We did this until he had rectified any problems but mostly they bobbed on the water the first time. For years he talked about the real boat he would build, until one day I said. 'Oh for goodness sake, why don't you get on with it before I'm too old and creaky to get into it.' He talked about that day as if it were the day I gave him permission, but looking back, I think it was more of an ultimatum. He enjoyed the boat for years, as you know." Beth nodded and Nan continued on a sadder note.

"But then Grandpa Doug decided to build a sail for it so he could take it out on the Bay, and he did so often, until the day he didn't come back."

"Now, what do you think, Beth? It looks sound enough to me." Matthew ran his hand over the gunwale, with a fond caress.

"It looks okay to me too."

"Can you find the life jackets then, while I secure it with ropes? Oh and while you're at it, go to the toilet! You too Mum!"

When Beth reappeared loaded with safety gear, Matt had the boat safely roped to the roof rack, but just to be absolutely certain the wind wouldn't catch it, he stretched occy straps over it and hooked them to the roof rack too.

"Sweet!" Beth said. Emily had appeared with an Esky containing water, a flask of tea, milk and lots of packets of sugar that Nan had pocketed at coffee shops. Another carrier bag contained cups and a packet of biscuits.

"Terrific," said Matt. "Now where did Mum go?"

"She's coming." A few seconds later, she appeared at the door wearing a strange assortment of hats.

"Beth, have you got a hat? Here, borrow one of Nan's," Emily said taking one off Nan's head."

"Is that okay with you Nan?" Beth asked.

"Of course." Nan smiled. "I brought them to share. Would you like your Dad's sailing cap, Matthew?"

"No. I've got this one," he said, pulling a very creased one out of his pocket. "You can get in the car Mum." Nan eased herself into the front passenger seat while the others finished loading up. Then they set off slowly. Emily knew Matthew was taking precautions in case the wind got under the boat and lifted it, as it had done once when they were children.

When finally they were on the river, they all fell silent enjoying the peace of it. Nan, spreading herself out comfortably on a beanbag in lieu of a wooden seat, drew attention to a spoonbill, then to a tiny blue kingfisher, and then to a cormorant drying his feathers in the sun.

"They remind me of Roman standards," Nan said. "It's something about the shape of them when they spread their wings out to dry."

Nan continued to point out interesting things about the river, such as the tide line above which the trees looked shiny and clean, and below which they looked muddy and spoilt.

"Those are the sort of details that make each outing on the river different. Many things affect how the river looks.

43

When it's cloudy or after a lot of rain it looks dark brown, and muddy with all the silt that runs into it. During a drought it's transparent and yellow like my birthstone. I love the days when it sparkles like an emerald. We saw a platypus in the wild, here." She looked over the side wondering if they would be that lucky again. She fell silent for a moment before announcing: "Elephant ears coming up," as they passed several huge leafy arrangements, the leaves of which did indeed resemble elephants' ears.

Matthew and Beth had fallen under the river's spell. They were silent and thoughtful. Beth finally broke the silence.

"I so get what you and Grandpa Doug loved about the river. When I meet someone special he has got to be someone I can do this sort of thing with." She fell silent again until she noticed a couple, out for their daily constitutional, waving to them from the riverbank. "Seeing people's reactions to us was always part of the fun." Beth waved back. "It's quite unusual to see a rowing boat on the river, isn't it?"

"Yes. Grandpa Doug never could understand why. You see the school kids on their racing shells, pulling with all their might during training sessions. Now and again you see people paddling Indian canoes, but in all the time Grandpa Doug and I travelled up and down the river, we never saw a rowing boat like ours – and yet the river must have been full of them during the time of the early settlers.

"Even if the river had supported a rowing boat or two, they wouldn't have been as quirky as Grandpa Doug's, with it's duck's head at the prow, and its beautiful curves." Beth's giggles were infectious. Matthew explained his father's intentions when he designed it.

"It's modelled on the Irish Curragh, but the duck's head is definitely a spoof of the Viking longboat. Your Grandfather had a sense of humour. He thought a lot about the design of it before he drew up the plans because the frame of the Curragh is covered with skins. Dad covered the Duck Boat with plywood, which must have been the thinnest and lightest material available.

"Everyone called it The Duck Boat, but he officially named her Kiss Me Kate, after me," Nan explained. "I don't suppose we could go up river as far as the Venus Pool?" Nan asked.

"What's the Venus Pool?" asked Beth.

"Oh that's a long way up the river. We can't go there today," said Matt.

"It's the most magical place," Nan enthused. "There were a hundred or more black swans there the day we found it, and it was the only time we ever went there. It was such a sacred sight, seeing an entire flotilla of them, floating on glass-like water like that. There were smaller birds too, floating besides them like tug boats."

"Wow! That must have been awesome," said Beth.

"It was. We certainly had some memorable times on the river. Like the time Grandpa Doug rowed us down river to a bat colony. Do you remember that, Matthew?"

"I do. There were hundreds of bats swarming overhead, and we had to have umbrellas so they didn't piddle on us. Dad couldn't hold an umbrella and row at the same time, so he played piddle dodging. I remember how we couldn't stop laughing and grandpa said we were rocking the boat so much that he was afraid he would fall in and then he'd get a second drenching." Nan left Matthew reminiscing, while another memory drew her back in time to another boat, on another river.

"Oh Nan! What is it?" Asked Beth. "You suddenly look so sad."

"Oh it's nothing. I don't know why being here would remind me of the night I left Liverpool to go into the Novitiate."

"Is that a sad memory then?" Beth was full of concern.

"It is and it isn't." Nan replied. "I was doing what I wanted. It was the first major decision I had ever made independently of anyone else. But I've often considered that sometimes you have to choose happy things at the expense of other happy things and that can make even a happy occasion sad."

"I don't get you." Beth said.

"What I mean is that in order to do what I wanted to do and enter the convent, I had to pay a huge price - that of not seeing my family. But life is often paradoxical like that."

"Tell me about it," Beth pleaded. Nan glanced at Matthew knowing he wouldn't want to hear it.

"Listen to your iPod Matthew," she said.

"It's okay," Matthew said. "I don't think I've heard this story." So Nan began:

"We sailed out of Liverpool on an overnight ferry bound for Dublin, we being me and Reverend Mother - the one who used to entertain me in her posh parlour in Liverpool. I'll never forget experiencing the overwhelming shock of sudden separation from everyone I loved, as I stood on the deck of the ship bound for Ireland. I had expected to sail out of port slowly, waving until my family disappeared from sight. But that's not the way it happened. One minute we were standing on deck waving and blowing kisses, and the next minute a heavy steel door, taller than us, was slammed across our field of vision, and they were gone, just like that. The suddenness shocked me and brought tears to my eyes.

'Arrah now, smile t'rough the tears, Sister dear,' Mother Anselm advised. 'Ye'll be fine. Ye'll see.' It was the first time I was ever called Sister. I suppose since I was experiencing a hard aspect of convent life, I had earned it.

Mother Anselm led me down into the bowels of the ship to our cabin. It was awkward because we were sharing and Mother Anselm put the light out while we were undressing. I had never before experienced a dark so complete in all my life. I managed to feel my way down to the bottom of the top bunk and I stashed my clothes there. Then fumbling I climbed up into it and lay on my back. I had thought, until then, that

46

darkness was limiting, but I found, lying on my back in that ship's cabin, that it was infinite."

Haunted

At Nan's, Emily was having a rest. Her thoughts kept returning to her girls, wondering how she could foster a better relationship with them. She had given up the hope that maturity would somehow conjure up interests in common, because that had not happened. No sooner had she got them through school than they were off with their friends, Maria to University, Laura to College to do a Diploma in Childcare and Beth… well she had been filled with wanderlust.

Beth left school after year twelve and then worked as a shop assistant, until she had enough money to travel the world. Her mother bought her a much longed for one-way ticket to London for her twenty-first birthday, and Beth managed to squeeze another five grand out of her father by making him feel he had neglected her for years. The minute she got her passport she was off and then messages began to arrive from all over the world.

Occasionally a rare text would turn up saying that she would be arriving home on Monday. There would be flight details and an assumption that her family would be at the airport to greet her. The subtext of these was 'I've run out of money so I'll be home for an extended visit to get a job and earn some more'. Each time she came home, she would adeptly manage to con more money out of her mother and father, so she could continue exploring the world.

On these visits Beth brought home José, the Spaniard, who they thought she would marry. She left him at the foothills of Mount Everest, for Luigi the Italian. A year later she left Luigi for Omar, the date farmer's son, returning to Europe with him, where she scored a job as an interpreter, working for the World Health Organisation in Geneva. When she finally came home to stay, she enrolled in a double degree in Philosophy and Politics with a long-term plan to work in academia or the diplomatic service, so that she could occasionally travel to academic conferences or political assemblies, in interesting parts of the world, for the rest of her life. The family was supportive enough not to tell her that she didn't have a diplomatic bone in her body.

Emily thought that Beth's wanderlust had been all used up by her travels, but when she had responded so enthusiastically to Matthew's invitation to go out on the river, Emily had seen traces of it again. She wondered how long Beth would stay put in Brisbane.

With no one around to intrude on them, Laura and Maria had taken themselves off into Nan's room. Maria wanted to look for more diaries, while Laura took her turn to read about Nan meeting George Harrison on the bus. Maria found the diaries in Nan's trunk, but the real find was a folder full of torn scraps of captured thoughts, buried under a stack of books on her writing desk. In among the scrappy bits and pieces were several longer texts. Maria sorted through them to see if there was anything worthwhile.

"Whoo hoo!" She cried. "I've struck gold."

"What?" Asked Laura.

"Some of it's about convent life," Maria showed her the opening quotation from the Holy Rule of Saint Benedict.

"Weird," Laura handed it back so she could continue reading about Nan meeting George Harrison. "You know, I suddenly feel as if I hardly know Nan."

"I know what you mean," Maria said. "It sounds like someone else's life because all we know of her is Nan the Gran. But she's so much more. She's a person who has led a sometimes strange and mostly full life and I want to know everything, because in some strange way, I feel the better we know her, the better we'll know ourselves."

"You sound like Beth," Laura said, climbing onto Nan's bed where she could read in more comfort. "I liked the Nan that was in my head – the one that made me feel happy and safe. Now I feel that the Nan in my head wasn't real. It's a bit disconcerting."

"I think she must have written this recently." Maria had obviously not been listening. "The pages are much cleaner and less crumpled than all the others. It was the last thing Maria would say for a while, for she too climbed up onto Nan's bed, where she and Laura read in companionable silence.

> **The sisters will observe the Grand Silence from after Compline at night, until Matins has been sung the following morning. This is a sacred time, wherein can be experienced the deepest, and most holy, communion of the spirit.**
> **(From The Holy Rule of St Benedict)**

I had completed six months as a postulant. Now I was a fully-fledged habit-wearing novice with a new nun name – a name that had been chosen for me. Postulants were always asked to choose three saints' names as possibilities. They usually got one of them, so you can imagine my astonishment when I didn't get any of the names I had chosen. The Bishop's voice had boomed loud and clear: "Katherine McBride, henceforward you shall be called Sister Jude." I was gob-smacked because Saint Jude was the patron saint of hopeless cases!

This ceremony launched me into my Spiritual Year, which was a time of arduous testing and fastidious commitment to The Rule. It was intended to filter out those who had a vocation from those who were dreaming! The Mistress of Novices decided who would be sent home and who would be allowed to stay. She lived with, and taught the postulants and novices, in a building set apart from the rest of the community. I thought I was doing okay, or else the big cheeses would not have let me receive the habit. My new name suggested, however, that my future might still be hanging in the balance.

I had expected the Novitiate to be a place of severity and deprivation that would mould your character for an even harder life on the missions. But it was no such thing. Unlike the novices who had entered the Novitiate from the elitist boarding school it was attached to, I found convent life luxurious in comparison to my tough Liverpool upbringing. It was nothing to see my mother divide six pen'orth of chips between six of us, when times were tough, and then steal a chip from each plate so she wouldn't starve.

For me, the 'life of poverty' (and I had enormous trouble calling it that) was a protected and sheltered life, with no deprivation at all. Poverty, I was told, was more to do with complete dependence on God's providence – in other words a nun's lack of choice rather than a lack of necessities.

Nevertheless, the more time passed, the more I loved the quiet peacefulness of the Novitiate. Home had always been overcrowded and was often noisy with bickering. In the convent, the Mistress of Novices might be severe occasionally, but that was nothing compared to Mum, who, if she saw you reading - or even worse doing nothing, would quickly give you a clout and a job. I didn't blame her. Overwork had run her into the ground. She suffered with bad health and she needed support. Even I could, reluctantly, see the injustice of us all sitting around doing nothing while she was run ragged.

At times the Mistress of Novices would accuse a nun unjustly. It was part of the training and was intended to foster humility. But it was nothing compared to the push and shove world I had lived in previously. I found such accusations mild as I embraced the Holy Rule fervently, and all was going well until I hit a time of very prolonged sleeplessness.

The novices slept in a dormitory divided into cubicles by wooden partitions. A curtain served as a doorway offering a measure of privacy. Being hung on metal curtain rings, they swished noisily when opened or closed.

I was lying in bed one night, eyes wide-awake, praying for a time when I might be able to sleep again, when my curtain swished and, as I turned towards it, I saw a vaporous form, with deep sunken skull-like eyes and hollow cheeks. I was sure I was awake because I was aware of my open, bulging eyes, and of trying to find a logical

51

explanation for the manifestation. As it came close it bent over me until its nose almost touched mine. I had the horrible feeling that if I didn't stop it, the creature would merge with me and I would be possessed.

"Sister!" I cried.

An emaciated nun had returned from the missions to die. She had been given a room on another level of the Novitiate building, and I told myself it must be her. Could she be sleepwalking? However, the moment I spoke, the phantom disappeared like the smoke rings Mum used to puff out of her mouth before she turned our bedroom light off at night, when we were children.

Now I was not only sleepless, but also afraid of the dark, and afraid to be in my cubicle, in case the spectre returned. So, when everyone was asleep, I would get up, dress, and make my way over to the chapel. The Chapel was on the first level of the main convent and the Novitiate was completely detached from it. To get into the main convent you needed a huge key, similar to the ones used in scary movies. I knew my Mistress of Novices hung the keys on a hook just inside her bedroom so it was easy for the on-duty-novice to open her door and take them, in order to go over to the Chapel and ring the bell for the Angelus, thereby waking the nuns and calling them to morning prayers.

The stairs to my Mistress of Novice's bedroom creaked more than Reverend Mother's joints. However, since the chapel was the only place I felt safe, I brazened it out. Taking the keys was simpler than I thought. Next I had to tiptoe from the Novitiate, blending into the shadows, in order to open the great gothic wooden stud-encrusted door of the main convent. I hoped the loud eerie creaks and groans of rust and metal would make anyone listening creep further down their blanket in fear, rather than bring them to a window out of curiosity.

I knew it was forbidden to break the Grand Silence, which required nuns to remain in bed until the bell summoned them to chapel the following morning. In this I was knowingly and willfully disobedient. So it was that I began to understand I would never be a humble nun, for I could not tell my Mistress of Novices of my fear for many irrational reasons. I dealt with the problem myself by bypassing God's representatives within the convent, taking my problem to God personally. Now how could that possibly be wrong?

After a few minutes of supplication for healing sleep and a way out of my fear and exhausted misery, I would gather up some cushions that the older arthritic nuns sat on, to make a mattress for myself on one of the pews - but not before turning on a very dim light at the back of the chapel.

On such a night, I was on my knees, saying my prayers, before the cross, when I became aware of a glow in the dark above the altar. The glow gradually got brighter and bigger, until I was so blinded by it that I had to shield my eyes. It was coming from a gold-domed grotto above the altar that housed a statue of the Virgin Mary. I tried to see what was causing the brightness, but it was like looking into the sun. I could see a shadowy form emerging from the blinding light and I thought it was the Virgin Mary coming to punish me for my disobedience. So, I prostrated myself on the floor, even more terrified than I had been of the phantom in my cubicle. I waited to be chastised, but instead I heard a rather gentle voice, obviously male, speak in Liverpool's vernacular.

'Hya! I'm lost. Yer couldn't tell me where I am could yer?' I raised my head from my prostrate position and realised it wasn't a visitation from heaven. It was a young man. I knew him. I'd met him on a bus once.

'I'm seeing apparitions everywhere,' I told myself. 'It must be the sleep deprivation.' I rose to a kneeling position and chanced another glance in his direction. He was still there waiting for me to answer. I plucked up the courage.

'George Harrison,' I said. 'What're you doin' 'ere?' I had been in the Novitiate for eight months now and I had picked up a brilliant Irish brogue. But the moment I heard George speak everything in me reverted to Scouse.

'I'm not sure. I couldn't sleep so I got up for a smoke… it relaxes me, yer know what I mean like… and the next thing I know, I'm 'ere. It must be bloody good weed! What's with the weird clobber then?'

'Do you remember me, then? Yer gave me yer Mersey Beat, on the bus about a year ago.'

'Of course I do,' he said, looking around. 'I never forget a face. But, yer know what? This place gives me the creeps. Where are we?'

'In Ireland - in a convent chapel!'

'Bloody Nora! That must've been **really** good shit!' He was quiet for a while and then he said. 'Oh well... since I'm here, I might as well light a candle.' He patted his hip pockets looking for money while his eyes scanned the chapel looking for the sort of candelabras usually found in churches.

'You can't buy candles here George.' I explained. 'It's not that sort of church. It's not a public place of worship.'

'Oh!'

'Like I said, it's a convent chapel and you gave me a terrible fright. I thought you were the Virgin Mary,' I said, pointing to the statue where he seemed to have come from.

'Arh 'ey girl! You've just offended me man'ood. Anyway, you needn't talk. Ye frightened the bejesus out of me.'

'Shush!' I cautioned. 'The bejesus is hanging just above your head listenin', I pointed up at the huge crucifix hanging from heavy chains.

'Sorry,' he said, giving the crucifix a glance. 'I've got no idea how I got 'ere. It must have been the marijuana. Are you a penguin?'

'I'm a novice.'

'So what're yer doin' 'ere?'

'I've been comin' here at night because I can't sleep. I'm not supposed to because it's against the Grand Silence.' Mention of the Grand Silence made me acutely aware I was breaking the rule even worse now, by talking to George Harrison. 'Oh God!' I said. 'I'm a bloody hopeless nun,' and I burst out crying.

'I actually meant what're yer doin' in Ireland?' George said, giving me his hanky.

'I joined an Irish convent,' I bawled. 'so obviously the novitiate is in Ireland. But I think I'll have te go 'ome because I'm always breakin' the rules. I can't even manage to hasten with modesty.'

'Ahr 'ey, girl,' George said. 'Yer can't be that bad. I remember something good about yer.'

'What?'

'Well, yer really luv the Beatles.' That made me laugh and cry at the same time. 'Now c'mon! Tell us what's up!' He sat down beside me on the front pew – the one I'd been sleeping on - and put his arm around me, and I remember noticing how gentle he was. Of course I was breaking the rule even more now. I'd have been thrown out of the Novitiate on my ear if my Mistress of Novices knew I was in the chapel with a man, who had his arm around me. But somehow, talking to George seemed even more sacred than obeying the rule, because he made me feel as if everything was good.

George got it all out of me. I told him all about the freaky ghost, my fear of sleeping in my cubicle, and about how Rip Van Winkle tired I felt. Finally he said:

'Maybe it would 'elp if yer thought about the Universal Spirit when yer afraid because then ye'll just know everything's part of everything else – even ghosts.'

'It sounds like yer sayin' ghosts are normal.'

'Well, I wouldn't exactly say normal. But, 'ey, don't be afraid, because who can say what's normal and what's not? Are you normal or is the ghost normal, eh?' He looked into my eyes but he knew that I was still going to be afraid and that I didn't get it. So he tried explaining further.

'Well let's put it this way,' he said. 'Worrif yer try thinking differently about the ghost and try thinkin' of it as a soul who's a bit lost and who's wandering around a place he doesn't know – just like me.' He could see I got that so he continued. 'It's probably just as scared as you, so be friendly. Just say: 'What are yer doin' roaming around in the dark? Why don't you bugger off into the light, or to 'eaven, or wherever you're supposed to go?' George's eyes were twinkling, and I couldn't tell if he was teasing me. I know it seems hard to believe, but I felt warmth right through me, which was funny because the Chapel, in the middle of the night, was like a morgue.

'You know what, George? I get it now that you put it that way.' We sat in silence for a while just thinking and then I said. 'Yer

55

know that ghost?' George nodded. 'Its face was ugly, like a skull!' There was another thought filled moment. 'Yer don't suppose it could've been Mick Jagger do yer?'

George couldn't half laugh when he got going. I turned my head to look at his big smile because I was sure George's smile could melt the Arctic. But George had already started to go back into the radiance, and I just knew I wouldn't have any more trouble sleeping. So I went back to bed and broke another rule by dreaming of him.

Secrets

Emily was making Spaghetti Bolognese, for dinner, when Beth, Matthew and Nan got back from the river. Meanwhile, Laura and Maria had discussed Nan's writing at length and this led to the sort of mateyness that included the sharing of confidences. That's when Maria discovered that Laura had already acquired some marijuana.

"It's a secret. I don't want Beth to know because she's quite likely to blab it out when we're arguing, or during one of her mood swings. It's only to be used in an emergency if Nan ever needs it."

"If you don't want me to tell her I won't, but she's not going to tell anyone because she's already got some too."

"Wha… But when we were in the car she was talking as if she could get some but hadn't yet. Why did she pretend she didn't have any?"

"She wasn't sure she should tell you now that you're a policewoman. She didn't want to put you in a compromising position. I'm not so worried about that now because you've already put yourself in one."

"So, what you're saying is that both of us scored some marijuana?"

"All of us," said Maria.

"You too! That means we could all be done for possession."

"I suppose so, but not for using, since we only want it for pain relief for Nan."

"It's still possession." Said Laura.

"Are you going to hide yours behind the pictures on the wall? I am." As she spoke, Maria was taking down a large frame on which eight Beatles LP covers had been mounted.

When Beth came looking for her sisters, Maria suggested that now might be a good time for Beth to hide her stash. Beth looked from Maria to Laura, her eyebrows raised in question.

"Don't worry. Laura's got some too. Now we're all sworn to secrecy and, just in case someone is tempted to go rogue, none of us is allowed to let Nan use it without the consent of the other two. Agreed?"

"Agreed!"

"Hopefully we'll never have to use it," Maria said, wistfully. Anyway as I was saying Beth, now's a good time to hide it while Mum's busy with dinner."

"Where's Matt?" asked Laura looking over her shoulder. "We don't want him walking in on us while we're hiding it."

"He's gluing a broken chair, downstairs," said Beth.

"And Nan? She must be exhausted after being out in the boat."

"No! On the contrary, she seems energised. Besides she had a snooze while we were out. She's next door looking at photos of Iris' new granddaughter.

"Here's my contribution," Laura said, fishing a small packet out of her bra. When she saw her sisters smirking Laura said: "What? It's the safest place! You hide it. I'll keep watch."

"Okay. Good idea," agreed Beth. Laura positioned herself on the front door step where she could keep an eye out for Nan, and she could bang on Nan's bedroom window if Emily or Matthew threatened to intrude.

Seeing Laura at the front door seemingly idling, Emily gave her the job of watching the dinner for a moment. She watched her mother open the door to the toilet and warned her sisters that she would be passing back soon.

"So be careful," she cautioned.

When five minutes had passed and her mother still hadn't returned, Laura chopped the onion and began to grind it into the mince with some garlic. Still her mother didn't come back. Laura had completed adding ingredients by the time her mother did return apologetically.

"Thanks, I'll take over now."

"It's all done. It just needs to simmer for a while." Before leaving the kitchen Laura turned to say sarcastically. "You know Mum, if you'd asked me I would have made dinner. Just be up front about it next time."

"What's up with you girls?" her mother was obviously startled. "Beth's just bitten my head off too, and now you."

"Why what did you do to her?"

"Nothing. I asked her a simple question, that's all. I don't know why you're all so tetchy."

"Ah, but what was the question?" Laura asked.

"She's was moving stuff around in Nan's room, and when I asked her what she was up to she bit my head off."

"Ah, well, there's the problem. Being up to something implies suspicion. You should have asked what she was doing, rather than what she was up to. Non-accusatory interrogation gets better results."

"Well, I don't care," said Emily defensively. "She looked as if she **was** up to something."

"In that case I'll go and arrest her," Laura said walking away.

"Smart arse," her mother muttered after her. Laura crossed the living room and opened the door to Nan's bedroom.

"You're under arrest," she said to Beth as she closed the door behind her. "You've been caught red-handed in the act of sneaking around Nan's bedroom." Laura made inverted commas with her fingers. "You have the right..." but Beth cut in.

"Hey, guess what I found," she said, sticky taping the last packet of cannabis to the back of a framed picture of George Harrison. She repositioned it and now that her hands were free she pointed to an old Newspaper advertising a Beatles concert. "Look!" It had been put into a frame and stuck on the wall with Blu Tack. Beth prised if off. She pointed to the handwriting above the headline, comparing it to George's signature on a framed photo of the Beatles.

"It's the same writing."

"Far out! Do you think this is…? No! It can't be… can it?" Her sisters were beaming. "It's George's signature?" They all jumped up and down excitedly. "Is it **the** Mersey Beat? The one George gave Nan?" They opened the frame and released the newspaper. Now that the name of the newspaper was no longer hiding behind the frame it was clear it was definitely a copy of The Mersey Beat. They all scrutinized the signature again. "It **must** be the one he gave her when they met on the bus. It's dated 1963."

"Far out," said Laura.

"She must have known, otherwise she wouldn't have framed it," Laura said.

"Did anyone bring their lap-top?" Asked Beth.

"No! Why?"

"I want to check how much George Harrison's autograph is worth."

"Who cares? It's part of Nan's stuff," Laura argued. "She treasures it."

"I know that. I want to know what it's worth so as to stop Mum from throwing it into a skip when... well, you know..."

"Oh! I see. Yes! We probably do need to protect it."

"Of course. But as well as that, aren't you a tiny little bit curious how much it's worth?"

As Matthew passed by Nan's room, glancing in as he did so, they fell to whispering. "We have to find a way of ensuring Matthew and Mum don't throw any of Nan's stuff out"

"You're right." Maria heard Matthew's voice in the living room and realised he must have finished his job. "Leave it to me." Casually approaching Matthew, who had picked up the newspaper, she asked.

"Matthew, if anything happens to Nan, can I ask you not to throw out any of her treasures? We'd like to keep her collection of Beatles memorabilia."

"Well I don't want it. I don't imagine Emily does either, do you Em?"

"No."

"Will you promise not to throw anything away, then?"

"Okay," Emily replied.

"You can have the lot as far as I'm concerned," Matthew assured her. Laura joined them in the living room, checking the time.

"You girls can have whatever you want of Nan's," Emily said. "But she's alive and kicking right now and she'll be back in a minute demanding her dinner."

"How long is dinner going to be?"

"It's ready," Emily, placed the pasta and Bolognese sauce on the table with a small dish of grated Parmesan cheese. As the vultures swooped, she reminded them to leave some for Nan. However, seeing how fast it was disappearing, she dished some up onto a plate. "I'll keep hers warm."

Later, Matt drove Laura home because she had to be back on duty by eight o'clock, leaving Maria and Beth to clear the table, while Nan, having picked at her meal, got ready for bed. Emily had offered to make her Milo to help her settle for the night. She had been harsh with her mother at dinner because, when Nan returned, having admired the new baby photos, and having learned the baby was called Penny, she kept talking about Penny Lane, and Eleanor Rigby, and about the time George and Paul went on a hitch-hiking holiday before they were famous.

"Oh Mum!" Emily groaned in the end. "Can't we just eat our dinner in peace?"

"Muuuum," complained Beth, annoyed that Emily was spoiling the story. "Go on Nan!" Emily bit her tongue. Nan didn't need much encouragement.

"They hardly had any money, so each night they slept on a beach. You can't imagine that, can you – the Beatles being that poor! Anyway, they reached Chepstow, but there was no beach there, so they went to the police station and asked if they could sleep in a cell. The duty officer told them to bugger off, but then must have realised they were trying to do the right thing. He didn't want them to be booked for vagrancy, so he told them to go to the local football stadium and ask the night watchman if they could sleep in the grandstand."

"Tell him I sent you," he told them.

"I wish one of the Beatles would walk into our station when I'm on duty. I only ever get wankers," Laura complained.

"It's not a true story," said Matthew. "She makes it up."

"Yes it is. It's in the Beatles Anthology," said Laura.

"Rubbish," said Emily. "She'd tell you anything."

"I read it myself," said Laura. "It's true."

"Well that's news to me," Matthew said.

"She makes most of it up," said Emily adjusting her argument. "Trust me. She told me the other day that they smoked tea when they used to jam at John's Aunty Mimi's. As if! Let it go in one ear and out the other."

"Or learn to check out the facts like I did," Laura said smugly. "I did a police assignment on checking out people's stories. My assignment was about Nan and her tall stories. I was surprised at how much of what Nan says is true. Some of it I couldn't verify, but I can tell you that they really did used to smoke tea when they jammed together – Typhoo tea actually. They weren't much more than kids. Boys wagging school! It's there in black and white."

"Where?"

"In the Beatles Anthology and it's reported exactly as they told it."

After finding George Harrison's signature, Beth thought, *I'm certainly not going to dismiss anything Nan says in future, no matter how far fetched.*

A Brush With The Law

As Maria was driving Beth home, a traffic cop on a motorbike flagged them down.

"Oh no! I don't believe it! Was I speeding?"

"Don't know," Beth shrugged! "I wasn't paying attention!" When Maria rolled down the window, she melted into the greenest eyes she had ever seen.

"Can I see your licence please?" Maria gave the traffic cop her business card by mistake. He studied it for a moment and then politely repeated his question.

"Oh, sorry! Here!" His eyes were flashing backwards and forwards between the card and Maria. Then he spoke again.

"Do you know what speed you were doing Miss?"

"I think I was doing 80 kilometres an hour."

"You were doing 86. Is there a reason you were speeding?"

"No officer. I didn't realise I was speeding. I'm usually very careful not to." The traffic cop looked again at Maria's licence and then at her business card.

"May I ask where you're going?" he asked.

"Home," she said.

"And where have you been?"

"We haven't been drinking if that's what you think." She was losing her cool a bit. "We've been visiting our Grandmother. She's got cancer." He bent down to see who was with Maria and seeing Beth engrossed in her mobile phone, assumed she was texting. She was, in fact, taking a photo of him. He took another look at Maria's business card.

"In the circumstances, Doctor" - there was a hint of a smile playing around his lips as he handed Maria her driving licence - "I'll let you off with a warning this time, but please be

63

aware of the speed limit." He put his helmet back on and walked back to his motorbike.

"Hey, my business card," she yelled, but if he heard her, he never let on. She wound the window up and, shrinking back into the seat, spoke her thoughts out loud. "God must hate me, or he would have let him arrest me." In that moment, one of Beth's legendary ideas was conceived.

"Yes, he is kind of cute. Oh by the way, Maria, I keep meaning to ask you, have you got plans for your birthday?"

"No."

"What would you like to do?"

"I haven't even thought about it. The up-coming conference has been a priority. I've been so flat out writing my paper, bringing my research up to date, and writing 'to do' lists so others can take over while I'm away that I haven't even given my birthday any thought."

"So you're not planning anything?"

"No."

"Good because Laura wants to organise something. We'll text you about it."

As Maria pulled into the kerb outside Beth's share-house, Maria hoped she and Laura were not arranging one of Beth's student parties for her birthday because she was so over loud and rowdy. She'd much prefer a nice intimate family dinner somewhere.

"I won't come in for coffee, Beth. I've got to get an early night because my flight's at seven fifteen in the morning. Text me if you need to, though, especially if Nan gets worse. I don't want any of this, Oh-best-not-to-worry-her, crap."

"Okay. And I'll let you know what I find out regarding the signature."

"I'd already forgotten about that. It's not a priority either. Goodnight!" Beth stretched across to kiss Maria on the cheek. "I love you Boo," Maria said.

"I love you too, Boo Boo." They both laughed.

"Nan's so right about memory. I haven't thought about the Boo story for such a long time." On the way home, Maria, determined to keep the Boo story in her mind, repeated it over and over, so she would not forget it again.

Once Upon a Time, there were three bears, they were sisters and they were all very pretty. The oldest was called Boo, the middle one was called Boo Boo, and the tiny one was called Boo Boo Boo. Maria remembered when the story had been about a single bear and how it had been altered when her sisters came along. How comforting it was to hear Nan's voice spring to life in her head. Death can rob you of people, thought Maria sadly. But it can't steal your memories.

Brother and Sister

Often when Matthew visited Nan she asked him what it was, exactly, that he did, and every time he would explain his work with enormous patience and in great detail. Whereupon, when he left, Nan would shake her head and remember the adorable little lad who, standing on a chair so he could access ingredients, used to mix potions in her pantry. The memory seemed very far removed from the present. *I'm buggered if I can understand what the hell he's on about anymore.* There was great pride, humour and joy in the thought.

Matthew had grown beyond his mother's IQ around the age of nine. He had asked her one of the many questions he often bombarded her with and had noticed that she had begun to give him evasive answers, such as a) that's an interesting question. Let's ask your Dad when he comes home, or b) I'd like to know that too. Shall we go to the library to find out? His growing out of Nan was complete the day he asked her a question that was as interesting to him as it was innocent.

"Mum, how come you don't know much?"

Nan acknowledged her lack of education, but it had not stopped her wanting Emily and Matt to have the very best she could provide. So, rather than take offence at his question, she told him how proud she was of him and Emily for being so much more knowledgeable than she was. It was then that he stopped evaluating her as a less than adequate teacher, and concentrated more on appreciating her as a mother.

When Mathew's father had died, he had been devastated because his father had always indulged his curiosity with a tolerant intellect and unwavering good humour. Doug's general knowledge was legendary and, because he listened to radio documentaries as he followed other pursuits throughout his day, he could put forward a good argument for almost any topic you threw at him.

Nan had a rather forceful personality and people assessed her dubiously before crossing her. Not so Doug. Once, when asked why he married her, he said, because she was a challenge. Nan was not formally academic, but she was insightful and witty, so he enjoyed sparring with her. She had a temper when crossed, and Doug taught his children how to navigate life with her. For example, if Nan complained that he had done something wrong he would hang his head and say penitently, "I will have myself shot at dawn, Mistress." If she went overboard with requests for help, he would finally say "Just a minute, dear. I'll go bury your last slave first."

"You manage Nan by making her laugh," he would say. "It's as simple as that." When he had left them for a life at sea – for that is how they spoke of his death – her children wanted to make her smile as he had done. Matthew began flinging the door open with the now predictable "Come on and kiss me Kate." But Emily and Nan rubbed up against each other causing unseen gashes and grazes.

Matt never slept over at Nan's because he lived just a short two-minute drive away. However, since she had been diagnosed with cancer he had called in every day, to make certain she had everything she needed, and someone to talk to. He had been with her when the diagnosis was made.

"Go home, enjoy your family and live life to the full," the doctors advised. They had all understood the sub-text, though none of them said so.

Matt called back after dropping Laura home. He wanted to make sure Emily was okay because she had always seemed vulnerable to Matthew. Her life had been tougher than his and, though she wanted so very much to look after Nan in her time of need, he wasn't sure she had the resilience. She was an efficient and capable career woman, but she was no domestic goddess.

"I left my mobile," he said as she opened the door.

"Oh, I didn't notice," she said looking around with him.

"I can't see it," he said. He dug deep in his pocket again and, finding it there, confessed to a very rare moment of stupidity. "Sorry! I had it all the time!"

"Do you want a cuppa?" Emily asked. "I'm making myself Milo."

"No. I'll get off. That was a big weekend, Em. Are you okay?"

"Oh well… you know, I'm worried about Mum… and the girls."

"Anything you want to discuss?"

"No." There was a moment's silence.

"I'll be off then, unless there's anything I can do?"

"No. I'm fine. I am. Don't worry."

"Okay. But don't forget. I'm only a stone's throw away. Ring me, day or night and I'll be here within a couple of minutes," he assured her.

"I will," Emily said. "Thanks." As she closed the door behind him, Emily felt lonely and inadequate, but nevertheless determined to do her best for her mother, who, in spite of everything, she loved.

It was nine-thirty by the time Matthew had gone and Emily crept into Nan's bedroom to check on her. She was fast asleep, so Emily went downstairs to the crypt. This room had been allocated to her when she was fourteen in an attempt to put some distance between daughter and parents. It was hoped this would diffuse some of the tension and frustration that regularly erupted between the two age groups. Emily looked around at the room that was once again her temporary home. Its very location symbolised to her everything that was wrong in her life. Emily wondered if Nan had any idea how many painful memories were entombed in this crypt. *Probably not*, she decided, sitting down with her Milo, and feeling some comfort while she sipped. *It's probably better that way.*

Christmas Letter

On Monday morning the following text messages flew between mobile phones:

From Maria to Beth. Time 7:55am: Re birthday. No fuss. Quiet dinner. Inc Nan.

Beth to Laura. Time 8:05am: Re party - quiet dinner. Find out who this is. (Beth attached the photo of the spunky traffic cop).

Laura to Gabby and Jinx, friends in traffic police: Time: 9:08am. Who's this cool dude? Send profile. High priority!

Beth to Laura. 9:37. Ring tone, no answer.

Laura to Beth. 9.40am. You woke me! Was on nights, as you know!

Beth to Laura 9:42am. Sorry!

Laura to Beth 9:45am. Grr! U did it again!

On the plane, Maria opened the folder containing what she thought was the hard copy of the conference paper she was to present that day, only to find it was the folder containing Nan's writing. *Bugger*, she thought, in a moment of panic imagining her paper on the table at home. Then she calmed down, realising it was in the side pocket of her laptop bag in the overhead locker. Should she ask the woman next to her to move again? No. She had been grumpy the first time. Maria imagined she was trying to meet some impossible deadline as she was furiously manipulating graphs on her laptop. So, instead of agonising over her paper again, Maria settled down to read the contents of Nan's folder.

She flicked through poems, short stories, and other more illustrative writing until it became clear that Nan's memories were not your usual sort of autobiographical writings. Some of the pages were novel in layout as if Nan had been playing on the computer. I wonder where Nan learned how? Maria asked herself more than once. But that's Nan in a nutshell. Just when you think you've got her figured out, she manages to surprise. However Nan had come by the computer know-how, Maria loved that she had set down her memories of exploring the river in such a way that the words wound down the page, in the shape of a meandering water course. *Extraordinary*, Maria thought, and leafed through some more pages.

The next piece was surprisingly minimalistic. Maria studied the piece in great detail. The words formed a cross that filled the page and read:

Veni
Sponsa
Christi
Destined
to a life of
abstinence.
Chosen by
God to
hasten
with modesty
through
a life of
holiness
always
keeping
custody
of the eyes.
Vanity nailed to the cross with self and all its lusts and lack of discipline.
Emotions thoughts and raging teenage turbulence captured and restrained beneath
the veil
Be
vigilant
my beloved
and do not
succumb
to
particular
friendships.
Always walk
in threes
or more.
Never
share
your
aloneness
With
anyone
but
your
Sponsa
for you
belong
to Him
and Him
ALONE

71

Maria felt that this piece of writing encapsulated something fundamental about Nan, and she dwelt on it at length. People had often asked Nan why she had entered the convent and she was always evasive. Was this poem the answer?

Among the papers Maria found an envelope addressed to Mr and Mrs McBride, Nan's mother and father and her own great-grandparents. Being a scientist, she took in every detail, of the envelope, noticing it was postmarked 'Eire' and dated nineteen sixty-four. She immediately recognised Nan's messy writing. Emily and Matt, and later her grandchildren, had tried to improve her handwriting while playing school, making her shape her letters over and over again in the way their teachers did with them.

"I could have been a doctor with this writing." Nan refused to feel ashamed of her handwriting. "I spent my early working life writing shorthand at a speed of one hundred and sixty words a minute. I don't know how to slow down."

Maria took the letter out of the envelope, smoothed out the pages and began to read.

Dear Mum, Dad and all,

I hope you had a lovely Christmas. Thanks for ringing and I'm sorry that you had to hang up before I could speak to you. I was disappointed. I suppose you were too. It's a long way from the Novitiate to Rev Mother's telephone. Mother said you sent your love so I got the message. Write and tell me all about your Christmas.

Two days ago it was the feast of The Holy Innocents and I was made Reverend Mother for the day. I tried to ring you, because, I could do what I wanted that day because I was the boss of the whole convent. But you were out - probably at work. It is easy to forget people work when you live in a convent. Perhaps I'm not meant to talk to you since we keep missing each other.

I didn't know it was a special day when I woke up. If I had still been a postulant they would have made me dress in the habit for the day, but as I already wear a habit, they couldn't do that. It is the custom, you see, for the youngest postulant to be made Reverend Mother for the day, on the Feast of Holy Innocents. But we have no postulants at the moment, so I had the honour. I made it a day of 'Licence' - that's a French word (we are a French order, remember) and it means freedom, so the rule of silence was relaxed for the entire day. Reverend Mother and Mother Pius, My Mistress of Novices (I am not sure if I told you her name), went out somewhere for the day, and I was told it was up to me to run the show.

The other novices were keen for me to get up to mischief, but after a year of being a nun, I found that really difficult (I know that's probably hard for you to imagine). I suggested a treasure hunt, an idea that was taken up immediately because everyone thought it would be pretty good fun, and if I didn't have the required measure of mischief, then the older novices certainly did.

I sent them begging through the convent because I knew some of the nuns must have been hoarding Christmas treats: sweets, biscuits, chocolate, or anything at all that might be considered a treat in our convent-world. Those who went searching for the treats were allowed to eat some of what they found, but I told them to pile the rest up in a heap for the treasure trail. It took most of the morning to prepare for it, because we had to think up clues with wit and guile (which seemed to be in short supply) and we often had to resort to stand over tactics to get the goodies out of the nuns, who behaved like Shylock when we raided their stashes! So the treasure hunt was timetabled for immediately after lunch. Lunch, by the way, was just as huge as Christmas, with special flowers on the table, delicious ruby coloured wine, and fancy serviettes and holiday food.

In the evening we had a huge concert and anyone could perform. The young professed nuns (they make their vows yearly until they make their final vows after five years) performed a scene from The Barber of Seville (in proper costume – not nun's habits). That was a big surprise for us novices. It was hilarious. I wish you could have heard their beautiful voices singing opera flawlessly, and what beauties the nuns are when dressed up in glitter and finery. Even for me it is difficult to imagine nuns like ordinary women, but I saw they were that night. And I saw how fun loving they are. I'm *sure some of them could go to the top of the hit parade if they had a mind to. But I wouldn't want them to compete against John, George, Paul and Ringo because then I would have divided loyalties.*

I was nervous in case the two Reverend Mothers came back and caught us. I was told I could bend the rules, but then the nuns seemed to take matters into their own hands and I didn't think they really should have done some of the things they did, such as tucking their skirts into their knickers in order to do the cancan.

That night some of us (novices) stayed up very late and built a pretend hearth with a pretend fire made out of red and orange cellophane paper and a light bulb. We did this because we all agreed that a nice cosy fire was one of the things we most missed about Christmas. We sat around and reminisced about Christmas at home until, at around 11:00pm, the door opened and it was Rev Mother wearing a long flannelette nightie.

"What are you doing?" She asked. Her expression was grim, and her voice was like flint. When we told her, she was furious and sent us all fleeing to our beds with the threat of punishment for breaking the Grand Silence. I tried to explain that I had understood that I was Rev Mother still and she said that I wasn't any more, and most certainly would never be again if this is what I allowed my nuns to do (It is against the rule to break the Grand Silence).

Those involved have been waiting to be summoned for our punishment, but it seems to have all just fizzled out and is, hopefully, behind us. According to the Holy Rule, we are required to leave all mail open so that Reverend Mother can read our letters, if she wishes. The Holy Rule does not say why and I suppose this is what we call blind obedience, meaning you do it without understanding the why and the wherefore. Personally, I don't think Reverend Mother ever reads our letters because she gave me a letter from Andy once, in which he asked me to leave the convent and come home and marry him instead. Anyway, if she does read them, that would be breaking the rule, because the rule requires us to keep custody of the eyes and Reverend Mother is far too holy to break a rule. I hope she does not read this one.

74

Now I'll tell you about Christmas. Mass was the nearest thing to angels singing that you could possibly imagine. We sang it in four parts. When we all sing together like that I feel as if heaven has come to earth. The best thing, though, was when we came down to breakfast. All the tables were covered in snowy white crisp linen tablecloths and all our napkins folded like Bishops' Hats. Someone had sprayed hydrangeas gold to make Christmas table decorations and there was Holly and Ivy everywhere. It was stunning and not at all like the austere Christmas lunch I had expected. We feasted all day. Yes, we did have turkey, and there was even wine. There was no exchange of presents, like we have at home, and I did miss our family Christmas together, but I wasn't unhappy because the whole convent was so full of such simple joy. That was present enough.

I asked Mother Pius why Christmas was so richly feasted when we had a vow of poverty. I think she thought I was ungrateful or insolent or something, because she answered rather huffily and then gave me a penance. I wasn't being critical though. I really wanted to know. Anyway, I understood more about the vow of poverty after she explained that it is not always about denial. It is about acknowledging God and trusting Him for our needs; it is about dependency rather than deprivation. I now understand that you could be as rich as a king and not break your vow of poverty. The vow of poverty is more to do with poverty of spirit – you are poor in that you give up the right to choose. Well, even that is not quite correct for you do have choice in that you choose to allow God, through others, to make that choice for you. In very simple terms, it is about being completely grateful with God's provision for your life, even if you do not like it much. Saints are people who can do this with joy. I think I am a very long way from being a saint.

Well as you can see God certainly provided well for us this Christmas. We did lots of special things and danced in the evening. The novices are wonderful dancers. You should see them dance jigs and reels, like those I learned when I went to Irish dancing classes, only they dance so much better because it is in their blood.

The highlight of Christmas day was when the mail was given out. As you know we were on retreat for eight days before Christmas so we were even more cut off from the outside world than usual, and not allowed to talk to each other at all. Consequently, Christmas seemed all the more joyful and celebratory because all restraint was lifted. I literally jumped for joy when I got my Christmas parcel from home. Oh thank you so very much for the beautiful warm scarf, Mum. I know you will have been up nights knitting it. We gorged on the Quality Street. As for the flannelette nightie you made me, Mum. It is perfect and feels like a warm hug from you when I put it on. You know that I particularly appreciate the gift of the time that went into its making, since you have so little for yourself as it is. Thanks Rita for the warm sleeves for under my habit in winter. The weather is freezing so I predict they will be worn day and night.

I am very happy here and I don't want you to worry about me. I am now three months into my spiritual year and imagining myself spending next Christmas in community somewhere else. I am hoping for France but of course we don't get a choice and we have to learn to accept with joy wherever we are placed.

We also had lots of celebrations on Boxing Day. It was as big a deal as Christmas. Then, just when I thought all the celebrations were over, imagine my excitement when I was woken and told I was to be Reverend Mother for the day on the Feast of Holy Innocents. The Christmas season has been all fun and games, as you can see. I am wondering what New Year will be like. I do love holiday times here. The nuns are smiling all the time (probably because the pressure's off from teaching) and some of them are allowed to come over to the Novitiate for visits. Otherwise we are not allowed to talk to them. I am not sure if I told you that. It is because the Novitiate is quite separate. Of course we share the chapel with the nuns, and we novices wait on them at table, and when we have 'Licence' the rule of silence is relaxed. But we are still not allowed to talk to them, though we can answer them if they speak to us, otherwise it would be rude, and anyway, they would not speak to us unless it was for something important.

Well that is all my news. I look forward to some from you and I hope you are all well and that you had a lovely Christmas.
Your loving daughter/sister
Kate

Maria folded the letter and put it back in its envelope. She took out a notebook and wrote the following:

THINGS TO ASK NAN.
Why can't novices speak to nuns?
Ask why Nan went into convent? No more fobbing off.
Ask about the cross poem
Ask why Nan left the convent.
Ask Nan if she ever found out if Mother Pius read her letters.

Battle of Wills

Emily had intended to sleep in late on Monday morning, telling herself there was no need to rush. *You're on holiday! Make the most of it.* She crept upstairs to the kitchen to make a cup of coffee and the oven clock told her it was only a quarter past seven. She trod lightly over to Nan's room and listened. There was no sound so Emily assumed Nan was still sleeping. She decided not to go back to bed, as she had intended, because the sun was dappling the trees with light, making the garden too beautiful to turn her back on. She would sit outside with her book and, for once, take time to enjoy her caffeine hit, without which she was hideous company. She picked up her copy of *Mao's Last Dancer* and sat on the front door step.

Brisbane was pretty. It was early spring and the flowering White May was budding. Bottlebrushes were attracting rainbow lorikeets and the wind tickled the treetops making them rustle. Emily smiled. Life was good…until… loud music broke the spell, and the voices of John, George, Paul and Ringo scared the birds away. Emily cringed. Her initial reaction was to jump up, rush in and turn it off. Then she remembered this was Nan's home and she was here to make peace. After filling the house with noise, Nan had filled the kettle by which time Emily had found the milk in the fridge.

"Here." she said, holding it out for Nan to take.

"Don't think because you're staying here you're going to take over, Emily. I can get my own milk thank you. I'm feeling tons better today."

"Well I'm glad you're feeling better, Mum. I'll make myself scarce then, but I'm just downstairs if you want me." Emily didn't want to start the week with a confrontation, so headed towards Nan's bedroom to gather up her washing. However, her mother's powerful voice stopped her dead in her tracks.

"Don't go in my bedroom!"

"I was just going to get your washing."

"I can do my own washing."

Emily's shoulders slumped. Yesterday had been so promising, but today was going to be a minefield unless she handled things diplomatically. Emily had become quite good at self-talk. She had to do it a lot in her job.

Okay! She'll probably forget about the washing soon, I'll do it later. It's not like work. There are no timetables or deadlines.

Emily was downstairs hanging out her own washing at ten o'clock when Matthew rang.

"Everything okay?"

"She acting like there's nothing wrong with her and making it clear she doesn't want me around."

"Try bringing up some old memories. That may turn her mood around."

"What, like the Beatles?"

"I wouldn't go that far. Try reminding her of birthdays, talk about Dad. Try for something that will make her feel happy."

"Good idea. Will you come for tea?"

"Yes. I'd better, in case you've killed each other."

"I'm determined to do this, Matthew."

"I know. I'll see you later." Matthew hung up and loneliness washed over Emily. *Don't get into a downward spiral*, she told herself. She wanted blissful days, despite the horror hanging over the house. That was when the word *paint* erupted into her mind along with a flow of painful memories that burned and seared as if a lava flow had passed through. She could not blot them out. Rather, it seemed that she must face each traumatic frame of a past she would sooner forget. Thank God for Matthew, she thought, knowing he was the only one who would understand.

Throughout the day, Emily went upstairs on the pretext of making tea, or a sandwich. There was some polite conversation, after which Emily retreated to her crypt. She noted that Nan had done her own washing, as she said she would, though in a fashion of her own, for Nan's underwear was now decorating almost every bush in the front yard. Emily resisted the temptation to rescue them for she had learned a lesson about that yesterday, from Laura. The only thing Emily insisted on that day, was preparing dinner – lasagne - to use up yesterday's leftover Bolognese sauce. She did this while Nan was having her afternoon nap, so there could be no argument. Emily and Matthew lingered over a cup of tea after dinner that night, while Nan rocked herself to sleep in her chair.

"The thing is, I don't want to make Mum miserable with unwanted help, Matthew. I want this to work. How do you care for someone like Mum, though, without intruding?"

"I think you've already worked that out. It's important to give her the freedom of her own home. A lot of people with cancer don't have family to look after them. They just have a carer visit once or twice a day to check up on them and take them shopping, if they're up to it. I think it's a good idea if you do the same. Be here, but not here, so to speak. Disempowerment's not the right approach, so avoid it, and do what you did today and let her do what she can while she can."

"Yes! Exactly! But I must have something to do. Here's the thing… I feel like painting and that way I could stay in the background. But I'm feeling guilty about it because of last time. I haven't painted since… Matthew, how can I know if I subconsciously want to escape from Mum like I wanted to escape from life before my breakdown? Also, I'm scared of it becoming manic and all consuming again."

"I don't think you can compare the present circumstances with that time, Emily. I know you remember it as a time when you let your children down, but you have to look at the bigger picture. Your marriage had broken up. Larry had buggered off leaving you with a lot of debt. You had 3 small children to provide for. Not to mention all those years with Larry's addiction. It didn't matter how much money he made – it was never enough, and, in the end, he gambled everything he had, including you and the girls..."

"I should have stopped him…"

"How do you stop a runaway train? You're being too hard on yourself again."

Silent tears had sprung to her eyes and were rolling down her cheek. They had touched on a grief that had taken her, tottering, to the brink of the abyss, and, just as she had begun the free-fall into it, Matthew had caught hold of her and held her fast. He helped her to work through her monumental problems, never taking them away from her, but enabling her to face them and deal with them. He handed her a tissue and she blew her nose.

"…Anyway, that's in the past. As for today, the way I see it is, you can either paint to nurture yourself - and this is your holiday, and that's what holidays are for - or you can paint to escape. Make the choice. Is it to be the nurturing story or the torturing story?"

"That's so simple and it makes so much sense. Thanks! Wow!" She leaned towards her brother and stroked his face. "It's a good job we have each other," she said, and they laughed. "Oh God. I sound like Mum!" She had just uttered one of Nan's catch phrases.

Matthew didn't leave right away after dinner. He made a second cup of tea and, turning the TV off, sat on the beanbag near his mother. She had woken up and he had brought a shoebox full of old photos that Nan had given him when he had moved out.

"Look, Mum. This is you and Dad. Do you remember your old Ford Escort?" Nan took the photo from him and scrutinised it. "This one is of Disneyland on the way back from England when we went to visit Granny and Grampy. Look, there's a squirrel in their garden."

"Oh yes. So it is." Nan did not seem in the mood for reminiscing because suddenly she asked. "When do I have to go for my radium treatment?"

"Wednesday - the day after tomorrow!" Then, as if Nan had pushed the thought away, she asked:

"Who'd like some chocolate?" Her eyes were twinkling as if she was being very naughty, and she was because when she ate chocolate, which wasn't very often, she ate several bars of it at one sitting.

Who cares? Let her enjoy whatever she wants. This was Emily's new attitude. *You're a long time dead.*

The phone rang. It was Beth about Maria's birthday.

"I can make dinner here for Maria's bir..." Beth was quick to interrupt before her mother took over. It had been hard work weaning their birthday celebrations out of Nan's clutches, and having won that victory, Beth didn't want to now surrender it to her mother.

"She wants to eat out. We'll all meet up at The Mexican at the end of the High Street. Do you know the one? Invite Nan to come too. Maria particularly wants her there; Matthew too." *Oh to hear those words spoken about me.* Beth broke into Emily's thoughts. "Do you think Nan will be well enough to come?"

"Well, she's okay today. Let's hope she'll be okay on Saturday. What time?"

"Is six thirty okay?" Emily confirmed this with Matthew and, putting the phone down, told Nan that Maria particularly wanted her to attend her birthday dinner.

"She always was thoughtful." Emily took comfort in a large piece of chocolate, fighting down the feeling of always being on the fringes of the love that existed between her daughters and her mother.

Phantom Pregnancy

At the conference dinner, Maria pleaded with Simon not to leave her side, because conferences were notoriously opportunistic for those interested in networking while shagging, and Maria, because she was spectacularly beautiful, spent much of her time avoiding unwelcome advances.

"For conference purposes, we're as good as married," she told Simon."And if anyone is over familiar with me, I give you permission to be as creative as you want. Just help me keep them at bay, okay?"

Maria could ask this of Simon because any chemistry between them was the sort that could only be shared in a laboratory and he knew that she did not want a repeat of the last conference when two lesbians and a swinger had, over dinner, presented vigorous arguments in favour of foursomes, in an attempt to outwit her into their bed.

Maria and Simon had discovered each other when they were studying biology at uni and had remained best friends since. They had both established themselves as plant biologists, though in different areas of research, and they had always worked together. When one of them left their workplace in favour of loftier or more lucrative positions, they would look out for a job to suit the other, or ring the other's praises so much that the new organisation would head-hunt them when a vacancy came up. In this way they had helped each other rise up the career ladder. Both now led their own research group in complementary areas, proving wrong those who said it was impossible for women to have a friendship with a man, without sex.

When Maria's phone rang during the conference dinner, she knew it was Beth. Beth's mobile plan gave her an hour in which she could ring anyone in Australia for free, so she always phoned between six and seven. Maria did not want to answer the call while networking with colleagues. Nor did she want to reveal any of her private business to them, so she switched her phone over to voicemail and stowed it back in her pocket, returning to the conversation around the table, which was mostly to do with the paper she had delivered that afternoon. This networking was useful for exploring areas of future collaboration and research. A colleague from another university was asking Maria to elaborate on a particular thread of her research when Simon's phone rang. It was Beth.

"Simon, is Maria with you?" she asked.

"Yes."

"Well why did she put me on voicemail?" she asked.

"Well, her talk went very well, thanks for asking, but at the moment she's at dinner with several people interested in her work. It isn't a good time for her to talk."

"Is that Beth?" Maria whispered. Simon nodded.

"Tell her I'll call her later."

"She'll call you later."

"Hmph," conceded Beth. "Tell her I might be busy."

"Okay," said Simon and pocketed his mobile. He whispered Beth's message into Maria's ear, adding, "Mmm. You smell nice." Maria smiled at the compliment. It was such an innocent and beautiful smile that David Marlow, who had repeatedly propositioned her at conferences all over the world, and who was now sitting opposite her with a hard-on, was prompted to present her with his business card.

"Think about visiting my research centre at the University of Melbourne," he said. Maria glanced at the card and noted his new title was Director. "I'd be very interested in discussing collaborative research projects with you. In fact we're hosting a conference in November, if you can get away."

"Well that might be difficult because of Horace," Simon intervened, annoying the hell out of Marlow.

"Who's Horace," Marlow asked Maria, who suddenly choked on a crumb and gestured between coughs for Simon to explain.

"The alpha male in her life!" Then turning his wicked gaze on Maria asked. "He is due in November, isn't he darling?" There was a communal gasp.

"A baby?"

"Was it planned?"

Maria, rendered speechless by this ludicrous proclamation, could say nothing in her own defence because her coughing fit was now convulsing her body. Those around the table read the head nodding caused by the very act of coughing as assent to all their questions and a low buzz of whispers travelled around the room. Despite the fact that pregnancy was not something she had ever contemplated, and deciding to leave career damage control until later, she saw an opportunity to promote a feministic cause that many of her married colleagues felt strongly about. So, buying time, by way of taking a long drink of water, she put her challenge out there.

"I'm sure that David's Research Centre would be a world leader in equal opportunities for women. He'd have a crêche for people like me, even if he had to man it himself, isn't that so David?" All eyes feasted expectantly on David's dilemma, especially the female ones. After a moment's quick thinking, he sidestepped the question.

"I will certainly put the idea forward to my Planning Committee."

While answering questions, Maria's eyes roved around the room wondering how Simon's announcement of her non-existent baby was going to affect her working reputation. It was true that government departments and academia, professed equal opportunity for women, but Maria had often wondered how many women had missed out on jobs because employers were concerned about the disruption pregnancy and family demands would bring to a woman's workplace.

Male academics would refute this, of course, but female academics were constantly raising it as a real issue. What on earth possessed Simon to say such a thing, Maria thought, hoping it would not interfere with her ambition.

In the polite networking that followed dinner, Maria was approached and taken aside twice.

"I'm here if you need a father for your baby," one man said. A little later there was another kind offer.

"I'm Renata and I just want to say that if you need another mother for your baby, I'd be very interested." Noting the sexual innuendo, Maria looked around for Simon with look-what-you-got-me-into desperation. She noticed that he was deep in conversation with Rick Walters and didn't respond to her frantic beckoning, so that she was forced to deflect such propositions on her own. Later, on the way up to their rooms, he told her that he had just been head hunted for a job.

"Rick said they have to go through the motions, but that he would make sure I got it."

"Where is it?" Maria asked.

"Perth," he answered. This brought Maria to a standstill.

"Perth?" Maria repeated incredulously. She considered this for a moment and then said with uncharacteristic vehemence. "Well what a bastard you turned out to be. You get me up the duff and then leave me!" Arriving at her hotel room door, she slid her card through the reader, opened the door, entered, and slammed it shut, but not before noticing the lesbian who wanted to mother her non-existent baby entering the room next door, mouthing the words, "I'm here for you."

Alone in her room, Maria rang Beth, who didn't answer, in retaliation for Maria not answering Beth's call earlier. Then she rang Laura.

"Hi!" Maria said hoping news of home would settle a nervous tension that had come upon her.

"It's not a good time, Maria." Laura said.

"Well, why did you leave me a message asking me to call you?"

"That was this morning."

Maria rang off. *Grr! What's wrong with everyone?* She thought. She decided to ring Nan, who was always good for a chat. Her mother answered.

"Hi Mum. Is Nan there?" There was a prolonged silence while Emily pulled the dagger out of her heart. It left her bleeding. "Mum? Are you there, Mum?" Emily stayed where she was putting her hand over the phone for a few moments, while she took control of her emotions. "She's asleep, sorry." Quietly, she put the phone down.

"Who was that?" Nan said coming into the living room at that very moment.

"It was Maria," Emily said.

"What did she want?"

"You of course!" Emily said dejectedly as she passed Nan on her way downstairs.

Maria sat on her bed wondering why, in a world full of family and friends, she felt so utterly alone. There was a gentle knock on her room door. It was Renata, the lesbian from next door.

"I have the makings of Margaritas," she said holding up two unopened bottles. "And I promise, I won't hit on you." Maria stepped back to let her in.

Cops

Laura's friends in 'Traffic' replied to her email about the spunky cop, which would have been fantastic, only so did the cop. The email said: *You've been checking out my ID. I'll wait for you after your shift and you can explain.*

"Shit!" she gasped. "Shit, bloody shit! Shit!" For once Laura didn't want work to end and, when it finally did, she left by the back door. "Shit," she said again when, creeping cautiously around the side of the building, she saw him waiting by her Motorbike. *So he has enough information on me to know I ride a Kawasaki Ninja. He doesn't look too pissed though,* she thought hopefully.

"G'day!" She put on her crash helmet as she approached him. "You must've been checking out my ID if you know what I ride. That makes us quits I think."

"So where did you get my photo from?" he asked.

"Internet," she lied, mounting her bike and pushing it off its stand. It rolled forward and he reached for the handle bar to detain her. "It's not an offence," she said.

"Why do you want to know about me and what are you doing with my photo?"

"I want to use it as a dart-board." He looked more bewildered than angry so she looked him in the eye and asked, without stopping for breath. "Are you married? Got a girlfriend? Are you gay?"

"No. What's it to you?" She turned the ignition key and luckily her bike fired first time.

"Phone me. If you know what I ride you must have my phone number." She pushed past him and gathered a bit of speed, but she was still in the car park so couldn't accelerate much. Just as she thought she was getting away, he jumped onto the pillion seat, forcing her to stop because it was illegal for a passenger to ride a motorbike without a helmet.

"Are you nuts?" Then she capitulated. "Okay, you win. I wanted to invite you to dinner."

"I don't date colleagues. Besides, I don't fancy you."

"We're not colleagues. You're in traffic, and I'm on the beat. Anyway, don't flatter yourself - I don't fancy you either, but come anyway!" This intrigued him and he searched her face for clues finding none behind her visor. She didn't appear to be flirting with him. "I promise you'll enjoy yourself," she said.

"Laura Taylor," he said. He repeated the name twice more, trying to place it. Then something clicked into place. "Have you got sisters?"

"Too many questions too soon," she smirked, enjoying having one up on him. "Be at The Mexican at the end of the High Street, Indooroopilly at 6:30pm on Saturday. Look in the window. If you see something you like, and I'm sure you will, come in and join us. Now, get off my bike before I do you for not wearing a helmet." He got off but didn't rush it.

"You're just a pissy cadet. I'll do you first for your damned cheek."

"Since when was cheek an offence?" she threw back at him as she sped away before he could jump onto her motorbike again.

Laura phoned Beth as soon as she walked through the door.

"He's hooked," she said.

"Excuse me?" Beth said vaguely.

"The traffic cop, I've invited him to Maria's birthday." That made Beth sit up and take notice.

"Wahoo! Brilliant! You're wasted on the beat."

"Beth, did you get through to Maria? Does she know which restaurant we've booked?"

"No! I keep ringing her and she keeps putting me on voice-mail."

"Surely she's rung you back? She always does as soon as she's free."

"I know. She has rung back."

"So what's the problem?"

"I keep putting her on voice-mail too."

"Why?"

"Because she puts me on voice-mail."

"What… you mean like tit-for-tat?"

"Sort of." Laura was too exasperated to speak. "Well, she did it first." Beth protested.

"You can't be serious?" There was a silence while each weighed up the other. "Well you know what? Call me back when you're out of nappies."

Brush Strokes

It was Monday night before Emily had organised the materials with which to paint. She had decided to make an early start the following morning, but instead, began to paint as soon as she had hung up on Maria. She had to, or the emotion would have exploded like a stick of dynamite, and might have been just as dangerous. Emily had learned enough about herself to know that this was her struggle and she must find a way of soothing her own hurts. As she prepared her canvas and her paint palette, she thought back to that time when her world had turned upside down, and asked herself what had made her so angry back then? What had been the trigger?

Without thinking why, she chose the largest canvas and began to paint life onto it with intense vibrant colours – reds, yellows, orange. She kept a notepad beside her to jot down her thoughts. As one memory triggered another, tears began to flow, softly at first, and then like a river that had burst its banks. They spilled onto her palette and mixed with the paint. She concentrated as she painted through the rush of tears, soon realising there was one dominant thought. She asked herself how and when she had come to believe the thought, and if it were true, and how, whether true or not, it had affected her life for many years. She translated the thought onto the canvas, working without a break throughout the night and into the early hours of the morning. Just as daylight was breaking on Tuesday morning, she put down her paintbrush and stood back from the painting to view her work critically. In the painting her mother and her children were on top of a rock face. She only had to paint herself now, but she needed a cup of tea first.

Emily took some rice-crackers out of a plastic biscuit container and ate them while the kettle boiled. She had made herself a make-do kitchen downstairs so she didn't have to intrude on Nan on those days when space was needed between them. The crypt consisted of a very large laundry to the back, a generous-sized living room housing an old fridge, a computer desk, bookshelves and a very comfy bed, beside which was an armchair. Directly opposite the living room was a bathroom. Emily's room had large sliding doors that opened onto the back veranda. During the day, this was where she used to paint, because the light was excellent and the view magnificent. The house was built on a hill and looked out over rooftops to distant mountains.

For this particular night-time project, Emily had made the laundry her studio, which turned out to be a good thing, because working in the laundry had jogged memories of how confined she had felt during the time she had been ill. She made a cup of tea and took it back into her room, where she could drink it in the comfort of her armchair. She was glad that Nan came down less and less. This meant she didn't have to share her work with her, and if she did choose to, it would be when she felt ready.

Emily reached down the side of the chair for her handbag and, finding her diary, noted that tomorrow would be Wednesday, the day Matthew had volunteered to take Nan for her radium treatment. This would give her time to shop for new paints. She had been astonished to find a stash of her old acrylics from years ago, and had asked herself why Nan had not thrown them out. Some of them were dried up but most were okay, though the tubes were almost empty.

Emily began to feel calmer and she was glad because it had been an intensely emotional session. Painting in this all-consuming way had crystalised the reason behind her anger. She had been hard on herself and had used a process of self-interrogation whereby in not letting herself off the hook, she had probed the darkest caverns of her soul in order to find the seed of resentment that had taken root there. Then she had brought it out into the open in order to examine it objectively.

It was a seed that had grown so large it had cast shadows over her entire life for, while painting, she had realised her anger was secondary to a feeling of overwhelming helplessness.

She drained her cup and went back to work fortified. It took her half an hour to paint herself into the picture and when she stood the finished result up against the wall and stepped back, she was happy. Her painting's perspective was different from anything she had ever done previously. In it she was an isolated person looking upwards towards her mother and children who were on top of a high rock, almost out of sight and way out of reach. Her face portrayed the grief, loss, helplessness and despair she had experienced when she had become too ill to care for her children and had been admitted to hospital. Nan had taken them to live with her until she was better. When she had recovered, the children did not want to return home. While Emily had been absent from their lives, they had turned to Nan for mother-love, and the more she mothered them, the more Emily felt she had lost them.

When Emily was able to return home, everyone thought it would be best if she adjusted in stages. So she went to convalesce at Nan's house, she downstairs, and her children upstairs with Nan. When it was time to go back to work Nan spoke frankly of Emily's struggle to manage as a single mother with all that it entailed.

"Why don't you stay here until you are ready to manage on your own?" Emily had agreed. It all made sound good sense.

Six months down the track Nan had another suggestion.

"You know, if you want to, you and the girls can stay here on a permanent basis. Then you could rent out your own house, which would give you more income."

Emily had not listened to her gut feelings. It seemed like such a good and generous offer, and she was so very strapped for cash. As the girls grew older they would cost more and there was high school to think about. She had always dreamed of sending them to St Francis Xavier's, which would cost money she didn't have. Sometimes you had to let go of one dream to realise another, she reasoned. So she agreed. She didn't see then that, with such an arrangement, Nan would become so enmeshed in their lives that it would be difficult to ever break free of her. But it had become crystal clear over time.

Emily yawned. She had faced her demons and it had left her exhausted. She decided she had earned a sleep-in. Having drained her cup, she closed her diary, put the laundry light out and climbed into bed, knowing Nan would not disturb her.

Telephone Tag

"Don't worry. I have no intention of seducing you," said Renata. "But you do look as if you need a friend. No strings! I promise." So it was that Renata stopped flirting with Maria, in order to befriend her. Maria confided that Simon was supposed to have protected her from unwelcome admirers, but that he had made a right pig's ear of it. It wasn't long before they were both rolling around laughing at the very idea of everyone thinking she was pregnant when she wasn't.

"You hid your feelings very well, and used the opportunity to put that revolting David Marlow on the spot." Renata soon eased Maria's worry that such a story could harm her career. "Beside, if motherhood really was an issue for some employers, would you want to work for them?"

"I suppose not. But I'd want to fight the mindset that saw it as a problem," said Maria.

"Attagirl!" Renata was bubbly after her third drink. "Cut off their appendages I say! It's the only way to make us all equal." Maria didn't stop laughing for quite some time. Later, when the Margarita-fired hilarity had quietened, Maria told Renata about Nan's terminal illness and they commiserated over the confused relationships that often existed within families.

"My parents don't really understand my sexuality," Renata said sadly. "I can't really talk to them about it." By this time Maria felt she could safely give her a comforting hug.

"You're okay," Maria said. "I like you just the way you are." Eventually they fell asleep together on Maria's bed. Later, in the middle of the night, when it was colder, they crept under the covers as if they had been friends since childhood.

Simon saw them leaving Maria's room the following morning and made the obvious assumption.

"I've always wondered what it would be like to sleep with a lesbian," said Maria, "and now I know." She spoke loudly, and deliberately, as they passed Simon in the lobby, giving him the cold shoulder. As the day progressed Simon was frustrated, because he could not find a moment alone with Maria to tell her about the other possibilities he and Rick Walters had talked about. Renata was everywhere he wanted to be - at Maria's side at conference talks, offering her canapés and pre-dinner drinks, sitting next to her at meals. The more he failed to get Maria alone, the more he resented it.

That evening, after the conference dinner, Maria went to her room alone.

"I need some space," she told Renata. "I hope you don't mind."

"No problem. I need to catch up on a few things too. See you in the morning," she said.

Alone in her room Maria phoned Nan.

"What's wrong with everyone? I've been trying to speak to someone – anyone for days."

"Have you dear? Well why didn't you ring?"

"I did... Oh never mind. How did the radium treatment go?"

"It was fine," Nan said. "I'm coming to your birthday dinner, dear. Thanks for inviting me." Since Maria hadn't yet been told the arrangements regarding her birthday, she was tempted to bite back *Fantastic Nan. Am I invited too*?

"I'm glad you're feeling better, Nan. How're things going with Mum?"

"Why don't you ask her yourself? She's right here." It was said before Maria could ask Nan to pass a message on. Emily, in fact, was not right there. Nan gestured to Matt to keep Maria on the phone while she went to call Emily up from the crypt.

"Emily. It's Maria for you." Emily guessed this was a lie. Maria's calls to her mother were few and far between.

96

"Hey kiddo! How's the conference? Did you wow everyone with your talk?"

"Yes Thanks Uncle Matt. It attracted a reasonable amount of interest."

"Good. So what's going on?"

"Simon's got a new job in Perth," she blurted out. "He's going to be heading up a new research centre."

"Wow! That's terrific. You'll miss him, though, won't you? What's the matter? Are you crying?"

"No, I've got a cold," she lied, blowing her nose. Matthew handed the receiver to Emily who had heard what Matthew had said.

"Hello Maria. How are you?"

"Okay. I'm just touching base, Mum. How's it going with you and Nan?"

"It's…um… interesting," Emily replied. "No knock-outs yet! Is the conference going well?" Maria's eyes filled again so that she had to blow her nose a second time. Emily did not beat about the bush.

"What's wrong, Maria?"

"Nothing," Maria lied. Emily tried again. "Is it anything I can help you with?"

"Not really. I don't even know why I'm crying."

"That's the worst sort of crying," Emily said. "Well I'm here if you want to talk. Email me if you'd rather."

"Thanks," Maria said and then hung up. She stared at her mobile for a minute trying to understand what had just happened. Had she and her mother just connected? Maria sighed. It seemed to her that there had been some cataclysmic shift in the universe, because everything was changing. Then her thoughts moved on to her sisters. *I'm not going to play telephone tag with them any more*, she decided emphatically, throwing her mobile onto a nearby armchair. She searched, instead, for the folder containing Nan's writing, and once having opened it, could not put it down.

Bluebell Bower

I had now been in the Novitiate for eighteen months and my community year was upon me. The entire convent and Novitiate were on retreat, at the end of which, postulants would receive the habit. Novices who had returned from their community year would make vows, and novices finishing their spiritual year would be sent off to live in community for ten months. I was the only one of these and when my ten months in community came to an end, I too would return to the Novitiate to make my vows.

Retreats usually lasted ten days and included an immersion in spiritual themes, a program of austerity that usually included fasting and complete silence. This, my Mistress of Novices taught, would heighten my relationship with God. We were allowed to roam the convent grounds at will, so long as we attended all the formal retreat talks, prayer times and silent, minimal meals.

I had a favourite place called Bluebell Bower. It lay parallel to a river that meandered through the convent grounds, which were extensive. It was an atmospheric place that I often imagined as a setting for Midsummer Night's Dream, because the ground rose up creating a natural platform, like a stage, with trees either side that formed a domed canopy over it. I thought it was cathedral-like, and, definitely, the most worship-full place I knew, decorated, as it was, with nature's offerings, and softened by the hand of God. My stout nun shoes did not echo there, as they did in chapel, because the ground was densely covered with bluebells.

I carried a book with me – the prayers of St Therese, and I intended to sit on Bluebell Bower's fragrant blue carpet, while reading it. I wanted to imitate the saint, otherwise known as The Little Flower who, before entering into contemplation, would position herself at the feet of Jesus, imagining she was a tiny flower in a great carpet spread out at His feet. She knew she was significant because without such as her, the carpet would not exist, and the carpet gave Jesus joy. She did not crave greater significance, or pride *of place before Him, It was enough for her simply to sit, inconspicuously, in his presence.*

As I sat among the flowers, becoming one with them, I became strangely elated and wanted to dance. At first I dismissed the idea. I had only ever stomped or jived at the Cavern. But soon the desire became overwhelming and, as if my soul left my clumsy body sitting there, I felt light and free, and began to move in a new way, totally devoid of inhibitions. I danced, at first, to the song in my head, but soon the music was outside of me, hypnotic and heavenly. Drawing me along the entire length of Bluebell Bower, which rose uphill. As I rose higher and higher it seemed as if the eagles soaring in the distance, and the clouds passing me by, were dancing with me.

Soon, my path began to descend and, in the distance, I could see a domed structure that suggested the entrance to a tunnel. It shone bright in the setting sun and I imagined it was the way to heaven.

My carpet of bluebells settled on top of a scrubby hill, transforming it into a forget-me-not place of unusual beauty. The dome, I could now see, was not a tunnel, but the roof of a great stage. Thousands of people were sitting in an immense amphitheatre screaming.

The sun had disappeared and the sky was full of twinkling stars. A hush fell over the crowd, as if something was about to happen – and it did. Four young men came onto the stage from the wings and, immediately, the crowd was on its feet screaming even louder than before. The young men took up instruments and started to sing a familiar song, that increased in volume as they made a four-staged approach to the microphones.

"Ahhh!" It was John,

"Ahhh!" George

"Ahhh!" Paul,

"Ahhh!" Ringo. Then all together they sang.

"Shake it up baby now, shake it up baby. Twist and shout!"

The crowd went wild and so did I. When they had finished their song, The Beatles said they were delighted to be performing live at The Hollywood Bowl and sang their way through many of their hit songs: 'You Can't Do That', 'All My Loving', 'She Loves You Yeah, Yeah, Yeah', and others that I had not heard since I had left Liverpool. As I sat, I knew the meaning of adoration. I loved The Beatles, but even more, I loved and adored the God who made them.

After the curtain call I sat there for a long time, while the crowds streamed out of the amphitheatre. I was still there when the stage-crew plunged the place into darkness. At last I got up for I had been away too long, and there was nothing else to keep me here. My bluebell path sloped up toward the sky again and I began to retrace my steps. As I looked down on a network of roads and by-ways, a voice rang out loud and clear.

"Hya girl!" It was coming from a speeding car that was climbing a different mountain. "We're havin' a bit of a party. De yer wanna come?"

"Sorry George," I said. "I'd luv to, but I'm on retreat!" At that moment he took the low road and my carpet of flowers continued to rise before bowing towards earth once more.

Maria breathed into the silence of the night, before putting the sheets of paper down. Obviously the story was not true. But Maria had just uncovered something interesting - that there was room in the heart of Nan's God for everyone, from nun to Beatle.

Head-Hunted

On Thursday morning after her shift, Laura realised that Maria's birthday was on Saturday and as far as she knew, the restaurant had not been booked and the traffic cop was the only one that had been invited.

"Stop stressing," Beth said. "It's just family – and the traffic cop. Who else is there to invite?

"I've been having second thoughts about him."

"It's a bit late for that, Laura. You've already invited him.

"I can uninvite him."

"But then we'll have to think of another way to put him in Maria's way. Maybe we should invite some other people so it's not too obvious or intimidating for him. I've got a couple of mates who would come and I'm sure you can think of a few people to invite."

"Beth! It's Maria's birthday. She's not going to want our friends at her party."

"Okay then, who are her friends?" At the same time, they both said

"Simon!" This was followed by a long silence.

"She keeps her friends and family separate." Laura said. Let's ask Simon who else we could invite."

"I don't know whether that's a good idea," said Beth. "I can see myself now, sitting next to a mad professor being lectured to on the incredibly riveting fact that I have 60,000 miles of blood vessels in my body, which, if I were to lay them end to end, which of course has been my life's dream, would circle the earth 2.5 times! Tell Simon he is not allowed to invite anyone over 35 years of age. That ought to eliminate the weirdo fact-book toting professors."

"Good thinking," said Laura reading a text. "Actually, will you do it? I've just been called in for an extra shift."

"Okay."

"Today!"

"Okay, okay! I'm onto it." Beth searched for Simon's number and pressed call. Annoyingly she got his voice-mail. "Simon. It's Beth. Ring me. I need you to invite people to Maria's party. It's urgent." She left the same message repeatedly for the next half hour only she started the repeats with bully tactics such as "Stop Ignoring me," or "I'm going to keep ringing until you answer me."

Simon saw Maria and Renata coming towards him as he was waiting for the lift, which had just arrived. He held the door open for them but they walked right past him and took the stairs.

"Damn," He murmured. Downstairs in the conference hall he could see no sign of Maria, but sat down beside Renata hoping Maria would join them.

"Hello, Simon. Congratulations on your new job."

"Where's Maria?"

"She went outside to make a phone-call. I'm holding her seat for her. She shouldn't be long."

"I might take a look," he said, not wanting to talk to Maria across Renata. "Will you hold my seat too, please?"

"Don't take too long. You don't want to walk in during Professor Von Klaut's talk. He's been known to have people shot at dawn for less."

Simon noticed Maria coming in and sat down again. When Maria had settled in he leaned across Renata.

"Beth rang. I've had a dozen calls about your birthday dinner. They've booked the Mexican near Nan's but they want to finalise numbers. Beth wants me to invite your work colleagues. Who would you like to invite? I need to get back to her."

"My work colleagues," Maria stared at him defiantly.

"Really?" Simon was so astonished that his eyebrows were practically hidden by his hairline.

"Really!" Maria confirmed. "Renata," she said smiling sweetly. "Would you like to come to my birthday party?"

102

"I'd love to. Thanks!"

Simon was now absolutely sure they were sleeping together, and technically this was true, only not in the way he suspected.

"Why are you angry with me?" Simon said. "You haven't spoken to me since Rick Walters offered me the job - and don't say it's because I got you up the duff again because that's totally unreasonable." Maria's face flamed red with anger.

"Think about it Simon! You told a whole conference full of colleagues that I'm pregnant. What if someone had been on the verge of offering me a job, three levels higher than the glass ceiling? Is it because you don't want me to succeed? Is that why you did it?" Simon was speechless. He told himself that she couldn't possibly believe that. Renata screwed up her face sympathetically.

"Umm! You know I think you sort of asked for that Simon, but maybe you have to be a woman to fully understand why." It was kindly said but totally ignored. It was Simon's turn to be mad now.

"I was trying to protect you."

"Protect me!" Renata tried to sink into the back of the chair in case the cutting tone of Maria's voice sliced at her too. "You practically sabotaged my entire future career."

"It kept the predators away, didn't it? I was only doing what you asked me to."

"Very badly," she snarled... "And as for you going to Perth, well whoopee doo!"

"She sounds mad at you for going to Perth," Renata butted in, very tentatively.

"Well I'm glad I'm going to Perth," he said "and I hope you'll both be very happy with each other." Simon and Maria glared angrily at each other, leaving Renata a fragment of time to make an observation.

"OMG!" she said to Simon. "You think… Woah! Wait a minute! Now I get it! You two are in love!" Two very

103

incredulous faces turned towards her and said at the same time.

"Don't be ridiculous!" Just then Rick Walters sat down next to Maria.

"Ah, Maria. I've been trying to catch you since the conference began. Any chance we can have coffee together after this talk? I've got a proposition for you. You haven't mentioned it yet, have you, Simon?"

"No! I haven't had the opportunity." There was steel in his eyes as he glanced again at Maria.

"Right. Good! I'll be in the coffee lounge after the lecture, Maria." Professor Von Klaut tapped at the microphone to make sure it was working causing Rick Walters to smile and make his way back to his seat.

"Good morning learned colleagues," Von Klaut said. "The subject of my talk is..."

Maria hardly heard a word of Von Klaut's presentation because she was wondering what Rick Walters proposition could be and what it had to do with Simon. Later, over coffee, Rick Walters revealed that Simon had set him straight over the baby rumour. Then he went on to recount how a world-renowned philanthropist had recently jetted some of the world's leading scientists to his Honolulu mansion to discuss the issues threatening the planet and how world hunger might be eradicated.

"We discussed many possibilities and later toasted the decision he had come to. He has donated billions of dollars - over a period of twenty years - to collaborative research across the globe, provided OECD countries match the amount he contributes to their country dollar for dollar. Australia is one of those countries."

"I've had meetings with the Prime Minister and he suggested that the Australian share be managed by the Australian Research Council and that funds should be competed for by application. That's where you and Simon come in. I want you in at the planning stage. You'll be my right and left hands and you'll be at every meeting I attend. Initially everything will be discussed openly within the context of a think tank that we are calling The Thought Court in order to distinguish it from other think tanks and because it is a unique venture. The Thought Court will be responsible for setting up research initiatives that, for now, we will call Flagships. These will be peopled by our stellar performers – science's elite. I have been nominated Executive Director and my brief is to set up the structure, location and direction of the enterprise."

"I'm overwhelmed," Maria said humbly.

"The Thought Court will be made up of industry experts such as leading Australian scientists, executive and senior public servants, business leaders, leading Australian and international environmental pioneers. In time the structure will emerge but I'm envisioning a fleet of Flagships, each with its own dedicated brief, and with its own working fleet. Each working fleet will have its own Ice Breaker. The purpose of an Ice Breaker is to investigate some of the more way-out and obscure research ideas and possibilities within their Flagship's brief, and to bring these back to the Industry Nexi for examination and evaluation. Depending on their merit an application for funding for pilot studies will be made. Once pilot studies are complete the findings will be presented for approval to the working fleet so that an application for research funding on a larger scale can be made. Once an Ice Breaker has brought new initiatives back to the Flagship it will be relieved of any responsibility for them in order to free them up to trawl for yet more newly emerging possibilities.

"What sort of research will be involved?" Maria asked.

"Everything and anything that relates to sustainability. I'm talking about blue-sky research that always has the bigger picture in mind. I don't need to spell it out for you. We have to look at making our oceans sustainable, our crops resistant to pathogens. We need to find ways of greening the deserts, eliminating plant diseases, increasing water supply and food production. We need to address problems of waste, from the disposal of toxic chemicals to the wastage involved in food industries – butter-mountains, and the like. Whatever we undertake, we won't be working alone. It will be an international endeavour and so there will be collaborative discourse between countries, and we'll have access to the best minds on the planet. Because this research will have the greater good at heart our objective will be altruism above egotism."

"There's no need to tell you how this will fast track your career, Maria. I'm offering you a supportive role initially, but it will prepare you for executive level management later. I will be mentoring you personally."

"No Flagship will work in isolation. Ideas emanating from one Flagship will be scrutinised by related Flagships so that connections can be made, sparking further new initiatives. There will be communal and informed input and problem solving. Blue-sky research involves seeing beyond our own needs – beyond our country's needs. We need a global vision and we need to get this right from the ground up."

Maria was overwhelmed but managed to find enough voice to ask.

"What exactly will I be doing?"

"Lots of things. For example, it'll be your job, initially, to locate research, and hook the ones you think would have good sustainability outcomes. You will have to look to the future with long-sightedness verging on the prophetic. You will pick your people well and make sure they have the right sort of heart for the job. We want people with a vocation – who want to save the world from a very bleak future, rather than people who simply want to line their pockets at the expense of a healthy and well cared for planet. In other words we don't want research centres full of selfish bastards. That's why I want you and Simon on board. I think I know you well enough to be sure you are both ethical scientists and that you really have a heart for the best outcome for all. You're both good at reading people, too." Rick smiled. "That's going to be important."

"I want you and Simon beside me, researching for me and feeding information back to me. I'll want you on steering committees, on employment panels, advising architects and planners, liaising with the ARC to set up the application process. For the first three months you'll both be practically eating and sleeping with me, so you'll need to appoint whatever support staff you need back in your current laboratories, and make sure that they're answerable to you for getting things done. You'll need 'can do' people who will free you up for other things. Don't do anything you can delegate. You're going to be too busy. If you don't think you can delegate, don't take the job."

"I can delegate," Maria was quick to answer. "I just have one rather significant personal problem to sort out at the moment." She was thinking of Nan. It was an exciting proposal, though badly timed.

"I thought the baby was a hoax?" Rick Walters said.

"No... It's not that. I mean it was a hoax. It's something else."

"I know this is out of the blue, Maria," Rick said. "I'm sorry if you need time, but unfortunately I don't have much to give you. Simon gave me his answer on the spot. I was hoping you would too. Look, I can give you till Wednesday. Then I'll have to call a meeting of all the key people; they're all standing by."

"I'll give you an answer before then," Maria said.

"Okay. But I have just one thing to say, Maria. Nothing, absolutely nothing, is more important than this."

A Novice Abroad

As was the way between Emily and Nan, the matter of Maria's phone call earlier in the week was dropped. Each retreated into her corner of the house and considered the situation. Nor did Emily show her mother her art. Nan had no idea that Emily filled her afternoons and evenings painting. Nan rarely ventured downstairs as it was, but since Emily had moved back in, Nan was careful not to intrude into her daughter's space.

Nan was usually up earliest in the mornings, and still insisted on making her own breakfast. Emily could usually hear her up and about and left her to it, rising only when the movement above had slowed. Then Emily would go upstairs and see to herself. By then, Nan was more inclined to chat. Emily usually helped herself to cereal while Nan would put the kettle on and make toast.

Each morning Nan liked to stretch her legs by walking to the end of the block, just a matter of a few houses, though, since having the radium, she relied on her walking stick more. Thursday morning was no exception. However, when Emily poured a second cup of tea and went to the door, as she usually did, to monitor Nan's progress, she found her in a crumpled heap on the ground, with a doozey of a bruise on her forehead. Nan looked shaken and Emily brushed away the remnants of twigs and grass clippings that were stuck to Nan's grazed forehead.

"I've become such a Klutz!" Nan was tearing up.

"Let's get you home," Emily said, struggling to lift Nan's diminishing frame. "Put your arm around me and let me take your weight."

"Thanks," Nan said. "There was a time I used to do this for you. Maybe I'd better stop going out on my own from now on."

"I can go with you," Emily suggested.

"Maybe," Nan said.

Nan's words created mixed feelings in Emily. She was happy – even hoped that her mother might need her, but not at the cost of seeing her mother's confidence slipping away. Though Emily felt her mother had stolen her children, she asked herself often, now that she had time to think, if she would have changed anything if she could have. Her children had given her mother so much joy. She realised she was glad about that, even if the gladness was confused with other emotions.

Emily made Nan a bed on the sofa, and when she was sure she was safe and settled, Emily brewed some tea.

"There," she said. "Hot tea is good for shocks." After a minute's careful consideration Emily broached a tricky subject. "I'd like to call the doctor, Mum - just to check that bruise on your head. What do you think?"

"I'm okay. The fall just gave me a fright."

"Yes, but I think we should get the doctor to check you out."

"There's no need. Nothing's broken. I'm just a bit shaken, that's all."

"Okay, but the nurse is coming today so, if you won't let me take you to the doctor, I think we should get her to check you out."

"I'm not a baby," she scolded. "If you were at work I'd be looking after myself. Lots of people in my position live alone and manage." Emily backed off. The nurse, however, diplomatically reported back to Emily when she left Nan resting.

"I've given her some morphine," she confided. "She's complaining of pain. She twisted her foot and that's how she stumbled. It may be best if you accompany her in future when she goes out walking."

"If she'll let me," Emily complained.

"Yes, well, if she doesn't she's likely to have more falls. You can tell her I said that, but I doubt if it'll make much difference. She's got a mind of her own, even Blind Freddie can see that. I've told her she's not allowed to go for walks on her own anymore, so you can quote me."

Nan slept for the rest of the day so Emily painted, climbing the stairs regularly to check on her mother. Once or twice she woke her to offer her a drink.

Emily painted through the quiet afternoon and early evening until Matt arrived after a late meeting.

"How is she?"

"She's okay… a bit shaken. She's been sleeping a lot because of the morphine. I haven't even started dinner yet. I wanted to see what she felt like eating, but she's been sleeping so much. Anyway, I wanted to keep going with my painting."

"Can I see?"

Emily's first painting was standing against the laundry wall in stark contrast to the one he had already seen, which was on the table.

'Wow!" Matt murmured.

"This one is about…"

"I can see what it's about. That's full of pain," he said, pointing to the first. "And this one… well, there's been a major emotional shift in this one."

"Yes, you're right," she said, remembering how, for the first time in many years, she felt pleasure in the thought that she had been able to give her mother something no one else could - grandchildren.

Later, as Emily and Matt shared honeyed prawns, sweet and sour pork and fried rice, Nan made herself a fluffy omelet because she didn't fancy Chinese. She insisted she could cook for herself. Then she joined them at table.

"Do you know where my photograph albums are?" Nan asked.

"You don't have photograph albums any more, Mum," Emily reminded her. "You said they took up too much room, remember? You bought a special filing box for your photos and, if I'm not mistaken, it's up on the shelf in your wardrobe. It's the box with the red roses on it."

"Would you like me to get it down for you before I go home?" Matt offered.

"Are you after a particular photo?" Emily enquired.

"Somewhere I have photos of the convent I taught at in Belgium, as a novice. I just want to look at them again. It's this fluffy omelet that's reminded me because that's where I first cooked one with one of my classes." Usually Matt and Emily would let such a statement slide but they hadn't heard this story.

"Oh! How old were the children?"

"They were twelve year olds. I taught the whole class English and, when I taught them how to make the omelets, I gave all the instructions in English."

"Good grief! That must have been a major undertaking," Matt said. It would be hard enough teaching a language to kids of that age. But to teach them to cook at the same time... well... were you successful or did you end up with egg on your face?"

"Of course not! They cooked it, ate it and asked for more. I taught them all the key words the week before - and of course, I demonstrated every step along the way."

"Even so, it must have been tricky."

"It was trickier trying to teach you two," Nan said looking from one to the other of them. "You didn't want to learn. They did. I was only nineteen at the time and I could wrap them around my little finger. The nun nearest to me in age was forty-two so you can imagine how much the girls loved having a young nun around." Emily and Matt looked at each other, wondering if this was one of Nan's tall stories. They couldn't imagine kids loving Nan when she was a nun because being a nun was one of those seriously weird things about their mother. Nevertheless, trying to maintain this new interest in their mother's life, Matt asked.

"And that was in Belgium? Or was it France?"

"It was Belgium. I did go to France for the first three months of my community year, but I didn't teach there. No! Actually, I tell a lie – I did. I taught myself French."

"I'd say that was impossible," teased Matthew. "How can you teach yourself something you don't know?"

"The hard way!" said Nan. "I was assigned to kindergarten as a helper, but my ability to communicate was so dismal that the teacher put me in the corner with a stack of picture books. I found a dictionary and looked up every single word for hours on end, every school day. But one day I knew enough to put my hand up with the infants. It was a bit humiliating being a grown up in kindy, but I was popular with the children. They all wanted to hold my hand if we did circle games, or partner me if we worked in pairs. Maybe that's where I got my love of picture books from."

It was true. Nan did love picture books. She could not resist coming home with two or three every time she passed a charity shop.

"So how did you come to go to Belgium?"

"Well, you see, in France - in kindy - I had built up a vocabulary of thousands of words, but I didn't have the grammar to go with it. Then an Irish nun in the order's only school in Belgium fell ill with cancer, and there was nobody to teach English and typing throughout the school. As I had been a short-hand typist before entering the convent, and now had a considerable French vocabulary, I was sent to replace her."

"But you weren't a trained teacher."

"No. That bothered me, but I was being trained in obedience and I didn't understand the politics of teaching. Most novices did a stint of teaching in their community year. It was the order's way of assessing whether a novice should go to teacher training college or not. Back then, I was too excited about the opportunity to think beyond myself, and it didn't seem to bother the nuns at all. The nun who had cancer, and Reverend Mother, mentored me and taught me the grammar I lacked."

"So how could you teach others if your own schooling was so poor?" Emily interrupted.

"Well, that's when I discovered that I wasn't as dumb as I thought. I learned all the rules of grammar before I went into the classroom, and the rest I put down to being a good actress. I think I was a good teacher, and the reason the children learned so much was because of my own enthusiasm. You see, I had just discovered the joy of learning myself and I think I infected the children with it. All of a sudden, learning wasn't boring, like when I was at school. It was really fun."

"I remember, during one lesson, getting a bit exasperated with the spirited eleven year olds when they began acting up because of a bee buzzing around them. 'Just ignore it,' I told them. 'A bee won't harm you unless it feels threatened. Perhaps it thinks you are a bunch of flowers. So, if it lands in your hair, be very still and when it realises there's no nectar there, it'll push off to somewhere more lucrative. If you show your fear you are likely to get stung.'"

"I bet you can guess what happened next, can't you?" Nan asked.

"No. What?"

"The bee came after me. It landed on my nose. For about five minutes, I continued to teach with the bee exploring the mountains and caves of my face as if it were Lawson, Blaxland or Wentworth negotiating the Great Dividing Range."

"Did it sting you?" asked Emily.

"No. Eventually, I opened a window and it buzzed off to find a sweeter flower. The girls all clapped. I had proved my point. So you see – I wasn't an awful teacher. Lots of teachers were untrained in those days. When I was in France, I remember the nuns being very worried in case Francois Mitterrand won the 1965 elections and wanted to close down the Catholic schools; at least that was my simple understanding of it."

"It doesn't seem right to have teachers, who had no formal training actually teaching in schools. I bet it doesn't happen now," said Emily.

"My memory of the nuns was that they were excellent teachers. I had first-hand experience of this because I learned so much from them. Lack of training didn't make them bad teachers. It just made them unqualified." Nan yawned. "Anyway, I think most of them were trained and I was excited about them wanting to train me." She yawned again.

"I'll get those photos down for you in a minute, Mum," said Emily. "Go to bed if you're tired. I'll be there in a tick."

When Emily entered the bedroom a quarter of an hour later, Nan was already asleep. She got the photo box down from a shelf that was too high for Nan to reach without taking risks and, stacking Nan's glasses, books and earrings into a pile, placed the box on her bedside table beside them. Before she realised what she was doing Emily bent to kiss her mother, surprising herself with the loving gesture. Just at that moment, Matt came to lend a hand and she was embarrassed by the surprise on his face.

"She's like a child when she's asleep," Emily whispered. Matt simply smiled and sat down beside Nan's bed, and took the lid off the box saying, "I'll sit with her a while, Em."

"I'll be downstairs if you want me. Will you give Mum her tablets before you go? They're in this drawer." Matt stood up to give Emily access to Nan's bedside table.

"They're these in the plastic tub. The nurse left them for her. You wake her, Matthew. She won't mind if *you* wake her, but she might get a bit tetchy if *I* do."

"Sure."

"Thanks for the Chinese, Matt. It was delicious."

"No worries," he said as he leafed through some of the photos.

The Wheatfield

Later, when Matt was long gone, Nan woke in the night and could not get back to sleep. She shuffled along the hall to the toilet, and just as she was getting back into bed she noticed the open box of photos; some of them had been set apart from the others. They were black and white, but that didn't matter because most of them were of black and white robed nuns. There was a post-card photo of the Belgian convent Nan had lived in, with its open shutters and large raised circular garden bed, enclosed by a wide gravel path that allowed parents to come and go, in their posh cars, without doing a three point turn.

The central mansion had once belonged to a nobleman, the school buildings being added at some point, making the whole a three-sided affair. Cloisters were added to the classroom buildings on either side of the mansion, to offer shade. These had been prettied up with cream paint and scarlet geraniums in planter boxes. The dormitories were situated above the classrooms. *That's where I used to sleep, when I taught there*, Nan thought, fixing her gaze on a specific window beyond which was her cubicle.

During her time in Tournai, Nan had been responsible for a large dormitory of ten year olds. Dormitory duty began after Compline, when the girls would go to bed. Nan had to make sure they brushed their teeth and washed themselves. When they were nicely tucked up, she too would draw the curtain to her own cubicle and do likewise. The following morning she would rise first and complete her own ablutions. When the morning bell rang, she was dressed and ready to get the girls up and accompany them to mass, after which she would sit with them for breakfast. The rule of silence was relaxed during working hours. In this way community life was very different from the Novitiate.

115

Nan sorted through the photographs until she found one of twins. Nan smiled affectionately. The twins were very cute ten year olds, who were always trying to find out whether Sister Jude had any hair, by lifting up her veil at the back. It was something they never discovered, but the story the twins put around was that Sister Jude had a long plait down to her knees. This was quite untrue because Sister Jude always cut off her own hair, keeping it very short like a boy's, for no other reason than because it was easier to wash and wear that way.

Nan picked up a photo of inside the chapel. A memory came back. It was of Sister Lucy who had been laid out in it, prior to her burial. This nun had made a big impact on Nan because she had never seen anyone dead before.

The next photo portrayed Mother Marie Joseph. She was opening a gate leading into the woods adjacent to the convent. Memories flooded back. She was there and the sun was festooning her habit with glorious yellow blobs as it filtered through the trees. The woods opened onto a radiant field of golden wheat and she strolled through it, unworried about flattening some of it. Somewhere near the middle of the field, she lay down, enjoying the warmth of the sun on her face. A few moments later, since she was well hidden, she took off her veil, her dress, her chemise and underskirt and wearing nothing but large modest nun drawers, her corset, a bra, and rolled down black stockings she lay down, and let the warm sun caress those parts of her body that showed.

Of course I'm breaking the rule! But, she argued in her head, *God made people naked, so what was he thinking? If they weren't meant to be, it was either bloody well asking for trouble, or alternatively, a clear statement that being naked wasn't such a big deal!* She relaxed into the moment. *Mmm… How absolutely divine… at least it was before that shadow spoilt it.* She assumed it was a cloud and waited for it to pass, but it didn't. Rather, it made a noise, like someone clearing a throat. Her eyes snapped open. For a moment she could only see sunspots.

116

Nevertheless she made a grab for her habit and dressed herself while she was recovering from her blindness. Eventually, she was able to see him, finding that he had responded to her embarrassment by turning his back on her.

"It's you. What are you doing you here?" She gasped.

"Never mind me, girl. What about you? Yer don't half get around, don't yer?"

"I'm a nun. I hardly go anywhere. It's you that gets around. What are you doin' 'ere?"

"Do yer mind if I sit down?"

"No. Please yerself."

"Okay. I'll tell yer what I'm doin' 'ere when you've told me what you're doin' 'ere.

"I'm gettin' a suntan."

"You're a nun. I didn't think nuns cared about suntans."

"Obviously yer wrong,"

"An how many rules have yer broken to get yer suntan then?" George asked. She had the grace to look ashamed.

"Stop interrogating me. Yer sound like the last of the Hitler Youth! Now you tell me what you're doin' 'ere! Yer a long way from 'ome, aren't yer?"

"'ome! I'm not sure where that is any more." George lay down on his back and took a deep breath. Having made herself decent, Sister Jude lay down beside him.

"What de yer think that one is?" They were looking at the clouds.

"A swan," George replied.

"Oh yes. I can see it too. That one's a yacht."

"I reckon that one's cloud nine." George stared at the cloud for some time before sitting up. He took a notebook and pencil out of the inside pocket of his denim jacket, and began to write.

"What're you doin'?" She asked.

"Writ'n lyrics," he replied.

"Oh! You mean a song?

"Yer."

117

"Are you gonna tell me what' you're doin' here or not?"

"I'm just a day tripper. Someone spiked our drinks."

"...Our drinks?"

"Yeah! Mine, and John's! We were at a mate's place in America. We were just 'aving coffee after a nice meal and the next thing, we 're 'ere."

"Is John with you?"

"Yeah. I lost him though, which a bit of a worry because I've no idea where I am, or where he is?

"You're in Belgium."

"In Belgium?" George repeated his words, sitting up again to have a look around him. He laughed. "That..." he said pointing to the woods, "...is Woolton Woods." Now Sister Jude, when she was Kate, had been to Woolton Woods many times, so she sat up too to see whether the woods behind her convent resembled it.

"No it's not! Woolton Woods isn't this flat. Belgium's flat."

"Okay, for argument's sake let's say it's Belgium." George said. "So what're yer doin' sunbathin' in Belgium? Ye've got to admit that it's not very believable, is it?"

"I'm 'ere for my ten months in community. It's part of becomin' a nun – ye know, tryin' out the real life, as opposed to being a postulant or a novice. I need to know what it's like so I can decide if I want to make me vows."

"And are yer going to?"

"Yeah. What about you? What are the Beatles up to these days?"

"We've been up to too bloody much. We're right up there with the stars," he said, indicating the vast blue vault of the sky. "We can't do anything wrong. It's great, but it's busy - too busy. I'd give anything for a decent night's sleep without any drugs."

"Well then there's a lot to tell me, if you can stay awake long enough," Sister Jude smiled. "Tell me about the other Beatles."

"Er… let's see. Well, Ringo's married."

"Is he?"

"Yeah. And we've been cutting records every couple of months. And oh yeah! We've been shoot'n a movie too– it's called HELP."

"First pop stars, now movie stars. Wow!" They fell silent for a while enjoying the peaceful warmth. It was Sister Jude who broke the silence. "A nun from here died you know. She was laid out in the chapel. She used to do all the washin' for us all. Her name was Sister Lucy. It's really sad. She was a nice old lady. One of the best!"

"That sounds funny," He said.

"What does?"

"Calling a nun a lady. Yer know, I'm not being funny or anything like that, but I don't think of yer as ladies."

"Don't yer? That's interestin'. Why?" George had to think for a while about this.

"Maybe it's because yer seem sexless. Except when yer undressed. I could see yer was a woman then." Sister Jude was glad they were both looking up at the sky so he couldn't see her blushing.

"I like to think of her up there sparkling like a diamond."

"Who?"

"Sister Lucy… the nun who died. It makes me feel better to think of her up there, watchin' over us."

"You know, the last time we met yer were telling me what a bloody awful nun you were."

"I think I've improved."

"Oh yeah! So that would be why you're lying, practically starkers, in a cornfield with a man." She had the grace to blush again.

"You're right! I'm still a bloody hopeless nun. But I'm a good teacher."

"I bet you are. But yer can quit and go 'ome if ye want to, ye know."

"I don't want to now. I luv it 'ere."

119

"I bet yer teach the kids 'ow te break the school rules and get away with it."

George's eyes are always twinkling, Sister Jude thought. George had been writing on and off while they had been chatting and Kate asked him to read out his song lyrics.

> *Take my hope*
> *Maybe even share a joke*
> *If there's good to be shown*
> *You may make it all your own*
> *And if you want to quit that's fine*
> *While you're out looking for cloud nine*

Kate smiled, pleased that George was giving significance to clouds. *They deserve it*, she thought.

Their encounter was cut short by a distant voice.

"George. Where are yer? Stop hidin', yer stupid get?" John was some way off but Kate shot out of that wheat like a rocket launching.

"Bloody 'ell! It's John!" She gasped, her eyes wide with hope. She took off like a bat out of hell, with her black dress and veil flapping like wings. She had one intention only – to reach the voice before it disappeared. Nun or no nun, she wasn't going to miss her one chance to meet the absolutely fab John Lennon.

"He's here John." She yelled at the top of her voice.

"C'mon on George! We're on in a couple of hours and we've still got to get to the studio." George had overtaken Sister Jude by the time John appeared, and she was losing ground, but she was still in with a chance to meet him. Suddenly she heard a different voice.

"Sister. Are you there?" She stopped dead in her tracks recognising the voice. Diving head first into the wheat she was just in time to miss being spotted by Reverend Mother. She could hear John and George talking not very far away.

"I've been talking to a scantily clad nun who said she was sun-bathing." John looked back over his shoulder and seeing only Reverend Mother who was at least sixty and rather porky, said: "Have ye. Well I hope it doesn't scar yer for life."

Propositioned

The air was charged with static as Laura and Beth jogged around the campus lake. It was a Friday ritual, when Laura was on late shift, to fall sleepily out of bed around 3 o'clock, and not bother showering because, what was the point, she was only going to get sweaty again.

She met Beth coming out of her last lecture of the week.

"It's going to storm," Beth grumbled, looking up at the darkening sky.

"Let's go to the coffee shop for dinner," said Laura. "We can watch it from there."

"Sorry! I'm a poor student," Beth said. "I'll make you a coffee at home."

"I'll shout you," Laura offered.

"No! Let's go back to my place. I can make you noodles."

"Okay!" Laura conceded.

"Storms still freak me out." This was the real reason why Beth wanted to get home to safety before it bucketed down. She and Emily had been caught in a flash flood when she was about four, and they had been forced to abandon their car, which was washed away. Returning to the present she got to grips with the task in hand. "We so need to get the guest list sorted. Can you believe that Simon? Maria's birthday is on top of us and he still hasn't got back to me with numbers."

Later they sent the following text to Simon: Re birthday. – U R dead. Look for hit men with violin cases at airport.

Simon and Maria were leaving the airport when his phone pulsed in his pocket He ignored it, otherwise he would have known just how pissed off with him Beth was. He had priorities of his own to attend to, one of them being persuading Maria to commit to the job offer.

"Of course you have to take it," Simon argued. "It's a fantastic opportunity."

"I know!" Maria said. "It's just that… Well it's Nan, Simon! How can I go to Perth when she's dying? I want to be here for her."

"I understand how conflicted you must feel, Maria, but you can't save Nan. This is an opportunity to be involved in a concerted effort to save… well, who knows how many lives you'll save? You've seen the statistics on world hunger."

"I know. The opportunity is huge… but to be honest, it scares me," she confessed.

"I bet everyone that has been approached about being a Flagship Head is shit scared," Simon said. "I know I am. The responsibility is monumental. But it's better than the alternative."

"Doing nothing, you mean?"

"Yes" said Simon emphatically. "And we'll have the world's best advisers. Imagine being able to pick up the phone and talk to people like Tim Flannery, or David Suzuki, or whoever else can offer their own particular brand of expertise. This is a worldwide initiative, Maria, and we can be part of it."

"I know. But Nan…"

"You think Nan would rather have you sitting by her bedside?"

"No." Maria knew she could be sure of that. "I just feel I should be making the most of this time with her."

"Throwing yourself into this is being there for her."

"I know you're right," Maria said. "It's just bad timing… I need to think about it." Simon was becoming impatient.

"I can't imagine why you would hesitate?"

"I'm not you," she threw back at him. "I have a family that I love, and Perth's a long way away."

"Is that what's worrying you – being away from your family?"

"That and other things," she admitted.

"Let me be your family then!" It was out before he realised he'd said it out loud.

"What? What are you saying?" she cast a bewildered look his way.

"I'll be your family in Perth."

"What! Like a brother?"

"You know what I mean."

"No, I don't."

"Marry me."

"Marry you?" Now she was even more confused. "You want me to marry you so I will take the job and go to Perth with you? What sort of reason is that for getting married?" Simon's face clouded with disappointment. He held her gaze for a moment. A feeling had grown during the conference, and he had dared to hope that her anger might have been about the unbearable thought of him being in Perth without her. The thought of being without her was certainly unbearable to him.

"You're right," he said making light of his clumsiness. "It's a really stupid idea. But come anyway."

"I haven't said no, yet."

"To my marriage proposal?"

"No. You don't get married so you can work together, Simon. You get married so you can live together because you love each other. As for the job offer, I haven't made up my mind yet. I can't see why you're pressuring me. Rick Walters isn't."

"I thought he was."

"Then you thought wrong. I have until next Wednesday." While she had been talking, Simon's proposal had been niggling at her. What on earth made him come up with such an idea? His ideas were usually brilliant. This one was just plain stupid. "Anyway, I am thinking about it. I want to talk it over with my sisters, with Mum and Matt. I want to talk it over with Nan."

"They'll all say the same. What's to think about?"

"And maybe that is just what I need to hear."

124

"And if they say don't go? You can't base your decision on what they want."

"Any more than I can base my decision on what you want - or Rick Walters for that matter." Simon's mobile pulsed in his pocket. This time he answered it.

"Hi Beth. We're just leaving the airport. How're you doing?" There was a short silence. "Oh Shit! Sorry! I totally forgot... No! It wasn't all drinks and canapés. We had a gruelling schedule. Something big came up and we had our mind on other things." Another silence. "No, nothing's wrong. Yes, I'll get back to you later. I will! I will!"

"That was Beth. She wants to invite a multitude to your birthday and she's after me for names and numbers from work."

"Oh no! That's all we need! I told her what I want." Maria was digging in her bag for her mobile and Simon, sensing Beth might be in for an ear bashing, tried to calm her down.

"Maria, she's just trying to give you a nice birthday. Be kind!" They had now worked their way to the front of the taxi queue.

"But she's so annoying. Call me selfish but I just want the birthday I want, not the birthday Beth wants."

"I'll tell her. Leave it to me."

"Okay! But if I have to put myself through an embarrassing fancy dress party, or a vicars' and tarts' party, or any other type of over-the-top party, I will be so annoyed. I just want a nice quiet family dinner. It's not that difficult!"

"Okay, okay!" Simon smiled opening the door of a taxi for her and lifting suitcases into the boot.

"It's good to be home." Maria said as he climbed in beside her. "Can you drop me off first?" The taxi driver nodded.

"Where to?"

"Chapel Hill, please."

125

"You're going straight to Nan's?" Simon was surprised. "I thought you would want some downtime first?"

"I feel too much on edge. I'm not going to wind down until I talk to my family."

Confused

Emily had returned from the supermarket and was putting shopping away when she heard voices in Nan's bedroom. She poked her head around the door to see who was there and found Maria sitting on Nan's bed.

"Maria! You're home!"

"Why don't you two go off and catch up on each other's news. I'm tired." Nan yawned to emphasise the point. "I'll catch up with you later, love. I can hardly stay awake." This was not true but she was determined to break this habit of always being there between mother and daughter.

"I'm sorry," Maria said. "I've tired you with my problems."

"Nonsense," Nan said. "But I can't help you solve them. That's what Mums are for. I'm not saying your news hasn't bucked me up though." She gave Maria a proud smile. "It makes me feel my life has been purposeful. After all if I hadn't given birth to your mother, she would never have given birth to you, and then where would the world be? Minus one person who wasn't in it for totally selfish reasons! Now, go away and let an old lady get a bit of shut-eye." She turned away from them and snuggled into her pillow.

In the kitchen Maria and Emily talked over tea poured from tiny pots.

"So! What's up?" Emily asked.

"A new job has come up, but it's really bad timing with Nan being sick. It's in Perth."

"Do you want the job?"

"Yes. It's a fantastic opportunity. It will fast-track my career while doing something I really believe in." Emily saw the passion burning in Maria and was proud of her.

"Perth's just a plane-ride away… and I'm here for Nan."

"Yes, I know. But if I go now I'll feel as if I'm letting her down."

"What did Nan have to say about it?" Emily enquired.

"Nan said it would give her precious time with you." Maria was unaware of the great significance this statement would have for her mother. Emily blinked away the tears that rose and swallowing hard, forced them back down to her heart where they had resided for so very long. Maria, engrossed in her own dilemma, did not notice.

"And how do you feel about that?" Asked her mother.

"I know as well as you do that you don't get on."

"Have you ever considered that the reason we don't get on might be that we never get time together without the three of you there between us?" Maria's shocked eyes stared into her mother's.

"What do you mean?"

"I mean she's my mother, not yours."

"Wow!" Maria said. "That felt like a punch in the guts." There was a long silence while they weighed each other up. "But you're the first to admit that you don't get on."

"Have you ever wondered why?" Emily said without malice. "You're my daughters not hers."

"But she's been so good to us all… to you." Maria knew as she spoke that this was not the point.

"Yes. I'm not denying that. I don't know what I would have done without her. But you're still my daughters, not hers." To Maria, this was just another confusing thought in a week of confusing events.

"I don't understand," Maria said.

"No. No one does," said Emily. "But think about it anyway." Emily reigned in her tongue before adding. "About your job, it's wonderful news and I'm sure that you will make the right decision. You're a clever girl and only you know what is right for you. As for Nan, she's lived her life. You're still building yours. I know you will choose what's best for you and that you will consider the greater good, because

128

you're a person who does that. I can't tell you how much I admire you for that. Now, you need to go home and rest and I need to go downstairs to paint."

"You're painting. I didn't know you painted."

"There's such a lot about me that you girls don't know," Emily replied sadly. "But that's about to change." She smiled at Maria. "I love you Maria. I'll see you at your birthday dinner."

When Emily went downstairs Maria sat for a while slowly sipping tea. There was a dawning awareness of something huge about her mother – but it was just beyond her understanding.

She slipped into Nan's room before going home. "I'm off, Nan. I'll see you at the birthday party tomorrow night."

"Here," Nan said. "It's an early birthday present. Open it when you get home." Maria kissed her and called a taxi. She sat on the doorstep and, not waiting to get home, as instructed, she opened the packet Nan had given her.

Inside were some pages clipped together and covered with Nan's messy writing. There were some photos too. She looked at these first. They portrayed a large four-storey mansion. It was not a building she was familiar with, and it didn't look Australian. A caption at the bottom of the page read 'Les Dames de l'Enfant Roi, Tournai.' The other photographs were of nuns. She looked for her grandmother among them. Maria didn't get a chance to read any of the pages because the taxi came, so she quickly put everything back in the packet. It was not a very peaceful ride home as her mind went over and over her mother's words. Letting herself into her unit she dumped her travel bag in the hall, deciding to unpack and shop the following day because it was getting dark. *If I get hungry later I'll go down the road to the Seven Eleven.* She wanted to read Nan's story before doing anything else. She made some coffee, slipped out of her business suit and into a strappy dress. Then she sat at her small dining table with the pages Nan had written.

Maria chuckled to herself as she read about George and Sister Jude in the wheat field. The tears came later, and when they did, they did not stop for a long time. Nor could she explain them. The story had been a joy to read and not at all depressing. *It's probably just the pent up emotion of the entire week*, she told herself. Later, when the tears stopped falling, she felt so much better.

I'll nip down to the Seven Eleven. Then I'll come back and have a long soak in the bath, with candles, bath salts, aromatherapy a nice glass of wine and the biggest bar of chocolate I can find. As she stood, she noticed something had fallen to the floor. It was a scapular that Nan used to wear. Maria remembered asking Nan about it when she was probably no more than seven years old.

"Why do you wear it?" The question was asked with childlike curiosity.

"Because it's holy." Maria had looked at it carefully again.

"No it's not," Maria had giggled as if Nan were pulling her leg. "It hasn't got any holes in it, Silly Billy," Nan had such a fit of the giggles that she couldn't stop laughing. It was the sort of uncontrollable laughter that was infectious so that Maria too got the giggles. That sort of laughter has to run its course and it wasn't until Nan was finally able to speak again that she said:

"Holy with an 'e' means there are holes in it. Holy without an 'e' means sacred."

"I know what sacred means. Why is it sacred?" Maria had asked.

"Because," Nan said as if sharing a very big secret, "John, George, Paul and Ringo wrote their names on it."

Maria looked at it closely. When she had first held it she had been able to see the names very clearly then. Now the writing was faded but she could still make them out. Sheesh! Maria had to admit that for someone who hardly ever left the convent, Nan hadn't half seen a lot of the Beatles. How on

130

earth did she get them to sign their names on a scapular? Crazy about the Beatles as Nan was, Maria could not envisage her forging the names. She made a note on her iPhone reminding her to ask Nan.

She stepped into the bath water while it was still running, and when she had soaked for a while, with water almost up to her chin, she came to a decision about the job. It was partly to do with what her mother had said. At first, Maria wondered if her mother had meant to be hurtful. Yet there had been no animosity or blame in Emily's voice though Maria identified a large portion of sadness. *Yes! That was it. 'She's my mother not yours'*, Emily had said. *Think about it! She had suggested she and Nan did not get on because the three of them were always there between them.* The more Maria thought about it, the more she thought she understood.

Emily had always been somewhat of a mystery to her daughters. Nan had filled their world most of the time and their mother had been someone in the background – someone who went out to work in the morning and came home at night, and who lived downstairs, like a lodger. The more Maria thought about this, the more she felt she had missed out on something important. As she picked up her mobile phone she realized, for the first time, that she didn't have her mother's number on speed-dial. *It's like she's never been important.* Maria thought.

Emily answered Maria's call and warmth flooded her soul as Maria spoke.

"Hi Mum, I was just wondering if you would like to do something nice with me on Sunday morning as a birthday treat. I was thinking let's make it just the two of us. We could go to the movies, or for a drive to the beach. What do you think?" That was when Emily learned that joy could stab and hurt just as deeply as sorrow. It was a moment before the tightness in her chest cleared enough for her to be able to speak.

"That would be lovely, Maria," she said.

131

"Do you think Matt would look after Nan?"

"Don't you worry about Nan," Emily replied gently. "I'll make sure she's taken care of. That's my job." Maria realised that her mother had done a very loving thing for her. She had lifted the burden of Nan from her shoulders.

"Thanks Mum." Emily, of course, thought the thanks were for agreeing to Maria's birthday wishes. But Maria knew that was not all she was thanking her for. "And Mum…"

"What?"

"I love you."

"I love you too Boo," Emily said softly, tears welling and heart tightening. Maria gasped as she remembered something important.

"Oh Mum! I've just realised. The Boo story - it was you all along," she said. "It was never Nan. It was your story. It was you!"

"Yes," Emily replied, and gently put the phone down, hardly able to contain her sobs. Another dam had burst, but Emily didn't mind. Walls were coming down thick and fast all around her. She sat in her crypt and, as rivers of resentment poured out of her, a new freedom and power poured in. It felt so right to be reclaiming what was rightfully hers. Nan was dying and her girls would miss her. She felt ready to clothe herself, once more, in the mantle of motherhood. Her girls would need her when Nan passed on, for their sorrow would be great.

Emily gazed at her paintings again. She was sure the paintings had built strength and resolve into her as she had worked on them. One painting showed how things were. The other showed how she wanted things to be – and now one of her daughters wanted to spend time with her as if, somehow, being with her mother on her birthday would, in itself, be a gift.

But her daughters weren't the only ones she wanted to reclaim. She wanted to reclaim her mother. She thought for a long time about this and then made a decision. She carried her two paintings upstairs and opened the door to her mother's room. Her mother wasn't sleeping. She was at her desk writing. She seemed to be doing a lot of writing these days.

"What's that you've got?" Nan asked.

"I've been painting. Would you like to see what I've done?"

"Painting?" Nan replied. "You haven't painted for years! Of course…yes, I would." Emily placed the paintings against the wardrobe and stood back so her mother could see. Her mother looked at them for a long time, her tired old eyes brimming with tears that spilled and zigzagged down her wrinkled face. Finally she turned towards her daughter and held open her arms. As Emily entered her mother's embrace, her tears spilled over too. So it was that mother allowed daughter to release the heartache of years. When Nan's tears had subsided, she held her daughter close until Emily's tears had dried up too, and as she held her, Nan sang:

"Cry me a river. Cry me a river…"

Mexican Spice

Beth was the first to arrive at the restaurant and in the centre of the table she placed a basket of flowers from which rose six helium balloons. Pleased with the effect, she approached the restaurant manager to give instructions about when the birthday cake should be brought to the table. That done, she spotted a face she recognised peering through the bay window that housed the family's festive table.

Oh no! It's him! How could I have forgotten about that? She beckoned the traffic cop to enter, at the same time as grabbing the arm of a nearby waiter.

"Can you seat another one, if need be?" she asked.

"Yes. No problem," he assured her.

The traffic cop did not come in. She saw him cross the road and pretend to look in a jeweller's shop window opposite. She didn't even know his name and now that she thought about it, Laura might have told her at least that much. Instead, Laura had been secretive, referring to him only as Officer Spunky. "Laura, where the hell are you?" Beth muttered under her breath.

It seemed that Officer Spunky's cold feet must have warmed up because now he was crossing the road again and this time she went to the entrance to meet him.

"I'm not sure what I'm doing here," he said, "but I was invited. Admittedly it was a weird kind of invitation, but your sister… I assume you're sisters. There's a resemblance. Your sister invited me."

"Yes. I'm Beth," she said holding out her hand, which he shook, awkwardly. And I'll kill my sister for leaving it to me to explain things to you," she smiled nervously. "Actually, we invited you because my sister likes you."

"Oh! In that case, I'll be off. We've already established we don't fancy each other. She's terrifying."

"Terrifying! No way!" Beth wondered where he'd got that idea.

"Give her my apologies," he said, as the door swung shut behind him. Laura breezed in half a minute later, causing Beth to wonder how she and Officer Spunky hadn't collided in their haste to arrive and depart.

"You've just missed what's his name…the traffic cop. I told him Maria liked him and he said she was terrifying."

"That's ridiculous!" Said Laura. "He doesn't even know her."

"I know! But it's just dawned on me. Maybe he thought I meant you fancied him."

"You told him she fancied him? Did you mention her name?"

"Er, no."

"Der! Why didn't you stop him leaving?"

"Hey! I'm not the one with the handcuffs." Beth said defensively. Laura was looking very frustrated.

"I hope you realise you've just screwed up a whole week of scheming."

Renata had to step aside to make way for Laura's pursuit.

"Is this where Maria's birthday party is?" Renata asked?

"Yes. Are you a friend of Maria's?"

"Yes. I met her at the conference. She invited me."

"Did she?" Beth was surprised "I'm Beth, her sister. Did she invite anyone else she didn't tell us about? Not that you're not welcome. I just need to know for seating purposes."

"I don't think so. Oh yes! Simon. He's coming."

"Yes, I know about him since they're practically joined at the hip. Have a seat. That was Laura you passed on the way in, by the way. She wasn't being rude. There's been a misunderstanding and she's just trying to stop someone leaving."

"No worries." Renata said completely without rancour.

135

"Excuse me," Beth smiled, liking her. "I just need to tell the waiter to set another place. I'll be with you in a minute."

"Okay. Do what you have to do." The waiter she had spoken to earlier was setting a table nearby and Beth interrupted his work.

"There's a new problem. My sister invited someone else and didn't tell me. Can you fit another one in?"

"Is that two more?"

"I'm not sure," said Beth looking towards the door to see if Laura had persuaded the traffic cop to come back. "Better set two more places. Sorry I can't be definite but one of them is a bit uncertain. We're hoping he'll stay." The waiter bestowed a dazzling smile on Beth, easing her tension.

"No problem."

Officer Spunky's car was just moving away from the kerb when Laura flagged him down. He braked and wound the window down.

"It's my other sister. You stopped her for speeding the other night, remember?"

"The doctor?"

"Yes. That's her. She likes you."

"Did she want me to come?"

"Well… she didn't say that exactly, but then she didn't exactly say she didn't want you to come either."

"What exactly does that mean? Does she know you've invited me?"

"Umm… well, not exactly."

"Well what exactly does she know?"

"Umm… not very much really."

"She doesn't know I'm coming?"

"Look, you don't understand. It's her birthday and you're her birthday present."

"I'm her what?" He was seriously indignant now. "You mean like a new handbag?" Laura knew she would have to gain the upper hand or lose him altogether.

"Oh for goodness sake, stop being so precious. You're spoiling everything. She really, really likes you. That's all you need to know. You like her, don't you? Of course you do." She deliberately gave him no time to protest. "She's completely gorgeous." She opened the door with her free hand. "It's your lucky day. Have you any idea how many men would kill to go out with Maria? But she doesn't even notice them. The thing is… we actually know she likes you, so you're streets ahead of the competition."

"Hmm!" It was a suspicious utterance that gave him time to weigh things up. "She'd better bloody like me," he muttered, negotiating his way back into the parking space he had been leaving."

Arriving back at the table, Laura smiled and introduced him to Beth and Renata. "Beth, this is… well… Umm… I'm sorry! I seem to have entirely forgotten your first name?"

"Mikey."

"Crikey! … Mikey, this is Beth." Laura had not meant to be flippant and was now trying very hard to stifle a giggle.

"Hi there," Beth said covering her mouth. She too was struggling to keep her face straight, but she made matters worse when she apologised for her sister. "Please excuse my sister for taking the mickey, Mikey…" This second very clumsy use of words took her by surprise, causing Beth and Laura to glance at each other in shock. It was the worst thing they could have done. They both buckled with laughter.

"Excuse…ha ha…us," they tried to say, looking and sounding more like a couple donkeys.

Fortunately Mikey saw the funny side of it too. He could not maintain his traffic cop face for long, and his amused smirk developed into an uncontrollable belly laugh just as Maria entered the restaurant. She stopped dead in her tracks, not able to understand what the traffic cop, who had come close to booking her the other night, was doing there. Beth, attempting to sober up, moved forward swiftly, to greet her.

"Happy Birthday Maria. I'd like to introduce you to Mikey… the bikey…" There was a new explosion of giggles. Maria's questioning eyes went from Laura to Beth, from whom she could get no sense and so moved on to Renata. But even she was giggling.

"Did you decide to arrest me after all?" Maria asked trying to overcome her awkwardness. But everyone was laughing too much to speak. "Well" Maria said, still trying to make light of her embarrassment. "If I'm to be arrested, at least let me look dignified. I just need to… you know," she said, pointing to her face. Beth, at last finding her voice between the guffaws, asked to be excused and followed her into the 'ladies'.

"In case you're thinking of escaping we've got the windows covered," Mikey called after them, causing a fresh outburst of laughter.

Maria and Beth took refuge beyond the closed door.

"God definitely absolutely and completely hates me!" Maria said banging her head against the wall"

"What are you talking about? You like him."

"I know. But why did I have to meet him just when I've agreed to move to Perth."

"Perth?" Beth repeated as if Maria had said she was going to live on Mars.

"Yes. I've been offered a really good job there."

"But Perth's on the other side of the continent," Beth stammered, quickly sobering up.

"That's called stating the obvious!" said Laura, who chose that moment to walk into the ladies. "Everyone else has arrived. Mum and Matt are looking after Mikey. He's not bad, is he?" Neither Beth nor Maria replied.

"What! Cat got your tongue for once?" Laura smirked.

"Maria's going to work in Perth," Beth blurted out.

"Perth? When? Why?" Laura asked.

"I got a job offer at the conference," she said.

"Well turn it down. You've just met the man of your dreams and if you're fed up at work you'll easily get another job."

"It's not just any job," she said. "Come on I'll tell you over dinner."

Nan sat at the centre of her family evaluating the dynamics. She reflected that dying seemed to heighten one's sensitivity. For example, she noticed how Simon's eyes kept returning to Maria. *He's in love with her*, she realised. *And if Maria takes the job she's been offered, that Mikey bloke isn't going to be devastated because he's interested in Beth. Emily can't take her eyes off her daughters. As for Matt… well, judging by the way he and Renata keep talking across me, could there be a possibility that love is in the air between them too?* Nan was forced to sit up ramrod straight so as not to obscure Renata and Matthew's view of each other. Renata noticed, with pleasant surprise, how Matthew tried to include his mother in their conversation and how sensitive he was to her needs, wrapping a shawl around her shoulders when she shivered. Her own mother's words came back to her.

'You can tell a lot about a man from the way he treats his mother, Renata. Remember that'.

Maria had been flattered by Mikey's attention at first, but her interest waned as she saw it was Beth he really wanted to talk to. Anyway, she didn't want any more complications in her life right now. There was enough going on. Noticing Renata's fixation with Matt she whispered discreetly.

"Am I imagining things or do you like Matt?"

"He's cute."

"But you're gay."

"I'm an Aspie." Maria knew exactly what Renata meant by this because the sciences seemed to attract people with Aspergers Syndrome. They were backroom people and most of them worked in a field associated with their interests, which bordered on obsessions. "Some of us don't have clearly defined sexual preferences," Renata explained.

139

"Are you 'bi' then?"

"Maybe! It's all a bit ambiguous really. I'm attracted to both men and women but I've never really had a proper girl-friend… only a few one night stands."

"At conferences?"

"Usually," she said laughing, remembering what had brought them together. "I usually fare better with men, even though they never last long. If I found a partner I could really love I wouldn't want to look elsewhere and I don't think it would matter if it were a man or a woman. For me, it's more about how people make me feel…" Then she whispered into Maria's ear. "Now Matt! Well, what can I say! Come on baby light my fire." After their laughter had died down Renata asked. "Is Matt a scientist? I bet he is."

"No. Actually he's in insurance, but recently he's decided he wants to go solo, as a consultant. He's an actuary. When he's ready, he'll set up his own consultancy, and I think that won't be too far down the track. I like him best when he's not droning on about probabilities and possibilities. He can be a lot of fun."

Maria's job offer was received in the family with mixed feelings. It had never occurred to anyone that reliable Maria would not always be close to home.

"That's the only problem with the job," she said.

"Nonsense. That's not a problem. It's a bonus." Nan's opinion was enthusiastic because it had settled on something she understood. "Being away from family makes you grow up. Anyway, it's not as if you will be alone. Simon will be with you and anyway, you ought to be thinking about starting your own family. You're thirty-five and it's time you settled down." Nan tried several times to bring Maria's attention back to Simon. They would make such a well-suited couple because they love each other already, Nan observed, noticing that Maria wasn't talking to him much. *Something has happened between them. I wonder what?*

"It's clearly not the time to settle down, Nan," Maria argued, rather too adamantly, Nan thought. "I don't have time for romance if I'm about to start a job that will require total dedication."

"Unless you marry someone who's in it with you," Nan said rather obviously, causing Maria to go on the defensive.

"If I take the job, it will have to fulfill me for now. I'll think about marriage later, if the right guy comes along."

"You'll be too old later," said Nan.

"Leave her alone Mum," Emily said coming to Maria's defence. "She's got enough on her mind at the moment. We should be supporting her, not pressuring her." Maria, astonished by her mother's sensitivity towards her for the second time that week, also thought, something has happened. What, I wonder?

After the main course, the sparkler-bedazzled, birthday-cake was brought to the table by a waiter, who started off the singing. The others needed no encouragement to join in and when the singing died down, Matthew proposed a toast.

"To Maria! To the future! To a sustainable world! To dreams come true!" Everyone wanted to make a toast after that and the time slipped happily by. At nine-thirty, Emily, Matthew and Nan rose to leave the young ones to their wine and chitchat. Laura looked at her watch.

"I'd better get going too. I'm on eleven till six tonight." She bent to kiss Maria's cheek. "Have a productive week sis, and I'm really thrilled about the job, although I don't know what we'll do without you." Maria got up to give Laura a hug.

"Thanks."

"She's only going to Perth. She's not snuff'n it." When Nan wanted to make them laugh she exaggerated her Liverpool accent. It gave Laura time to get her brimming tears under control.

"I haven't actually accepted the job yet."

"Well, if we have to lose you, I'd rather lose you to the greater good than to anything else." Laura headed for the door where, remembering something, she turned back. "I'll bring your present round tomorrow after I get up. Is three o'clock okay?"

"Yes. See you then." Maria remained standing.

"Sorry to party poop my own birthday, but I could do with an early night. I've some serious decisions to make. Thank you for coming, Mikey. I hope we'll see you again." Maria and Beth caught each other's eye assuring each other that if anyone would be seeing more of Mikey, it would be Beth. Simon got up to leave too, intending to walk Maria to her car, but Renata stepped between them and took Maria's arm.

"It was lovely to meet all your family, Maria. Thank you for inviting me." Mikey, noticing Simon's awkwardness got up to shake his hand. Simon reached his car just as Maria and Renata were hugging goodbye. Simon was shocked at the resentment he felt. *So, I haven't been imagining it*. He was remembering how they had been whispering in each other's ears through dinner. *This is so not right for Maria. Maybe Renata's what stopping her making her decision,* he thought with a downhearted sigh. *She has to come to Perth. Maybe with the two of us working together I'll stand more of a chance.* Taking their relationship to the next level had become the most important thing in his life. After all, on a personal level, what was the point of improving the world if she wasn't going to be in it?

Mikey

"So! It's just us left!" Mikey said this as the door to the Mexican closed on Simon's departing figure. "Now I need some answers. Suppose you tell me what I'm doing at your sister's birthday dinner."

"Suppose you tell me?" Beth flirted.

"You know the answer to that. Your sister invited me."

"You didn't have to accept."

"That's true. Call me curious if you like but let's just say she threw me a challenge and I accepted."

"What challenge was that, then?" Beth's face was alive with changing flirtatious expressions that fascinated and delighted Mikey.

"She said I should come and look in through the window and if I saw anything I liked, I should come in."

"And did you see anything you liked?"

"Yes. But what I liked wasn't what I was supposed to like."

"How awkward for you. So what do you think was supposed to take your fancy?"

"Your sister."

"You mean Laura?"

"You know I don't."

"Oh! Then you must mean Maria."

"Yeah! Well, I think I was supposed to be smitten with her, but Blind Freddie could see she's obviously spoken for."

"What do you mean?"

"Simon."

"Ha! You're deluded!"

"Whatever! Anyway, I don't fancy her."

"But she's gorgeous."

"I agree, but she's not my type."

"Why did you come in, then?"

"Because I saw something else I liked."

"What would that be then Tortilla? Taco? Margaritas?"

"Nah! I'm fussy about food. I like my own cooking best…and I rarely drink."

"You cook?" By now toes were touching under the table and electricity was sparking between them.

"Actually I do - really well," Mikey smiled confidently.

"Not only can he cook but he's modest with it."

"It's not shooting your mouth off if it's true. Would you like some more wine, or a Marguerita, perhaps?" Mikey offered.

"Mmm! I love Margueritas. Thankyou!" Mikey called the waiter and ordered one.

"Are you a dinky die Australian?" When Beth spoke she usually got straight to the point.

"Why?"

"I don't think that's just suntan." Beth wet her finger and rubbed the back of Mikey's hand vigorously. Mikey raised an eyebrow half expecting a racist comment. It didn't come. Instead Beth smiled and said. "I bet you come from somewhere exotic, like Mauritius?" Mikey shook his head. "Bali then? Tahiti? Vanuatu? The Solomon Islands?" Mikey continued to shake his head through all the guessing. Eventually Beth sighed, "I give up."

"New Zealand," he said. "I'm Maori."

"Cool!" She said. "Have you got tats?"

"I'll show you mine if you'll show me yours." There was more than a hint of naughtiness in his eyes.

"You never did tell me what it was you liked the look of when you looked in through the window."

"I don't think I need to," he said.

"But I want you…" A waiter interrupted them with Beth's Margarita. Mikey poured himself a large glass of water then leaning closer to Beth, took her hand in his and, raising it to his mouth, whispered huskily.

"Now, what was that you were saying about wanting me?"

An Elusive Woman

Arriving home, Nan went straight to bed. Emily fluffed up her pillows and pulled the doona over her, straightening it as she did so. Matt hesitated at the bedroom door with a glass of water.

"It's all right. I'm decent. You can come in. It was a lovely night, wasn't it? Maybe I'll sleep in tomorrow. I feel tired enough." Emily noticed the strain in Nan's face, and was not sure if it was the cancer, or whether she had just overdone things. *She's losing a lot of weight and she's ashen.*

"Here," Emily said. Nan took the small tub of medication from her and upturned it into her mouth, washing it down with the water Matt offered.

"Goodnight," Nan said. "Thank you for a lovely family night."

"Goodnight Mum," Emily and Matt said, wondering just how many more family nights they would have together.

Emily waved at Matt's departing car and thought about going to bed too, but it was only ten o'clock and she didn't feel tired. Instead she went downstairs, made some coffee and stood on the veranda, thinking about the events of the evening. Soon she made a decision and changing out of the purple georgette dress she was wearing, she donned her oldest jeans and paint-stained t-shirt, and began to apply colour to a canvas, seriously at first, and then more playfully, bringing out the ghosts of her family's past. This time her painting was not full of angst, but of fun. When she stepped back from it several hours later, she smiled.

On his way home, Matt's thoughts were divided between worry about his mother and fascination with Renata, the only woman he had looked twice at in the last twelve months. The trouble was, he had no way of contacting her without involving Maria, which he was reluctant to do. He had established that Renata's field of research was to do with desalination processes. He knew also that she worked at ATARO. He wondered, if he did a search on their website, would he find her. Not with only her first name to go on, he decided. On the other hand, Renata isn't that common a name. It shouldn't be that hard. Matt wondered what statistics might have to say about his chances of finding her. No, he thought dismissing the idea of calculating the odds. Sometimes you just have to go with your gut.

Arriving home he opened his laptop and turned it on. He typed ATARO into Google and waited. A map of Australia showing ATARO's many locations told him that it might be like looking for a needle in a haystack. He clicked on Queensland locations and found there were four ATARO locations in Brisbane. He took a long shot and clicked on the location where Maria worked and found that Australia's rivers and waterways were being researched there, with the aim of providing the water resources needed for future increases in population. He thought he might be in with a chance of finding Renata so, clicking on the search button again, he came up with seven pages of references bearing her name. He scanned through them but any of them could have been the Renata he was searching for. Wanting to be sure, he opened up a few of them looking for a photo, or the mention of something he could link to her, but found nothing concrete.

Sleep on it, he told himself. This would give him time to consider the one thing about Renata that worried him. She was, he suspected, about ten years older than Maria, which would make her around forty-five. He was fifty-seven, making him around twelve years older. If she was a young forty-five, the age gap might appear greater. He had colleagues that had been brutally rejected by feministic women, and made to feel as if they were dirty old men. It puts you on your guard. Some men are a lot more sensitive than women give them credit for. As he got into bed he decided he would find out what he wanted to know about Renata indirectly, if he could. In the meantime she came to him in dreams.

Planets Align

On Sunday morning, Maria rang Emily early.

"Hi Mum. Do you want to go to the movies or to the beach? I fancy the movies because it's not an all day thing, time being tight at the moment."

"Well, if you're busy, we don't have to go anywhere." Emily wondered if Maria was having second thoughts.

"No, I'm looking forward to it but we didn't get down to talking about which movie to go to," Maria said.

"You choose. It's your birthday."

"Well there is a movie I've been wanting to see… I've heard it's really good. It's about a camel that cries."

"Sounds riveting," Emily replied rather sarcastically.

"No! Honest! It's had really good reviews. The actors aren't movie stars. They're just the real people who own the camel, and their neighbours."

"Like I said. It sounds riveting." There was a short silence. "I'm kidding, Maria. I'm sure I'll love it." Emily wasn't sure she would, but that didn't matter. What mattered was that her daughter wanted to spend one-on-one time with her.

"I've accepted the job in Perth, Mum, so I thought we might go for coffee after the movie and have something really decadent to celebrate – like a vanilla slice!"

"Congratulations, Love." Emily glowed. To herself she thought: *Coffee, movie and vanilla slice! All my planets must be aligning.* "What time shall I pick you up?"

"I was going to pick you up."

"It's your birthday and your success we're celebrating. I'll pick you up."

"Okay, if you're sure. See you around ten o'clock then. The movie starts at ten thirty."

When Emily put the phone down she realised she was nervous. She had time to work on that. Later, straightening Nan's bed, she hummed – humming calmed her, causing Nan to turn from her desk.

"Do you fancy a bit of a walk today, Mum?"

"Yes. That would be lovely."

"Maria's accepted the job."

"I'm glad."

"Matt's coming round at ten to look after you," Emily was straightening the bed as she spoke. "I'm going to the movies with Maria." Emily didn't see Nan's raised eyebrows because Nan hid her interest by scrutinising her paperwork, but she did notice Nan's hand stop writing. When Nan did turn to search her daughter's face, her eyebrows were back in place, and her face was as inscrutable as her daughter's.

"Good. I'm glad." Nan meant it more than her daughter would ever know.

Matt arrived at nine thirty so he could have coffee with Emily before she left.

"How's Mum?" he asked cheerily.

"She's up and we've had a little walk. She's got a better colour this morning."

"I wonder if she's up to an outing?"

"Where to?"

"I thought I might take her up to Mount Coot-tha for lunch."

"If you feel you can manage an outing, why not, if she wants to? She loves the view of the coast from up there – you know how she likes to be able to see into the distance."

"She did okay last night, didn't she?" Matt observed.

"Yes. Did you enjoy yourself Matt?" Matt was deep in thought and didn't manage the transition from his own thoughts to the question he had been asked. He merely looked at Emily vaguely.

"Last night?" Emily repeated. "Did you have a nice time?"

"Yes. I did. Very much so," he said reflectively. Emily looked at him thoughtfully for a moment and then grabbed his hand.

"Come with me. I've got something to show you." Matthew followed her downstairs and when he caught up with her she was excitedly holding her painting for him to see. He looked very taken aback at first and then he began to laugh and so did she.

"Have you shown Mum?" He chuckled.

"No."

"You should." He urged. They were still laughing when they burst into Nan's room with it a minute or two later. Such was Nan's reaction that they couldn't tell whether she was laughing or crying. In fact, she was doing both.

Woman to Woman

Maria was just putting on her makeup when the phone rang.

"Yes," she said. "I've spoken to him and I said yes." Maria smiled, glad that Simon was pleased.

"What are you going to do about Renata, then?" Asked Simon, deciding to take the bull by the horns.

"What do you mean?"

"Well… you know… you've practically been joined at the hip lately. I thought…" Maria remembered how she had tried to give him the impression they had spent the night together at the conference.

"Well you thought wrong. Renata's got the hots for Matt."

"But she's…" There was a long silence. In the end Maria broke it.

"She's what?"

"A lesbian…Oh never mind," Simon said. "It doesn't matter. Anyway, what I rang for was to ask if I could take you out for dinner… to celebrate our jobs?"

"Why not," she answered. "I'd like that."

"Seven then," he suggested. "Dress up, we're going somewhere fancy."

Maria had a present for her mother tucked away at the bottom of her purse because she wanted to acknowledge her mother's contribution to her life. She was now feeling this was long overdue because, without her mother… well, she simply wouldn't exist. In actual fact the present symbolised much more - that Maria had taken on board what her mother had said, and that Maria was ready for her mother to take her rightful place in her life.

The movie turned out to be a brilliant choice because it was about a newborn camel whose mother had rejected it.

Maria certainly had not chosen it because of it's content, but it gave them an opportunity to chat about the idea of motherhood in general.

"I don't think I have a maternal bone in my body," Maria confessed.

"Maternal love sometimes doesn't kick in until a child comes along," Emily said on reflection. "Some people are better at it than others."

I'm not sure if I want children, Maria thought. *I've just committed to a project that might take years of research. I can't imagine ever having time for them.*

"What was having children like for you, Mum?" Maria asked. Emily considered this for a moment and then said.

"I'm going to answer that question woman to woman, rather than mother to daughter. It's a compliment and it is important to state the difference so that you don't take it amiss. It means I think you are grown up enough for me to be frank with you. The truth is that I think I was one of the less able mothers. Not that I didn't want you. I did. I loved you all so very much." Emily smiled remembering.

"You say that as if you have regrets."

"I do. I regret lots of things… I don't think I did a very good job." Maria didn't often think about her mother as a mother and so didn't feel able to comment. She moved on to the next question.

"I don't quite remember how we all came to be living with Nan. It's all a bit hazy. Tell me about it, Mum?"

"Well, although I don't think I'm very good at motherhood, having children was the best thing that ever happened to me. I didn't find it easy, though. **Lots** of mothers find out the hard way that they're not as good at mothering as they would like to be. In fact, most mothers I know have all experienced self-doubt about their competence as a mother. Perhaps it's the constant demands. The thing that sent me over the top, though, was separating from your father and his gambling addiction. It wasn't so much bringing you up… It was doing it alone... and there was so much debt."

"So how did you cope?"

"I didn't," Emily said simply.

"What do you mean?" Maria said in puzzlement.

"Surely I don't have to spell it out, Maria. You must remember. You were ten at the time."

"Remember what?"

"My breakdown." Maria looked incredulous.

"You had a breakdown?"

"Yes… but… you knew that." Emily was watching Maria's face closely, waiting for her to remember. But she clearly did not.

"It's the first I've heard of it." Now it was Emily's turn to register incredulity.

"You mean nobody told you? W… Well you must have memories of that time."

"I remember moving in with Nan. Laura was a baby and you'd gone into hospital because there was something the matter with you. But nobody ever told me what. When I asked Matt and Nan, they just said your head was a bit poorly and the doctors were fixing it. I thought you had one of your really bad migraines. You used to say your head was hurting often enough."

"But I was away for weeks."

"I was a kid. I just accepted what grown ups said."

"I didn't know. I can't believe nobody told you." Emily said. "I always assumed you knew."

"When you came back, I remember you asking me if I would prefer to go home to our own house, or whether I would rather stay at Nan's. I remember asking you whether, if we chose to stay at Nan's, you would be there too… and you said yes. I remember thinking that if we stayed at Nan's, Nan and Uncle Matt would make up for Dad not being there, and it would be like living in a family again… and Nan could continue to do the school run so we didn't have to go to after-school and vacation care. I remember weighing up the pros and cons in my very immature way, and deciding that living at Nan's would be the cosiest option."

"And were you right? Was it the cosiest option?"

"I think so. We had the best childhood. We all think so." Emily marvelled at the simplicity of children. All these years she had just assumed the children knew, but they had absolutely no idea.

"So... tell me about the breakdown," Maria said.

"There's not much to tell, really. You've just said it all. Nan looked after you while I was in hospital. When I came out we all thought it best if we stayed at Nan's and I assumed responsibility for my life and my commitments gradually. I was still on very shaky ground emotionally and financially, and you all loved being at Nan's. It was only supposed to be temporary, but then Nan suggested that I rent out our own house to pay off your father's debts. I thought about it long and hard because you were doing well at school, and Laura was still in nappies. I needed to provide for you, and it seemed to me that the only way I could give you a really good start in life was by taking up Nan's offer. The rental money would pay for your schooling. Nan was the answer to all my problems."

"Why didn't you make Dad pay his share?"

"He did, when he had it. He was generous when he had money, but that wasn't often. You know what he's like. Any serious money went into promoting his business ventures."

"How did you feel about us living at Nan's?"

"It was a generous offer and there's no doubt that it helped me get on my feet. But I felt like a failure. Eventually, as you well know, I sold our old home to buy my current house, but not until I got a job at Uni and began to work my way up the administrative ladder. I had to study hard for that. My head was always elsewhere rather than with you girls and Nan filled the gap. The trouble was, you were all grown up by the time I could provide what I'd always wanted for you - a home of our own - and you'd all grown so fond of Nan that I felt selfish depriving you of her. I missed your childhood and I began to resent Nan because I felt she had stolen you. I'm learning to think more kindly now and I don't see things quite as I used to. Now I can see that Nan didn't steal you. Nobody did anything to anyone else. It was just life, happening."

"And it wasn't so bad, was it Mum? We were all happy."

"You were all happy, yes. But I wasn't, because you were all upstairs with Nan and I was downstairs resenting everything - feeling like she was more like a mother to you than me." There was a long silence as both women reflected on this.

"Mum, I have something for you. It's not new. In fact I feel a little embarrassed giving it to you because of that. But it is something I searched and searched for because I wanted to find exactly the right thing. I know it looks a bit tacky and everything, but I want you to accept it simply for what it is – an acknowledgement of what you are to me." Maria opened her purse and took out a small box and put it into her Mother's open palm.

"What is it?" Emily said.

"Open it and see." Emily did, and the sun caught the small object causing a hundred rainbow sparkles to dance around it.

"It's beautiful," Emily's eyes were wide with astonishment. In her palm lay a small marcasite heart-shaped brooch. It had the word 'Mother' written across it.

"I want you to know that I took on board what you said the other day, Mum. I understand the sacrifice you made for us. I'm glad you told me and I want to acknowledge you as a wonderful Mum. It's long overdue." Emily snuffled into her handkerchief. "I understand now why there is tension between you and Nan at times." Maria went on.

"I'm glad," Emily said. "But I want you to know that I'm trying to fix that. I'm trying to fix everything."

Later, when Maria sifted through the events of the day, she admitted to herself that life was not always as it appeared. *All this time I thought Mum wasn't that interested in us, because Nan did all the caring things, such as washing our clothes, cooking our meals, cleaning the house. Nan did everything that you could see. But Mum did all the unseen things. She took on what has traditionally been the man's role. But it cost her dearly. It cost Mum her motherhood.* Maria was now beginning to understand something of the labyrinth that was the relationship between her mother and Nan.

A Twenty-Four Hour Birthday

Beth jogged over to Maria's. She was the only one of the three girls who liked to exercise. Although Laura often jogged with her, she didn't love it like Beth. It was just as well that Beth liked it because exercise was good for depression, which she was prone to. Beth felt the difference in her own mental state after the adrenalin rush she often experienced.

Nan often wondered if Beth's bouts of melancholy were due to middle sibling syndrome. It was true Beth had often resented her position in the family, though not so much these days. During teenage, she had raged against the perceived favouritism that was, in her opinion, shown towards Maria because she was the eldest, and Laura because she was the youngest. Nobody else saw this favouritism and, indeed, her sisters heatedly argued against it. Maria believed that too much responsibility and blame fell on her. Laura wished her family would see her as someone worthy of responsibility and stop treating her like a kid. That nobody else saw this favouritism only caused Beth to rage more.

Beth arrived at Maria's, on a high, at a quarter past three, only to find Laura already there and gift-wrap covering the table.

"Laura brought cake. Would you like some?"

"Yes! A big piece! I'm starving!" Beth handed Maria an envelope containing a homemade birthday card to which was attached a homemade gift voucher. It announced:

To make your birthday very special I promise to wash and vacuum your car monthly for a whole year.

"I'd already made it before you told me about Perth. But it's the thought that counts, isn't it? How about I do it every time you are in Brisbane over the next couple of years?"

"That's lovely, Beth. Thank you." Laura had given Maria a book voucher saying: "Maybe there's a 'for Dummies' book out there on how to become an executive overnight."

"Thanks… I think," Maria chuckled.

During their chitchat, the question of Nan came up and Maria told them what she had learned from her mother earlier.

"Did either of you know Mum had a breakdown?" Both sisters shook their heads.

"That's how we came to live with Nan and how Mum came to live downstairs."

"Poor Mum" Laura said. Beth remained thoughtful while Laura and Maria caught up on each other's news. Laura's life was fairly uneventful, and the demands on Maria's time were intensifying. For the next few weeks she and Simon would travel back and forth to Perth every week, with little or no time for anything but work.

"But it's exciting," Maria admitted cutting more cake for her sisters.

They talked about Nan's health, and then Laura and Beth commented on how much they liked Renata, speculating about whether Matt had paid her a lot of attention out of interest or politeness. Maria was silent on that particular subject, distracting them with reprimands about them inviting the traffic cop without even asking her. But when Mikey became the subject of everyone's curiosity, Beth picked up her water bottle.

"I've got to go," she said, heading for the door. Half opening it she mentioned casually over her shoulder.

"You don't have to worry about Mikey the Bikey bothering you any more, Maria. I've got a date with him."

"Whooo!" Maria and Laura said. Beth must have known that they'd be after her in a flash to worm more details out of her. The door slammed behind her and she ran. By the time they had the door open again, she was bounding down the stairs two at a time and when they reached the footpath she was jogging down the street. Laura, jumping onto her motorbike, caught up with her halfway down the road and crawled the pavement beside her for a short while, trying to learn more. But Beth just kept pointing to her ear buds saying.

"Can't hear you." Eventually, Laura managed to get her to stop and take her ear buds out.

"Mikey's on an early shift this week, and I've got evening tutorials. We can't have a date until next weekend. Now go away. There's no more to tell." Beth jogged off, leaving Laura to text Maria this news."

Ups and Downs

There was a clear view of the city from the top of Mount Coot-tha, where Nan toyed with a smoked salmon salad, while Matt tucked into a very satisfying plate of fish and chips.

"If people had told me when I was a girl, that one day I would be sitting on top of a mountain eating a posh meal in one of the most beautiful places in the world, with a son who was a mathematician, I wouldn't have believed them."

"That's not a posh meal, Mum. It's just a salad."

"Yes, but it's a posh salad," argued Nan. "It's got lots of different fancy leaves in it. Look, this purple lettuce, for example… and this one too."

"That's just spinach."

"I know that Matthew, but when I was a girl spinach was something only Popeye ate out of a tin." Matt didn't say anything because he knew what was coming, his mother being given to repetition. "It gave him super-strength," she said. "And look, there's capsicum and bacon bits as well as that funny white cheese."

"It's fetta."

"I know. I'd rather have Cheshire myself, but I like this too. It goes nice with salmon."

"Well eat a bit of it, then. You've hardly touched it." Matthew had nearly finished his fish and chips.

"I don't feel hungry any more. Can you eat it?" Just then Nan winced with pain. "Ooh!" She gripped the table with one hand and spread the other one over her stomach. "Oh! Dear God, please help me!" Matthew saw the fear in her eyes.

"What is it, Mum? What can I do?"

"It's my stomach… and my back. It hurts Matthew. I don't think I can stand. Just let me sit here for a few minutes. Maybe it will pass."

161

The pain did not pass so Matt called an ambulance. They heard the siren at the bottom of Mount Coot-tha and it seemed to take an age to reach them. Later, at the hospital, a doctor said:

"We need to do more tests. We'll be able to tell you more tomorrow. In the meantime we've put your mother on a morphine drip until we know more. She's comfortable, so you can sit with her now if you wish, but she'll be sleepy."

Emily had dropped Maria at home around two because her sisters were calling in with birthday presents. She herself was planning to shop, until her mobile phone rang minutes later. She pulled over and took the call, then headed straight for the hospital, arriving at Nan's bedside breathless. Nan was more peaceful now, and sleeping.

"How is she?" Emily's eyes were beseeching Matthew's.

"We'll know more tomorrow. In the meantime they've given her morphine so she's not in pain."

"Was it all too much, do you think? I mean the dinner last night… lunch today?"

"I don't know. She seemed to be enjoying herself one minute and the next she was doubled over in pain… unless she's been putting on a brave face." Matthew shook his head helplessly. "I didn't imagine things taking a turn for the worst so quickly. They're going to do more tests and then they'll be able to tell us more. She's comfortable; at least that's something."

"Had we better tell the girls?"

"I think we should," Matthew advised. "Especially as Maria's flying to Perth tomorrow. She doesn't need that sort of call while she's there."

"Yes, you're right. It's such bad timing. She won't want to go."

"Well you'll have to persuade her to," Nan said, opening her eyes for a brief moment before drifting away again.

"Mum?" Emily leant over her mother. "How do you feel now, Mum?" But it was no use. She had drifted off again, so

162

Emily and Matthew chatted about the girls across Nan's bed in the hope that she would participate in the conversation again. She did not.

Matthew stood looking out of Nan's hospital room window while Emily went to the ladies. It had a beautiful view of the Brisbane River and Matt was remembering how significant the river had become to his parents when his father had finished the Duck Boat. They had navigated the river and its creeks entirely, in small lengths, from boat ramp to boat ramp or pontoon, and back the same day. *When Mum passes on, I'd like the Duck Boat. It's the only thing I really want.* Just as dusk was falling a nurse came around to check on Nan's intravenous drip.

"You should go home and rest," she said. "She's probably going to sleep right through the night, which means you can too, without feeling guilty."

Emily returned while the nurse was talking and they agreed that she was right. Together, they made their way to the car park.

"I'll treat you to a curry if you like?"

" I'd really like that." Emily's unshed tears began to flow. Matthew put his arm around her.

"How am I going to tell the girls?"

"There's nothing to tell the girls yet," he cautioned. "Lets not let our imaginations run away with us, eh?"

"Yes, you're right. It may not be as serious as we think, after all Nan has had a history of tummy trouble…"

"…And back pain!" Matthew added.

"That's true."

They drove separately to a local Indian restaurant and by the time Emily had parked her car Matthew was already seated. Emily, smelling the delicious aromas, said, "I think I've found my appetite. I'll have butter chicken and some naan bread," When it arrived she tucked in, eating hungrily. Matthew called the waiter to order some more naan because Emily said "Gerroff! It's too delicious to share," before

163

relenting and letting him have some, since he was paying for it.

"I'm done," Matthew said putting down his fork. "Now, I suppose we'd better call the girls."

"Yes. But let's wait until we get home. I don't want to break down here. Do you want to come back to Nan's for dessert? The mulberry tree's full of ripe fruit and I've got that frozen berry yoghurt that goes perfectly with them."

It was eight thirty before Emily and Matthew rang Beth and Laura, and both insisted on going to the hospital, despite the fact that Nan was sleeping. They left a message on Maria's landline and mobile: Please ring. Mum.

Spanish Albarino

Simon was prompt. He was dressed in an outfit Maria had never seen before – casual but classy, rather than crumpled and homeless which was more his usual style. He had brought flowers - orchids, which, being a researcher, he had chosen because they meant 'beautiful lady' which Maria was. The Chinese, he had discovered, saw orchids as symbolising many children, but he had discarded that meaning. Somehow, he couldn't see he and Maria – assuming there ever was a 'he and Maria' – ever having time for children.

Maria was wearing a velvet dress the colour of her violet eyes... the colour of the orchids, Simon thought. She had never looked so stunning. Simon could not possibly know that ever since he had brought up the idea of marriage, Maria had begun to speculate upon the idea. Not that she would have admitted it to herself, or anyone else. She was too sensible for idle daydreams... and yet her mind seemed to return to the memory all too often. Now, seeing Simon's new clothes, she chided herself. *They're not for your benefit. Get a grip! He's just marking our good fortune.* She extended her arm to let Simon put the orchids on her slender wrist. Though they had often been in close physical contact she had never before felt the frisson that ran through her body as his fingertips touched her.

"They're beautiful," she said meaning it. *You're beautiful*, Simon thought, not yet having summoned enough courage to say it out loud.

Simon opened the car door for Maria and, as she passed him to sit down, her perfume wafted over him. *She looks and smells intoxicating.* He thought. *I wonder what she feels and tastes like, and will I ever be lucky enough to find out?* He did not want to frighten Maria with his recent ardour, so he tried to chat casually about her birthday on the way to the restaurant, which was on a large pontoon on the river.

"What did you get?" Simon asked, "Apart from the job?" It had been agreed that no presents should be exchanged at the Mexican restaurant. This was fairly typical of Maria's birthday, since she had argued, aged nine, that because she had been born at four minutes past six in the evening, her birthday should go from four minutes past six on her actual birthday, until the same time on the following day because, for twenty four hours following her birthing hour, it was still, technically, her birthday.

"Nan gave me another chapter of her story." Simon was privy to Nan's eccentricities because he was practically part of the family and, of course, Maria's partner in crime when it came to the illegal appropriation of marijuana. "Beth gave me an IOU by way of a year's worth of car washes because she claims she is a poor student. She did provide the flowers and balloons for the restaurant table, though, which was a lovely gesture. We know what it's like to be a student, and poor, don't we?"

"We do," laughed Simon, "…but she gets more mileage out of it than we ever did. Did Matt give you a gift?"

"Yes. He gave me a new iPhone. He said a swanky executive needs a swanky phone for her swanky new job."

"That was generous of him."

"It was. Mum gave me a massage voucher for two, so I can go with a friend. Otherwise I can go twice."

Simon wanted to say that he wished he were that friend, but it wasn't the right time.

They arrived at the restaurant exactly on time and entering, were warmly welcomed by the Maitre d', who escorted them to their table. He was at pains to ensure they were happy with their table, offering them another one if not. Satisfied their seating was to their liking, he pulled Maria's seat out, allowing her time to position herself so that she had the best view of the river, before he pushed it back in.

166

A waiter approached their table.

"Your menu Senōr, Senōrita," he said with a smile. "Our Chef's signature dish is on the menu tonight. It is Lobster Thermidore. I can recommend it."

"Thank you," they both said.

"I will leave you a moment to consider your choice."

It did not take Maria and Simon long to decide on the Lobster. As soon as they put down the menus, the waiter was beside them again.

"Are you ready to order, Senōr?

"Yes, we'd like the lobster, but we're not sure what to drink with it," Simon admitted.

"May I recommend a nice Spanish Albarino?" The waiter suggested.

"Can I have red wine?" Asked Maria. "I know it's unusual with fish, but I like red wine."

"If the Senōrita would permit, I must say...no no! Is no good for choice! Isa because of the tannin in red wine. The lobster, he will react... make everything taste of metal. Isa basic chemistry...sorry, No no!"

"Oh!" Maria smiled disarmed by the Spaniard's knowledge. "Then I will have what you first recommended, thank you."

"Albarino," said the waiter again. "You will not be sorry. This wine isa perfect. Is come from my country where I live... Galicia. Is on Atlantic coast, where is much fishing. Galicia is famous for this wine. Is acidic and goes well with fish and especially lobster, and is not expensive. Isa very fine wine! You will see!"

"You've convinced us." While they waited for their meal, Maria continued to describe her presents and when the food came, aromatic and colourful, they discussed their new jobs, and particularly what the change meant for them.

"I've drafted an ad for someone to take over my research."

"Yes, I'm thinking of doing likewise," Simon said. "There are so many things to consider, aren't there? We'll have a better idea what we're in for after Thursday's meeting." Both of them had been invited to attend a Thought Court in Perth. It was to be held at the University of Western Australia and they would be accommodated in one of the Colleges. "Maybe we can have a look what the renting situation is like while we're there. I was thinking of renting a unit until we get settled, and maybe something a bit more permanent later on," Simon suggested. "What about you?"

"I haven't really given it much thought," Maria said. "I've never been to Perth."

"Me neither," Simon admitted. "We could share, if you like," he said tentatively.

"Really?" she said smiling. "That's a great idea."

Simon looked into her happy eyes. *Is she really as innocent as she appears*, he wondered? Maria's lack of guile was one of the things Simon loved most about her. He had been out with a number of women and most of them would have been happy to have a live-in relationship with him. But either they had been too manipulative, too much in love with themselves, or just didn't interest him enough. It was Maria's lack of guile that set her apart. Her authenticity had attracted him to her all those years ago at university. It had taken Maria's friendship with Renata to make him realise how much he wanted to keep her in his life – and not just as a friend. He was about to broach the subject of marriage again. It was true, he was worried he might frighten her away completely, but one way or another, he felt he had to know. *Let's hope I get it right this time.*

"That was the most delicious meal I have ever eaten," Maria said, putting her knife and fork down on the plate and taking another sip of wine. "This is delicious too. In fact that was THE perfect meal." After their dinner plates had been cleared away, Simon took the bull by the horns.

"Maria," he said. He didn't dare take hold of her hand as he wanted to in case she noticed how much his were shaking. "There's something I need to say to you." Maria's eyes stopped wandering around the restaurant and fastened on him expectantly.

"The other day, when I asked you to marry me. I wasn't joking. I'm in love with you Maria and I want to marry you." Maria's eyes widened with surprise. She opened her mouth to speak but had no words. "Is it such a terrible idea?" He asked.

"No… No… It's not. I've been thinking about it a lot, too, since you brought it up last time."

"You have?" It was his turn for surprise.

"Yes… I mean, I don't know. It's all such a surprise. It's different… I mean it changes things. What if it doesn't work out? Will we be able to continue as friends?"

"I don't know. It's a risk, but life changes everything anyway. Nothing stays the same forever."

"We could have a trial run at it. I'm thinking about your suggestion of moving in together?" she said.

"You want to?" Simon was overjoyed.

"Well, it's all a bit sudden…and when you mentioned it before it was for the wrong reasons, but you've just given me a different reason. You said you loved me. It makes all the difference. I'd like to say I love you too, Simon, but I'm not sure what it's like to be in love. I haven't really thought about you that way until recently… I have to say that the idea feels good. I am so very comfortable with you. But I don't know whether feeling comfortable with someone is what love is. We've never even kissed. Marriage seems a bit premature." Simon looked crestfallen, but it didn't stop him taking her hand and bringing it to his lips. Maria continued. "So what do you think about moving in together and seeing whether we're compatible in all the important ways before committing to something as monumental as marriage?"

"Spoken like a true scientist," Simon teased. "A pilot study, you mean." Maria pulled a face indicating that now he was being silly. "Okay! I'm teasing and you're on to me. I think it's very… well, very you … sensible and cautious. It's a better outcome than I dared to dream of," he said. "So I'll take it." The tension eased between them, and Simon poured them both another glass of Alberino.

"I haven't given you your birthday present yet," said Simon taking a small box from his pocket.

"Yes, I noticed that," Maria said. "I thought you were being tight."

"Far from it. I've been trying to pluck up the courage to give it to you because I didn't know if you would want it," He opened the box to reveal a diamond ring. "This is definitely the most expensive birthday present I've ever bought," he smiled. "Will you wear it, because I am going to do the best I can to make sure I meet your needs in all the right ways." Simon smiled suggestively causing a flamingo blush to wash over her. "Once we're living together, as far as I am concerned, it will be forever." He took the square of diamonds out of the box. "Can we make it official?"

"You make it very difficult for a girl to resist," she smiled. *His eyes are shining*, she thought. *I wonder what they're like when they're smouldering*. "So! This job's turning out to be a job with perks," she said, as he slipped the ring on her finger. They laughed causing the waiter to look their way. Simon beckoned him over.

"That's bloody good wine. She's agreed to wear my ring on the strength of it." The waiter smiled clearing away the empty Alberino bottle, so that Simon said, taking it from him. "I think we'll keep that one as a souvenir, but do you think we can have another bottle. I'm hoping its magic might even bewitch her into setting the date!"

"Congratulations," the waiter said beaming with pleasure. "For you, is ona the house."

"Really! How generous!"

"Thank you!"

The rest of the night was wonderful. They had raspberries, cream, and coulis, layered between brandy snaps which they ate from each other's spoon.

"Why didn't I realise how hot you were before now?" Simon murmured. "I feel like a blind man who can suddenly see."

When it came time to leave, Simon apologised. "We can't drive home. We're over the limit. I'll ask if we can leave my car in the restaurant car park and we'll take a taxi."

"Is no problem, Senõr." The waiter had already sought the Manager's approval.

Drawing into the kerb outside her unit that evening, Maria sent the taxi away without Simon.

"I think we should get some practice in before we go to Perth."

"You mean a sleepover," Simon asked hopefully.

"No. School kids have sleepovers. I'm offering you something far more..." She whispered into his ear,

"I don't have a toothbrush."

"I've got spares." She walked away from him, knowing he would follow. When he did catch up with her, he drew her into his arms.

"You're making me crazy."

"How disappointing," she teased. "I was trying for well and truly insane... but we've still got the rest of the night to work on that." They were now standing close to the entrance of her unit, and he swivelled her round and pinned her to the door, his arousal on her pubic bone, melting her.

"Come inside," she said her eyes misty with longing...

Loving Kindness

When Laura's motorbike pulled to a halt outside Beth's share-house, Beth and Mikey were kissing each other goodbye.

"Hey Mikey!" Mikey waved before mounting his motorbike. He pulled out into the traffic and sped off into the night, Beth sighing as he disappeared into the distance.

"I thought you couldn't have a date until his shift changed?" Laura said this with 'please explain' eyebrows.

"We can't, but it doesn't mean we can't snatch the odd hour together. What's the latest on Nan?"

"We'll be there to see for ourselves soon. Hop on," Laura chivvied. "I'm due at work at ten o'clock."

"Okay. Let me lock up and grab my bag." Minutes later Laura, with Beth riding pillion, was speeding along the motorway, skillfully weaving through what little traffic was on the road at that time of night. Beth claimed riding pillion always gave her a high. When Beth said the same about jogging, Matt had observed that every family seemed to have a junky these days. However, as long as Beth was only getting high on adrenalin, he conceded that things could be worse.

When they were approaching the hospital Beth yelled that Laura should not go into the hospital car park, digging her knees into her sister's ribs to make sure she had her attention.

Laura pulled to the side of the road thinking something was wrong, since she had not heard Beth for the wind rushing by.

"Park here!" Beth said. "You don't want to pay for car parking."

"You stopped me for that? You know, I did work that out for myself, so stop being a bossy boots. I was going to park in that side street, but this is just as good." she turned off

172

the ignition. If she were on duty she could have parked in the car park free of charge, but she wasn't the type to compromise her job by taking advantage of the perks when she was off duty.

The duty nurse was alarmed by the arrival of a police officer but when Laura explained she wasn't on duty until later, and that she had come to see her grandmother, the nurse relaxed.

"She's a bit restless. On the bright side, though, at least you can talk to her." They were disappointed therefore to find, on entering her room, that she had drifted off. They waited a while and occasionally tried to waken her with a quietly spoken question, but when it got to half past nine, Laura said she would have to leave for work.

"I'll drop you home Beth."

"Okay." Beth replied reluctantly. "I don't suppose there's any use me staying on my own. It's not as if she's even aware I'm here. I wonder where Maria is?"

At that very moment Simon and Maria were getting out of a taxi outside the hospital. How quickly things can change, Maria was thinking. Only a short time ago she and Simon had experienced their first kiss, which had ignited desire and the need for more physical expression. But it had been interrupted the moment Maria had pressed the play back button on the answering machine.

"Don't answer it." Simon had pleaded.

"Alright." She said between kisses. "But I think it is probably urgent, otherwise they'd leave a message on my mobile. Whoever it is must really want to get in touch. I'll listen, but I won't answer. If I don't, it will be beeping all night." She was unbuttoning Simon's shirt as she put the phone on loudspeaker.

"Maria, it's Mum. Please call me… it's very urgent." Maria stopped undressing Simon.

"It must be Nan," she said beseechingly to Simon.

173

"You have to call," he said. "Go on!" She stroked his cheek.

"Thank you for understanding." He kissed her briefly one last time before their intimacy was stolen completely. She smiled sadly and punched the speed dial button. Her mother picked up her call.

"What's wrong?"

"Nan's in hospital Maria. They're doing more tests. We don't know anything yet. We'll know more tomorrow." There was a long silence. "She's comfortable and she's sleeping." Another silence. "Maria, I know it's going to be very hard for you to go to Perth tomorrow but you have to go. It was the last thing she said before the morphine kicked in. She told us to persuade you to go."

"Of course I can't go to Perth," she said. "How can I at a time like this?" Simon was signalling her… wanting to know what was wrong. "Hold on Mum." Maria explained the situation to him and then began to tell her mother, again, why she could not go to Perth, but Emily interrupted.

"Maria, can you put Simon on?" Maria handed the phone to Simon who did a lot of nodding and agreeing and promised he would do his best, before he finally hung up.

"I have to persuade you to go to Perth," he said. Maria did not answer.

"Let's go," she said. "I need to see Nan."

"Of course you do," he said, hiding his disappointment as he put his shirt back on.

"I'm so sorry," Maria said, hugging him one more time.

"We have the rest of our lives," he said smiling. "Time with Nan is precious. I get that."

"You're amazing…" Maria said, "… and I want to spend the rest of my life with you."

A New Arrival

Beth and Laura were heading for the lift to the car park when they came upon Simon and Maria.

"Laura, are you okay?" Used to being the caring big sister, Maria held her arms wide to embrace her. Laura accepted the hug but said that she was fine and that Beth probably needed a hug more than she did. Maria hugged Beth too, and remembered quickly that Beth was the most sensitive and deep feeling of them all. *It's probably why she writes poetry and journals.* Maria thought. *Why have I never realised that before? Probably because Laura's the baby!*

Maria had watched Laura grow resilient this past year. Sometimes, these days, she appeared to be the oldest, and definitely the toughest and most cynical member of the family. It must be to do with being a police officer. This observation was very true. Laura, in the short time she had been in the police force, had confronted the spectre of death head on, since it was now part of her working week. She was not as daunted by the events of the evening as Maria imagined.

"What about you?" Laura asked, but before Maria had time to answer, Beth interrupted.

"Laura, if it's okay with you, I might go back with Maria and Simon so I can sit with Nan a while longer. Maria, or whoever's driving" she said changing her gaze to Simon, "Can I cadge a lift home with you?"

"We're over the limit so it'll be a taxi, but yes, we can drop you off on the way home."

"Okay. I hope Perth's a blast," Laura said moving off with a hurried goodbye. "Let me know if there's any change. I'm on the desk tonight so you can get straight through to me at the station."

On their way to see Nan, Maria and Simon's eyes met with longing, though they didn't have long to think about what they were missing for they soon arrived at the ward, where the duty nurse said it was fine for them to sit with Nan for a while.

"I'm supposed to be going to Perth tomorrow," Maria told the nurse. "How bad is she?"

"Is that where you live?" she asked.

"No… at least, yes, that's the plan. My work is taking me there. That's why I need to know how bad she is. I will be back next weekend."

"Well it would be very unlikely for your Nan to… you know… pass on this week. She's not at that stage yet and the doctor will be doing everything he can for her." Everyone bucked up immediately.

"Oh" Maria sighed with relief. "Are you sure?"

"Yes. Now you go and give her something to look forward to…" she said. "…because that's what she needs right now." Maria and Simon smiled at each other. "We have the very thing," they said.

When they entered her room Nan looked the picture of peacefulness. Leaning over her, Maria took hold of the hand that wasn't punctured and bruised by a drip.

"Hello Nan," she said, kissing her grandmother's forehead gently. "I've got some wonderful news for you." Nan's eyes snapped open and she looked piercingly at Maria as if trying to understand who she was. "Hello Nan," Maria said again. "How are you?"

"What news?" Maria smiled thinking *she doesn't miss much.*

"You're invited to a wedding! Simon and I are engaged."

"Whoah!" Beth murmured totally not expecting such an announcement. Not so Nan who, with a strong Liverpool accent said:

"About bludy time too."

Nan's hospital room suddenly became festive with talk of weddings and rings and the setting of dates. They would have arranged everything right there and then, but Nan drew Maria's ear close to her mouth and whispered something about her mother to her. Maria nodded and engineered the conversation away from the wedding.

"Settle down, everyone. That's enough about weddings. If we want a wedding planner we'll obviously ask for one. But what I want right now is for Nan to tell us one of her Beatles stories." Somehow Maria felt, that if Nan could recount one of her stories, it would be a sign that nothing monumental was wrong.

"Oh… well… Give me a moment to think," Nan said.

"Well, while you're thinking, I'm going for coffee," said Simon. "Who'd like one?" Everyone did.

"Since you're not an octopus, I'll come and help you," said Maria. "You think up the story Nan and we'll get the goodies."

"You just want to snog!" Beth said. "You're not fooling us."

"Have I told you about when George visited me at Weybridge?"

"No, Nan. But hold that thought because I want to tell you about Mikey before the others come back."

"Oh I know all about Mikey and you," Nan said, astonishing Beth. "You can keep all that for your Mum. I'm getting past all this lovey-dovey how's-your-father." Instead, Nan and Beth shared a long heart to heart about Emily that involved the shedding of tears. The nurse, walking into the middle of this, brought medication and comfort food - sandwiches and Milo. By the time Simon and Maria returned Nan and Beth were over their emotional interlude and were tucking in.

"You took your time," said Beth. "The nurse found us dying of thirst and brought us refreshment."

177

"Well, the coffee machine was a long way away." Simon grinned. When everyone was sitting comfortably on or around the bed, Nan began.

"George came to visit me in Weybridge. Did I ever tell you that?" They all shook their heads. "It would have been September of nineteen sixty-seven, after my second stint of teaching in Belgium, after I made my vows. It was July, and I'd just returned to our convent in Weybridge to find out where I was being placed next, when I was told I was to stay in Weybridge and study so I could go to teacher training college.

Weybridge was lovely… Posh! Classy! There was a school attached to the convent and I had charge of a small dormitory of four children. My bed was curtained off giving me some privacy. It was a beautiful room furnished with plush counterpanes that looked as if they'd been woven out of gold. They had definitely been made professionally. Rich people's kids came from all over the world to the school so everything was affluent and comfortable."

"What did you do while you were there?" asked Beth.

"I made a big impression. On my first morning there, I was told to make breakfast for a sick nun. Of course I didn't know where anything was and, trying to keep the rule of silence, I found a teapot in the kitchen. It was full of stale tea so I found a sink. It was full of lettuce but that didn't matter because I only needed enough water to swill the teapot out into a bucket I found under the sink. Well, the water came out of the tap like Niagara Falls and the small pot overflowed in a nanosecond, dotting the lettuce with tea. If there had only been enough lettuce for a family it wouldn't have been a problem. However, the sink was huge, like a trough, with enough recently washed lettuce to feed an entire school. It was now covered in wet hard-to-get-off tealeaves. Bloody bloody shit! I thought. Now I'm for it. The lay sister, who had washed every lettuce leaf under intense magnification, if her glasses were anything to go by, pounced on me. I had ruined her

178

entire morning's work. She threw such a hissy fit, that I'm sure if I scrubbed the entire convent, floors, walls and ceilings, with my toothbrush, for a hundred years, it would not have been enough penance. Fortunately all the other lay sisters gathered around me telling me not to worry or I might have stabbed myself in the heart with the large butcher's knife that was draining near the sink.

"I'm really sorry," I said, "I feel awful."

"Aragh don't worry," one of them said with a lovely Irish brogue. "Tis only taylayves! Sure dey'll wash off."

"I'll wash them," one of them volunteered as others started asking me who I was, and where I'd come from. Before I knew it I'd broken everyone's rule of silence big time. They kept calling me Sister Beatle, which surprised me as I thought only the nuns in Ireland called me that. They knew about my Beatles hair cut too. I soon realised that the culture of convent life, being one with no televisions, had a strong oral tradition. Whatever happens becomes part of folklore that gets told and retold not only at international level, but down through time as well.

When all the fuss of the tealeaves had settled down, I suddenly went cold as I remembered I'd left an egg boiling while I went about my tea-making. Oh God, I prayed. Please don't let it have boiled dry! I had a very bad feeling about my egg as I 'hastened with modesty' at full pelt, skidding to a halt in the corridor where I had left it. On the way I considered my options. I could either sin against love by serving the poor old sick sister an inedible egg and legging it before she realised, or I could sin against the vow of poverty by binning the egg and starting from scratch. I never had to decide because, when I went back for the egg, it had gone. That's when it struck me what a bizarre place it was for a stove to be, in a corner on the bend of a corridor. Nevertheless, that's where I was, beside the stove, forefinger to cheek, asking myself: Where's the bludy egg gone! The pan was there – it was dry and blackened - and the gas was still on. I turned it off quickly telling myself

179

I'd sinned against the vow of poverty by wasting gas, while at the same time asking myself if I was in the right place. I weighed up the possibility of there being two stoves on the bend of two different corridors. No. I told myself. There's the pan – true, it's black now – but it is definitely the same pan… I think…

There was only one answer: a thieving, greedy nun must have nicked it. The trouble was that I couldn't think of a single nun I knew who would do such a mean spirited thing – but then I didn't know anyone in this convent, did I? Anyway, the more I thought about it, the more unlikely it seemed because, to take the egg and eat it would involve breaking numerous rules, and nuns who were not me, just would not do that. I knew this because of Chapter, when you have to kneel in front of everyone, including Reverend Mother, and confess your faults. Some nuns were so holy that all they had to confess were things like:

I confess, Reverend Mother, that I wasted my tacking thread because I couldn't be bothered taking it out of my work and reusing it.

Or

I confess, Reverend Mother, that I took two pats of butter for my bread on two occasions in the last hundred years.

I, on the other hand would be there for hours while I confessed my faults against the rule:

I confess, Reverend Mother that I broke the rule of modesty by wanting to see myself as a nun in a mirror. I did this by waiting until evening and hanging my black apron outside my dormitory window so I could see my reflection better. I also broke the grand silence because when I was climbing up onto my wash-stand to put my apron outside my window, I accidentally knocked my washbasin and jug onto the floor smashing it to smithereens and spilling water everywhere, causing the novices to slip and slide, so that they ended up with broken knee caps, eye sockets and pinkies. I offended against the rule of poverty by needing a replacement bowl and jug for my ablutions.

Also reverend mother I committed faults against the Holy Rule by dropping my apron into the night outside because of the fright I got at making such a clatter when my jug and bowl broke. I confess that when I looked for my apron the following morning I found that it had fallen through the greenhouse roof, breaking a pane of glass above Sister Dympna's rare plant collection, causing them to catch a chill and die of the plant equivalent of pneumonia. So now she won't be able to sell them to raise money for Biafra, which may lead to millions of people starving, and all because I had a first stone in my apron pocket.

It was rare for Reverend Mother to interrupt our confessions so I was surprised when she asked.

'And pray sister, do tell us all what a 'first stone' is.'

'Umm! It's a stone with the word 'first' written on it, Reverend Mother,' I said. She looked perplexed. 'I keep it in my apron pocket to remind me of the scripture: *Let he who is without sin cast the first stone.*'

"Anyway, getting back to the mystery of the vanishing egg, I was so engrossed in my own dilemma that I was only distractedly aware of another dilemma in progress just a short distance from me further down the corridor. Two nuns were bending over a nun lying on the floor.

The horizontal nun was pointing up at the ceiling. The vertical nuns were looking up to where she was pointing, and so I looked up, as you do when everyone else is looking up. And there it was - my egg. I had no idea how it got there, but was told later that it had probably exploded. It was now hanging precariously from the ceiling. I have no idea why it is that Reverend Mothers always turn up when you don't want them to, but she rounded the corner, and seeing the horizontal nun, hurried to see what was up with her. She followed the gaze of all the vertical nuns, which now included me, and that was when the stupid sodding egg dropped off the ceiling and landed, splat, on her face. It was so hard-boiled that it gave her a black eye. Well, as if I wasn't in enough trouble for what moved into folklore as the great egg and lettuce fiasco of 1967, I got the giggles – as any normal person from Liverpool would. Reverend Mother and I never quite saw egg to eye much, after that.

But that's not the story I wanted to tell you about because that's not about the Beatles. The one I wanted to tell you is about George."

"Well that might have to wait until I've freshened you up a bit," interrupted the Nurse, who asked Nan's family to wait outside, or get another drink, while she attended to Nan.

"She seems very hyped up to me," said Maria once they were out of hearing.

"They've increased her medication so maybe that's why," suggested Simon.

"I'm not complaining," said Maria. "It's just that you can't get a word in edgeways and I've got so many questions to ask her about what she's just told us."

"Maybe they've got her on speed or something. She's like uber-Nan. I'm surprised she didn't tell us that story while doing laps of the ward," added Beth, stopping beside the coffee machine while Simon inserted coins. "Put it this way, Maria. I don't think there's any chance of her having an early night. Anyway, if you want to ask her questions you just have to be forceful enough. I'll show you how to do it when we get back up there."

A Psychedelic Mini

When the young people got back to the ward a quarter of an hour later, the nurse intercepted them warning that Nan might begin to get drowsy soon because she had just had a sleeping tablet.

"Normally I'd ask you to say goodnight to her now but she begged me not to send you away yet. Just keep the noise down, though, because all the other patients will be sleeping. She's in a room of her own, so I don't see why you can't stay a while longer. It might help her to settle better if she tires herself out first. By the way, did your Grandmother really know The Beatles?" They all looked at each other and smiled.

"I see," said the nurse.

When they gathered around Nan again she was chomping at the bit and keen to continue her story telling.

"Well now, it was probably a couple of months after the egg and lettuce incident, when I was well settled into the convent at Weybridge, and studying feverishly for my exams, that Reverend Mother said I could go with some older nuns for a walk along the canal. I was pretty excited about it because it was actually my first time out since arriving in Weybridge. We walked for about ten minutes through the town centre, and on towards the canal. I was following on behind the older nuns, marvelling at the 'outside world' while they were deep in some teacher-related conversation I wasn't interested in. I wanted to savour the freedom of being out and about.

People did tend to gawp at us a bit… I was getting used to that. But a passing car shouted something at me as it passed and, as usual, I smiled but didn't really pay much attention, until I heard the screech of brakes and knew, because the noise changed direction, that the car was now reversing. I remembered to keep custody of the eyes and just kept walking as sedately as if I were auditioning for sainthood. The older nuns, I thought, could have done with revisiting the 'hasten with modesty' rule sometime soon, because they were streets ahead of me. A loud, excited male voice interrupted my thoughts.

'Hey Jude.' Now that really did stop me in my tracks. When I looked back a man resembling Jesus was running towards me waving. It never crossed my mind that he might be waving at me, so I turned to walk on. 'Hey Jude', he shouted again. I didn't know what to do. The man made me nervous, feral as he looked with his untidy growth of beard and weird clothes.

'I think you might have mistaken me for someone else,' I said nervously, as he drew near.

'No I haven't. You're Jude...' I must have looked blank because he said. 'Okay, you're Kate, then.' when this didn't get the reaction he was hoping for he smiled and said.

'Remember? I met you on a bus in Liverpool, and in a convent in Ireland, and in a field in Belgium.' That's when it dawned on me.

'Nooooo…' I said looking at him more closely 'No… No-no-no-no-no… You can't be…? You're nothing like him!' The man began to nod. 'I don't believe it…' I said, parting his beard in an effort to recognise the face beneath.

'Honest!' He said. 'It's me.'

'But you… You don't look a bit like….' Then I saw the twinkling eyes. 'Glory be!' I gasped. 'What've you done with my mate George?'

'It's the beard,' he said smiling.

'Well I don't like it' I said. 'What're you doing hiding your lovely face.' Liverpool people don't usually take offence at such observations and George didn't.

'What're you doing here?'

'Studying for teacher training college…'

'I thought yer were thinkin' of leaving.'

184

'I'm waiting for them to kick me out! I thought I was wearing them down but what can I say. They're all saints. They tell me I'll still be here when I'm old and decrepit. Well not exactly here, but still a nun - somewhere.'

Aware that the older nuns I was supposed to be walking with were now tiny little nun dots in the distance, I absolutely had to excuse myself.

'It's… well… what can I say? It's great to see you George,' I said. 'But I have to go. The other nuns are way down there,' I said, pointing down the street. 'If I don't catch up to them I'll be defrocked. But before I go, tell me quickly what you're doing 'ere?'

'I'm on my way to a party at John's,' he said.

'You mean John Lennon's?'

'Yeah.'

'Does he live around here?'

'Yeah. He lives in the St George's Hill Estate.'

'A council estate?'

'If it is, it's a bloody posh one. It's where the rich and famous live. He's got a brilliant mock Tudor house there… in Wood Lane. It's where the party is. You can come if you like?'

'I'm not allowed.'

'How do you know? You haven't even asked.'

'Trust me, George. I'm not. I shouldn't even be talking to you. Do you live here too?'

'Not in Weybridge! I live nearby though,' he replied. 'You'll have to come over.'

'That wouldn't be allowed either,' I said, wishing for the first time ever that a nun's life were not quite so limiting.

'Maybe we can figure out a way,' he said. I couldn't help teasing him.

'It's true that you've achieved amazing things, George, but I don't rate miracles among them. I turned round to see where the other nuns were. 'Oh oh!' I said worriedly. 'Do those nuns look bigger to you? They're coming back to find me. I'd better go. It was lovely to see you again George. I'll see

185

you around then eh?' Again I pushed the hasten-with-modesty rule to the limit, in my anxiety not to draw the other nuns' attention to the fact that I had been talking to a man in the street."

Nan drew breath.

"I need to go to the bathroom." When she returned her granddaughters did not give her time to speak.

"Why did you leave the convent, Nan?" As usual, Nan evaded the question.

"That's another story. I can't tell you that story in the middle of this one and you do want to know what happened next, don't you?" They nodded.

"Sister John of the Cross, wanted to know who I'd been talking to. Fortunately she was one of those people who never listen, so she didn't expect an answer. She just kept firing questions at me: 'Why didn't you keep up with us? Do you think we've got all day, sister? How would I ever explain to Reverend Mother if we lost you?' Sister John was a very grumpy nun and she was even more grumpy than usual for the rest of the walk, which made me consider that the word 'cross' in her name had several layers of meaning.

The second time I saw George in Weybridge was not much more than a week later. Reverend Mother had just told me my parents had telephoned.

'They want to visit you and bring you a Christmas present. Your sister's fiancé has offered to bring a statue of the Virgin Mary from the convent in Liverpool.'

I remembered that statue; it was gargantuan. A bad feeling washed over me, though I didn't say so, because Reverend Mother was in a really good mood and I didn't want to spoil the moment. *Forget about it*, I told myself and I concentrated on the happiness I felt to be seeing my family soon.

When the day dawned I was impatient to see them so, by eleven o'clock, I was practically crawling up the wall, asking myself: *When are they going to get here*? I had plenty to keep me busy as I was in the middle of exams. I swotted to make the time go faster. The nun on parlour duty that day was Sister Aurelia, who was, to be honest, a bit three-sheets-to-the-wind. She was very old and Spanish, and her eyes were always dripping tears. She had a hunched back, causing her head to loll sideways, so she was a bit – let's say, unusual. She really didn't understand much, and when she came to tell me I had a visitor waiting for me in the parlour she was making a 'loco' sign with her finger.

'He theenk he a beetle,' she said.

To be honest, what she said did not register. She announced one visitor and I expected others. I literally skipped down to the parlour, threw open the door and there, to my utter dismay, found, not my family, but George Harrison.

'No!' I said. 'No! No!' My disbelief was profound 'I don't believe it! Wh...What... What are you doing here?'

'I found out where you lived...' he said, all smiles, '...so I've come for a visit.'

'You can't just keep turning up in my life!' I protested.

'Why not?' He said. 'I know yer like seein' me.'

'That's true. But I live according to strict rules.'

'Oh stop worrying girl! I'll donate a big fat cheque. They'll be asking me back next week, you'll see. Money talks – even here!'

'You've got to go!' I insisted, not very graciously grabbing him by the arm and manhandling him towards the door. 'I'm a nun. I don't have visitors – especially not men!'

Just then, Sister Aurelia entered carrying a tray loaded with a teapot, milk-jug and sugar-bowl, all silver, as well as scones and pretty fondant cakes. They looked delicious and it was years since I had had an iced cake. It was in the short silence, while Sister Aurelia was placing the tray on the table, that I opened my mind to the idea of being given a cheque. I wrestled with whether I could brazen out having a male visitor, while choosing which cake I wanted. A big fat cheque is a big fat cheque for the missions, after all. And well… those cakes! Just to check if it was worth the risk I asked George.

'How much?'

'I dunno! What do ye think? Five grand maybe…?'

'You'd pay five grand to visit me? Why?'

'Cos yer better value than a shrink! You don't know how luvly it is to sit down and talk te someone who dusn't want to rip me clothes te shreds, or cut off a tuft of me 'air. You… well, yer nearly threw me out. It's really refreshin'.'

'It's because I'm a nun, George. I'm not supposed to rip men's clothes off. I've taken a vow of chastity and I have to keep custody of the eyes even if I so much as come upon a pair of men's undies on a washing line. I'm supposed to behave with decorum at all times, but somehow I can't seem to do that when you're around.'

'Arh 'ey Jude! Yer can't blame me for yer lack of decorum in the cornfield in Belgium. Yer took yer clothes off long before I arrived!'

'Grr…' I murmured, blushing, and annoyed that he would even mention that incident. 'Write the stupid cheque now George, before I change me mind.' George looked at me funny, as if he was suddenly disappointed in me.

'Yer mean yer only want me for me money? I'm really cut up about that!'

'Firstly, I don't want you! Secondly, you can console yourself that I won't get a bean of your money. I haven't even 'eard the jangle of small change for years. I can tell Reverend Mother yer want yer money to go straight to the missions if yer want some added reassurance.' George took a cheque out of his pocket and filled it out.

'It's a good job I always have a blank cheque in me pocket,' he said, as he wrote.

'Why don't you just carry a cheque book like everyone else?' He continued to write before answering.

'The business pays for everything and for accounting purposes it gets confusing if lots of people carry chequebooks so they just give us blank cheques to use. I'll get another one tomorrow.' George handed me the cheque and I felt more like a hooker than a nun, as I took it. However that didn't last long for as soon as my eyes fell on the iced cakes I smiled. I placed the cheque safely under my saucer and said with the first hint of politeness I had shown George. 'You go first.' I moved the iced cakes towards him, mentally attempting to put a force field around the yellow one and ready to break his face if he took it. He didn't.

'Whoohoo!' I said taking it with complete and utter delight. I closed my eyes in order to savour its sugary sweetness. George spoiled the moment:

'It's the dearest bloody tea party I've ever been to,' he complained. It was a good-humoured complaint, and he seemed much happier now that I was relaxing. Sister Aurelia appeared again, and began opening cupboards and rattling cutlery. I instantly knew she had reported back to Reverend Mother and had been told not to leave us alone.

'I think she's been sent in to chaperone us,' I said. 'But it's okay. She won't understand our Liverpudlian accent if we pileitonthick. So! TellusowotheBeatles'redoin' George?'

'Te be honest, I'mbludyfedupovit. Yer can't go outforfear o' gett'nmobbed. Weevengetdeaththreats.'

'Why Warravyerbeendoin?'

'Nott'n'! It's like beinaprisoner, only worse cosyeraven't dunanything wrong.'

'Sounds awful! Woulditelp ifIprayed forye George?' He smiled as if he liked the idea of being prayed for.

'Dunno, Ye can givirragoifyelike.'

'I will. Sobeinfamous isn' all it's crackeduptebe then, 'ey?'

'Well, tebe'onest itcanbegreat, but it can also beabloodynightmare,' and he told me this awful story about the way Imelda Marcos treated The Beatles when they went to the Phillipines. But that's another story.

189

'Burritdusavadvantages.' He said. 'Wegotthree Grammiesthisyear.'

'Terrific!' I said.

'And John's got a psychedelic Rolls.'

'Wouldn' I justluvaride inthat?' I said dreamily.

'I'vebeenlearning thesitar withRaviShankar,' I had absolutely no idea who Ravi Shankar was, or what a sitar was either, but I didn't interrupt him because, even though his coming to see me caused me problems, I loved him telling me all his stuff. It was a window into a world I had chosen to leave and was beginning to miss.

'Maureenadababy.' When I looked puzzled he said 'Yeknow. Ringo's wife. They called him Jason.'

'Arrh that's great! I beteelikesplayin 'isDad's drumswithim,'

'We allwent tohearthe Maharishi giveatalk at the Hilton. I reallydigim. What about you?'

'I've neverheardofhim.'

'No, I meant wharravyou beenupto?'

'Oh! I'mstudyin'. Theywantme tebeateacher. Ye know whatsnice, George?'

'What?'

'Findin' out I'mnotassoft asIthoughtIwas. The only thing is, I'mbeginin' toavemedoubts about beinanun again.'

'Areyegirl? Why?'

'It'snotbecauseit's'ard beinanun.'

'No! Wellitwouldn'be whenyerbreak asmanyrules asyoudo.' I flicked my nice Irish linen serviette at him. It caused Sister Aurelia to frown in our direction, so I let his comment go.

'But tobehonest,' I confessed. 'I don'treallythink Ibelong. It'sallabit posh ifyerknowwhatImeanlike. Thenuns usedtotellme about the missions, whenIvisited them in Liverpool, and Iusedtethink, wouldn't it be lovely tego out tethemissions andluv poor sufferin'people – yer know, reallyluvthem… maybe evenpeoplewith leprosy. I usedto imagine meself huggin'lepers, yerknow, and showin'them I wasn'afraid of the consequences, likecatchin'leprosy fromthem because, well, all yer need is love, isn't it? I'ad this odd notion that if I luvdthemenough, Iwouldn'tcatchit fromthem, 'cos I'dbe nearly asaint andthereforeimmune. But whenyergetdown tothenittygritty, George, I wouldn't even beallowedte touchlepers, never mind hugthem, even if our nuns did 'ava lepercolony, whichtheydon't. Ye see, theruleforbids us tobefamiliar with people. We're notevenallowed to walk intwos whenwe'reout walkingtogether. Anyway, asI toldyerbefore, I'm havin' secondthoughts. Maybe it's 'cos I'm in a reallyrichschool fullospoiltbrats. I suppose it's justasimportant teluvrich people, butferme… well, it's just not me, yeknowwhatImean George?' George was looking at me very intently at that moment. Then he smiled… he did 'ave a nice smile.

'Yersee. That'swhatImean,' He said. 'That's what I luvabout yer. Yer wannaleavethe convent because yernotallowed to'uglepers.' I was a bit miffed because he was laughing at me but Reverend Mother chose that moment to breeze in. I was just about to explain what I was doing having morning tea in the parlour with a man without permission, but George beat me to it.

'Hello,' he said holding out his hand with a big smile. 'I just happened to be driving down the street one day when I saw Kate… erm… Sister Jude. I used to know her in Liverpool, so I made enquiries and people told me there was a convent here, so I knocked on the door and here I am. I just wanted to catch up and make a donation.'

'May God bless you for it,' Reverend mother said, inclining her head towards him dubiously.

'I also wanted to see if there was any possibility of startin' up a leper colony, which I would totally finance, on condition that you send Sister Jude to it.' Reverend Mother gave me a very weird unreadable look.

'Indeed there is nothing I would like better than to send Sister Jude to a leper colony,' Reverend Mother replied, with a very tight smile, and I couldn't tell if she was being mean, but that would be unkind, and Reverend Mother was holy and therefore would never... She broke into my thoughts. 'Our work is teaching, not nursing, so it is very unlikely. But I will let our Mother General know of your generous offer, Mr... er...'

'Harrison. I'm George the Beatle...' he said.

'If, however, you would like to sponsor one of our teaching endeavours, Mr Harrison, That would be very welcome.'

'No. I've got nott'n' against schools, Sister, but I just have this thing about lepers... What can I say? I just wanna hug them, and I thought if I sponsored a leper colony I could do that to me heart's content.' This made me choke on my tea, which I slurped up my nose instead of down my throat. When it fell back down into my throat unexpectedly, it caused me to splutter as if I were in the early stages of drowning. Water splattered out of every orifice above my neck, with the exception of my ears and it was a while before I stopped coughing and wheezing.

George's eyes were twinkling with merriment. He had just managed to get a rise out of me, and wrap Reverend Mother around his little finger all in one go. That, in my opinion, put him up there in the higher echelons of finger wrapping.

'Look, Reverend Mother, it's a cheque for the missions,' I said, when I had recovered. I waved the cheque about before handing it to her. 'Isn't that generous of George?' You could almost read her thoughts. Somehow the five thousand pounds was at odds with this long-bearded-wonder in scruffy clothes. Personally I liked him clean-shaven, but it was his face.

'God bless you for your generosity, my son!' Reverend Mother said.

192

'It might be the most expensive elevenses I've ever had,' he said, 'but I'm really enjoying it.' I could tell that Reverend Mother was ready to steer him towards the door, but he sat down and started tucking in again. 'I don't suppose you could put some water on the pot, luv?' He handed the empty teapot to Reverend Mother who, rather taken aback, went in search of Sister Aurelia whom she had dismissed.

When she came back she wanted to know how George knew me, and he couldn't so very well say that he met me while astral travelling, when he was tripping on marijuana and LSD, now could he? But George remembered that I had told him I used to go to the church a few doors away from his Mum's and so he said he met me there occasionally. It made him sound holy, like a churchgoer.

'It wasn't a lie,' he said later. 'I could have met you dozens of times without realising it.'

'And what do you do for a living?' asked Reverend Mother, when she joined us at table.

'I'm a Beatle,' he said, looking quite puzzled because he had already told her that a minute ago. I don't suppose George could conceive of people not knowing who The Beatles were. However, Reverend Mother had already had a very bizarre conversation with Sister Aurelia about the beetle in the parlour. 'A beetle... a beetle', Sister Aurelia had repeated several times. 'He mucho loco.' Reverend Mother was not so quick to dismiss him as crazy. I had a feeling she'd be asking a lot of questions about George but she did go off smiling with the big fat cheque safely in her pocket.

"I'll see you in my office in ten minutes, Sister." That put a damper on things because I knew I had to give George his marching orders.

George and I chatted on for a while and I told him my family were coming for a visit that day and how, when I came to the parlour, I expected to see them not him.

'I'm sorry I was so shocked,' I said.

'No! Don't be! It's what I like about yer. You always say and do the unexpected. You're the only girl I know who makes me feel like she's disappointed when I turn up. Yer real, ye know what I mean like?' Not knowing whether that was a bad or a good thing, I changed the subject.

'I haven't seen my family for over a year.'

'I dig that,' he said. 'Sometimes I don't see mine for a long time and you really miss them don't yer?'

'Why don't you stay and meet my family?' I said. 'They'd be blown away to meet you.'

'I'd luv to. Some other time, though,' he said. 'I've got an Apple Corps party to get to.'

'Apple Core?' George spelled it out for me.

'Apple C.O.R.P.S. It's a recording studio we're opening soon.'

'Well don't let me keep you,' I said. 'Thanks very much for taking an interest in us…' I said, '…and thanks very much for the donation.' Then I broke the rule and gave him a hug. 'You're so nice…' I said. '… I'm really sorry I was so unwelcoming.'

I rang a clangy handbell and Sister Aurelia came to see George out. I watched her accompany him to the door with tears in my eyes, thinking God brings such unlikely people together to achieve his purposes, for they were such an odd sight as they walked down the corridor together, she small, bent, insignificant, and listing badly, George so tall and famous.

I looked in on Reverend Mother, as she had requested. It wasn't really unusual because the rule required us to do so when a parlour meeting ended.

'George has gone, Reverend Mother,' I said, kneeling beside her desk. There was a short pause. I waited.

'Your family has been involved in an accident, Sister.'

'Oh no!' Worry must have been written all over my face because she quickly added.

'Don't be concerned! They're safe. However, they will be late. Our Lady didn't make it. Five thousand pounds should cover it.' I backed out without saying a word. Sometimes I managed the rule of silence very well.

Plans

Early the following morning, Maria and Simon woke up groggy not so much from their late night with Nan, but more from the passion of the night. However, before leaving for the airport, Maria rang her mother, as Nan had suggested.

"Mum, Simon and I are engaged so I guess sometime soon we'll be getting married and… well… I really need my Mum right now."

"Wh… wha… Is that you Maria?" Emily was still surfacing from a deep sleep.

"Yes, Mum. Sorry. Did I wake you up?"

"Yes. What did you…? I thought you said…"

"Simon and I are getting married. Well we we're going to live together first – give it a try, we thought, to see if it worked. But it seems to have escalated from that and all of a sudden we seem to be talking about weddings."

"It's a bit sudden." As Emily heard her own thoughts being spoken, she realised it wasn't sudden at all. "Although, you've always been best friend. It's obvious now that I think about it. Oh, how absolutely wonderful! When is it to be then?"

"We haven't fixed the date yet, but soon… very soon. I love him Mum. I have a ring and everything. We'll talk about it when we get back from Perth. We weren't going to announce it just yet but with Nan… well, I think we're thinking sooner rather than later. I wanted you to know right away. Oh! There's the taxi. I'll email you Mum, and we'll talk more when I get back."

"I'll be here. What time's your flight?"

"We have to check in at seven thirty."

"Are you travelling Qantas?"

"No. Virgin."

"Okay. Have a good flight." As soon as Emily put the phone down she raced up to Nan's room to ask if she needed anything because, if she hurried, she would just about make it to the airport in time to see her daughter's engagement ring. She was half way upstairs when she realised Nan was in hospital. She did an about turn, hurried downstairs, and in a flurry of arms and legs, shrugged out of her pyjamas and stepped into her clothes. Her shower could wait. The phone rang. It was Matthew.

"I can't talk. I'm just racing to get to the airport before Maria and Simon fly out."

"Why? What's wrong? Is it Mum?"

"No. Nothing's wrong. In fact, it's quite the opposite. Maria and Simon have just got engaged."

"Oh! In that case I won't keep you. Give her my congratulations. Unless you want company?"

"No thanks Matt. I want to do this on my own." Emily thought about phoning for a taxi but then remembered that taxi drivers don't always know the quickest way from A to B. She picked up her purse, not stopping even to comb her hair. Her hair was very short and had a natural kink in it so that she didn't have to fuss much with it. Getting into her car she wound the window down and was soon speeding along the river road, her mind on Maria and Simon and how even great sorrow could be punctuated by joy. She was thinking of Nan, of course, and wondered how this news would affect her. She had heard that a sick person's life could be prolonged if they had something important to live for. Emily hoped this would be so for Nan, but if it wasn't, then she hoped that this new joy would outweigh the pain of life.

Emily slammed the car door and raced towards the Virgin terminal. Maria and Simon were nowhere to be seen. She checked the flight times on the departures screen and saw they were due to fly out at eight o'clock. It was seven thirty-five. She hoped they weren't on board already. Unencumbered by luggage, she excused herself as she tore through the crowd of people heading towards security. Then she saw them. They were some distance ahead of her.

"Maria! Simon!" she yelled at the top of her voice. Everyone but Maria and Simon looked her way. She yelled again, gaining ground as she sped along.

"Maria! Simon!" But still they walked on. Emily noticed, despite her hurry that they were not holding hands. She had expected them to be totally wrapped up in each other, holding hands, kissing and generally announcing to the world that they didn't just love each other as they always had, but that they were **in** love. But then she realised, that such was not their way. They would be too practical for that. In fact they just looked like everyone else, each of them pulling their cabin luggage and carrying laptops over their shoulders. "Maria! Simon!" She thought her voice would have been drowned out by the announcement of their flight over the loudspeaker, but they stopped and turned round.

"Mum!" Maria's face registered astonishment. The worst-case scenario came to mind.

"Has something happened?"

"Yes," Emily said. "My daughter got engaged and I wanted to give her a hug and…" Suddenly Emily felt stupid, "…see her ring."

"Oh Mum!" Maria smiled, eyes dewy with tears and arms reaching out for her. "That's so lovely!" Releasing her mother from her embrace, she held out her hand where diamonds sparkled.

"A square setting," she said looking up at Maria. "How beautiful. I'm so very happy for you Maria; and you Simon." Emily hugged them both at the same time. The last call for their flight was blaring over the loudspeakers.

"That's us," Simon said apologetically.

"Go on then. I've done what I came for. Go save the world!"

Maria gave her mother one last hug and then it was their turn to run while Emily retraced her steps. She had often heard it said that when a daughter marries, you don't lose a daughter, you gain a son. Emily felt she was gaining a daughter and a son.

A Game of Cards

The next week was busy for everyone. Maria and Simon, in Perth, were almost off the family radar. Busyness was setting in and Rick Walters was not joking when he said he would be counting on them to do his legwork. It was unfamiliar territory but they had each other to confide in and bounce ideas off and they learned that the power of two was far greater than the power of one.

In truth, they were glad to be somewhere where they could focus on their new responsibilities, although it was looking more and more unlikely that the entire initiative would be managed from Perth. Too many of the key people were from the East Coast, and many of them were protesting against Perth as a relevant location for the initiative. Most people said The Flagships must be situated close to universities and industry if they were to be attracting the nation's innovative genii. It was not a matter of creaming off these gifted people, but of working with them wherever they were so that their ideas could serve the greater good and not just the bank balances of industry. So, just as important in the master planning of the Flagships was the introduction and location of Industry Nexi with a Charter of Ethics that focused on the common good. Much of this would come later. For now the location of the management centre was what was pressing.

The indecision around the location of the management centre did not stop basic infrastructure planning. Indeed, as plans were documented, the more it was realised that a central facility was needed, and Perth was not central. Perth had lots of space, but its dislocation from all the key participants made it unviable. Maria and Simon were charged with the job of finding that central location. They shelved the idea of moving into a unit together until they knew where they would be working. They were too busy, anyway, for these personal considerations. From morning to evening they were on the go and at the end of the day they would fall into bed together and ease their tensions by finding new ways to delight each other.

Beth was studying hard for exams, and Mikey made excuses to call on her each evening often with a take-away, before his night shift. So the long wait until they could have a proper date did not seem quite so bad. They called in on Nan who was having some more tests, but would soon be allowed home with a line inserted into her chest so that other medication could be administered easily and efficiently. Nan guessed that Mikey was a bit intimidated by visits to the hospital, not knowing quite what to do or say. He wandered off for cups of coffee and magazines, flowers, or anything else that would give him a role to play. Nan could see how much Beth liked him and hoped that he was the reliable type. Beth was the one who Nan thought could most do without getting her heart broken.

Matt still had Renata on his mind, and was still trying to decide if he should try contacting each Renata listed on the ATARO website. While he was procrastinating she beat him to it ringing his mobile on Monday night.

"I really liked talking to you the other night, Matt. I was wondering if we could have coffee some time?"

"Yes." He said trying to hide his astonishment. "Why, yes. I would have contacted you to invite you, but I only had your first name. I should get your contact details right now?"

"What's your email address? I'll email them to you," she suggested. That started off a lot of on-line communication, so that by the time they met on Wednesday evening, they already knew a great deal about each other. Points in common were a love of live theatre and art-house movies, swimming, bookshops, rock-climbing and beautiful gardens. Their coffee date led to even more things in common, such as chess and backgammon, sudoku, hiking and boating, although boating was more of an extrapolation, really, because Matt loved it –

and, on the basis of all he had told Renata, she was sure she would too. They had arranged an outing up one of the Brisbane River's creeks for the following Sunday.

Emily was astonished to get a call from Laura, who, having considered Maria's tale about Nan always being there in the middle of any relationship between mother and daughter, asked Emily if she fancied going to see the play Doubt which was on at a local theatre.

"I thought we might go on Thursday week," she said.

Emily didn't much fancy going to see a play about nuns. Perhaps it was too close to the bone, but she did not say so.

Misunderstanding, and thinking Emily was going to see Doubt the coming Thursday, instead of the Thursday after, Matthew said he would look after Nan because Nan was coming home from hospital that day.

"No, my date with Laura is next Thursday, not this Thursday, but come anyway. Nan will be pleased to see you." Emily agreed.

When he turned up, Renata was with him. As Matt had given Emily no inkling of this, her astonishment was considerable. Normally Matthew and she talked about prospective dates or the lack thereof so this seemed a bit like secrecy.

"Nan's resting," Emily said. Matthew went off in search of playing cards.

"I rang Matt a few days ago. I just couldn't stop thinking I would regret it if I didn't." Emily didn't get a chance to respond to Renata because Matthew's search had taken him into Nan's room and she had decided to get up for a while.

"She fancies a game of cards too." He announced. The phone rang and Matt went to answer it.

"I hope you're good at cards Renata. Mum's ruthless," warned Emily.

"I can play a mean hand of snap," Renata laughed.

"It's Maria for you!" Neither Matthew nor Renata noticed the smile on Emily's face as she crossed the living room to speak to her daughter, who had asked for her, not Nan.

"Yes?" she said.

"I'll teach you how to play rummy," Nan offered, padding into the kitchen to put the kettle on. "I'm glad you're no good at cards. I might win for once."

"I bet she'll be playing like a pro before we finish the first game. Renata's smart. She learns things in a fraction of the time it takes others." Renata protested.

"Oh come on Matthew! You're a mathematician. I bet you've got formulas worked out. I'm not playing for money."

"That was Maria." Emily took up the hand she had been dealt. "They've set the date."

"Oh! When?" Matthew and Nan both asked.

"I can't tell you. She doesn't want me to steal her thunder." Emily couldn't believe how very good it felt to be nursing one of her daughter's secrets close to her chest. The lean years make the years of plenty so much more valuable she thought.

Baked Alaska

With all this relationship building going on, the week soon passed. Maria and Simon would be home on Friday evening and Emily became absorbed in gathering the family for an engagement celebration.

"I'd like to make a special dinner to celebrate, but I'm an atrocious cook."

"You'll be a fabulous cook once you get a bit more practice. If you want, I'll teach you," Nan offered. Emily felt this was real progress. It had been a long time since her mother had taught her anything.

"I don't want you doing anything stressful," Emily said. "Stress is not good for you."

"I won't be the one stressing. You will. I'll just be issuing orders from the wings. It couldn't be easier. Now ring everyone and, if they've got plans for Saturday night, tell them to cancel them."

Under Nan's instruction, Emily made a very early start. She decided on Moussaka, with side-salad, and Nan's pièce de résistance, Baked Alaska, by way of an engagement cake. She had started very early, buying a sponge cake at the local supermarket as soon as it opened.

"That's the easiest way to do it. You don't want to be making a sponge cake specially. It's okay to take shortcuts to make life easier." Next Nan told her to cut the sponge in half through the middle and put the bottom part on a pie plate.

"Warm it slightly in the microwave, prick it all over with a fork and then soak it with Tia Maria. Warm sponge absorbs liquid better than cold. If you'd rather use a different liqueur that's okay? I use anything I've got. I've made it with sherry and wine and even orange juice, but the nicest one I ever made was a canned cherry one. I soaked the sponge in the juice and put the cherries on top of the meringue when I took it out of the oven. You can begin to experiment when you get confident."

Opening the liquor cabinet Emily looked to see what they had in. "I'll do the Tia Maria one," she said. "It's Maria's favourite." She took a large swig. "Mm… that IS nice," she said, taking another one." She took the sponge out of the microwave.

"Just a little tip, Em," said her mother. "Don't take to the bottle while you're cooking because, if you are anything like me, you won't have all the ingredients and you might have to go out half way through to buy something that's missing. You don't want to be done for drink driving."

"I'm very organised. I've checked and I've got all the ingredients," Emily said, drenching the sponge with the Tia Maria. "Anyway, this is just the first stage. You said it has to go into the freezer for quite a while before I have to do the next bit."

"So, go on then. Put it in the freezer. You might as well freeze the other half of the cake too," Nan said. "It will do for next time you make one."

"You know what I'd really like? I'd like to make some flowers to decorate it with. Do you make them out of icing?" Emily slid the base of the dessert into the freezer.

"Yes. You'll need to get my cake decorating tools down, then. They're in a tin in that top cupboard. Not that one, this one," she said pointing to the cupboard over the oven. Better check whether you've got enough icing sugar."

"Yes, there's an unopened packet and one that's half full."

Soon mother and daughter were engrossed in the moulding of delicate flowers, petal by petal. Emily's talents as an artist were useful when it came to painting them with food colouring. Nan had taught her grandchildren how to make these sorts of flowers years ago, and Emily still remembered the resentment she had felt watching Nan work with them in the kitchen. *She never taught me how to do it.* Emily had since learned to be kinder for she now knew that Nan did not have the skill when Emily was a girl. Nan had taken lessons when Emily was grown up and she finally had time to do the things that were important to her.

"You can leave the flowers drying on a tooth pick like this," Nan said, sticking the other end of the toothpick into an orange so the flower could dry out. "Normally I would leave the cake base in the freezer overnight, but you put it in about three hours ago so I think it will be frozen by now. Okay, now pile ice cream on top of it. Pack it down. You don't want air pockets where the heat can get through and melt it. You don't have to be so gentle with it Em. I press it down with my hands so the layers of ice-cream get really packed down. That's it. Yes the best part of doing it like that is licking your fingers clean."

Emily glanced at the oven clock while trying to find space in the freezer. "It's lunch time. What do you feel like, Mum?"

"I forgot to mention that you need to make sure there's enough room in the freezer, especially when you cover it with meringue. It's a dessert that keeps getting bigger and bigger so you need enough freezer space for its growth spurts."

"Okay. Good. Thanks. Now, what about lunch?"

"I'm not hungry, love. I'm going for a lie down."

"You have to eat, Mum."

"I will, when I'm hungry. Now I'm just tired and I need a rest."

"Well at least let me make you something nourishing to drink. What about a banana smoothie?"

"Yes, I fancy one of those," Nan smiled.

Later, when Nan was rested, she told Emily to whisk up five egg whites, adding ten tablespoons of caster sugar, one spoon at a time, making sure each time the mixture formed stiff peaks before she added more. Emily took the base of the Baked Alaska from the freezer when the ice cream was sufficiently frozen.

"Now cover the ice-cream with the meringue making sure it is sealed all the way around. You don't want the heat to get at the ice cream. The meringue insulates the ice cream from the heat and stops it melting. Now you can leave it in the freezer until you need it. The secret is to cook it in a really hot oven for about five minutes so that it browns very quickly without melting the ice cream. You'll have to heat the oven in advance to about 220° giving it time to warm up while people are finishing the main course. Talking about the main course, hadn't you better make a start on it?"

"No. That's enough for today," Emily said. "I'll do the Moussaka tomorrow."

The cooking lessons continued the following day and Nan's tuition didn't stop until the table was laid and the wine glasses sparkled. When everything was ready Emily looked at the table proudly.

"That is one of the most empowering things I have ever done," she said with satisfaction. When the Baked Alaska came out of the oven Emily would place the flowers on it before taking it to the table. She imagined how stunning it would look and how surprised her children would be.

"We'll have it with raspberries," she told Nan. "We all love raspberries. I'll put them in a separate bowl though because I want the Baked Alaska to look more like an engagement cake than a dessert."

The Cavern

As Beth and Mikey arrived the phone rang. It was Laura.

"Start without me. I've been delayed. I shouldn't be too long."

"We'll wait for you."

"No don't, just in case I'm delayed more than I expect to be."

Matthew and Renata were welcomed and, for a while, the conversation focussed on embarrassing Matthew with all the funny stories from his childhood. So it was that Renata learned that Matthew had tormented neighbours with his musical 'manque' when, in a moment of madness, Nan had bought him a set of drums for Christmas so that he could be like Ringo Starr. Someone explained that Nan had lived as a nun in France and Belgium for a while and liked to intersperse her stories with oddments of French for no other reason than, musically, they sounded better than English.

"Manque means lack." Beth explained.

"You were a nun?" asked Renata, studying Nan with new interest. "Wow! I wanted to be a nun when I was young."

"You'd be surprised how many women tell me that."

"What was it like?" There was a loud groan from Matt as Emily counselled Renata not to go there. She was just about to ask them why when the doorbell rang and the lovebirds breezed in. Renata leaned towards Nan and said.

"Maybe you can tell me all about it some other time."

"Of course." Nan agreed. "Let's keep tonight about Maria and Simon."

Renata thought this was a generous answer. *I think I'm going to like my Mum-in-law-to-be* she thought, for she was already certain that, one day, she would be a part of this family.

There was a wave of excitement around Maria as each of them admired the ring and hugged the gift-showered happy couple.

"I made this for you." Beth handed over a gift-wrapped parcel.

Everyone waited with bated breath wondering if this was another of Beth's cheapskate, poor student presents. But when Maria opened it she was pleasantly surprised. It was a clock with a small photo at the centre in the shape of a heart. It was of Maria and Simon and around the photo were printed the words "Will you?" and "I will" as well as the date they had become engaged. The words were intertwined with beautiful folk-art convolvulus. The fingers were permanently fixed at 7:36, which was the time Simon had produced the ring. The photo was one Maria had asked 'Spanish Alberino' (a nickname the waiter had earned) to take, using her iphone. She had emailed it around the family a few days later. Beth and Mikey had also, very thoughtfully, brought along a bottle of Alberino for a souvenir of the night.

"For your first wedding anniversary," Beth suggested.

"Oh Beth! You've captured the moment perfectly. Thanks."

"My turn," said Nan. "I haven't been able to get out to the shops so I've given you something of my own that I think you'll like."

"You can open this one, Simon." Maria handed the parcel to him. It was something in a box.

"I'm guessing it's a vase," He lifted the lid, took out two items wrapped in tissue paper and gave them to Maria for unwrapping. She uncovered two tiny teapots. They all laughed as Maria hugged her grandmother.

"Our turn," said Matt handing Maria a long thin parcel. Again there was much shredding of wrapping paper.

"Bud lights! Perfect for romantic evenings."

"We're hoping for lots of them," Simon said. "Thanks Matt."

"Hi everyone," said Laura bursting in with apologies. She too was carrying something gift-wrapped.

"You're just in time," said Maria reaching out for the gift. It was a large white platter.

"It's for the prawns for your first Christmas. I hope we're all invited."

"Have you set the date yet?"

"Yes Nan." All the faces around the table turned towards Simon who teased them with a long silence before announcing, "We're getting married on Christmas Day."

"It's the only way we'll be able to have a honeymoon…" Maria explained. ATARO will be closed between Christmas and New Year, you see, and so is the new research enterprise. It seems silly not to take advantage of it."

"That's only about 8 weeks away." Emily was thinking practically. "Everywhere will be closed over Christmas."

We haven't fixed the venue yet but you don't have to worry about anything Mum. What I would like, though, would be for you to help me choose the dresses. Laura, Beth, You'll be bridesmaids of course, and Renata, I would like you to be my Maid of Honour." Three faces lit up with delight.

"And Matthew. Would you be my best man?" Asked Simon.

"I'd be honoured." Matthew said sincerely.

"There's lots for you to do, Mum, but it's stuff you can do from here – the invitations, for starters."

"Where will you honeymoon?" Beth asked.

"Maybe somewhere in the Whitsundays. We've been too busy for the details, haven't we Simon?"

"We sure have. A Pacific Island holiday might be nice…"

"Or a Norfolk Island one maybe?" Interrupted Maria again. Happiness is often infectious and soon there were many more suggestions of good places to honeymoon so that Emily had to interrupt everyone.

"Can I give you my present now?"

"Of course," said Maria.

"I'll have to go downstairs for it, and it isn't wrapped, but it's still a present. Is that okay?"

"Of course," Maria was not the only one who was curious. "Go get it quickly! I'm intrigued."

Emily was soon back, awkwardly struggling with a large framed picture. When she turned it round, they all gaped. She had captured everyone's likeness as they sat around the table in the restaurant on the night of Maria's birthday. But there were two ghostlike figures standing behind Nan – the two important men in her life: Grandpa Doug and George Harrison. A few moments passed before the laughter began and became contagious. Emily had to wait until the laughter had died down to find out if they did actually like the painting, or whether they just found it hilarious.

"Did you paint it Mum?" Maria was awed rather than astonished.

"I did. But you don't have to hang it if you don't like it."

"Are you kidding? It's clever... it's fun, and it's absolutely brilliant. I had no idea you were such a good artist."

"Well, it's been a while since I painted, and now that I've started I don't think I'll ever stop."

"It's such a personal present, Mum. How could we not like it?" Maria took hold of Simon's hand. "It's got all my favourite people in it. Do you like it Simon?"

"I do."

"But who's that?" asked Renata pointing to George.

"Oh! That's someone who's lived with us for a very long time," said Nan, piquing Renata's curiosity even more.

Mantle of Motherhood

It was Thursday night and, as she got ready to go to see 'Doubt' with Laura, Emily still had Maria on her mind, which wasn't surprising since she had been designing wedding invitations all week and had emailed three for Maria's approval. Maria and Simon had returned to Perth, to prepare a submission on where the new site for the research enterprise should be. As it turned out they had found the perfect location in Brisbane but could not tell anyone because it was still confidential.

Emily smiled, pleased with the improvement in family relationships. She told herself that she was done with self-pity. She had never realised before how empowering the right attitude was. *Nevertheless*, she thought. *Don't go at it like a bull in a china-shop. Be careful of feelings and make changes with kindness.* Things had gone very well with Maria and she hoped things would go as well with Laura.

She went over the events of Saturday's engagement dinner. This brought Mikey to mind. Emily liked him and hoped he and Beth would make a go of it because, despite his macho job, he was gentle and not afraid of his feminine side. Even Nan had commented on it when the Baked Alaska had been brought out.

"Oh Mum," Maria had said happily. "You've excelled yourself." Emily had noticed Nan's smile of satisfaction. Nan had always been the one to make the Baked Alaska, and now she was passing on the role to her daughter.

"You're a top cook, Emily."

"Why thank you Mikey. I'll teach Beth how to make Baked Alaska. Then she can make it for you." Astonishing her, Mikey had smiled.

"You can teach me, then I can make it for Beth." Nan was overjoyed by Mikey's unexpected response and contributed a piece of wisdom.

"Nothing is as powerful as gentleness and nothing is as gentle as true strength."

"Yes, he is gentle, isn't he?" Emily had whispered to her mother who was sitting beside her. Beth, on the other side of Nan, overheard and smiled, glad that Mikey was finding approval within her family.

"Will you make me Baked Alaska?" Simon had asked Maria, hopefully. Maria had thought about this for a moment, but being a young woman of integrity she said:

"Probably not. We'll have to go to Beth and Mikey's for that treat."

Both Nan and Emily noticed the hopeful look that passed between Beth and Mikey.

Emily realised that the clock was ticking. *All this daydreaming is not going to get me to the theatre in time for Doubt.* She had 20 minutes to get there at the specified time. She ran the comb through her hair and quickly applied some blusher, eye shadow and lipstick followed by the final touch - mascara. It was all Emily ever wore on her face and, truly, it was all she needed because she had inherited Nan's English rose complexion.

Beth, who had no lectures or tutorials for the next week, had decided to stay at Nan's for a few days so Emily didn't have to worry about her.

"Ring Matthew if there's anything worrying?" This was said more for her own sake than Beth's.

"Don't worry Mum. I've done a first aid course."

"Call Matthew anyway," she said. "He's officially next of kin."

"I know that, Mum." Beth said, a little impatiently. "Go! Enjoy yourself and stop worrying."

Emily met Laura outside the theatre. As they settled into their seats Emily hoped her boredom would not become obvious. However, the play proved to be quite gripping though she could not imagine her mother as a nun in a similar context.

For Laura, it was interesting from the point of view of a police officer. In her working life she came across sex offenders, but within Holy Orders, well that was hard to understand. She had many questions. Later, over coffee, she raised them.

"That older nun was terribly severe, Mum," Laura said. "I can't imagine Nan like that. Do you know much about her convent life?"

"Only that it appears to have been densely populated by Beatles."

"Did she ever mention it was… you know, unreasonably severe or strict?"

"From what Nan says, they were remarkably kind and patient, and she seems to have loved them dearly."

"Why did she leave then?"

"Who knows? Maybe she just wasn't cut out for it. She often says she should never have gone into a convent… that she was running away from life."

"Surely her life couldn't have been that bad."

"Life was different then. Her family was poor and Nan often used to tell us her memories when they surfaced, like wanting a small blackboard for a birthday present, just so she could have something to write on. She even used to draw on things like swimming certificates. She said the best thing about wallpapering a room, for her, was that there might be some wallpaper left over."

"Why did she want wallpaper?" asked Laura, for whom this was a truly puzzling statement.

"So she could draw on the back of it."

"Well hello! Why didn't she just use scrap paper or buy a notepad?" This was said with the intolerance of one who was ignorant of hardship.

"They didn't have the luxury of scrap paper, and it cost money to buy a notepad. There was no money to spare for those sorts of luxuries. We've always had scrap computer paper to draw on – reams of it. I can't imagine having nothing to write on. After the war, when she was born, there weren't many luxuries. They were even, sometimes, deprived of necessities."

"Would it make you go into a convent though?" Asked Laura.

"Who knows why you'd do that? It's a complete mystery to me, because from what she says she was a fairly typical teenager. She had a boyfriend and went to dances – as you are well aware, she even went to the Cavern Club where The Beatles used to play. She told me once that she had the list of items she was supposed to take into the convent stolen from The Cavern."

"I can't imagine why anyone would want to steal that."

"It was her money they wanted. They would have been disappointed.

"I wonder what was on the list?"

"Stays, black stockings, floor length flannelette nightdresses, staunch black lace-up shoes, a black shawl, galoshes…"

"I don't know what half of those things are. You sound as if you know the list by heart. What are galoshes, anyway?"

"I believe they are plastic overshoes."

"Why didn't they just wear wellies?"

"God knows!"

"I wonder what the thief made of the list!"

"They probably didn't even look at it. There wouldn't have been much money in the bag because she hardly earned anything, and what she did earn she had to cough up."

"What do you mean?"

"She had to give it to her mother."

"What all of it?"

"Nearly all. I remember she told me once she earned three pounds, fifteen shillings, and she had to give her mother the three pounds. She was allowed to keep the fifteen shillings, but out of that she had to buy clothes, pay her bus fares to work, and pay for anywhere else she wanted to go during the week."

"That's practically slave labour."

"That was the way things were then. Mothers looked forward to their kids going to work so they could contribute to the home."

"Maybe a convent would appear attractive, in those circumstances."

"Maybe. She wasn't allowed money in the convent, though."

"None?"

"No. Any money nuns received would have gone into the convent purse. From what she says she didn't need it. Everything the nuns needed was provided for them. She often says that life in the convent was rich compared to home. She wanted for nothing. She told me once that the nuns had to make three vows and one of them was to live a life of poverty. Most of the nuns came from very wealthy backgrounds so convent life was like living in poverty for them. But Nan always felt like it was a step out of poverty rather than into it."

"It's a very unusual thing to have done. I mean how many people do you know that have done it?"

"Well, Nan is unusual, isn't she?"

"What do you mean?"

"It's nothing I can put into words. She's just different."

"I've never thought about it. She's just… well, Nan! I wonder what it was like for Nan, living in a convent. I just can't imagine it."

"Nan always says that convent life is just a reflection of any other community, that you get the nice nuns, the horrible ones, the gentle ones, the severe ones, the clever ones, the not very bright ones. People are people wherever you go. It's a good thing to remember." Laura thought about her police work, which brought her into contact with such a variety of people.

"I guess so," she said.

The Book of Hours

When they got home Nan yawned and rose from the table where she was sitting with Beth.

"I'm off to bed."

"Who won?" Emily asked seeing the playing cards still strewn over the table.

"I did," said Nan grumpily. "I feel like I'm six. She let me win."

"I did not. You know how bad I play. Tell her Laura."

"It's true. Beth's crap at cards."

"If anyone would like to bring me some Milo, I wouldn't say no."

"I will." Beth volunteered. "How was the play?"

"Very disturbing," Laura said.

"In what way?"

"Ask Mum. I'll do the Milo if you like. I want to ask Nan something." Laura relieved Beth of the mug of milk, and used the microwave to heat it. After adding the Milo, she took it into Nan's room, but Nan was in the bathroom. She deposited the Milo on Nan's bedside table and walked along the corridor to where Nan was cleaning her teeth. Since Nan had never had much privacy with the girls always being around to intrude on her ablutions during their growing years, Nan did not complain about the invasion of privacy.

"Nan, did you ever come across any sexual abuse in your convent?" Nan gestured to the frothy toothbrush in her mouth. Most people would take this as a hint to wait elsewhere, but Laura did as she had done as a child and waited for her to rinse her toothbrush and wipe her mouth.

"Did you?"

"No. Never. Why do you ask?"

"Because the play we went to see was about nuns. Were the nuns you lived with nice?"

"Most of them were... most of the time." Then she thought about it further. "Everyone has a darker side that emerges sometimes, but because we had a rule of silence, and because we were all trying so hard to be good, we never saw much of that side of each other. Excuse me!" Nan tried to squeeze past Laura who was blocking the bathroom doorway. Laura followed her along the hall and into her bedroom.

"There are a lot of allegations of sexual abuse in the Catholic church, Nan. Did you ever come across any?"

"No. Maybe I was lucky, but I never did. Besides the rule had preventative measures written into it to stop that sort of thing."

"What do you mean?"

"Well, in The Holy Rule - a modified version of the Rule of Saint Benedict, there were rules about why we were not allowed to give our love to anyone but God. For example, we were never allowed to talk after Compline – that's part of The Office, which is a mixture of sung psalms, prayers and bible readings. We sang The Office several times a day and Compline was the part we sang before retiring for the night, after which the Grand Silence was observed. The Grand Silence lasts for all the hours associated with going to bed, including being in bed, being asleep and rising from bed. It starts in chapel and ends in chapel. It was implemented so that even a nun's sleeping hours could be dedicated to God. Our whole day was governed by rules, so there was little opportunity for anything that might be considered unseemly."

"It all sounds very negative."

"Yes, I can imagine how it does to an outsider. It wasn't, though... not at all. We weren't told 'don't do this' or 'don't do that' as if we were living under a dictatorship. The Holy Rule had an immensely positive side to it. It was more like: don't do this or that so that you can do something much better. For example the rule said that nuns should maintain the rule of silence except for those periods, such as recreation, when they were allowed to talk. This was so nuns could be praying for the world. Now is that a good thing or a bad thing? Or, for example, there was a rule that nuns should not walk in twos because this would lead to special friendships and your special friend was always to be God. The rule's intention was to help us find strength within ourselves - in the Almighty within us - rather than from each other. One could say that the Ten Commandments were negative, but let's take Thou Shalt Not Kill for example. Nobody could call that negative because it has a hugely beneficial side to it, for example, it leads to a better society, where killing each other is forbidden, and where people feel safe because of it."

"Why do priests sexually abuse kids, then?" asked Beth determined to have her questions answered. "Surely they have rules too."

"Yes. They do. But people deviate from rules. That's why they earn the name of deviants."

"But you never experienced any deviants first hand?"

"No. Never... though, now that you ask me, I do remember one nun insinuating something a bit sus. She was the only really horrible nun I ever came across, and it needs to be said that you do get horrible people everywhere, even in convents." Nan made this point emphatically. "It's a mistake to assume that nuns are perfect or even good. They are just people like everyone else, with both positive and negative sides to their character. This happened when I was in Belgium. The horrible nun accused Reverend Mother of having an illicit relationship with a nun who was ill with cancer – the nun I replaced actually. It was a terrible thing to say. I thought she was vindictive and mean spirited. I never saw any evidence of anything other than sisterly caring in Reverend Mother's behaviour, and I slept in a room very close to the nun who had cancer. I would have known if anything was going on. I didn't sleep that well when I was in Belgium. Anyway, she was very ill – dying actually. Reverend Mother was kind to her, as you would expect if someone was dying."

"So the rule was written up to make it difficult for any hanky-panky to take place?"

"Oh yes. Absolutely."

"And what about the children you taught? Did any nuns ever take advantage of them?"

"Never - not to my knowledge. Some kids got very silly about some of the nuns. What I mean is that it wasn't unusual for a school child to have a fascination with a nun. It happened to me when I was in Belgium, probably because I was so young. A few of the girls would follow me around all the time hoping for some special attention. It troubled me and I was very careful to be fair, making sure all the kids got some attention, since, being away from home, they craved it so much."

"Feeling loved was important to junior boarders because they were deprived of the physical affection usually received from family members. Nuns were also starved of physical affection too. It would have been so very easy at times to hug a child and I did once. It was against the rule of course. Afterwards, I tortured myself thinking I might be a deviant – it was so lovely to connect with someone physically like that. It wasn't until I held your newborn mother in my arms, years later, that I recognised the feelings I had worried so much about. They were quite normal maternal feelings, but nuns tend to get scruples about their behaviour. In my opinion, it's not such a good thing to be that introspective. It's a sort of obsession with self really and I think it is unhealthy."

"Why did you leave the convent, Nan?"

"Because I fell in love with the young English Dominican priest who used to come once a month to hear our confession."

"Did you?" Laura's eyes were round with interest.

"No silly!" Nan said laughing wickedly. But that's what people want you to say. "The truth isn't nearly as interesting and much harder to explain."

And the truth is...?"

"I can't honestly put that into words. I think sometimes it is because of one reason and then I remember another and another. There were so many reasons, in the end, that I can't isolate one major one. I can only say that I loved convent life, and I realise now that I'm old, that it was one of the most beneficial experiences of my life. But a time came when I knew I had to leave because it wouldn't be right to stay. Nor would it be right to say it was for this reason or that reason, because it wouldn't be the whole story, and even I don't really understand the whole story. I think that's locked away somewhere deep inside me and maybe one day something will unlock it. What I can tell you is, that I left because I became certain there was another path waiting for me. I don't think I made a mistake in going into the convent. It was part of my journey and, more than anything else I have ever done in my life, I can never regret it. It's where I began to understand the source of my strength."

"Do you still believe in God, Nan?"

"Oh yes. I'm surprised you would even ask that. I would have thought that was obvious. Now, no more questions. I'm tired and I need my sleep."

Laura's mobile rang as she left Nan.

"Hi Sarge. Yes… Okay, I'm on my way!" As she terminated the conversation she realised she had forgotten to tell him something. She speed dialled work and said "Hi Sarge. I'm at Nan's and I have to go home for a uniform. I'll be about a half an hour." Laura had made a snap decision to accompany her mother home to Nan's for a sleepover. She had not expected to be on duty until the following night. Her mother overheard.

"You have to go?"

"Yes. They're short staffed."

"I'll run you home then."

"Thanks Mum. That would be great."

Broken Trust

Later when Beth got up to go to the toilet before turning off her light, she looked in on Nan whose light was still on. She was writing and prolifically, judging by the untidy spread of ink covered pages on her desk.

"Why aren't you asleep?" Nan seemed to wince so Beth said: "Are you in a lot of pain, Nan?"

"A little, but that's not your worry, love."

"It's just that…well… This is a big secret Nan, and you must swear not to tell a soul." Wrinkles appeared on Nan's forehead as she raised her eyebrows expectantly. "If you need it for your pain, there's some marijuana stuck on the back of the memorabilia on the Liverpool wall." Nan's eyebrows lifted significantly higher. "We got it in case you needed it. We thought we'd hide it there so Matt and Emily wouldn't find it. It's for if things get too painful." Nan said nothing, but got out of bed and walked over to the Liverpool wall, studying it intently. Turning round she asked.

"Which one?"

"I forget. We put a small packet on the back of the some of the biggest pictures." Then remembering she said: "Definitely that one," pointing to the biggest of them all. Nan was going to unhook it but Beth stepped forward and did it for her. Nan looked behind it and sure enough found a small packet. She looked at Beth questioningly and Beth nodded her head.

"Isn't it illegal?" Nan asked, eventually.

"Yes. That's why you must never tell a soul."

"Does Laura know?"

"She got some of it."

"You, Maria and Laura did this?"

"Yes."

"For me?"

"Yes."

"But why?"

"We didn't want you to be in too much pain."

"Oh!" Said Nan shaking her head, speechless for once in her life. "You… you… you're such amazingly kind girls," Nan was overwhelmed, but then fear got the better of her. "But I just feel like I want to spank the three of you with a wooden spoon. What were you thinking?" Nan gave a big sigh as if suddenly burdened by more than she could carry. "You do know I've never used it, don't you? And I hope you haven't?" Beth answered that question indirectly.

"Cannabis is quite legal in some countries, Nan, so if we lived in Holland, for example, it would be fairly normal for people - anyone - to smoke it, and us getting it for you wouldn't be a big deal." That made it seem more reasonable to Nan, but still she said.

"I have no idea what gets into you girls! If you got caught with it you could ruin your lives!" Nan handed the picture back to Beth and got back into bed. Beth fiddled with the picture until it was hanging straight. Then she bent over Nan to kiss her. Nan spoke, very quietly, as if confiding a secret.

"You know, it was often George's way of reaching me. I never tried to connect with him that way, although I've thought about it many times. But I wouldn't know where to begin. You need papers to roll it don't you?"

"We got some of them too. They're stuck behind one of the album covers. I think it's that one."

"Sergeant Pepper's Lonely Hearts Club Band?" Nan asked.

"Yes. Now you go to sleep, Nan. Would you like me to get you anything for the pain?"

"No love. It's not that bad. Goodnight," she said.

"Goodnight Nan," said Beth, closing the door, quite unaware that she had left Nan in a quandary.

Mysterious Behaviour

Breezing into Nan's room the following morning Emily found her on the floor beside her writing desk, with several sheets of paper scattered over and around her. Her first thought was Nan's time had come and nervously she touched her mother's hand. It was warm and Nan stirred. Emily felt for a pulse and found it beating strongly. She crept down the corridor and opened Beth's bedroom door.

"Beth, can you come and help me with Nan. She's on the floor. Don't ask me why because I've no idea. I can't lift her on my own. I need some help getting her into bed." Beth was halfway down the bed under the doona. It took a few moments for her to appear.

"Go back to her," she said wiping the sleep out of her eyes. "I'll be right there." Once her mother had gone Beth threw off the bedclothes. She was naked, but it only took her a moment to slip yesterdays clothes back on. By the time Beth got to Nan's room Nan was awake and sitting up. With one of them each side, they helped her to stand and then get into bed.

"What happened, Nan? What's been going on?" When Nan did not answer, Emily reframed Beth's questions. "Who took your fly-screen out and opened your window wide like that?" Again there was no answer.

Beth noticed Nan scratching at red blotches all over her arms.

"Nan, you've been bitten everywhere. You look like you've got the plague."

"What have you been doing, Mum?" Again there was no answer. "I'll go and get something for the mozzie bites. Beth, don't leave her side, do you hear?" When Emily had left the room Beth stooped to pick up several pages, scattered around the floor.

"Nan, what's going on?" she asked bunching the papers together.

"I've been very, very naughty," Nan whispered. "Quickly! Take those!" She was pointing at the papers in Beth's hands. "Don't let Emily see them! Hide them!" It began to dawn on Beth what might have happened, and if her mother cottoned on, all hell would break loose. Beth tried stuffing the pages under some books, but this made Nan agitated. "No, not there! Not in here! In your room! Put them in your bag. Take them all home with you." There was such urgency in Nan's pleading that Beth realised she must hide the pages quickly, so she tiptoed along to her room and quickly stuffed them under her doona. She was just entering Nan's bedroom again when Emily came running with itch relief ointment and anti-histamine.

"I told you to stay with her," she scolded.

"I was busting to go to the toilet. She's fine. Look."

"There's a really funny smell in here," Emily said.

"I can't smell anything," Nan said, looking at Beth with a do-not-say-a-word threat in her eyes.

"It's familiar but I just can't place it." Applying a soothing gel to Nan's bites she returned to her interrogation. "Are you going to tell me what you were doing on the floor, Mother? You could have caught your death of cold."

"Mum, we live in the sub tropics. Nobody dies of cold here."

"Of course they do."

"Not in October."

"There was a story in the news not so long ago, of people dying of hypothermia."

"Yeah, but that was in the mountains…in winter… not here in Brisbane." Beth chose argument as a method of distraction, which was a stroke of genius because it released Nan from their scrutiny. Relaxing back into the pillows Emily had just pumped up, Nan closed her eyes and got out of trouble, with faultless strategy, by falling asleep. *Or is she*

226

pretending Beth wondered? Emily shushed her out of the room.

"Best to let her sleep while she can. I might get the nurse to come and check her out later though."

"Well I think she's fine," said Beth, trying to relieve Emily's worry. "She probably just wanted to see the night sky properly without the barrier of the screen. When you're dying all sorts of things become important to you. I honestly think you're over-reacting."

"You're probably right, but that doesn't explain why she was lying on the floor with papers strewn around her, as if she'd fallen and let go of them."

"She'll have some explanation." Beth said evasively. "I'm going to get my shower and then I'm going to meet some friends for coffee. I'll be back in time for tea."

"Okay."

"And Mum?" Emily stopped unloading the dishwasher and turned to Beth. "You've been to a play with Laura, and a movie with Maria, but you haven't done anything with me. I don't have much money but I thought I could hire out a video. Would you like to come over to my place sometime and have a girls' night in?"

"You mean just us?" She was thinking of how full of people Beth's share-house usually was.

"Yes. I'll try to get rid of everyone, but if I can't, we can watch it on my laptop in my room – on my bed."

"That sounds great, love," Emily smiled.

"Well let's do it soon. What about a Saturday night? Everyone goes out on a Saturday night and we'll probably have the house to ourselves."

"Okay. Email me the details and I'll ask Matt and Renata to stay with Nan. What can I bring?"

"Popcorn, or ice-cream," Beth suggested. "I'll get the DVD. Is there anything you particularly want to see?"

"No. You choose."

"Okay. Make it about eight o'clock then."

Emily's tension over Nan seeped away in the afterglow of this short conversation with Beth. When she peeped in on Nan, a couple of minutes later she was sleeping peacefully and didn't seem as fragile now.

Beth returned to her room to get dressed after her shower and, retrieving Nan's writing from under her doona, she folded the pages neatly and hid them in her bag, fighting the temptation to read what Nan had wanted to hide from Emily, which was just as well because Emily knocked and asked what she had done with all the papers that had been strewn on Nan's bedroom floor.

"Nothing!" She replied.

"Well this is all I found," her mother said. "They can't have disappeared." Beth's heart froze and she offered up a silent prayer. *Please God, if you stop her finding any more pages of Nan's writing I'll give up sex!* Then, thinking of Mikey, she changed her mind and promised to give up margaritas instead. She really didn't drink enough of these for it to matter much.

"Bye Mum." Beth shouted ten minutes later as she left the house.

"Bye love!" Emily opened Nan's bedroom door too late. She had been going to tell Beth that she had found two of the pages on Nan's desk, but Beth was half way to the bus stop by the time Emily got to the front door. *Maybe Nan picked up the other pages when I was getting the cream for her stings,* Emily thought. She made a cup of tea and sat at the dining room table to read the two pages she had found.

I'd seen lots of pictures of George as he aged, but he hadn't seen me since I left the convent. I have no idea how he recognised me but he just said 'Hiya Jude' and stood there beside me blowing smoke out of the window and gazing up at the sky. Every now and again he hummed a song that I didn't recognise.

Emily stopped reading. More crap, she thought anchoring the pages under a Diana Gabaldon book Nan had just finished. Emily picked up her cup and, glancing in on her mother, decided she could safely leave her sleeping, though she wouldn't go downstairs, as she usually did. Instead she picked up the box of photos that had not been put away since Nan had asked for them a while ago. She tipped all the photos out onto the table and began sorting them under headings: Doug's family; Doug and Boat; Grandchildren; Matt and Emily. She made file cards with labels that stuck up above the photos so it would be easy to find each set of photos when they had been put away in the box.

It was when she was sorting the 'Nan/late teens' that she found a photo that she could not put down. At first she had wondered what Beth was doing in the photo. Wearing cool cheesecloth, and carrying her ban-the-bomb fabric bag, she looked as if she belonged in a sixties student protest. It didn't take long to realise that the photo wasn't of Beth, but of her Mother. Beth looked like Nan's doppelgänger.

Beth, meanwhile, took a bus into the city, and then another to West End. The Three Monkeys would be perfect, she thought. I'm bound to find a secluded corner there at this time of day. She walked the short distance from the bus stop to the café and paused on the threshold to smell the intoxicating aroma of freshly brewed coffee. She was on friendly terms with the staff - one of them was a fellow student.

"Coffee and baklava please, Jayne." Beth said.

"As usual," replied her friend.

"Yes. I'm predictable, aren't I?" she joked. "I'll be near the back door," she smiled not bothering to take a number.

Beth had chosen a spot near the back door because it had a large table with cushioned built-in benches. Light streamed in through the open door and she needed light to read by because the café was dimmed by swathes of dark, ethnic-looking fabric that seemed to absorb the light. Taking Nan's pages from her bag, she laid them out on the table and began to sort them so one page continued on from another. When her coffee and baklava arrived and the polite chitchat was finished, she began to read.

I knew it! She thought. *It was the marijuana.*

Using The Force

Maria and Simon had flown to Perth early on the Monday following their engagement celebration, having done enough research to know that Perth was never going to be a good centre for the newly conceived research initiative. The East coast of Australia had many advantages, though it might be difficult to convince the Federal Government of this. The politicians had a wider political agenda and were keen to open Perth up as an international centre because of its proximity to Africa and India. Academia preferred Brisbane because of its central location on the East Coast, offering easy access to most big Australian cities, universities, industrial and commercial research centres, plus good links to Asia and the USA.

Maria and Simon had found the perfect site for the centre on the outskirts of Brisbane and they had presented their findings to Rick Walters, who then presented it to the Steering Committee when they met on Tuesday morning. There was vigorous debate about it, especially from government representatives. Nevertheless, Rick put up a brilliant argument.

"Academics, on the whole, do not want to uproot their families… and let's consider for a moment the problems we'll have with industry if they have to travel too far. Time is money and that's the basic disadvantage with Perth. Think about it. People in Melbourne could be in Brisbane in a couple of hours - even less for people from Sydney. They could do return flights in a day. But nobody wants to do two and three-day stopovers whenever a meeting is set up, and nor will industry want to move their families to the other side of the continent. We, who are totally committed to the project don't want to do it, so how can we expect industry to? It's an ill-conceived idea and I respectfully ask our government to reconsider locating the Centre to Brisbane."

Back in Brisbane, Matthew and Renata were getting to know each other better. They were taking things slowly in preference to rushing things. They had both been on their own for many years and were fairly set in their ways. Change did not come easily to them as they each, in the absence of the other, considered how much they stood to lose or gain if their relationship developed into a long-term one. Nowadays getting married or living together was not the sole option. There could be spaces in their togetherness that suited their individual needs. They liked being able to retreat to their own separate homes, giving each other space, independence and, arguably, the best of both worlds.

"It will be very interesting to see which way they choose to go," Emily said one day, over morning tea.

"They'll work it out, in their own good time." Nan looked at her daughter closely. "Do you miss him?"

"I feel happy for him. I like Renata, and he deserves some happiness of his own." It was an unselfish answer, Nan thought, dropping the subject.

Beth phoned Laura at the police station.

"Nan's smoked some of the marijuana." Laura checked that there were no other police officers around.

"Are you crazy calling me about this here?" But then curiosity got the better of her. "How the hell did she find it?" When Beth didn't answer Laura guessed. "Oh Beth! You didn't!" There was more silence. "What were you thinking? It's not supposed to be for now. It's for later when she's in a lot of pain."

"I think she's in a lot more pain than she lets on."

"How do you know that? Did she say so?" Beth could hear the icicles in Laura's tone.

"I could tell," Beth said.

"You could tell! You think that's a good enough answer? You shouldn't have told her, Beth. We agreed we would

232

discuss it more when the time came." Laura was getting angrier by the second.

"I know. But it seemed like the right thing to do at the time."

"SAYS WHO?" Laura's anger had changed to fury and the ice in her voice could have frozen the sun. "YOU HAD NO RIGHT, BETH. WE MADE AN AGREEMENT." Laura ended the call and stuffed her mobile in her shirt pocket just as a senior female police officer entered the station.

"You look upset! What's up?"

"Oh nothing!" Laura took a moment to get her voice under control. "Just an idiot." Laura said.

"Ah! You'll get used to it." The officer briefly laid a hand on her shoulder as she was passing, in a gesture of encouragement.

"Do you think you could hold the fort for me? I need to go to the happy house."

"No worries," the officer said helpfully. Laura didn't go to the toilet. Instead she went out of the back door and speed-dialled her mother to see how Nan was. Then she speed-dialled Maria.

"Hey! What's up?" Maria's voice was chirpy.

"Beth told Nan," Laura said.

"Told her what?" Maria answered, puzzled by Laura's clipped statement.

"About the Marijuana."

"She what?" Maria's tone had moved into the high octave.

"I've just given her a serve!" Laura said. "And I just spoke to Mum. She said she found Nan on her bedroom floor this morning. She had taken the screen out and her window was wide open. There were a lot of pages of Nan's writing strewn on the floor around her, and they've disappeared. Maybe Beth's got them. I didn't pursue the details because I was so mad at Beth. Mum knows it's more stuff about Nan meeting George Harrison. The first two pages were still on Nan's desk."

"Why did Beth tell her?" Maria asked. "Has Nan deteriorated?"

"Not when I saw her last night." Laura replied. "She was in fine fettle and as grumpy as hell because she said people had let her win at cards."

"Keep in touch with Mum and let me know if you find out anything else… and can you get Nan's writing from Beth and send me a copy?"

"I'll try, but what if she won't give it to me?"

"You're a police officer. Use the force!"

"How are you anyway?"

"Fantastic. Couldn't be better actually." Laura picked up on Maria's bright tone.

"Why what's going on?"

"Sorry. Top secret at the moment."

"Oh! I'll leave you to it then Octopussy! Give my love to 007." Laura knew better than to try to wangle top-secret information out of Maria. In fact Laura admired the way Maria would never compromise the trust placed in her. As this was not conducive to inspiring telephone chatter, Laura said goodbye and switched off her mobile. She would leave Beth until later. During her official coffee break, she went outside again and phoned her mother.

"Hi Mum. Just checking in again. Is everything okay now?

"I think so. Nan won't tell me why she was sleeping on the floor. She says she doesn't remember, but I'm sure she does. She gets that mind-your-own-business look about her and says: 'It's not a sin to sleep on the floor, is it?'"

"But does she seem any different?"

"She's fine. In fact she's better than I've seen her for a long time." Laura breathed a sigh of relief. "The nurse is coming soon. I'll tell her and see what she thinks."

"Good idea. I rang to tell you that I've just spoken to Maria. Everything is going well, or in Maria's own words, 'extremely well', so, no worries there. I thought you would like to know."

"That's very thoughtful of you, Laura. Thanks."

"See you at the weekend, Mum." Laura sent a text to Maria telling her Nan was okay. While she had been talking her coffee had gone cold and so she went inside and put it in the microwave for 30 seconds. Just as it pinged her mobile rang and she answered Beth's call.

"How rude of you to cut me off!" Beth said. Laura had learned in the academy that a culprit's strongest line of defence was attack, and Laura had been trained to put the focus right back on the culprit.

"This is not about me, Beth. It's about you and what you did. How rude of YOU to change the rules without consulting us!" Beth backed down somewhat.

"Yes, well okay. We did agree and I should have mentioned it first, but I don't know why you're so cranky. Nan's okay, so there's no harm done." The apology was so grudging that Laura interrupted her.

"I don't want to discuss this while you're in a mood Beth. I'm going to hang up now because I'm still really, really mad at you. And another thing, you'd better not discuss this with Mikey, or anyone else for that matter. You've already broken a trust once. Do it twice and you'll be sorry! You need to understand how serious this is. By the way, I'll be dropping in after my shift. Maria wants me to send the pages you've got to her. Don't give me a hard time about it." Laura hung up. Beth looked at her phone again and muttered.

"What's your problem? The poor old bugger just smoked some marijuana. She didn't turn into a serial killer." Beth's mobile beeped. It was a text from Maria. All it said was 'Why'? It was enough to make her feel some remorse. It was one thing for Laura to be mad at her - she and Laura argued all the time, but when Maria was mad at her, it hurt, because Maria was never mad at anyone.

When Laura called at Beth's share-house, after her shift, Beth was conveniently out. Knowing Laura was Beth's sister and, furthermore, knowing she was a police officer and that she had a key to Beth's room, one of the students in Beth's share house let Laura in. Laura didn't have far to look. The pages of Nan's writing were on Beth's desk, on top of a pile of study materials. When Beth returned home late that night and found Nan's writing gone, and that her sister had taken them from her room, she was very angry. She rang Laura's number and woke her up.

"You had no right to enter my room without permission."

"So, go call the police!"

"Don't smart-arse me, Laura. I'm going to call the police and I'm going to tell them you entered my room illegally and took something that belonged to me."

"In the first instance you gave me a key to your room and secondly, Nan's writing doesn't belong to you. But please yourself. Go ahead and report me!"

Drug Worries

It was now Friday and Maria called Nan's to touch base.
"Hi Mum."

"Hi Maria. I hear things are going well in Perth?"

"Yes. It's mad busy, busy, busy! Simon and I are run ragged, there's so much to do. How are things there?"

"Good, except for the scare with Nan. I was worried she had maybe had a mini stroke or something so I got the nurse to check her out. The odd thing is that she said she could smell marijuana in Nan's room. I think she's right. I sometimes get a whiff of it around the University."

"Marijuana?" Maria was terrible at lying so she hoped her mother would not ask her any questions.

"Beth was here that night. Maria, she's not into drugs is she? I mean you would tell me if she was, wouldn't you?"

"Don't be silly Mum."

"You never know with Beth."

"Mum, do you really think if Beth was smoking marijuana she would do it in Nan's room?"

"Well the nurse must be mistaken then. She suggested I have a word with you all, but Laura would never do drugs, would she?"

"No Mum."

"And you wouldn't either, would you?"

"Absolutely not, Mum."

"But Beth… No, Beth doesn't have the money for it, does she?"

"Maybe it was George Harrison, visiting Nan in the night." This made Emily laugh as it was meant to.

"The thing is that I could smell it too." Emily said. "Anyway, it seems to have gone now. Is that why you called - to ask after Nan?"

"No actually. I rang to tell you we've decided to have the wedding in Nan's garden if that's okay. I just wanted to run it by you."

"The last time you mentioned it you were thinking about a park?"

"No, we've abandoned that idea because it's probably going to be a very small wedding with everyone busy with their own Christmas commitments. We've found an Indian celebrant who's happy to do it."

"But what about the food?"

"Matthew's booked us into River Bend – you know that Event Centre, down the road from Nan's?"

"Yes, I know."

"Well, they don't usually do Christmas weddings, but they've changed their policy this year. Isn't that lucky?"

"It'll cost a fortune."

"Not really because a lot of people won't be able to come because it's Christmas. Uncle Matt has offered to pay and he's got it all under control. He's organising it all as his wedding gift to us – that's if it's alright with you too?"

"Oh! He didn't tell me." Emily was overwhelmed. "Of course it's alright with me."

"He's not taking over Mum, and it's only provisionally booked at this stage, so if you're not okay with it now is the time to say."

"I'm more than okay with it, love."

"He offered to look around for a venue when he saw we were stressing about all we have to do. He said he didn't want us neglecting the most important day of our lives. The garden was Uncle Matt's idea too, and I don't know why we didn't think about it before now. It's perfect. He said it'd make things manageable for everyone. I think, by that, he meant you, Mum, because you've got more than enough to do just looking after Nan. So, are you cool with all that?"

"Yes. If you are, I am. It's your day and you're the one who has to be happy."

"Thanks Mum. Now, on the subject of weddings, Renata will be the Maid of Honour and Beth and Laura my bridesmaids. I want us all to go shopping for outfits on Saturday week. Uncle Matthew's paying for it ALL. He'll be at your place at nine o'clock to look after Nan, so be ready to leave right away."

"You want ME to come?"

"Of course. You're the mother of the bride. I want you to look beautiful too. Renata's borrowing a friend's people mover, so we can all travel together, and we intend to make it fun. After we've been shopping we're going to have a late lunch at The Irish Club, and then we're all booked in to a day spa for a massage. Are you okay with all of that?" Emily was too astonished to speak. "I'll take that as a yes, then, shall I?"

"Yes. It all sounds fantastic. I didn't expect..."

"You're my Mum," Maria said. "I want my Mum with me all the way to Simon and the celebrant. Oh that reminds me, Dad can't make it because it's Christmas Day and he has to be at home for the kids."

"You're not disappointed?"

"No! Believe it or not it's worked out really well because I want you to give me away, not him."

"Oh!" Emily was speechless again.

"You're not saying very much Mum."

"I can't," Emily replied, between sniffs.

"Oh Mum. I didn't mean to upset you."

"You haven't. They're happy tears."

"See you tomorrow then, and don't forget to mark the following Saturday in your diary. Write across the entire page: WEDDING SHOPPING."

The phone rang again a couple of minutes later. It was Maria again. "I forgot to tell you Simon's Mum is coming too. Okay?"

"Of course. Of course."

Repercussions

When Maria got home on Friday evening she rang to organise a meeting with her sisters.

"Tomorrow afternoon then, at around four o'clock? Good." She and Laura meant to lock horns with Beth over the marijuana incident.

The following afternoon, as she placed an informal agenda before them in a business-like manner, her siblings began to get an inkling of Maria as a team leader. She looked the part too as she had not had time to change since coming home from the laboratory and weekend meetings with colleagues regarding her research programme. She was the picture of efficiency in one of her newly acquired business suits, carefully chosen to enhance her image for her new role.

"Now then, first we'll look at item one. Beth, do you now understand that you broke a trust?"

"I do, but I think you're being stupid about it. It's hardly an agenda item. You're not at work now, and it's up to Nan if she wants to smoke the marijuana we got her." Maria remained firm but cold.

"No it isn't. It's up to us. There was an agreement that all three of us would decide when and if she needed it and that it would only be administered as a medicine, not as a recreational drug. Only on this understanding did we decide we would offer Nan the option."

"Well I think she needed it," Beth said stubbornly.

"You broke a trust, Beth. I'm taking the marijuana away from Nan's room this weekend and Laura and I will decide when she needs it."

"That's not fair!" Beth was highly indignant.

"Yes it is. You don't get to ride roughshod over our carefully considered decisions. An agreement is an agreement.

Furthermore you don't even acknowledge the seriousness of what you did."

"Yes, I do," protested Beth. "Okay, I was wrong. I admit it. I give you my word that I won't do it again."

"You see, the problem is that Nan can help herself to it now, and we can see, from her writing – thank you for sending it through to me Laura, by the way - that Nan wasn't using it for her pain. She used it to see if she could meet up with George Harrison one more time. At least that's what her writing claims and that's not a valid reason in my opinion."

"Well it seems to have worked... at least it made her happy enough to write about it."

"Yes, but we still don't know why she was sleeping on the floor. Did she pass out? Did she have a mild stroke? Did she fall?" This time it was Laura asking the questions.

"There's nothing wrong with her according to Mum so what's the problem?"

"The problem now, Beth, is that Mum thinks you smoke marijuana. A further problem is that the nurse knows there was marijuana in the house that night. None of this is good. It's attracting unwanted attention. If we had been able to discuss it and make a decision that Nan could have it, we could have had someone sleep in her room all night to make sure she was okay. But there are now a lot of unanswered questions that can't be explained away easily. Now we have to make sure it doesn't happen again. We'll put it somewhere else. So to clarify, three of us must make the decision about giving Nan the marijuana. If one of us can't be there to reach agreement, then two must reach agreement about it together. One of us cannot make such a decision alone. Agreed?"

"Agreed!" Laura and Beth said.

"Good," said Maria. "Now, moving on..."

"Wait a minute. Where are we going to hide it now?" Laura asked.

"I'll tell you later, Laura." There was a short volatile silence. Beth broke it.

"You're not going to tell me are you?" She was indignant with rage.

"No."

"Why? I've said I'm sorry and I won't do it again."

"It's called consequences, Beth. Suck it up."

"You're a bitch!" Beth said, jumping to her feet with a Medusa like glare at Maria. She picked up her bag and headed for the door, where she stopped and retraced her steps.

"Give me back my key," she snarled at Laura, holding out her hand. Laura raised her eyebrows but struggled, nevertheless, with her key ring, breaking a nail in her effort to return the key. Beth made to leave again but paused at the door to throw her sisters a scowl full of contempt. 'Screw you!' were her final words on the subject as the door slammed.

"I'll go after her later," Laura said. "She's not used to you being assertive. The new job must be stretching you."

"It is. We don't have time for egos and awkwardness and I'm sorry if I'm bringing the tensions home with me. Was I too hard on her?"

"She'll get over it. So where are we going to hide it?"

"In the shed, I think. No one ever goes in there these days. I'll wrap it up in lots of old dirty plastic so it will just look like something that's been left there for years."

"Okay, but show me when you've finished. Just in case you're not around when and if it's needed."

"Okay, but I'm hoping to be around. We're moving the entire operation to Brisbane." Maria said. "It really is a relief. Perth was a bad idea from the start. All the scientists thought so, but the politicians were leaning on us. Simon, Rick Walters and I are flying down to Canberra on Monday, with the architect. We've been asked to brief the Minister directly. Usually we'd work through his aides. There's lots of space in Boondall near the Brisbane Entertainment Centre. It would be a perfect location for us, and with the backing of some of the politicians, we can hurry things through. There are lots of economic advantages for the community in building there."

"So you won't have to go and live in Perth?"

"No."

"Where will you live, then?"

"At my place. Simon's agreed. We'll rent out his place."

"How much do you want for it?"

"I don't know. How much do units go for these days?"

"I pay $230 a week for mine." There was an excited glint in Laura's eye.

"Well, Simon can work it out."

"Can I have first refusal?"

"Oh! That would make everything easy," smiled Maria. "I didn't think of you."

"His place is awesome and it's not that far from work."

"Okay. It's up to Simon. I'll talk to him about it and get back to you," agreed Maria.

"Right. By the way, what did you think of Nan's writing?"

"Did you read it?"

"I tried to," Laura said. "It was about Nan and George reminiscing, really."

"Yes. And more stuff about what it's like to die. She must be worrying about it."

"I don't blame her." Laura picked up the agenda. "Now then, what's this about?" Laura was pointing to the next item on the Agenda. "It looks very much like my kind of agenda item. 'Shopping!'"

"Oh yes. That's about next Saturday – a week from today to be exact. If you don't have to work I'd like us all to go wedding shopping." Over another cup of tea, Maria told Laura about all the latest developments with regard to the Christmas Day wedding.

"Not many people will come on Christmas Day," Laura said. "What about all the invitations Mum's made?"

"We can still send them to everyone, but we just won't expect everyone to come. We've had to make it meet our own needs rather than those of others, and in particular, I do want

243

Nan to be there! If we leave it too long she won't be. We can honeymoon during the Christmas shutdown. Those who can't make the wedding will understand why we've done it this way." Laura glanced at her watch.

"I'd better go and smooth things over with Beth," she sighed. "I hope she's cooled down a bit."

"Tell her Renata and I will pick her up at eight-thirty next Saturday, and that we're picking Mum up at nine. Tell her she can choose her own bridesmaid's dress. Oh, and tell her about lunch and the spa. It's all booked and paid for so she's got to come, tell her."

A White Lie

Later on, Beth was at a loose end because Mikey was working, and so was Laura so she could have the following Saturday off for shopping.

Maria and Simon were also working the weekend, and had gone into their respective laboratories to meet with colleagues and interview applicants relating to the delegation of their research work. This had become very urgent but hard to organise during the normal working week because Rick Walters needed their full attention. Not that Beth wanted to see Maria and Laura. Right now she hated her sisters.

The three other tenants of Beth's share-house were going out. That just left her Mum who would probably be looking after Nan. Nevertheless, Beth wondered if this might be a good day for the chick flick night they had planned.

"I'll have to see if Matthew can look after Nan," Emily said. "Can I ring you back?"

"I've already asked him. He'll be at your place at 5 o'clock. I'm cooking Indian, so come with an appetite."

"Wow! Okay," said Emily. "I'll be there."

When Emily arrived at Beth's, plans had gone awry. Justine, the youngest and dizziest of Beth's housemates, had fallen out with Fran, her more responsible and very academic older sister, who also lived in the share-house.

Beth was consoling Justine as Emily's car drew up. Neither sister wanted to go out with the other as they had planned. So it was that Emily walked into a cold war that Beth was stuck in the middle of. Neither Justine nor Fran had the sensitivity, or the courtesy, to take the fight elsewhere so Beth suggested moving the movie night into her room.

"Do you mind having your meal on a tray?" Emily thought of offering to move things over to Nan's but was careful to accept Beth's hospitality rather than rearrange things.

"Fine by me." She replied.

"Good. Here you are then," Beth said dishing up. "You take your tray and I'll follow on with the chapati and water. Unless you'd like your wine now?"

"If it's curry I'll have water for now," Emily said.

"It's Butter Chicken," Beth said. "It's quite mild but I'll bring a jug of water anyway."

Emily led the way from the kitchen to Beth's bedroom, which was up a short flight of stairs that you got to by way of the veranda. Emily forged herself a pathway across the small room, kicking a mountain of clothes to one side, while looking for somewhere to sit down. There was only the bed, so Emily climbed aboard and sat with her back against the wall, while Beth set up her laptop. Emily plumped up some pillows for Beth because the wall was hard. Beth put the two glasses of water down on her bedside table, and then offered her mother a chapati before setting it down between herself and her mother.

"Have you seen Calendar Girls, Mum?"

"No. You know I don't go to the movies much."

"It's got some big stars in it, like Helen Mirren and Julie Walters."

"Great. I like both of them." She kept the conversation on neutral territory for a while before plucking up the courage to ask her daughter a question that had been interfering with her sleep.

"Beth, I've got something to ask you and I don't want you to get cross. Whatever you answer will be fine with me." Beth was taken off guard in the middle of inserting the movie into the computer. Emily bit the bullet and asked: "Do you smoke marijuana?"

Beth's entire body froze for just a fraction of a second and her heart sank. There was no way Beth could dissolve into tears, which is what she felt like doing. Why was everyone picking on her? She told herself she couldn't break down because that might lead to her telling her mother about the row she'd had with Laura and Maria and what that had been about. No matter how horrible they'd been to her, she couldn't do that. Anyway she was in enough trouble with them already, and they'd never trust her again. To avoid a difficult situation she went for the smart Alec reply.

"Only when I've got no heroin," she replied totally deadpan.

"Tell me the truth, love. I need to know if you do."

"Get real Mum. Where would I get the money for pot?"

"Only the nurse said she could smell it in Nan's bedroom the day we found her on the floor."

"Well don't look at me. I know I'm a uni student, but I'm a mature student. I don't do drugs. Besides, if I did, Mikey would soon have something to say about it." It was true that she no longer dabbled and Mikey was the reason for this. But even when she had, she was too sensible to get hooked. When she returned to Australia to study, she wanted to depend upon her own fortitude to get her where she wanted to be. "Maybe the nurse was mistaken. They can make mistakes you know."

"No, I don't think so. I smelt something too."

"How do you know it was marijuana? Maybe next door were using one of their joss sticks – or maybe it was their marijuana. I've smelt it coming from next door before. I think Jack smokes it."

"Maybe you're right. It explains the smell but not why Nan was on the floor." Emily cleaned her plate with some of the chapati. "I guess we'll never know unless Nan tells us. But you know what, I'm not going to let it spoil tonight. That was delicious. Thanks." She gave her daughter a kiss on the cheek and said. "Now what about the movie."

But Beth was on a roll now.

"Of course there is another possibility."

"And what might that be?"

"That Nan's got a stash somewhere."

"Now you're being daft," said Emily.

Beth pressed the play button and soon all thought of marijuana smoking grannies sank into the mists of time.

Begging for Supper

Another week went by and there was little contact between the sisters. Nan's phone rang about four times daily, usually around dinnertime, and Emily reassured each family member that, if anything, Nan had improved significantly. There had been no repeat of the sleeping on the floor incident and Nan seemed to be handling any pain she had, without complaining. Things couldn't be better.

"Everything's moving forward, both wedding wise and work wise," Maria told her mother when she rang.

When Beth rang she wanted to speak to Nan. Emily was self-aware enough to notice she didn't have the usual heartache when her children asked this. Cheerily she handed the phone over to her mother.

"Hello!" Nan said.

"Nan, I've got some questions about your convent life. Can you answer them now?"

"I can try."

"When you were in Weybridge, why were you studying?"

"I was studying so I could get into teacher training college."

"So where did you study?"

"In my dormitory."

"But who taught you."

"No-one."

"Why?"

"I didn't ask. I was just given the course materials and told when I would take the exam."

"Couldn't you have sat in on the classes the nuns taught?"

"I didn't ask. Anyway, it would have taken too long."

"What do you mean?"

"Well I had to do the equivalent of Junior and Senior Certificates in a year."

"In a year? Without a teacher! That's impossible!"

"No it isn't. I did it... and I got a place at Teacher Training College on the strength of it. But I never went, because I left the convent."

"I see," said Beth. "I've got another question now."

"What?"

"Mum said you had to kneel when you spoke to Reverend Mother? Why was that?"

"You know what? That's a good question. I think it was out of respect, or humility, or obedience. It was an acknowledgement of her being as God to us."

"Did you find it demeaning?"

"No. If I had harboured those sorts of feelings I wouldn't have been there long."

"Why?"

"Because convent life is based on a life of humility and love."

"Okay, here's another one. What did you have to beg your supper for?"

"As a penance," Nan said. "You understand the concept of penance, don't you dear? Anyway, why are you so interested?"

"I'm trying to get to grips with identity – how we see ourselves in society. It's for an assignment. We have to look at a microcosm of society and analyse it. I'm thinking of doing convent life, after all, I know so much about it now."

"Oh." Said Nan. "Are you going to write about me?"

"No. I'm going to write about me, but I have to do that by drawing from the bigger picture and how your convent life might have affected how I see myself today."

"I don't imagine it has had much bearing on your life, dear."

"You'd be surprised, Nan."

A Kindly Man

"Pay for everything with this, Em." Matthew handed her a wad of notes. Emily looked at the money in astonishment.

"Goodness Matthew! Did you rob a bank?"

"No. I've just finished a couple of consultancies and I'm loaded." He smiled modestly.

"Oh Matthew! How can I ever repay you? You're like a benevolent father, a caring, thoughtful brother, and better than any husband. You're the very best of best friends to me."

"Well where would I be without you and your girls, Em? Your family has filled my empty life with happiness. Without you all, my life would have been empty and loveless. I'm lucky to be in a position where I can help you out from time to time. If you need more, ask for it."

"How much is here?"

"Enough. Just make sure you all get what you need. Don't skimp."

"I appreciate it Matthew. Don't ever think I take it for granted."

"I don't." Matthew reassured her. "I probably wouldn't give it to you if you did." Emily stuffed the bankroll into her bag because it wouldn't fit into her purse.

"Just call me Moneybags!" She laughed. "Do you want to hear something amazing?" Emily asked.

"I do." Matthew said expectantly.

"Maria has asked me to give her away."

"And so you bloody well should. You're the one who has worked to get her where she is."

"Ah! Be fair! I think she might have put in some effort herself. Give her some credit."

"Yes, but you gave her the foundation on which to build. Her success is yours too."

"I didn't think girls these days wanted anyone to give them away."

"Some don't. Take it as a compliment and don't analyse it. Just accept it."

"Sound advice that I'll follow," said Emily.

When the doorbell rang a few minutes later she had just put the final touches to her make-up, and looked stunning in a simple turquoise sheath, causing the bridal party to gasp when she opened the door.

"You look lovely, Mum. We just want to say hi to Nan." Laura charged past her mother. Maria and Beth followed, leaving the two mothers to hug and share the happiness of their children.

"Come on in Violet." Emily had met Maria's future mother-in-law a couple of times before. Once at the hospital when Simon had been rushed in with acute appendicitis, and once just after Violet's husband had died and she had spent Christmas with them. "We don't want to miss any excitement, do we?" Emily and Violet found Maria, Beth and Laura had woken Nan up after a disturbed night.

"What's your favourite colour Nan? I like you in mauve."

"No, she suits blue."

"Yes, I like her best in sky blue."

"My favourite colour is green," Nan said, rubbing her eyes.

"What size are you?"

"The same size as I was yesterday. Who wants to know and why?"

"I need your dress size," Maria said.

"I used to be a size twelve but as you can see, I've put on weight," she joked.

"Would you say about an eight?" Maria asked her mother.

"I'd say that would be near enough."

"Do you want a fascinator, Nan?" Laura beamed with excitement. We'll find you something gorgeous."

"Don't worry about me. I'm sure I already have something I can wear."

"We are going to worry about you because you are going to look exquisite," Beth said. "We'll make sure of that."

"Then I'll leave it in your capable hands," Nan said. "And yes, I do want to be fascinating so bring me one of those things you mentioned."

Maria added 'fascinator' to her list.

"What size shoes, Nan?"

"Size six; a 'C' fitting," Nan said.

"We'll have a fashion show when we get back," Maria said. "So you don't miss all the excitement." Receiving kisses on both cheeks, Nan did not say that she was quite content to miss all the excitement. She felt so tired these days that even just being awake was exhausting, and yet something made her cling to life. Maybe she wanted to enjoy the happiness in her family. New things had begun there and she wanted to see where they were going.

"Matt can tell you all about the wedding plans, Nan," Maria said. "He's the man! He's booked the wedding reception and is paying for it and everything."

"And he's given me a bag of money to pay for our shopping spree." Emily, too, was flushed with excitement. The room was full of merry giggling women, but Nan wasn't paying much attention to any of them. She was looking at her only son thinking how proud Doug would have been of him.

An Awkward Invitation

"It's nice to have the house to ourselves, isn't it?" Nan said. Matthew looked up from his laptop noticing that Nan was now dressed and groomed.

"I'd like to be a fly on the wall in the bridal salons our girls go to, with all their strong opinions flying around." Matthew being the only man in the family for so long, often felt overwhelmed by the views of too many females.

"I suppose they do all have strong opinions," Nan said. "It makes them interesting, though it can be wearing at times!"

"Are you feeling tired?" Matthew was careful not to fuss. He knew that would make his mother turn into stoic Nan.

"I do feel a bit weary today," she said honestly.

"I was going to suggest we go out for morning tea – not far – just somewhere local, but if you don't feel like it we can just have coffee here."

"You look very busy, so I'm guessing that you've got work to do which suits me fine because the girls want more of my story. I've got a pain in my shoulder, though, and it hurts to write."

"Is that from sleeping on the floor the other night?" Nan avoided the question and eventually Matthew made a suggestion.

"Maybe you could use this." Matthew rummaged in the pocket of his brief case.

"What is it?" Nan asked, taking a small black machine from him and turning it over in her hands.

"It's a digital voice recorder. I use it for work to note things I have to do, and also for things I need my assistant to type up."

"I didn't know you had an assistant Matthew." Nan wondered what else she didn't know about her son. "How do you use it?"

"Here." Matthew took the recorder back and crouched in front of her chair. "You press this button to record and this one to stop. That bit of metal with the holes in it is the microphone so that's what you speak into. You can pause it if you want, using this button, and go forward and back with these arrow buttons. Now show me how to record. Speak into it".

"Testing one two three," Nan said timidly.

"Don't feel self conscious. It's quite normal these days for people to walk along the road or drive their car talking away to someone on the other end of a hands-free mobile phone. That's it. Good. Now press the rewind button and listen to it. No, that will erase it. This one. Now stop it." Nan pressed the stop button. "Now hit the play button. No that's record. If you press that one you'll record over what you've just said. That's it." Nan's voice filled the silence.

"Testing one two three."

"Do you think you can work it now?"

"I think so. If I can't, I'll ask for help."

Since it was a glorious day, Nan asked Matthew to carry her rocking chair into the front garden to the shade of the orange Bougainvillea, which was a magnificent mass of blossom. From there, Matthew could keep an eye on her through the living room window and she could watch what was happening in the street. It was mid-November, and signs of Christmas were beginning to appear as one or two people fixed Christmas lights to their homes. Some of them took weeks to complete but prior to Christmas they would attract tourists from all over Brisbane. The house diagonally across from Nan's had won last year's competition and raised thousands for charity.

Nan pressed record and spoke into the small machine.

"When I was a girl, the excitement of Christmas was condensed into a few short days. Mum would begin the cake making in a huge enamel bowl. She would enlist the aid of the entire family, because food mixers were still beyond the means of most people. Pounds of butter and sugar had to be creamed and numerous eggs beaten in quickly so they didn't curdle. The hardest bit was mixing in the fruit and nuts because the mixture would be so dense by then that it was hard for a child to force the wooden mixing spoon through it. But every little bit of help saved my mother's weary arms.

There would be enough mixture in the bowl to make a large Christmas cake and four two-pound bun-loaves; the bun-loaves were usually given to sisterly neighbours, without whom my mother's life might have lacked vital support. Normal mixing bowls were too small for so much mixture so we used the large enamel bowl that was usually used for dishwashing. Someone's contribution would be to scour it clean.

I was usually given the job of greasing the cake tins, and lining them with greaseproof paper. Once the mixture was in the tins, Mum would wrap the outside of them with thick sheets of newspaper tied in place with string. Without this insulation from the heat, the cakes would burn on the outside. One of the rare pleasures of childhood was the spicy aroma that came from the cakes when they went into the black-leaded oven beside the open coal fire, filling the house with Christmassy smells."

Nan pressed the pause button for a moment, giving herself time to dwell on the memory, and decided that she would make a Christmas cake this year, as she had done almost every year of her life. Then she had decided not to because there would be wedding cake this year. *Even so*, she had decided eventually, *some things are important rituals for memory's sake.*

Thinking about Christmas brought back memories of another special Christmas, in which George Harrison had loomed brighter than the star on the Christmas tree. She smiled wistfully, pressing the 'on' button again, as her eyes glazed over and her mind travelled back in time.

"When I was a young nun studying in Weybridge so I could get into teacher training college, I received an invitation. It was unusual for a nun to receive an invitation because mostly people knew we weren't allowed out. It was a given, when you entered a convent, that you cut yourself off from the world. However, these were the days following on from Vatican Council Two, when nuns, priests and monks were encouraged to leave the seclusion of the cloisters in order to mingle with their local communities. The order I belonged to was lagging behind in this. True, our habit had changed, but we were still very much cut off from what went on in the world outside of our convent. So an invitation was unusual enough to be a really big deal.

Of course it was from George. Who else would be cheeky enough to ignore the protocols involved? There was a formal invitation with a hand-written note that I read again and again. 'Just come as you are. You'll blend in really well.' He was right, I would, because it was to be a fancy dress party to celebrate the end of filming 'The Magical Mystery Tour'.

Reverend Mother could choose to open our mail and read it, and letters always came slit open by a paper knife so you never really knew if it had been read. That bit of the rule came under the vow of poverty. In choosing the life of a nun we chose to be 'poor in spirit' so that nothing belonged to us, not even our private letters. I always kept my letters to read during my alone time, so I could savour them to the full. Naturally, the politics of the occasion required me to discuss the invitation with Reverend Mother, because George was someone in the public eye. Of course I knew I'd never be allowed to go, so I dropped the note that came with the invitation into my waste paper basket, because it was just George being silly. Leaving my dormitory, I went next door to Reverend Mother's office. There was a short delay before she answered.

'Enter!'

I opened the door and moved across the room, falling onto one knee when I reached her desk, as was the rule when speaking to a seated Mother Superior.

'This came for me, Reverend Mother.' It felt more like a confession than a statement. She didn't look up but continued to write. She wrote on for another minute and, feeling very awkward, I wondered if I should ask if she would prefer me to come back at another time, but I was sure that would be misconstrued as a lack of patience. Finally she put her pen down.

'Ah yes!' She said. 'The invitation.' Oh no! She already knows! I cringed at what might be coming. 'Now then, your friend, the cockroach...'

I thought about correcting her but I thought this might be a deliberate attempt at humour. It didn't matter because she corrected herself.

'Ah yes, Beetle!' She said, referring to a notebook that had been set aside on top of her writing bureau. 'Beatle! Spelt with an 'a'! Extraordinary! Your friend has contacted me saying that you are invited to an erm...' again she referred to the notebook '...sedate dinner' to celebrate some achievement of The Beatles.

'This young man - this George Harrison, has informed me that The Archbishop of Westminster will be attending the dinner which will be held at the Royal Lancaster Hotel, and that it will be a rather formal affair at which a young nun would be quite safe and inconspicuous among all the other well-respected guests. I understand there may even be some members of the Royal Family attending. As His Grace the Archbishop of Westminster himself will be attending, you will be placed at, what Mr Harrison terms, the holy table – assuming, of course, you are allowed to go. He enclosed another cheque for five thousand pounds, by the way, which is most generous, and he says he will give the convent an even larger Christmas donation, which you will receive personally, on the convent's behalf, at the dinner.'

'His Grace's aide has telephoned to confirm that you will sit at his Grace's table. He says Mr Harrison is extremely generous to the Archdiocese and, therefore, it would be awkward, politically

speaking, if I offended him by refusing his request. In the circumstances, you will be allowed to attend. As the dinner is to take place at 7:45pm you will not be returning home afterwards. The Archbishop's aide has assured me that he can house you at the Bishop's Palace and will return you here the following morning at his discretion. He assures me you will be under his Grace's patronage the entire time and so I have reluctantly agreed. In these post-Vatican Council days, His Grace says, it is expected that we will move more and more out into the world. When I protested he said I should 'get with it'. Benedicite, Sister.' This was my dismissal and meant Go in peace!

Peace! Peace! I felt like a nuclear explosion had just gone off in my head, yet, even so, I did register a protest – well it was more of a whimper really.

'Oh but Reverend Mother, I don't want to go.' I was already trying to overcome doubts about whether I was suited to the religious life and, now, here I was being thrown back into the chaos of Beatlemania!

You total bastard, George, I thought, wondering how he had managed to get one over on Reverend Mother. I bet he omitted words like 'fancy-dress party', 'Magical Mystery Tour', not to mention 'drugs', 'fornication', 'open bar' or anything else that might insinuate the riotous knees-up it was bound to be. I bet he never mentioned the dubious list of possible drug-addicted rock-stars that would almost certainly be there.

At my protest Reverend Mother looked up in shock.

'I beg your pardon?'

'I don't want to go, Reverend Mother.'

'It has already been decided, Sister.'

'But…'

'You will go!' Reverend Mother's eyes had spread all over her face and though I knew she was very kind in many ways, I couldn't help lowering my gaze, to escape her Medusa glare. Nevertheless, it takes a lot to shut me up when I'm rattled, so I hazarded another protest.

'Bu…' This was as far as I got.

259

With an exasperated expression, that made me feel like I was the only nun in the history of Christianity that had ever attempted to put forward an argument against what obedience had decreed, the hand came up. Thus she shut me up.

'To whom did you make your vow of obedience, Sister Jude?' I had never noticed the great chunks of flint in Reverend Mother's eyes before.

'God?' I murmured.

'I was thinking, rather, of God's representative on Earth, Sister.' There was an electric silence that I so wanted to fill, but was thrashing around in my mind for the right answer. I was considering giving it another shot by answering, 'You, Reverend Mother?' But she fired another question at me before I could.

'Who was that representative before whom you made vows of poverty, chastity and obedience?'

'Oh! You mean the Archbishop?'

'I do. Yet, you would argue with his authority?'

'Well, it's just that…'

'Silence, sister!' I had never heard Reverend Mother use that how-dare-you-argue-with-me tone before. Most nuns were so compliant that she didn't need to. The next time she spoke she was far more controlled.

'If I have to obey the Archbishop, so must you. You will go to this dinner. You will attend in all humility and obedience. Now for your disobedience, you will beg your supper tonight.'

The injustice of this reprimand stung. If I was given such a punishment for trying NOT to break ten million Holy Rules, I wondered what punishment I would get for obeying Reverend Mother. I'll probably have to clean out the septic tank with my tongue for the rest of my life, if my photograph gets splattered all over the News of the World, I thought. I realised there was no point arguing and, against my better judgement, I heard myself say:

'As you wish, Reverend Mother.' She had already returned to her writing and I was surprised when, as I neared the door her voice halted me in my tracks.

260

'You can get up off all fours now, Sister!' I hadn't even realised I was still on my knees.

A nun On a High Horse

I was just leaving Chapel, having sung Terse and Sext with the rest of the community, when Reverend Mother beckoned me. It was the day I was due to attend the Magical Mystery Tour 'sedate dinner'. She said that the Archbishop had telephoned to confirm accommodation arrangements and someone would pick me up around 6:00pm. Great, I thought. I don't know what's making me more nervous, being a guest of George Harrison at a Beatles knees-up, or being a guest of the Archbishop of Westminster afterwards. I found myself pining for those uncomplicated days in Liverpool when I used to dance at the Cavern and the Beatles were just in the pictures I would drool over.

I was given to understand that George had arranged transport for me, and I was glad when Sister Aurelia summoned me to the parlour in the middle of Vespers because that meant Reverend Mother was officiating and I could slip off with just a bow to her, rather than with all the usual formalities of prayer for safe travel, and a lecture about what was seemly behaviour for a nun, and of course her blessing.

I did think about pleading with Reverend Mother one last time but by that time, I had reasoned that, if I really did have to go to the party, then God must truly want me to go. From there I moved on to feeling that if I was meant to attend the party, I should probably bloody well try to enjoy myself.

I had a secret notion that God was big into enjoying Himself. In fact I frequently imagined him sitting on his throne in heaven having a rollicking good laugh at the messes I got myself into. I bowed towards Reverend Mother on the way out of chapel, so she could silently, as the rule required, deliver me into God's hands – or, in this case, possibly Satan's. In the parlour I found George waiting for me and he sure knew when I had arrived because I slammed the door and stood hands on hips, feet apart, spewing wrath.

'What the hell are you playing at?' I accused.

'Arrh Ay girl! Yer don't 'ave ter thank me or anything.' I had never realised how sarcastic George could be.

'Thank you?' Seeing how high on my horse I was, he tried defensive tactics.

'I was just trying to give yer a treat because yer life seems really - well, I was going to say boring, but nobody could call you boring. Let's just say that your life seems a bit lack-lustre.'

'And why exactly is that your problem?' There was a short silence. I'd never seen George stuck for words before. 'My life, for your information, is anything but lack-lustre. It's full of God's bedazzling glory and it's exactly how I want it to be.' I continued. 'How dare you take it upon…'

'Whoah! Okay! Let's stop right there. I can see I've done the wrong thing. I'm sorry! I thought it would be a treat. There are people who'd kill for a ticket to this party, but I can see you're not one of them, so let's just forget it.'

As he was speaking George had opened the door to the parlour and was speeding towards the front door. I had a sudden picture of me confessing to Reverend Mother that I wouldn't be dining with the Bishop after all, because I'd just savaged my host. I pictured me possibly having to beg my breakfast, lunch, tea and supper for the rest of my life, and so it was that I found myself running after George.

'Where do you think you're going?' I asked. Sister Aurelia was hovering around at the far end of the corridor and looked very concerned about the fracas.

'You don't want to go. I get it. You're off the hook… uninvited. I'll give your ticket to someone else.' Now I was even more deranged.

'You can't do that after inviting me,' I said. George stopped on the spot and his hand went to the back of his neck where he pulled at muscles that were obviously tensing.

'You know what, for a nun you're one contrary soddin' mare. Do yer want te go or don't yer?'

Thankfully Sister Aurelia, being Spanish, had no idea George was swearing but she could see the tone of our conversation was anything but seemly.

'Why you shout?' she asked as she approached the front door that George had just passed through.

'It's alright, Sister,' I said trying to smile. 'It's just a misunderstanding.' I followed George, pulling the door to so that she was shut inside, while I was reasoning with George outside.

'I've got to go now. Mother has ordered me to.' George calmed down a bit but walked down the garden path onto the street. Fortunately there was nobody about.

'Well she must have trained with the Gestapo, that's all I can say.'

'Ha!' I spat.

'Huh!' he grunted. I had caught up with him and we were both now standing arms folded across our chests in a defensive position. The next minute we both burst out laughing.

'I'm sorry George,' I said. 'I'm just really scared. I haven't been out in the world on my own for four years. Have you any idea how terrifying that is for me?'

'I'll look after yer, honest. Trust me!' He said, putting his arm around me.

'Gerroff!' I said. 'Touchin's not allowed.'

'I don't fancy yer if that's what yer think. It's nothing like that.' Strangely, that hadn't even crossed my mind.

'Hold on while I get me overnight bag,' I said, running back through the door and past poor bemused Sister Aurelia.

'Is okay Sister,' I said, doing her finger thing. 'Men! They loco!'

Scousers

Nan switched off the recorder and left it on her rocking chair while she went indoors.

"Would Sir like some coffee?" she asked.

"Oh sorry Mum," Matthew said. "I'm supposed to be looking after you. Go on back outside and I'll bring you one out."

"No, I'll make it. My throat's getting a bit scratchy with talking and I need to stretch my legs. Actually, why don't we make it together, then we can both stretch our legs. It can't be good for you to be bent over your computer all the time like that."

"You're right. Occupational Health and Safety are always coming round at work to check we move around a bit so we don't get RSI."

"And numb bums." Nan's manner was deadpan. Matthew smiled, pushed his laptop away from him and standing, rubbed his bottom.

"You make the coffee. I'll find something to eat." Nan said. "I bought a lemon meringue tart just for you. We can't have you giving everyone treats and not getting any yourself."

"You're a bad woman. It's a good job I love you."

"How's the work going?"

"Well enough," Matthew replied. "What about you?"

"Good! My mind's nice and clear today," she said. "But I want to know how things are with you."

"I know you mean between me and Renata," he grinned.

"So, how are things?" Nan persisted.

"Good. She's nice… different! We're thinking of going on the river in the boat tomorrow."

"Oh that's a pity. I've already promised it to Mikey. It's a surprise so don't tell Beth. Can you and Renata take it out another day?"

"We'll have to, won't we?" Matthew and Nan chatted while he practically ate the entire lemon meringue pie, but Nan, not wanting to keep him from his work, soon said:

"Well, I'd better get on while my head's clear." She resisted Matthew's attempt to see her safely back to her rocking chair. Instead, he watched her go down the front steps into the garden, noticing how frail she was becoming and wondering how much time she had left. She picked up the recorder and switched it on again. When he heard her speaking he sat down and pulled the computer towards him, content that, for now at least, she seemed okay. Soon he was lost in his work.

George didn't pick me up in his car, as I had imagined. He came in a psychedelic bus.

'It's the bus we used in the movie,' he said. 'The Magical Mystery Tour bus.'

'It's a charabanc.' I exclaimed. 'A very colourful one.'

'Yeah. Great isn't it?'

I had only ever been in one other charabanc and that was when I was a child. Mrs Williams, who lived up our street, organised one to Blackpool. It was one of the few times we ever left Liverpool. I always saw Mrs Williams as a human bank, because she collected money every week and saved it, when an event like this was planned. This was the way working-class families afforded such outings. Most families in our street lived from hand to mouth and saving and banking money were practically unheard of. Mum would definitely miss a few shillings out of the shopping money week by week, but she'd economise by perhaps buying only a half-pound of stewing steak for the scouse, instead of a pound. In fact the weekly pan of scouse was a good indicator of how flush a family was in any given week. When people were really skint, it would be blind scouse, which was scouse without meat. George Harrison would have probably eaten scouse once a week like me. While I'm thinking about scouse, here's how you make it.

266

Scouse.

Put a large pan of water on the stove to boil.

Add as much chopped up stewing steak as you can afford.

Cut up a couple of onions and add to the pan. Put a couple of whole ones in too if you like boiled onion like I do.

Slice up a pound of carrots and add to the pan.

Add five pounds of potatoes.

Add salt and pepper to taste.

I like to put a couple of bay leaves in and a stick of chopped celery, but you have to understand it's not strictly proper scouse then.

Bring everything to the boil and let it boil for a few hours until everything breaks down and the water becomes thick. Add water if it looks like it is boiling dry.

Now back to the story. Going to Blackpool was like going to heaven. We looked forward to seeing the Blackpool lights – a mile of illuminations that lasted a few short weeks. People came from all over England to see them. The lights featured bikes, cars, clowns, aeroplanes, animals and other objects, all set in motion by a trick of flickering lights. It's not a big deal now because neon lights are ten a penny. Then they were very rare.

There was a fairground too, so the kids would be given money out of the bank to go on the rides, while the grown-ups would go to the pub. A few mothers would accompany the kids to make sure we came to no harm. On the way back home, on the bus, we would have a good old singsong because all the adults would be merry with drink. You couldn't board a charabanc without singing all those Liverpool folk songs that I learned sitting underneath the windows of the pubs on three of the four corners of our street.

Nan stopped recording for a moment. I'm supposed to be talking about George and the Magical Mystery Tour Fancy Dress Party, she thought. She considered rewinding and recording over the last bit, but she thought that might be too

267

complicated for her, so she pressed the start button and continued.

Satan was on the bus, disguised as God's representative on earth. He invited me to sit on his knee in the back of the bus, an invitation that I made light of by saying I was going to sit up front near George to pray for reprobates like him.

'C'mon then luv! Give us a kiss for Christmas under me mistletoe,' he slobbered. The mistletoe I noticed was swinging precariously from the top of his mitred head. 'Arrh C'mon luv!' he pestered. 'We're a matchin' pair.'

'We're not a matching pair, luv,' I said, 'because I'm a real nun and you're a fake Archbishop, Anyway, trust me, you wouldn't want to get on the wrong side of my fella!'

'Hey George,' he said. 'She 'asn't 'alf got a mouth on 'er, 'asn't she?'

'Out o' the mouths of bishops an' nuns...' George said more to himself than anyone else. I was glad the Archbishop was at the back of the bus and I was at the front.

'This is just the sort of thing I was afraid of.' I grumbled to George.

'Don't give us an 'ard day's night, girl,' he grinned. 'Lerrit be.'

'You.' I said. 'You're always laughing at me.'

'Yer make me laugh!'

I heard my mother's voice in my head saying 'There'll be tears before bedtime'. Oh shut up Mum! I thought.

'Who is the archbishop anyway?' I asked glancing back over my shoulder. The prelate was paralytic, and in the company, I now realised, of a drunken monk. I hope those two aren't at the holy table, I thought.

'A mate from Liverpool.'

'Surely he didn't convince Reverend Mother he was the Archbishop of Westminster?' I asked dubiously.

'Oh that wasn't him. I 'ad ter get one of me posh actor mates for that.'

'Where am I sleepin' then? I was told I would be sleeping at the Bishop's Palace.'

'Well, te be honest. That won't be happenin'. I've sorted out something else for yer though.'

'So I'm here under false pretences, then?' It was more of a challenge than a statement.

'Well, inviting yer te the party started off as a bit of fun, te cheer us both up. Yer sounded a bit down the last time we talked. If yer remember, yer were having second thoughts about bein' a nun.'

'I'm astonished that you even remembered that.' George looked at me for a while and I remember wondering if I'd underestimated him to think he could so easily forget me, or whether I'd undervalued myself, to think I could be so easily forgotten.

'Whatever your motives were, George, I shouldn't be here. I tried to tell Reverend Mother I didn't want to attend but she insisted because, of course, she doesn't know that it's probably going to be one hell of a hooley! She wouldn't listen when I tried to explain that it wouldn't be a sedate boring dinner with a holy table – that it would probably be a drunken orgy, and she might have to bail me out of jail tomorrow after she sees me in the shock-horror Sunday morning headlines. She just wouldn't listen.'

'It's not gonna be that bad. Actually the press don't even know about it. We've kept it hush-hush so far.'

'Well praise the Lord for that,' I said, relief flooding through me.

'Yer know what I think?'

'What?'

'I think that as far as ye're concerned, if it's meant te be, yer should just lerrit be.' He sang the last bit and someone with a guitar struck up the chords and before we knew it there was a good old sing-along happening. I was so wrapped up in myself that I hadn't taken much notice of the others on the bus until then. When the music stopped George started to laugh.

'Don't you ever take anything seriously?' I asked.

'Here, cheer yerself up with a jellybean and let's get going, or we'll be too soddin' late for the party.' George switched on the engine

269

and revved up as I caught the bag he threw at me. I took a black jellybean. It tasted of liquorice, or was it aniseed? It brought back memories that soothed me. Maybe I could enjoy myself after all, I thought, popping another black one in my mouth.

'With all your millions, George, I'm surprised to see yer working on the buses.' He laughed.

'Ah but it's not just any bus. It's the Magical Mystery Tour bus. It's fun an' I like drivin' it, so I decided to pick up a few people just to get the fun happenin' sooner rather than later.'

'Sorry, I don't get to 'ear what's goin' on in the world, George. The magical mystery thingy is still a magical mystery to me.'

So George told me all about how they'd filmed the movie, The Magical Mystery Tour, using friends, family, employees, their fan club secretary and mostly ordinary normal people. It was due to be released over Christmas as a special Christmas television treat, and he hoped it was going to be huge. I learned later that it was a flop because the BBC presented it in black and white. Nutters! Fancy screening something psychedelic in black and white when colour was central to the whole concept!

'I luv drivin'. I used to go to motor races before I became a Beatle. I'll have a drive of anything, I will.'

'I liked the car you were drivin' through Weybridge.'

'That's me Mini Cooper,' he said. 'I 'ad that and the bungalow I live in painted in psychedelic colours. It was a really straight white cottage when I bought it but it's the gear now.'

'Am I sleeping there tonight?'

'Er... no actually.' My heart plummeted. I still had no idea where I was sleeping. That's very worrying for someone so used to a quiet life and strict routines.

'I'm not sleeping at his place,' I said, indicating, with a jerk of my head, the pretend prelate with the skew-whiff mitre on the back seat.

'Well, I was gonna tease you about it all night, but I can see yer going to have a nervous breakdown if I don't put yer out of yer misery. I've booked rooms in the 'otel where the party is, for me

guests, but I've booked somewhere special for you. But if I tell yer, it has to be a secret between you and me, okay? No tellin' anyone else.'

'Who am I going to tell, George? I live in a convent with a rule of silence.'

'Funny that, 'cos for someone with a rule of silence yer don't 'alf give me an 'ard time.'

'People do tend to talk a lot when they're having a nervous breakdown, George! It's called hysterics.'

'Okay. So yer won't tell anyone?' I levelled with him.

'I might have to tell Reverend Mother if she interrogates me.'

'Okay. Yer can tell her. I doubt if she'll tell the News of the World.'

'I doubt very much if Reverend Mother even knows what The News of the World is.' This seemed to reassure George.

'The thing is, I want te move out of me bungalow. It's too small now for me needs an' interests, so I've got me eye on a new place. It's a convent at the moment, and findin' somewhere for yer te stay gave me the idea of booking yer in there, so I can have a decko at it, without the nuns suspectin'. I've told the nuns that yer'll arrive late and leave early and if yer've got a rule of silence yer won't have to talk to them will yer? An' yer won't be givin' me an 'ard time about having te tell too many porky pies. We don't want yer 'aving te beg yer soup for the rest of yer life, do we?'

'Hmph!' I have to admit I was extremely relieved. 'Where is this place, and how am I going to get there?'

'It isn't that far from Weybridge. It's in a place called Henley-on-Thames, and I've arranged a private car to take yer there. I thought a taxi might be a bit scary for yer. It's all organised.' Somehow that didn't comfort me.

'It's not going to be him, is it?' I asked, pointing at his buddy the Bishop, who blessed me every time he caught me sneaking a worried peak at him and said loads of prayers with the 'F' word in them.

'No, it's a good friend. She's very reliable.' I was reassured by his use of the word 'she'. I was used to women and I was glad I was staying in a convent rather than at the Bishop's Palace.

271

'Thanks, George,' I said 'Now I can relax. I had visions of being swept up by a heavily intoxicated crowd and of finding myself compromised by irregular sleeping arrangements involving a bedroom full of naked people and me – fully dressed of course.'

'I think you might have to confess that little fantasy, Sister.' I blushed. 'In fact, I'm starting to wonder if this party might prove a bit boring for someone with your fertile imagination.' I didn't want the conversation to linger around my fertile imagination so I changed the subject.

'So where's your psychedelic bungalow then?'

'It's in Esher. It's called Kinfauns. Me and Patti live there.' There was a map on the dashboard so I leaned over and grabbed it and opened it up.

'Esher could be on the moon for all I know,'

'It's only five minutes up the road.' George explained.

I hadn't been watching where we were going. It didn't matter because I didn't know the area, but we seemed to have only just started when we stopped again outside a mock-Tudor house. George didn't get out, he just beeped the horn repeatedly until the door opened and a teddy boy came out. I had to look twice before I realised it was John Lennon dressed in the tightest pants I'd ever seen and wearing a black and white leather jacket. His hair was greased into a DA. In case you don't know, that means a duck's arse.

'I'm runnin' late,' John said. 'I'll follow on. Will yer take some of me people?'

'Okay,' said George.

A crowd got on the bus and that's when the singing began in earnest because most of them were musos. Some of them began handing out drinks and smokes and soon it was as if I was experiencing everything through a veil because the bus was so dense with pungent smoke. Things livened up a bit then and somehow, as if passive smoking made me loosen up, I accepted a nice glass of tonic water from one of the newcomers. After a few of those, my anxiety totally lifted, and I joined in the singing of the old Liverpool songs that were so much a feature of my childhood. I was very surprised at what a merry occasion it was turning out to be.

272

Nan turned off the recorder at the same time that Matthew got up to stretch his legs.

"I think I might have a nap," Nan said.

"I was just about to make you a poached egg on toast. Will you eat that first?

"Thank you. I will, but I need a toilet break first," she said. By the time she came back Matthew had made a cup of tea and though she wasn't hungry, she ate as if she was, for the sake of her son. She told him to go back to work when they had eaten.

"But do you think you could get the recorder for me. It's outside on the rocking chair. I think I'll record the rest of the story on my bed and then I'll be comfortable if I drift off."

More Than a Party

In her room Nan pumped up her pillows, turned the fan on high and settled herself comfortably on the bed. She rewound the recorder a bit and listened to what she had said about the journey to the fancy dress party on the bus, chuckling to herself now that she could listen rather than construct the story as she went. Coming to the end of it she began to record again.

By the time we neared the Royal Lancaster Hotel where the party was waiting for us, we were all getting on famously and me and the Bishop were asked to sing a duet - something holy, but I couldn't remember what we sang until George reminded me the following day that we sang one hundred, thousand, million, bottles of holy water, standing on the wall. But that was as far as we got, it appears, because of the booing, for which George apologised. He didn't need to. I couldn't remember any of it.

I don't remember much about the party at all, other than meeting a multitude of really famous people I didn't know, and none of whom I could remember properly the following day. I saw them all in a very biblical way, as if through a glass darkly. When the Magical Mystery Tour Bus arrived at the party, George said.

'Come on, girl. Let's go.' He escorted me, solicitously, to a table where I learned there was no such thing as a 'holy table'.

'Sorry I didn't come in fancy dress,' I said to Paul McCartney and Jane Asher. They'd come as the Pearly King and Queen.

'I'm Sister Jude.' I held out my hand and Paul grinned,

'Hey John... I wondered vaguely how John had managed to arrive before us, but Paul interrupted my thoughts. "...say hello to Sister Jude."

'Yer not!' John said, obviously amused by something I didn't get.

'Yesh I am,' I declared.

'Yer not,' he said. The Beatles were all grinning now. I didn't get why.

'Stop arguin' wiv me,' I said. 'I know who I am much better than you. I am a holy nun…nun… nun…ion and I don't tell liesh.' John laughed out loud.

'Yer really believe in getting' into yer character, don't yer?' he said.

Mostly I remember vague things about the party, like Maureen and Ringo; he was dressed like a regency dandy and she looked like Minihaha and I couldn't help wondering why they hadn't come as a matching pair.

I remember lots of tinkling of glass and much toasting of the recent movie. I remember Lulu having a go at John Lennon because he was paying too much attention to George's Patti, telling him he should've been looking after his own wife. I have a very hazy memory of trying to work out how dogs could play instruments, and George told me the next day it was the Bonzo Dog Doo Dah Band, one of whom was dressed up as Tiny Tim. I couldn't tell which one he was because there were three Tiny Tims.

I didn't realise until a lot later that I was probably suffering from alcohol poisoning due to all the dubious tonic water I drank for my ever-increasing thirst. Also, I think I was suffering from a drug overdose from the marijuana I had passively inhaled on the bus and at the party.

At one point I was dancing with a court jester with gold jangly bells on his hat and shoes.

'That,' I was told by my next partner, Prince Phillip, 'was Tony Bramwell.'

'Who'sh he?' I asked digging around in my lack of worldly knowledge for something to talk about.

'Oh! You must know him. He's an old mate of The Beatles and their right and left hands. Who are you by the way?'

'I'm Shister Jude, long time mate of Jeshus Chrisht and hish right and left hand!'

'Ah well, any mate of John Lennon's is a mate of mine,' he said, twirling me round. His bizarre statement went totally over my head. 'You probably won't remember me tomorrow but I'm George Martin. It's been a pleasure. Here, have a dance with Hunter

275

Davies,' he said, handing me over to an overgrown boy scout, who swung me away. That was when I really felt woozy and had to fly off to vomit in the loo.

I vaguely remember dancing with John Lennon and being thankful for my stout nun shoes because he kept treading on my toes with his brothel creepers.

There was a lot of chitchat about the making of the movie and I was introduced to various members of the cast, like Miranda Ward, The Beatles Fan Club Secretary. I remember being impressed with her, in a vague sort of way, and I remember thinking that The Beatles must be really nice to remember the people to whom they owed much.

I remember seeing someone wearing a see-through raincoat with plastic eggs stapled all over it and asking who he was?

'He's The Eggman,' someone answered.

Shopaholics

By the time shopping Saturday came round, the dust had settled over the marijuana incident and as if by some sort of silent agreement, the sisters had buried the hatchet and Beth's fall from grace was never mentioned again. Prior to coming face-to-face, tentative texts had passed between them, and these served to indicate that no animosity remained. As Beth received the odd joke or email, the subtext was that she was still loved. So her anger cooled.

There were several bridal shops in Queen Street. Laura and Beth wanted to go in all of them. However, Maria had already viewed their online collections and knew exactly where she wanted to go. She had made appointments and, at the first salon, three gowns were waiting for Maria to try on. She chose none of them.

"Thank you," Maria said, leaving the salesperson a bit deflated.

Next stop was Eliza de Vega in Queen Street. Unusually, they found a parking spot easily enough. They were cordially welcomed and offered a flute of French champagne.

"No thanks," Maria said, not wanting to let down her guard in case the saleswoman talked her into buying a dress that didn't feel quite right. "But the rest of the bridal party might like one."

The salon manager had the four dresses Maria was interested in hanging on a rail ready for her to try on, but she only tried on one of them and fell in love with it. It had a simple oyster satin skirt with the hint of a train and a lacy round necked overtop with matching oyster satin lining and belt. The feature buttons down the back were exquisite.

"I'll have it." Maria was emphatic.

Maria did not choose a veil, but rather, a lace mask to cover her eyes. It matched the bodice of the dress. The total effect was stunning, original, and gave Maria an air of sweet innocence mixed with a mountain of mystery.

"This is the one."

"Try this one," the sales lady urged.

"No. I don't need to. I want this one." The salon manager knew there was no arguing with this sort of decisiveness. She'd had years of experience with brides, and she knew when not to waste effort. Besides, she was satisfied. It had been an easy sale, or so she thought.

"Can I try the others then?" said Beth.

"Is there something you aren't telling us?" Her mother asked.

"No," she replied, though nobody was certain she meant it.

"It's Maria's day not yours," said Laura.

"I don't mind," said Maria. "She can try them if she wants. It would be fun." So Beth tried on the other dresses. One was very simple and unadorned. It didn't fit Beth's artistic temperament or figure. The other two weren't quite 'her' either so she didn't try them on. However, searching through the racks of dresses, she came upon one that was like the dress of a Spanish dancer and had a fan and a mantilla attached to a tall comb.

"I love it," Beth said. "This is my wedding dress. But please don't tell Mikey I said that."

"We have that one in black and red, as well as white," said the salon manager.

"Black? No thanks!" Beth said.

"You would be surprised how many brides like black these days – and colour. Would you like to try it?"

"Yes," said Beth.

"No!" said Laura.

"We do still have a lot to do Beth. Would you mind coming back in your own time to try it?" Turning her attention to the salon manager Maria asked if they could now look at bridesmaids' dresses.

"Do you have any idea what you are looking for?" Enquired the Manager. The three bridesmaids began to speak at once.

"I'll have that glass of champagne now, if you don't mind." Maria had cleverly stopped the argument between the significant members of the bridal party. "Violet! Mum! Won't you join me?" The salon manager poured champagne for the two older ladies, while Maria took her first sip.

"Mm." She said with an appreciative smile. "It's delicious." Now I can tell you what I want very simply, and then it is over to each bridesmaid. You can all have the same dress in different pastel colours. Or you can all have the same fabric but different styled dresses. Or you can all wear the same dress in the same fabric. You can choose. I want you to wear something that complements my dress, so nothing fussy. I would also like them to be sleeveless, like mine."

Maria guzzled two glasses of champagne while the girls quickly resolved the issue of the dresses. Beth and Laura chose a pale shade of lemon in a matching style. Renata chose the same dress in a pale apple green. The three colours were tasteful and springlike. Maria congratulated the salon manager.

"I thought it might take several days to sort them out."

The bridesmaids' dresses had to be made to measure, but Maria's lucky-off-the-rack number fitted perfectly, except for the length.

"We can sort that out within a week, but the bridesmaids' dresses will take longer."

"How long?" Asked Maria.

"Four weeks to first fitting," replied the manager.

"I'm getting married on Christmas Day," said Maria. "They need to be ready by then."

"In that case, I will hurry the order through for you. They are simple in style so shouldn't take too long. I'll ring you when we need to fit them."

"What about shoes?" Maria asked. The salon manager suggested a shop they did not know of, located in one of the arcades in Queen Street, but not on the beaten track because it was up two levels.

"But first we need something for my mother and mother-in-law to be," Maria said. "Also, my grandmother. I'd like to take hers home on approval, since she was not well enough to come with us. I am happy to pay for it now on condition I can bring it back and get a refund if she doesn't like it or if it doesn't fit."

"We will be happy to swap it for another outfit," the salon manager reassured her.

"I don't want a swap. She may refuse to have an outfit, but it's in your interest to let me try to buy her one."

"We prefer our customers to come in and be fitted properly so that we are sure the outfit is what they want and fits perfectly," the salon manager asserted.

"As I said, my grandmother is too ill for that."

"Well, it is not our usual practice, but in this instance I'll be happy to let you take an outfit home on approval."

"Thank you," said Maria, happy to have won a little victory.

Terms of Endearment

When Matthew checked on Nan an hour later he found her asleep, with the recorder still running. He pressed the stop button and pocketed it.

Renata had phoned to say they were done shopping and were moving on to the spa.

"We're skipping lunch. We used up our entire calorie intake for the month on coffee and cake in a swanky French coffee shop we found, on the way to get shoes." Simon decided that he would make a salad for mid-afternoon. He was thinking ahead. *They'll be hungry if they've skipped lunch, and I don't want to be kept here too late, so I'll just take a break and get it ready now.*

Matthew took some lamb cutlets from Nan's freezer and put them in the microwave to defrost. He made a green salad and peeled some chats and put them on to boil with some eggs. Then he sliced up some spring onions. Finally he put the kettle on to make himself a cup of tea, and when he had read the newspaper, he made potato salad. Matthew helped himself to a small plate of the potato salad and then put everything in the fridge to await the arrival of the girls, who breezed in around three thirty, each bearing several bags.

"Did the money you gave us include make-up, Uncle Matthew?" Beth asked. "I hope so because I can't afford what I bought."

"It had better then, hadn't it?" Matthew replied, amused by Beth's cheek. He didn't begrudge it though, remembering his own poverty-stricken student days, and he didn't even have to get a student loan to do his degree.

"And jewellery?" she asked, chancing her luck even further.

"Is it gold, diamond or silver jewellery?"

"No, but it is very expensive costume jewellery."

281

"How expensive?" he asked.

"About a hundred bucks each?" Laura said, which caused she and Beth to argue about whose purchases were more expensive and how much they were on sale for. In actual fact there was only a couple of dollars between them, because both sets of jewellery were practically identical, except for a slight variation in design. Matthew got the gist of the cost and was not unduly perturbed.

"If it had been gold jewellery, amounting to thousands, I would have said on your bike! But a hundred dollars each is fine." He assured them.

When they then started arguing about shoe prices he threw his eyes up to heaven and decided to curb any further bickering.

"Look, I don't need to know what everything has cost, or whether one person has been more extravagant than another. Did you have enough money, Emily?"

"Yes, there's heaps left over."

"Good! That's all I need to know. Now shut up and stop arguing. Nan's sleeping."

"Mine was only seventy dollars, but I got a necklace and earrings to match." Renata said. "I wanted to buy them myself but Emily wouldn't..." Matthew held up his hands to silence her.

"No more talk of what anything cost. Moving right along, I have to announce that Nan has been recording more of her story on this." He took his voice recorder out of his pocket. "I could do with it back tomorrow, though, because I need it for work on Monday so can you listen to it today or tomorrow?"

"We could listen to it now?" Maria suggested.

"I'm too tired," said Laura.

"Me too," Beth agreed.

"That just leaves tomorrow," Maria said, "and I've got work to do."

"And we're going out in the Boat," complained Beth. Matthew regretted not having been able to explain this to Renata on the quiet. He saw Renata's disappointment and shrugged his shoulders when she caught his eye.

"We could go out in the boat instead if it's inconvenient," Matthew suggested.

"No!" Beth replied. "Mikey's surprising me."

"So how come you know?" Laura asked.

"I know everything," Beth grinned.

"Sorry darling. They got in first. Shall I book it for next weekend?" Several pairs of wide eyes peered at Renata. In all the time that Matthew had been bringing women home, this was the first time he had used a term of endearment in front of them. *It must be serious*, everyone thought while Renata blushed.

"Okay. Why don't you do that… darling?" Now tennis match eyes turned towards Matthew, but he didn't blush. The corner of his mouth lifted, instead, into an almost imperceptible smile, at the idea of Renata returning the endearment. Maria was first to break the loaded silence that followed.

"Okay, getting back to the recording, we have to do it now," Maria said. "Matthew needs his voice recorder and that means he'll probably need to record over it." Because they were tired this started a new bout of bickering between Beth and Laura.

"Oh do shut up!" Maria's voice was firm. "Arguing doesn't solve anything." Then, remembering her mother-in-law, who had found a chair in a corner where she could sit and kick off her shoes, Maria apologised. "Violet, we're not usually a rude family." Then to save more embarrassment she exclaimed. "Food! That will put us all in a better mood. Let's not spoil a lovely day." She communicated volumes to her sisters with her very expressive eyes. They didn't dare argue. "Now, Matthew, what needs to be done?"

"I'll cook the lamb chops while you set the table. I've already done the rest."

"Come on then, girls," their mother said. "I'm tired too, so you can all help. No, Laura, no sloping off to the toilet with a book. Put the table cloth on."

Laura responded indignantly. "I need to go."

"Well leave the book here," her mother said grinning. "I'm timing you." But Emily didn't time her. With Renata, Violet, Maria and Beth lending a hand, it was all done before Laura returned and Matthew was just putting the food on the table.

"Sit down everyone!" Matthew said. "Has anyone checked on Nan?" Nobody had, nor did they have to, because the smell of the lamb brought Nan out of her room and to the table.

"Hello Violet, love. How did the day go?" Nan sat down at table and pleased everyone by helping herself to some salad.

"Very well indeed!" Violet smiled.

"Well, have we got a wedding dress?" Nan asked.

"Yes, but it's being shortened." Maria's face was radiant with happiness.

"It's awesome," said Beth.

"Very elegant," said Emily. "Show her the photo, Maria."

"We didn't want you to miss all the excitement." Maria searched for her mobile phone and pressing a few buttons handed it to Nan.

"Look."

"Well, don't you look a picture, dear?" Nan smiled.

"I'll download it onto my computer when we've finished lunch," Maria promised. "You can't see the detail on such a small photo."

"I'll be going home after we've eaten then," Matthew said. "I want to be surprised on the day." More to the point he couldn't imagine anything worse than sitting through all the small talk involved in recounting the details of their day.

"Since I live near you, would it be a trouble for you to drop me on the way, dear?" Violet asked.

"You don't need a lift, Violet." Maria interrupted. "I'm sorry, I should have told you. I'm taking you home with me. Simon is treating us to dinner tonight, and then he will take you home. Is that okay?"

"Wonderful," she echoed. "Thank you for including me in your special day, love, and for your generosity." She looked from Maria to Matthew not quite knowing whom she should thank for her beautiful emerald silk dress and fascinator.

"Simon bought your outfit," Maria said. "He insisted."

"Did he?" I must thank him then. She seemed surprised and delighted.

"So what are we going to do about the recording?" Maria said. "What made you record it rather than write it, Nan?"

"Because it's uncomfortable to write." Nan confessed. "It puts too much pressure on my shoulder. Anyway, there's not much more of my story to tell. I'm nearly at the end." These were ill chosen words that threw a damper momentarily over the entire table until Renata distracted everyone with a suggestion.

"I have an idea," she said, taking some more potato salad. Everyone's eyes switched to the woman who was fast becoming an important member of the family. "What if I go home with Matthew and take the recorder with me so I can type it up for you while he works? You would then have a hard copy to keep. That's if it's okay with you... darling?"

"Fine by me," Matthew replied. Again there was that little curl of the mouth as he cut into his chop.

"Thanks Renata." Maria was smiling, glad that in a very short time, Renata had become her new best friend. This was just as well because she was about to marry her old one.

After dinner, Matthew and Renata made a quick getaway leaving the girls to clear away and then clear out. As

285

they washed dishes, they told Nan about their shopping exploits, and about the dresses, shoes and jewellery. Mobile phones gave Nan a good idea what the bridesmaids dresses would look like, and shoes and jewellery were brought out and tried on for Nan to admire. Finally, Emily said.

"We bought you an outfit too, Mum, but if you don't like it, we can easily take it back."

"I've got lots of clothes I've hardly worn. You don't want to be wasting good money on me."

"Well what were you thinking of wearing?" Emily didn't want to tell Nan she had lost so much weight she would be lucky if anything fitted her. "Why don't you get it out so we can see if it needs cleaning?" Nan padded into her bedroom and came back with a nice amber georgette outfit that that had a heavily beaded bodice.

"Oh I remember that outfit, Mum. You looked stunning in it. Why don't you try it on to show Maria? It's her wedding and she's the one who has to be happy about everything." Nan padded to her bedroom once more and this gave Emily time to ask the girls to back her up if she needed them to. But she didn't need them to because Nan rejected her outfit herself.

"Goodness me," Nan said pulling at the waist of her skirt as she returned to her family for approval. "I've finally lost weight. All the diets I've ever done must have kicked in all at once." The skirt was too big by about ten inches and the jacket bagged around her small frame.

"Here, try this one on Mum." It was the new outfit.

Nan liked the warm autumnal colours, and Emily had sidestepped any discussion of weight loss. Nan emerged from her bedroom beaming.

"This outfit reminds me of autumn in England. How does it look?" They had been clever and had selected a very small sized garment with a bit of stretch to it.

"You look beautiful, Nan," Beth said. "Maria, you'd better watch out, Nan's going to steal the show."

286

Cushla

Renata made coffee for her and Matthew, to keep them alert so they could meet their respective deadlines. She plugged in headphones and began to rewind Nan's story. She wasn't very far into it before she stopped.

"Can I interrupt you for a moment Matt?" He didn't answer right away – just held up a hand. Eventually he said:

"Sorry! I was in the middle of complex maths! What is it?"

"I don't understand. I thought this was supposed to be Nan's life, but it doesn't sound like it is. It's Nan speaking and I know she used to be a Nun, but this isn't anything like what I expected. She's talking about going to a fancy dress party with George Harrison."

"Yes. Well... there are things I need to tell you about Mum."

"What do you mean?"

"Well, she maintains she had quite a relationship with The Beatles – or at least with George Harrison."

"And did she?"

"What do you think? When it comes to Nan's convent and Beatles experiences, Emily and I just don't go there. The girls seem to have a weird fascination with it though. They are certain some of the things really happened because, they say, there's evidence to support their conclusions."

"Where?"

"You'll have to ask them. I think they mentioned The Liverpool Wall."

"What's the Liverpool Wall?"

"Ask Nan to show you the next time we're at her place."

"Can't you tell me?"

"I can, but it's best that you see it. In short, there's a lot of Liverpool memorabilia covering one of her bedroom walls; most of it is to do with The Beatles. Ask her to show it to you."

"Why?"

"Because she loves to talk about it. Or you could just ask the girls. As I say, they're totally into it."

"Right."

"The thing is that some of Nan's storytelling makes her sound nuts. Emily and I have learned not to ask questions about that time because it seems to unhinge her and she becomes an instant crackpot. It used to embarrass us when we were kids so we tend to just leave that bit of her life alone."

"But it's absolutely fascinating, whether it's real or not."

"I'm glad you think so, but if you had been hearing it for a lifetime, you might think differently." Renata could see signs of tension in Matthew.

"Thanks. I'm sorry to interrupt your work, Cushla."

"Cushla?" Matthew's eyebrows were raised in question.

"It means beat of my heart." This explanation came with a big smile followed by a long kiss. Renata loved that slight lift to the corner of Matthew's mouth when he was pleased and embarrassed at the same time.

"I like it. I've never heard the word before."

"It's Gaelic, that's why, and you'll hear it a lot from now on."

"Good." By now Matthew was positively beaming. "I'm really sorry I have to work, darling. I've got a presentation to do first thing Monday. It's just as well Beth and Mikey claimed the Duck Boat because I would have had to work through tomorrow night to have this ready for Monday. Bummer eh? But it's really important. I'll make it up to you tomorrow night. Would you like to go out for dinner? You can ask me anything you want then."

"That would be lovely," Renata said, deciding to make notes on what she didn't understand. She turned on the recorder again and began to type. At 8:00pm she stopped for a break.

"Are you hungry?" she asked.

"No, I don't think I am."

"Do you have any Cornflakes?"

"Yes. Help yourself. I wouldn't mind some hot chocolate if you feel so inclined?"

At the same time as Matthew and Renata were having Cornflakes and hot chocolate Maria, Simon and Violet were in an Italian restaurant. Simon was tucking into a huge plate of linguini del mare, a creamy combination of marinated prawns, calamari, fish, and mussels sautéed with some deliciously flavoured herbs. As Maria and Violet had eaten well at Nan's, they decided to order an entrée of Spiralli Arrabbiata, which was the simplest dish on the menu, being a mixture of capsicum, onion, sliced mushrooms, chilli, garlic, basil and baby spinach in a Napoli sauce. This, combined with a carafe of light white wine, filled a hunger that neither of them felt, and solved the romantic problem because now each lovebird had consumed equal amounts of garlic.

Violet complimented Maria on the hospitality of her family. Now, all that remained was for the list of guests on the groom's side to be settled. These did not amount to many because Simon's parents both came from small families. The wedding menu was also settled. Since the wedding reception was to be held on Christmas Day, a Christmas lunch seemed appropriate. There would be a choice of pork, turkey and ham, with oven roasted potatoes and stuffing and the usual assortment of vegetables. For dessert, rather than Christmas pudding, they would have the family all time favourite - Baked Alaska.

"I am amazed that you found anywhere open on Christmas Day, dear," Violet said.

"Are you?" responded Maria. "Well, when you think about it, more and more people are going out for Christmas lunch these days. A lot of the hotels are open and offer a

Christmas Menu to non-residents. I was at an island eco resort, a couple of years ago at Christmas, and the number of people that came over from the mainland, especially for Christmas lunch, was extraordinary. The guests were most put out, actually, because we thought we were there for a very quiet sumptuous Christmas, but the place was overrun. It was impossible to find a sun-lounger anywhere so we just went and read in our rooms until all the day-trippers had gone. It was the most disappointing Christmas of my life."

"Well I hope this one won't be," Violet said.

"It won't be," said Simon. "I'll make sure of that." Maria couldn't help thinking of Nan at that moment. The only thing that could possibly spoil Christmas was if Nan were not able to celebrate it with them.

"Does anyone want coffee before we leave?" Simon asked.

"Not me," said Violet. "It'll keep me awake."

"We need to be kept awake, but since your Mum must be tired after a huge day, how about we have coffee at home, Simon. Then we can get an early start on our work." Maria suggested.

"Don't tell me you have to work tonight!" Violet exclaimed.

"Yes. We have to put in some long hours if we want a honeymoon," Simon said.

Later, after taking Violet home, Simon worked slouched on a comfy chair, balancing his laptop on his knee, while Maria worked at her desk in the corner of her lounge room. After a while the telephone interrupted the silence and Maria picked it up because she was nearest.

"Oh I forgot to ask him," Maria said. "Just hold on." Maria covered the phone. "Laura wants to know if she can rent your unit when you move in here, and she also wants to know what the rent would be so she can work out if she can afford it. She knows you're busy and hates to bother you but she has to give notice to her landlord if you agree to it?"

"Oh! Well…Great! That saves me advertising. Ask her what she pays now."

"She pays $230 a week."

"Tell her she can have it for the same." Maria passed on the message and smiled, as she put down the phone.

"Thanks." Maria said approaching to kiss him on the head from behind.

Duck Boat

Beth was up early the following day to pack a picnic for the much looked-forward-to day on the river. Mikey arrived by car rather than bike, and Beth was ready when he beeped his horn. He had attached a roof rack and had begun untangling ropes while he waited for Beth. He would need them to tie the boat down tight enough so that the wind could not lift it as they were driving along.

"Hello Sailor!" Beth said. She smelt delicious and Mikey stopped unravelling the ropes to hold her and whisper in her ear.

"You take my breath away, and you cause all sorts of disruption in my nether regions." Beth smiled pressing herself teasingly against him for a moment.

"Save it for later," she smiled. "Now, how can I help?"

"Well you can try getting the knots out of these. Where's the picnic?"

"On the kitchen table. You can't miss it!" Mikey was glad that everything was ready because if they set off now they would be able to catch the outgoing tide, making the rowing easier, and if they were lucky they'd be able to come back with the tide when it turned. His hopes for the day bubbled over:

"I hope we can find somewhere nice for our picnic," he said, putting the Esky on the back seat.

"Nan said it's sometimes difficult to find anywhere to moor. The banks are usually muddy and spiky with mangroves."

"I'm the optimistic type. I've got a rug, just in case." Beth couldn't imagine anything more pleasurable than lying with Mikey, somewhere private, on a rug, in the warm sunshine.

"Nan and Grandpa Doug used to stay in the Boat to eat most of the time. They say the best time on the river is that still time between tides. On a calm day the river can be like

292

glass. Oh good!" Beth sighed. "You brought the umbrella I put out."

"I hope you aren't expecting rain?"

"No, the forecast is good but, nevertheless, Nan said to bring one because it gets hot on the river and you can get burned. Have you got sun cream on?"

"No."

"Well there's a big bottle of it on the table. Go and put some on." Mikey would have preferred Beth to rub it on him but being anxious to get off, only enjoyed the thought of it.

Queensland kids were taught in school to slip, slop, slap which was short for slip on a shirt, slop on some sunscreen, and slap on a hat. New recruits in traffic had it drummed into them too, by Workplace Health and Safety, because they were vulnerable being out on the road most of the time. Too many traffic cops had fallen foul of skin cancer, so much so that now sunscreen was mandatory. Returning as he rubbed in the sun cream, Beth explained the umbrella's other important use.

"It can act as a sail. If a wind comes up you might be glad of it."

"You can't hold an umbrella and row at the same time," Mikey declared. "You are rowing, aren't you?" Beth didn't rise to the bait.

"While you are rowing, Michael, sweetheart, I will be reclining on the beanbag."

"A beanbag?"

"Not any old beanbag - THE beanbag! It's so much more comfortable than a hard wooden seat, and you'll be able to admire me as you row!"

"I really do think you should take a turn of rowing!"

"Yeah well… dream on lover boy! However I will assist your rowing with my umbrella acting as a sail."

When they arrived at Nan's she was sitting on the doorstep waiting for them. Beside her was another small Esky.

"Rowing's thirsty work. When you feel tired, tie up to a tree branch and let this restore your energy. It always worked

293

for Grandpa Doug." She handed it to Mikey, with a sly wink. "Be careful," she whispered. "It's got breakables in it."

"Thanks Nan," he said, pleased that she seemed to have taken a liking to him. Under her careful supervision, they positioned Mikey's car in exactly the right place so The Duck Boat could be lowered onto it.

"It's so simple it's ingenious!" Mikey had quickly worked out how easily it could be lowered onto the car from where it was stored up near the carport roof, suspended on a couple of ropes attached to a pulley system.

When they had lowered it, Nan declared it perfectly done. She picked up the thick heavy ropes.

"I remember Doug splicing these to make the loops. I think he learned how to do it in the Sea-Cadets. These are just those elastic things for the roof rack."

"Occy straps!" Mikey picked up various bits of wood. "What are these?"

"They're detachable seats to make the boat lighter to carry. Doug used to put all the loose parts of the boat in the boot or on the back seat. If you put them in the boat on the roof rack, the wind might catch them and lift them out causing an accident. But you're used to road accidents. I'm sure you'll figure out a safe way to transport everything."

Beth came alongside with the red velvet beanbag, and Mikey laughed as he pictured Beth reclining on it, while he did all the work.

"That had better go on the back seat," Nan suggested.

"It's a good job we didn't invite anyone to go with us," Mikey said, pointing to the back seat and the boot. "We're chockers!"

"Don't forget the lifejackets! I'll get them." Nan climbed the steps, disappearing into the depths of the house and reappearing a short time later with two of them. "Best to be safe," she said. "Have you got enough water?"

"Yes," Beth replied.

"How much have you got? Rowing is very thirsty work."

"I've got two litres, but I've got flasks of hot water to make tea and coffee with too."

"Good. Have fun, then."

The Missing Bit

Maria and Simon began work early on Sunday. Later, the phone rang. It was Renata.

"Maria, I've transcribed Nan's recording. I have to say, it's not what I was expecting. The word enigma comes to mind."

"I know exactly what you mean."

"Matthew says you claim to have found some proof to support some of what she says, and that it's on the Liverpool Wall? Other than that he avoids talking about Nan's early life."

"I know. Both he and Mum say they've had enough of her tall stories to last them a lifetime. The thing is, there are a couple of things that do seem to support what she says, but obviously a lot of it is a bit off-the-planet. Whether it's true or not, though, it's part of who Nan is."

"She's certainly an interesting woman. What I typed up last night probably falls into the off-the-planet category. It's the way she talks about George Harrison as if she really knows him."

"I'm convinced she did. You do know, don't you, that she really did spend part of her life at a convent in Weybridge close to where John Lennon and George lived?"

"I know she used to be a nun, but Matthew doesn't talk much about the past and I'd certainly never heard anything about Weybridge until last night."

"Well that bit's true. She did live close to where George, John and Ringo lived, but Mum and Matthew just dismiss that. They say she was locked up in a convent so how could any of it have happened?" There was a short silence.

"I've checked out some of the facts relating to what she writes about and what I typed up last night fits perfectly into the real history of the Beatles. For example, she's got the names of the houses George Harrison's lived in right; there was a Magical Mystery Tour Fancy Dress Party, and she even has the people she met all in the correct fancy dress. You've got other parts of her written story, haven't you?"

"Yes. I made notes before I forgot it all. Beth took it for a while because she was doing an assignment on some of it but I'm pretty sure I got it all back."

"Do you think Beth and Laura might have written down any of her stories?"

"I think both of them have done an assignment on Nan's stories. I doubt they've written anything else though. They're both so busy."

"Well so are you, yet you have."

"True. I haven't written anything, though, since before you and I met. I've been too busy. I'm sure Beth and Laura would have mentioned it, if they had. Ask them, though. I might be wrong. But you should ask Beth and Laura for copies of their assignments, especially Laura's, because her assignment was a fact checking exercise."

"I will. Matthew's busy working today and I have time on my hands, so can I come over and pick up anything you've got? I'll take good care of it and give it back to you as soon as I can?"

"Of course, but I really do want it back."

"My word of honour! Can I come by soon and pick it up?"

"Yes, of course. The only thing is both Simon and I have got to work so it will be a case of here's your hat what's your hurry."

"There's no need to stop work on my account. I'll just pick up the folder and run."

Renata called in around 9:30am with a chicken salad she had considerately made for their lunch.

"Here," she said kissing Maria's cheek. "It will save you precious time."

"Thank you. You're amazing. That's so thoughtful."

297

Renata decided to use the university library, just a few streets away. There, she found a space near a leafy water feature and plugged in her laptop. Making herself comfortable she opened Maria's folder. It was a bit like a jigsaw puzzle and she spent a couple of hours reading through all the papers and sorting them into topics. The first topic she looked at more closely, was the one called 'convent life'. She began to check out details, such as what the terms 'The Holy Rule' and 'The Holy Office' meant. By the time she had finished, she had a good idea of the pattern of a nun's day with its many calls to prayer.

She learned that most convents and monasteries lived, and still live, according to the Rule of St Benedict, which was established to order and facilitate the spiritual growth that a vocation requires. She discovered that The Holy Office involved chanting psalms, prayers, and requesting blessings. These were all sung in Plainchant, not to be confused with Gregorian chant which uses more notes, whereas Plainchant used very few.

Renata had managed to establish that the convent day was broken up by calls to prayer, but her research and Nan's writings were at odds. Renata assumed from this that different monasteries and convents ordered the Holy Office in accordance with the work they were engaged in. The pattern of Nan's day suggested that the office was always sung in chapel, 'Matins' and 'Lauds' before and after the nuns' early morning meditation and 'Prime' immediately after Mass and before breakfast. Next came 'Terse' and 'Sext' both of which were short, and chanted before lunch. 'None', another short set of psalms and prayers, was chanted after lunch and not at the ninth hour as was traditional. Before the evening meal came 'Vespers'. After the evening meal the rule of silence was relaxed for recreation, a time when nuns would assemble to chat, walk, knit, sew or play games together and this was usually when letters were distributed.

The last office of the day was 'Compline' which was always followed by the 'Grand Silence', a much deeper silence than that imposed during the day. She guessed the rule must have been relaxed in the daytime because you had to talk to teach.

Renata downloaded a copy of the Rule of St Benedict so she could look at it more closely some other time. Then she began to check out information about the Beatles. Thus the time flew by and suddenly she realised it was mid afternoon, and she was hungry.

Renata picked up a burger and while eating it in the car, she decided to call in on Nan since she would be passing nearby on the way to Matthew's for the promised dinner date. She rang first to see if Nan was up to a visit.

"She's sleeping at the moment, but I'm sure when she's awake she'll be very pleased to see you."

When she arrived Emily greeted her with a smile and a hug.

"She's still asleep, but it's time she woke up or she won't sleep tonight. I'll put the kettle on and you can take her a cup of tea. Was there something specific you wanted?"

"Oh nothing urgent. I wanted to have a look at Nan's Liverpool Wall. I hear it's a bit of a sore point with you and Matthew, though, so I don't want to bring up anything difficult for you."

"You won't." Emily put the kettle on. "Don't get me wrong. Mum's stories used to embarrass me no end when I was younger. But now that she's got cancer – well it makes you think long and hard about a person's life and I realise now that the Liverpool Wall is part of what makes Mum who she is. Her life experiences make her pretty special."

"Yes, they do. Whether they're imagined or real, Nan's stories are extremely personal and unique…"

"Quirky, zany, weird…" Emily added.

"Yes… all those things, but in a nice way."

"If you don't mind me saying so, you speak as if you know her well. So, how is that? Has Matthew been spilling the beans about our crackpot Mum?"

"No, it wasn't Matthew that got me hooked on Nan. It was typing up the recording Nan made yesterday. Did you know that Maria's got a file on Nan and it makes for very intriguing reading? I've just spent a few hours at the library going through it all and checking out the details. I wasn't familiar with some of the more technical terms of monastic life, but I'm a bit more knowledgeable now. Your Mum's absolutely fascinating, Emily. I've never met anyone who was a nun before."

"It's not so much the nun stuff that Matthew and I avoid talking about. It's when she starts combining her nun story with The Beatles that we switch off. I think it's because she really believes her own stories. I mean, think about it. It borders on insanity."

"I can see you feel really strongly about it. If you'd rather not tal…" Emily interrupted her.

"I used to feel strongly about it. What kid wouldn't when you would see people covering their faces to hide the smirks and ridicule. Kids used to tease us because of it, especially at school. I couldn't care less now, because, as you say, it's all part of who she is, and weird or not, she's… well, she's Nan. Here!" Emily said. "Take this in and wake her up. This one's yours."

"Thanks." Renata picked up the two mugs.

"I think the medication makes her drowsy. She tells me to wake her up after a half an hour because she doesn't want to miss out on the rest of her life by sleeping it away, but when I do, she complains, turns over and goes back to sleep. She always enjoys a cup of tea before she gets up, though, and she won't grouse on you like she would on me."

Renata knocked on the door and heard the noise of bedclothes rustling, followed by a yawn and then a stretch. She opened the door slightly.

"May I come in, Nan?"

"Oh it's you Renata!" Nan's voice was sleepy. "Is Matthew here too?"

"No, it's just me. I've got some questions about what you recorded." Nan looked blank. "You know... what you recorded..." Nan still looked blank. "On Matthew's voice recorder!" Understanding dawned and Nan beamed.

"Oh! Have you typed it up already?"

"Yes. Want some tea?" Renata handed Nan the mug and she took a tentative sip before putting the cup on a coaster on her bedside table to cool.

"Fire away then!" she said.

"Well, first of all I want to see the Liverpool Wall." She said looking around. "This must be it."

"Yes, my memories are all wrapped up in those souvenirs. It was great living in Liverpool when The Beatles put us on the map." Nan picked up her cup again as Renata went from picture to newspaper cutting, to frames containing small items such as concert tickets, to lyrics and posters of the Beatles albums and movies.

"This bus must be the Magical Mystery Tour bus that you were talking about on the recording?" Renata said, pointing to an album cover. "Did you really know them?"

"Of course. How could I tell you about them if I didn't?" Renata did not know the answer to that. She felt like a little child, being told for the umpteenth time: "Of course Santa's real. Would he leave you presents if he wasn't?"

"You didn't really go to the Magical Mystery Tour fancy dress party, though, did you?"

"Yes, I did."

"Does anyone believe you?"

"Possibly my granddaughters. I don't know. I never ask them. Matthew and Emily don't."

"It takes some believing, though, doesn't it? I mean, if George's mate rang and spoke to Mother Superior trying to convince her that you were going to stay at the Bishop's

Palace, surely she wouldn't have believed it, would she? Anyway, would the Bishop really go to a Beatles party?"

"Yes. Some of the clergy are fond of a little tipple. Maybe that's a generalisation. I'm just going on priests I know. I don't really know about the rest of them."

"I suppose they can't spend all their time polishing their halos." Renata commented, making Nan laugh.

"I've often wondered myself how George pulled it off, and who rang Reverend Mother pretending to be the Bishop? Don't forget, at that time the Beatles moved in pretty influential circles. Maybe it was one of George's really posh friends, like George Martin. They'd have known actors like Peter Sellers and Spike Milligan. Someone like them could've pulled it off. Is it so hard to believe that he might talk them into convincing Reverend Mother to let me go to the ball? I never really asked him how he did it. I spent the journey to the party getting high on very dubious tonic water and passive smoking and my memories of the evening are confused. I remember the following morning very well though, when George picked me up – especially the headache I had."

"But you didn't write about that?"

"Yes I did. It's all on the recorder."

"No. There was nothing about who took you to wherever you stayed."

"Yes! It's all there." Nan argued. Renata looked very puzzled and then she remembered how she had stopped the tape when the speaking had finished. Her hand went to her gaping mouth.

"Oh no! I've got an awful feeling... Excuse me Nan," she said. "I need to phone Matthew." She called his number on her mobile phone and, answering quickly, he seemed in exceptionally high spirits.

"I've finished what I had to do. Now I can really enjoy the evening with you."

"Matthew, have you been using your recorder today."

302

"Yes, why?"

"Much?"

"Quite a bit, why?"

"Please don't use it any more until I get there." Renata said.

"I told you. I've finished for the day."

"Did you fill up your recorder?" she asked. "Only I don't think I typed all of what Nan recorded. I hope it hasn't been recorded over. I'll be there in ten minutes. Please don't record anything else."

"I can tell you now what I said if you want." Renata gathered up her two bags, and her car keys.

"Let me see if it's still on the recorder first. If not I'll come back and type it up as you speak. I'll get back to you." She was already heading for the door where she turned back to Nan and said. "I feel like such an idiot. I'm so sorry Nan."

Shipwrecked

Laura had been on an early shift, and the following day she had agreed to swap an early for a late. She decided to unwind by picking up a DVD and, realising she could have a late night without it affecting her work the following day, decided to take it over to Nan's and watch it there with her mother. She called Nan's and her mother answered.

"What's for dinner tonight?" she asked.

"Sausages and Mash. Why?"

"I thought I might sleep over. What do you think?"

"Great."

"I've got a movie."

"Which one?"

"Bugsy Malone."

"Haven't you grown out of that yet?"

"I can watch it at home if you'd rather?"

"Don't be silly. I love watching that movie with you because you laugh like you did when you were a kid."

"Okay then. I just have to pick up my uniform from the cleaner's so I'll be there soon."

"Great."

Just as Emily was replacing the handset, Beth and Mikey arrived home from their day on the river. Beth had caught the sun despite the umbrella and she complained wishing she had dark skin like Mikey.

"How was it?" Nan asked opening the door.

"Brilliant. Except we had a little accident with the Boat," said Beth.

"Oh! What happened?"

"We were trying to tie up at one of those big square mooring platforms they have for canoes on the river," Mikey explained. It had big U-shaped bolts sticking out of the side of it and as we were approaching it, the current slammed us against it and the bolt went right through the boat. I didn't realise it was made of such thin plywood." Nan smiled in response.

"Doug made it out of thin plywood so it would be light to carry. He didn't like using trailers so it had to go on the roof rack, and for that he had to be able to lift it single-handed."

"I'll never again approach a mooring platform with the current," Mikey vowed.

"I don't get what you just said," Beth admitted.

"Well, if you approach the mooring against the current you're not going to get slammed into it are you, because the flow of the tide is pulling you away from it."

"Oh! Of course," said Beth. "Anyway, Nan, the short story is the Duck Boat's got a big hole in the side of it now."

"A small hole, and fortunately it's high up." Nan smiled noticing Mikey's role had become one of toning down Beth's exaggerations.

"We could have sunk!"

"But we didn't." Mikey turned to Nan apologetically. "I'll fix it sometime this week before Matthew takes it out next weekend. Can I come around when I'm off duty? It'll be in the next couple of days, probably. I'll ring first, though."

"Of course. And you'd better tell Matthew what happened so he doesn't do the same thing."

"I'll email him and tell him not to forget the life jackets," said Beth. "I so thought we were shark bait. Good job the hole wasn't lower or we might have been. It was pretty scary. What's for dinner Mum?"

"I wasn't sure if you were staying or not but I made enough for you. It's sausages and mash. Laura asked if she could come too."

"Do you want to stay, Mikey?"

"Sure. Love to. I'll go and unload."

"What time's Laura getting here?" Beth was anxious to get home and shower. She was hot and sticky after her day in the sun.

"I expected her by now." Emily glanced at her watch. "It's not like her to be late."

"I'll phone her and see where she is. I'm starving. Is it nearly ready? By the way Nan, thanks for the bubbly. That was such a cool touch. It was just like you said, between tides, tranquil... serene. I had a feeling of sheer bliss. I'm hooked on the river now. It was everything I remembered and just as beautiful as the times I used to go out with you and Grandpa Doug." While she was speaking Beth had called Laura's mobile but there was no answer. "Oh come on Laura. Pick up." Voicemail asked Beth if she would like to leave a message. "What time are you getting here?" Beth chided. "We're waiting for you and I'm starving. Call Mum!" Mikey dumped the esky and life jackets on the floor, not far from the front door.

"Beth, you know where they go. Does the esky need cleaning out?" asked Nan.

"I'll do it," Beth said taking it to the sink and getting in the way of her mother who was forced to put down the saucepan she had been about to drain. Beth wiped the Esky out with a damp dishcloth. "It's only had bottles in it. It's fine." She said. "Come on Mikey, you might as well learn where they go. Pick up the life-jackets." Nan did not miss the provocative smile Beth gave Mikey as she led him down the corridor to the end of the house.

"They've gone for a snog!" Nan whispered to her daughter. Emily smiled inwardly as she busied herself mashing potatoes and turning sausages. She and Nan were on easy terms now, in a way they had not been since she had been newlywed. She was glad she had moved in to look after Nan because, little by little, her mother had let her shoulder more and more of the chores.

Emily realised she had been hard on her mother and had made a lot of wrong assumptions. Nan had been there for her when she needed her. Emily enjoyed the blissful feeling of being closer to her daughters than she had been for years. She

306

had desired this for a very long time, and now she had so much to look forward to. She had begun to think that with all the changes in family life recently. *I might even be a grandmother before too long, although not if Maria has anything to do with it*, she was remembering their conversation, after the movie about the weeping camel. *But Beth loves kids. Who knows what life will surprise me with next?* As for Nan, well since she would not be there for the joy to come, Emily could not begrudge her what little joy remained.

Battered by Batteries

"Can we eat soon? I'm starving and Mikey's on the nine o'clock shift and needs to get home to get changed."

"Not to mention the fact that it'll take them a couple of hours to say good night," whispered Nan to Emily. "They seemed to be constantly joined at the lip. I think you'd better serve up."

"I'll try her one more time," Emily was used to the girls being late but Laura had said she wouldn't be long. "I wonder where she can be?" Emily let the phone ring for longer than usual and then hung up. "No answer! It's not like her. She usually phones to say if she is running late."

Over dinner, Beth and Mikey told Nan and Emily about their day.

"We launched at College's Crossing and went upstream as far as we could. But then we couldn't get through because it was overgrown with trees, and very narrow. We went as far as we could by lying down and pulling ourselves through the overhanging bushes, just like intrepid explorers. But then Mikey thought he saw a snake in the tree above us, and so we panicked a bit and reversed out as quickly as we could."

"So we were just getting over that bit of excitement when a fish jumped into the boat." Beth was now recounting the story. "It did! Honest! We were still freaked out because of the snake, but now we just went berserk, kicking the fish to one another in panic until we realised it was a fish, not a snake. We threw it back into the water, close to some fishermen we felt sorry for. They'd been fruitlessly fishing all morning, and here we had fish jumping on us." Everyone saw the funny side of this, but the ringing phone interrupted their laughter.

"Hello," Laura's voice said with a bit of an echo.

"Where are you?" Emily asked.

"I'm at the hospital. I'm sorry I'm late, but believe it or not I wandered into a robbery on my way over."

"Oh No" Emily said. "Are you okay?"

"Yes. I'm fine. I stopped at a service station to pick up some chips and lollies so we could have a nice chick flick night, and it all got a bit over the top."

"Are you hurt?"

"Just a few bruises."

"I'll be right there," Emily said. "Which hospital did they take you to?" Everyone had stopped eating at the mention of trouble.

"I'm at the Royal, but Mum, I'm all right... You don't need..." But Laura found herself speaking to a dial tone.

"Laura's been hurt in a robbery."

There were astonished cries all around Emily. Within seconds the surprise and consternation spread to mayhem with everyone talking at once, and wanting to go to the hospital and relieve their shock by doing something – anything.

"Absolutely not!" Emily said to her mother. "I don't want to have to worry about you as well, Mum. Beth, can you stay with Nan?"

"But I want to go to the hospital too," Beth said.

"I need you to look after Nan," said Emily controlling her distress. Everyone began to argue about who should go to the hospital and who shouldn't. In the end, Emily raised her voice, letting go of years of self-control.

"Oh for crying out loud, can't you see I need to go. I'm Laura's mother and I get to make the decisions for once. Nan, please stay here! Beth, please stay with Nan!"

Mikey had his mouth open ready to speak.

"No, I don't want you to drive me, Mikey, but thanks for your thoughtfulness. I can drive, and I want to go on my own, please." Mikey's mouth closed cooperatively. Emily eased her tension with a little diatribe: "It's all the more reason why you need to get to work, Mikey, because people aren't safe on the

309

streets. Get out there and stop these lunatics." As she spoke, tears sprung to her eyes. She found her bag and car keys. "I'll ring as soon as I can." She blew her nose, said goodbye and left everyone gaping.

Later, at the hospital, where Laura informed her she was to stay at least overnight, Emily learned that it wasn't just a robbery; it was an armed robbery featuring a gun-toting madman and her superhero daughter. The armed robber had thrown Laura backwards into a display stand and slugged her with his gun as she tried to get up and grab his legs. She had been X-rayed and the skull was dented, rather than fractured, but they wanted to keep her in under observation.

"It could have been much worse," the nurse told Emily. "She's lucky she didn't arrive here with a bullet through her brain. She's a very brave girl."

A female police officer was sitting by Laura's bedside when Emily was shown into the ward.

"I'm fine Mum," Laura said, playing things down. Emily's eyes overflowed with emotion and her tears wet her daughter's hair as she hugged her. "I don't know whether to be angry or proud," she said in the end.

"I was just doing my job," Laura said.

"You were off duty."

"Mum, this is police officer Frances Miller," Laura said, choosing not to argue the point.

"Pleased to meet you, Frances," Emily said loosening her grip on her daughter. "Are you from the same station as Laura?"

"Yes. We went through the academy together."

"So," said Emily turning again to Laura. "Tell me what happened."

"Well, I was at the back of the store when a guy asked for the money out of the cash register." Frances took a notebook out of her breast pocket.

"We can make this your statement, if you like. It will save you having to go over it all again later."

310

"Okay," Laura agreed.

"He didn't know I was there, so I had the advantage of surprise," she continued. "As he entered, I was bending down to get something off the bottom shelf, and so he didn't see me. He began waving a gun about and screaming at the cashier at the top of his voice. She was just a kid. The robber wasn't much older. I could see the cashier was totally losing it, and panicking so much that she wasn't listening to what he was telling her to do. The girl's shrieking was making the robber very jumpy and I was afraid he was going to use violence to shut her up, so I came up behind him, stuck my mobile phone in his back and said. 'Police! Drop it Mate,' and he did. He was just about to turn around. I didn't want him to because I didn't want him to see that I wasn't in uniform and that it wasn't a gun that was pressed into his back. So I pushed him up against the counter really hard and said: 'Don't move a muscle and you won't get hurt!' Then, trying to be as cool as I could, I said to the cashier, 'please ring 000 and ask for the police. Tell them that a police officer has apprehended a thief in your petrol station and needs backup'."

"I thought if I emphasised I was a police officer the thief would behave, but I think it freaked him out more and I thought he was going to do a runner, so I pressed him up against the counter even harder and said, 'I wouldn't run if I were you, Mate. You'll only end up tired in jail.' Then my phone rang and he realised I didn't have a gun. That was when he lost the plot. He punched me in the gut with his elbow and as I doubled over he shoved me back into a shelving unit stacked with batteries, torches and other stuff. He picked up his gun as I was getting up, and I tried to grab him around the knees so he didn't kill someone with it. He belted me over the head with it instead, and shoved me into the display stand again. This time it toppled and everything fell on me. Some batteries are bloody heavy! Meanwhile, he ran for his life, but he didn't get far because a patrol car in the

311

vicinity responded immediately. They picked him up as they were turning into the service station."

"It was probably me phoning you that made him realise you didn't have a gun. I can't believe I nearly got you killed. I am so sorry."

"It might have been you, Mum, but other people do call me you know, so it could have been anyone."

"Just look at what the brute did to you." Emily took hold of Laura's chin and moving it from side to side said. "You're going to have a nice shiner. Are you hurt anywhere else?" she was attempting to pull up Laura's t-shirt as she spoke.

"Mum!" Laura was embarrassed by this solicitude, especially in front of a fellow officer. "It could have been a lot worse, but I'm fine, as you can see."

"Did they say anything about concussion?"

"Are you looking for things to be worse than they are?"

"It's a perfectly reasonable question."

"They want me to stay awake for a couple of hours - just in case."

"Sleepiness can be one of the symptoms," added Frances.

"I know," Laura said. "I'm wide awake, right now, though. I don't feel at all sleepy."

"That's probably Adrenalin," Frances explained.

"What will happen to the thief?"

"He's nicked!" Frances assured Emily.

"Good," she sighed. Frances asked a few more questions, and when she was satisfied she had all the information she needed, she closed her pad and turned her attention to Emily.

"How long are you going to be here?"

"Until they throw me out." Emily had a defiant air about her, as if nobody was ever going to boss her about again.

"Well, I might as well go and get this typed up." Frances pocketed her notepad and got up to leave. Emily caught her arm.

"I don't suppose you could stay with Laura a few more minutes, could you? I need to phone the family. They're waiting for news and probably imagining the worst, so I need to put them out of their misery." A nurse entered the room just as Emily was speaking.

"I'll stay with her. I need to do her obs. and give her a bit of a wash and get her into a gown, so take your time." Emily and Frances left the ward together, and as the swish of the curtain screened Laura from view, Emily said.

"Thank you for being there for Laura, Frances."

"You're welcome," she replied. "Cops are like family. They look out for each other."

Outside the entrance to the hospital, Emily rang Nan's.

"She's fine," she told them. "A bit bruised, but fine. They're keeping her in for observation so I'll stay a while longer."

"No worries," Beth said. "I'll sleep here tonight and keep an eye on Nan. Stay as long as you like."

"What about your exam tomorrow?" Emily asked.

"It's not until 3:00pm. I can go home and change tomorrow lunch time."

"Did you have study to do?"

"No. I cram as I go. Let them bring it on! I'll be brilliant." This was not entirely true, but she didn't want to give her mother any more unnecessary worry.

"Great. I won't hurry home then."

313

A Bad Hangover

When Renata arrived at Matthew's, he was having a shower. She found the recorder beside his computer and pressing the play button heard Matthew's voice dictating instructions to his secretary. She pressed fast-forward several times despairing every time she heard Matthew's voice. The next time she hit the play button there was nothing, but then suddenly Nan's voice filled the silence and Renata listened to a part of Nan's story that she had already typed up. She fast-forwarded it a few times until she was sure she was at the beginning of the bit she had not yet typed up.

"Do you mind if I just finish this before we go out?" she asked as Matthew walked into the room with only a towel around him. "Although, I don't know how I will ever concentrate!"

"Fine. I'll get dressed. Can I make you a drink while you're working?"

"Yes, a cup of tea would be lovely." Renata typed as fast as she could, stopping now and again to wind back the recorder because it was running faster than she could type.

I haven't the foggiest idea what time I left the party. It was some unearthly hour. I do remember waking up bleary-eyed the following morning because a nun was knocking on my door. When I opened it, she pushed past me to put my breakfast tray down on an elephant table that graced the centre of my room.

'Mr Harrison says he'll wait for you downstairs, Sister.' I inclined my head to show I had understood. 'He says you're not to hurry and you're not to skip breakfast because you'll feel better after you've eaten. Is there anything more we can do for you?' I shook my head.

I showered and ate some dry toast, thinking about how much I wanted to die. George was wrong. I did not feel better for having eaten, but I felt I could, at least, face the day. When I was finally

314

ready to go downstairs I realised that I was in a very large house because of the many rooms I had to pass in order to find a staircase. It was a wide one and, as I looked over the banister rail, I could see I was one floor up. I began my descent and judged, by the many paintings of the house, that it had been a grand house in its day. A bend in the stairs brought me into a large hallway where George was waiting.

'Hya!' He said. He was in the company of two ageing nuns. 'The sisters have offered to show us 'round. Isn't that great?'

I smiled inclining my head, hoping my face was not showing my real state of mind. I followed George and the nuns, counting the rooms as I went, giving up at sixty-nine. I discovered later there were over a hundred. I remember thinking that Jane Eyre could have trodden the floorboards of this convent, and felt very much at home. Dracula, too, for that matter! Out in the garden I realised, looking up at the front face of the building, that it was a gothic mansion with extensive gardens.

'It's known to most as Friar Park and was built by Sir Frank Crisp,' the nun in charge said.

'Was 'e someone famous?' I knew George was doing his homework.

'He was a Baronet,' she replied. 'He was also a lawyer, a microscopist and a liberal activist.'

'A'rrh 'ey! Did he have anything else wrong with him?' George asked, making me burst out laughing, which didn't do my head any good. His humour was lost on the nuns, who only looked puzzled.

'Sister, I can't help thinking, this place is far too big for your needs.' George had become serious now. 'I'm wonderin' if yer planning to stay 'ere long, or whether yer've ever thought about downsizin'. The nun did not respond. 'I'm only askin' because, if you are, I'd be very interested in buyin' - if the price's right.' There was another silence. 'Well it wouldn't do yer any harm te take me number, would it? Just in case!' George handed the nun a card with his telephone number scribbled on it. 'Give us a bell if yer'd consider selling the place to me. I'd give yer a fair price, so long as you don't

try to rob me soft, eh?' After a moment's silence one of the nuns replied.

'Actually, we ARE thinking of selling. There are only four of us now and you're right - the house is far too big for us. However, convent matters are not usually settled quickly. We have protocols, Mr Harrison. How soon would you want to occupy Friar Park?'

'Yesterday.' He replied, but modified that on noticing the nun's disappointment. 'That was a joke. No rush, Sister. Whenever it becomes available! Just give me first refusal when you make up your mind eh?'

'We would have to have our Mother General's permission, you see, Mr Harrison,' the nun smiled. 'The sisters are not used to things changing quickly and out of kindness to them, I would want to give them time to get used to the idea. Huge changes have been taking place in monastic circles, and some of us are already finding it hard to adapt. We need time to breathe in the new. Can you be patient?'

'I can,' George said. 'As I said before, no sweat! Thanks for showin' me 'round. I luv it! It's brilliant.'

'What would you do with it?' Asked the nun in charge. 'Will you open a nursing home, or a school?'

'No,' George said. 'I wanna live in it!'

George raved about Friar Park as we drove away.

'I've got a feelin' I'm gonna live there...' he said. 'I'm gonna call it Crackerbox Palace. Imagine only four nuns rattlin' 'round in somethin' the size o' that.' I imagined him and Patti rattling around in it but said nothing. My throbbing head could not stand the tension of disputing the commentary.

'The upkeep of the garden itself must cost them a fortune,' he said. 'The nuns are probably past it. Do yer think so? Yer know all about nuns. Would yer say they'd be too old for gardenin'?'

Being as on this particular day I felt too old to breath air, never mind for gardening, I didn't feel qualified to answer the question. He was so excited about Friar Park, though, that he didn't notice he might as well have been talking to himself.

316

'I luv gardening,' he said wistfully. 'Imagine what I could do with that one!' I did imagine it, but, alas, through the eyes of one whose early gardening attempts had resulted in a garden fork through my boot.

Clearly I didn't know George as well as I thought, because I found photos on the Internet, years later, showing how he had transformed the gardens at Friar Park, with his siblings and his Hari Krishna friends, thereby making something already beautiful into something glorious.

George brought the car to a stop. I had no idea where we were. When I asked, he said:

'Kinfauns.'

'Kinfauns?' I repeated, knowing the word but not being able to put it into context.

'Me bungalow.' George explained.

'Oh! I said brightening up a bit. Why've we come here?'

'So I can get yer some money. I usually have a blank cheque in me pocket, but I forgot to get one and I promised your boss another donation.'

'Oh! I'd totally forgotten about that. Have you got any coffee, George?' I followed him into the house.

'Of course.' He assured me.

'And Aspro?'

'Yer can have any drug you want,' he smirked cheekily.

'Fifty Aspro should do it,' I said. 'And make that a bucket of coffee.'

'Is yer 'ead that bad?' George was more than a little amused.

'You could say that. It's not funny.'

'Ye'd be better off just having water, yer know. Coffee'll only dehydrate yer more.' He opened the front door and ushered me through into the kitchen, where he offered me a large glass of water, which I drank greedily. After that he showed me to the loo while he went in search of money. When I returned I found him in the kitchen.

'I've just vomited into your toilet, George. I'm sure I'm not the first. I am sorry though.'

317

'Yer the first nun to 'ave done it.' You'll probably feel better for that. Here, have some dry biscuits. They might settle yer stomach a bit. 'De yer still want that coffee, 'ey?' I nodded and he put six big scoops into the percolator. 'I'll put the kettle on in case you want to water it down.'

'Good idea! When did you move in here?' I asked.

'Nineteen sixty-four! I liked Esher as soon as I saw it and I liked the idea of living near a royal residence.'

'Oh yes?' I asked. 'Which one?'

'Claremont Estate.'

'Who lives there?

'It's one of the houses owned by the Royal Family.'

'Does the Queen ever use it?'

'I don't think so. She bought it for the Duke of Albany when he got married, but he's dead now. His widow's still there, though.'

I picked up a framed photo of George with Patti. She was wearing a fur coat.

'That's our wedding,' George said.

'Oh! Didn't Patti want the big white wedding most girls dream of?' George gave me two large glasses of tap water. I emptied them one after the other.

'No. She was gonna get a white fur coat, but in the end she settled for a ginger one. We kept the weddin' very hush hush. I didn't even tell my parents until 4 days before and they didn't tell my kid brothers until hours before the weddin'. We 'ad our 'oneymoon 'ere. We had a proper one later but we loved it here. I've got me recording studio here, ye see.'

'There must have been a lot of broken hearts that day,' I smiled weakly. 'That coffee smells good,' George poured it into two large mugs.

'Here.' He said. I took the coffee from him and helped myself to another Marie biscuit. He opened a drawer, and pulled out handfuls of unopened yellow packets, and dumped them on the table. 'Here,' he said. 'Open them and start counting.' I looked at him bewildered.

'They're me pay packets.'

'They're like the ones I used to get,' I said.

318

'I hardly ever open mine because the studio pays for everything for us.' I was astonished at how little was in the pay packets, considering George's fame. I can't remember how much it was but I know I had to open stacks and stacks of them to get the amount he wanted to donate. He had promised more than five thousand pounds. In the end, we had to leave before I'd finished opening them. 'Just take them all, that'll make it easier.' So I stuffed them all, including the loose money that I'd already started counting, into my overnight bag and into the large detachable pocket nuns from my order wore hooked round their waist, under their skirts. That really tickled George. I looked enormous and weighed a ton. Later, when I waddled into Reverend Mother's office with my overnight bag, looking like I was pregnant, her eyebrows went up to her hairline again, and when, for ages, I kept unloading handfuls of little yellow pay packets, well, I don't think Reverend Mother quite knew what to make of it.

'Yer a case!' George said when I started walking funny.

'So yer keep tellin' me,' I answered back.

I only ever saw George one more time after that. It was just before I left the convent and he'd just moved to Friar Park. Though millions of girls fell for George, I was not one of them. We didn't have that sort of relationship. I never saw him once I left the convent, because then the relationship would not have worked. I would have been just another fan. As a nun I think he felt safe with me. I was someone he could be himself with and who wouldn't talk to the world about him. We were just mates and I wanted nothing from him.

But now I'm going off the point. I was telling you about the last time I saw him, not long before I left. I had to take a sick child home in a taxi to Henley-on-Thames. I asked the taxi driver if we could go past Friar Park on the way back, and, approaching the gates I asked him to stop. I wasn't expecting to see George. I just wanted to have a look to see if it was as I remembered. He was there, sitting up high, on top of a huge earthmover, just staring into space. He was close enough that he would have heard me if I had shouted, but I could tell he was deep in thought and I didn't want to disturb him. I imagined he was away somewhere, on one of his trips, only this time I wouldn't be there. I was in the real world.

319

I was glad that he had achieved his dream and had bought Friar Park. I whispered a quiet goodbye to him, and just as I turned to make my way back to the taxi, he turned his head and saw me, and shouted my name. But that's another story, and I need to finish the one about the Magical Mystery Tour fiasco.

So, getting back to the kitchen at Kinfauns, now where was I? I finished my coffee quickly and, with the money well hidden beneath my skirts, I got back into George's little Mini Cooper and he ran me home. I half expected that small car to buckle under the weight of my moneybags.

'Thanks for all the money, George.' I said as we stopped outside my convent. 'You must've given me a small fortune.'

'It's not. It just seems like that to you because you haven't got any. Anyway, It's the season of goodwill,' he said. 'It's the least I can do.'

'Thank you.' I said. 'You're a good man. I hope you have a very blessed Christmas.'

'You too,' he said, pulling away from the kerb outside my convent, as I waved goodbye.

When I got undressed for bed that night I realised that, sometime during the Fancy Dress Party, The Beatles had all signed my scapular."

Renata pushed her computer away, sat back in her chair, and stretched her arms over her head.

"There, I'm done," she said with a sigh.

"You let your tea go cold."

"I tend to do that when I become engrossed," Renata said. "Do we have time for a fresh one?"

"Dobby will make a fresh cup of tea for Mistress," Matthew struck up a Dobby pose making Renata burst out laughing because it was so unexpected.

"I can make it," she said, thinking perhaps Matthew felt taken for granted.

"No! Never let it be said that Dobby would not make tea for mistress." When he came back from putting the kettle on, Matthew was wearing two tea towels knotted at the shoulder.

320

"If Dobby makes mistress a nice cup of tea," said Renata, "Mistress will give him his freedom as a present."

"But Dobby does not want his freedom," Matthew replied. "He wants to be enslaved to Mistress for the rest of his life."

"What a good elf you are, Dobby. Mistress loves you very much." The pet name Dobby would stick. Renata asked if she could print out what she had typed up on Simon's printer.

"Of course."

"So where are we going for dinner, Dobby?"

"I was thinking of Greek."

"I love Greek. Are we passing by Maria and Simon's?"

"Close," he smiled.

"Can I take these back to her, please?" Printing was in progress and Renata began to gather together the contents of Maria's folder.

"Of course. Had I recorded over any of it?" Matthew asked.

"No. We were lucky. It was all there." Matthew handed her a cup of tea.

"Dobby you're not going to take me out dressed like that, are you?" Renata grinned as she looked up at Matthew."

"Mistress only has to say the word and Dobby will take his kit off," Matthew said with a very elfish gleam in his eye.

321

Buying Time

On the drive home from the hospital the following day, Laura told her mother, in a no-arguments kind of way, that she would be doing the late shift at the police station. She had informed her boss, and he had put her on desk duty.

"Much as I hate desk duty," she said on the way home. "I feel as if I need to do something very normal." Emily did not argue. She knew better. Instead she made light of her daughter's determination.

"You don't usually talk much about work. What happens when you're on the desk?" Emily was finding out that there was much more to her daughter than she had ever imagined and she wanted to know more.

"All sorts of things happen - like the time some idiot walked in. He'd stolen over a thousand dollars from a corner store and when we were taking down his statement he asked if he could go home on bail."

"Have you got money for bail?" I asked.

"Yeah," he said. "I've got the thousand dollars." He was deadly serious too. Emily laughed out loud. Laura cast a sideways glance at her mother, enjoying amusing her.

Beth came running out to the car when Laura and Emily swung into the drive. Nan waited by the front door to welcome them home.

"How are you Laura?" Beth threw her arms around her youngest sister, who winced with pain. "Oh sorry. Where does it hurt?"

"Everywhere. I was battered by batteries," she said.

"She says she's going to work tonight," Emily said on the side to Beth.

"Surely you're not going to work!" Beth said tactlessly, because she really was horrified at the idea. "Here, lean on me."

"I don't need to. I'm fine." Ignoring Laura's answer Beth persisted in grabbing her in places that hurt, so that Laura lost her temper. "I said I'm okay!" Then she made an effort at patience before continuing. "Look, I appreciate your concern, but please, can you get out of my way or I'm going to fall over you."

Beth moved from 'in Laura's face' to beside her.

"Okay, but please don't go to work. You need to rest."

"Don't tell me what's best for me. I'm telling you I'll be better off at work. Not only will it take my mind off everything, it will make me feel useful. I will take it easy and if I feel I need to rest, or go home, I will." Beth was not the only one this sermon was aimed at. It was aimed at anyone who would try to smother Laura rather than allow her to manage her own life.

"Okay, okay!" said Beth. "You're fine! I know nothing! I'll just shut up!" There was a short silence. "But at least listen to Mum, Laura." Beth chimed up again. "She knows what's good for you."

"I know what's good for me better." Laura shot this back, in a will-you-for-goodness-sake-stop-trying-to-boss-me-around sort of way. She headed indoors with Emily following on her heels, only to find Nan doubled over in pain, having retreated indoors while this power struggle was going on.

"Nan! What's the matter?" Laura called over her shoulder, "Mum! It's Nan, Quick!" Laura stepped aside so Emily could pass.

"I need to go to the hospital," Nan said. "I'm sorry. I was hoping not to have to bother you."

"Oh Mum!" Then turning to Beth, Emily asked: "Why didn't you tell me?"

"I didn't know." Beth was defensive and as surprised as her mother.

"I thought it might pass," Nan said. "Sometimes it does."

Now Emily was in a pickle. She did not want to leave Laura, but she needed to take Nan to hospital for pain relief.

323

She knew Matthew was doing a presentation and would not be finished yet. *Maria and Simon have probably been working through the night, and would be right up until the wedding. Beth will have to stay with Laura. No! She's got another exam tomorrow. Who can I call?* Laura interrupted her thoughts.

"I'll be fine Mum," Laura promised. "Do what you have to do for Nan."

"You're not staying here on your own. Anything could happen."

"I don't know what the fuss is about. I'm going into work later."

"Yes, but that won't be for hours and there'll be people with you there. It's the time in-between I'm concerned about." *Think! Think!* Emily told herself.

"I can miss my exam," Beth proffered generously.

"I hope that won't be necessary," Emily said. "I have an idea." She rang Renata's mobile and Renata picked up immediately.

"Renata, are you busy?"

"Well, sort of. I'm at work, why?"

"Can you get away?" Renata picked up on the urgency in Emily's voice.

"Yes, if it's something urgent."

"Nan's in a lot of pain. I need to take her to the hospital, but I've only just brought Laura home from hospital on condition she's kept under careful supervision. She was in an armed robbery and got slugged."

"Shot! Oh no!" Renata gasped.

"No. Not shot. Bashed with the gun."

"Oh good! Oh God, I can't believe I said that. I meant not good but not dead! What happened? Why didn't you call?"

"Too many questions. Here's the question I need you to answer right now. Can you come over to stay with Laura right away? I've called an ambulance for Nan."

"I'm on my way. Go if the ambulance comes before I get there. Laura can let me in."

"Great. Thanks Renata."

"No worries."

When Nan was examined in Emergency, the registrar prescribed something for the pain, and she was taken for a scan.

"Can I go with her?" Emily asked.

"Of course," the nurse smiled. Emily sat by her mother's side waiting for the scan to be done. Then she had to wait another 3 hours for Nan's consultant to show up.

"I've been in theatre," he said, by way of apology. "How are you?" He directed his question at Nan.

"I've been better," she said as he put the negatives up to the light and studied them.

"It's not good news," he said.

"So tell me something I don't know," Nan said. "For example, will I make Christmas?" The Consultant took time considering her question, but before he could answer she said. "Okay, I get it. Let me put it this way then. Can you try your hardest to give me Christmas? My grand-daughter's getting married on Christmas day and I'd hate to spoil her big day." The doctor took a little bit longer to consider things and then came to a decision.

"We could try one more treatment," he said. "It might shrink the tumours and give you some more time. I can't make any promises, though."

"I know that. Thank you," Nan said.

"I'll get things moving then. It may take a few days to organise. I'll have to play with schedules. I'd like to keep you here until we get the pain levels sorted out."

"Done," said Nan. When the doctor had left, Nan turned to Emily.

"Now, Emily. Just for once I want you to do something for me and there is to be no argument about it."

"What?"

"I want you to go home and look after your daughter."

"I can't leave you Mum."

"I appreciate that you don't want to, love, but I don't need you. Let's get this right for once, shall we! You're Laura's mother and she needs you."

"But you're my mother and I need you." The words were out before Emily even knew she had thought them. After all the counselling Emily had undergone, after all the self-analysis, here was a truth that had never surfaced. She was dependent on her mother. Her mother was trying hard to set her free, but she was resisting. Had it always been so? Nan caught hold of Emily's hand and pulled her close. She held her face still, grasping her chin, and gazed into her eyes. Emily remembered how she used to do that when she was a child and wanted her to listen carefully. She resisted Nan's gaze.

"Look at me. No! Look at me." Emily was forced to make eye contact. "Now listen and listen well. You don't need me. You only think you do, because I've always been here. Soon I'm not going to be and you will realise how strong you are on your own. Go and get some practice in! Be there for Laura! You've been doing so well at that lately."

"Have I?"

"Of course you have. How can you possibly doubt that? Go and relieve Renata. Laura doesn't need her. She needs you. Everyone else is a poor substitute." At that moment, a man came to take Nan back to the ward. "Don't you dare follow me Emily," Nan ordered. "I mean it." Emily watched her mother being wheeled away not allowing herself to think of anything other than the words Nan had just spoken. Then she turned and made her way to the hospital car park.

When Emily arrived home, the place was empty and horribly quiet. A large A4 piece of paper near the kettle drew her attention. It said. *I rang for an ambulance. Laura unwell. Confused and vomiting! Come as soon as you can. Renata.*

326

An unexpected Diagnosis

When Emily arrived at the hospital for the second time that day, Matthew was in the Emergency waiting room, hoping Renata would bring him news of Laura soon. He told Emily what he knew.

"Renata said Laura began to complain of a terrible headache and about five minutes later she collapsed and Renata couldn't wake her up. She's having a CT scan as we speak."

Emily thought of Nan telling her to go home, that Laura needed her, and wondered where such a premonition had come from.

"I'll just go and see the nurse." Matthew couldn't help noticing how white and pinched Emily's face was. The nurse checked on Laura coming back a minute later with a smile.

"You can come through, she's just back from X-ray."

Emily was shown to Laura's cubicle.

"Here, sit down." As Renata rose to greet Emily she explained that they were waiting for a neurosurgeon's report on Laura's scan. Then she returned to Matthew.

"How are you?" Emily asked.

"I don't know. My head hurts. They've doped me up. I don't think we're meant to watch Bugsy Malone," she smiled in an attempt at bravery.

"Have they said anything yet? Is it concussion?"

"Probably. They say that might explain the headaches, but they're ruling out other possibilities, so I've just got to sit tight while they get to the bottom of it."

About a half hour later the neurosurgeon breezed in accompanied by a nurse. Opening the report on the CT scan he quickly read it. He held the images up to the light one after the other. He was grave when he turned back to Laura and Emily.

"It was probably concussion that caused your headache and the blackout. How do you feel now?"

"I feel vague, as if I'm only partly here."

"Well there's some good news and some bad news." He waited for this to sink in before continuing. "It was lucky for you that you were concussed because, if you hadn't been, we wouldn't have discovered that you have a brain tumour." Laura paled and there was a sharp intake of breath. Emily felt as if she had been hit by a four-by-two. She heard her daughter's voice as if from a long way off.

"A tumour?" Laura was shaking her head. "No! A lump, maybe - because of the dent in my skull?"

"We need to remove it as soon as possible." Laura did not miss that the neurosurgeon had come straight back to the point.

"Are you talking about cancer?" Laura was never one to hide from the hard things of life, but she sounded incredulous.

"I can't answer that at this point. We have to go in and remove it and then we'll send it off to the lab for analysis. They'll be able to tell us if it's malignant."

"But I'm young," said Laura. "I'm a police officer. I'm working tonight." It was not that she was in denial. She was just voicing the thoughts in her head.

"Have someone call work. I have a cancellation tomorrow so I can operate first thing. We'll know by the end of the week whether or not you'll need any further treatment."

"Like chemo?" Again it was Laura who asked the hard question. Emily wasn't yet able to frame a sentence.

"Yes." Said the doctor. "Exactly. Any questions?"

"What's the recovery rate for removal of a brain tumour, Doctor?" Again it was brave Laura who asked the question.

"It depends what we're dealing with. I had a very courageous young woman once who needed surgery to remove a tumour on Christmas Eve, and on Christmas Day she was sitting up in bed, with her make-up on, waiting for her family to bring in Christmas treats. She's still sending me Christmas cards and that was 20 years ago."

"I'm guessing that was a non malignant tumour?"

"Yes. Well then, I will see you tomorrow morning." Before the nurse left with the doctor she said:

"I'll leave you for a minute or two. I'm sure this has come as a shock. I'll be nearby though, so if you have any questions, or need me, just press this." She put a buzzer into Laura's hand before leaving. Finally Emily found her voice.

"I'm so sorry you are going through this Laura," she said.

"It's not your fault. In a way, the events of the last twenty-four hours might have happened for a reason because, if the tumour's malignant, better to find out now rather than when it's too late."

"Yes, you're absolutely right. When did my baby become so old, and so brave, and so wise?"

Laura put her hand to her mother's face, caressing it tenderly. "When I inherited your genes, I suppose."

"You're incredible, Laura. I'm so very proud of you." The nurse interrupted them.

"They're going to take you up to the ward now. Is there anything you want to know before you leave here?"

"Yes, heaps," said Laura. "But I don't think you have the answers yet."

"Can I stay with my daughter?" Emily asked.

"Absolutely. You can see her settled in. They put off most of the lights in the ward about now, but I'll ask the ward nurses if you can stay awhile. Just be mindful, though, that patients cope better with surgery if they get a good night's sleep."

"What time is the surgery scheduled for?" Emily asked.

"You're lucky," the nurse said turning to Laura. "You're first up. 7:00am. I hope you realise how coveted that time slot is."

"So how come I got it?" The nurse took a moment to think of an answer and in the short time it took her, Emily had worked it out. Someone died

"You must have done something to deserve it, that's all I can say, because having your surgery early has a good omen about it. Let's hope the news will be good. Now when was the last time you ate?"

"I don't know. Maybe eleven o'clock this morning."

"Good," she said as a wards-man arrived to take her to Ward 3G. The nurse wrote on Laura's file that she was nil-by-mouth and he wheeled her away, Emily gave her daughter a brave smile.

"It might take a while for her to get settled into the ward. You know how it is – there are procedures to follow. Go and have a cup of coffee and give the ward nurses a quarter of an hour. I'll tell them you will be along shortly."

"Do you think it would be alright to call in to see my mother? She's a patient here too."

"Where is she?"

"I don't know. I have to find out. She was brought in a bit earlier."

"Really? You poor thing! You're not having a good day, are you? What's wrong with her?"

"Cancer. She's not going to get better though. We're resigned to that. We're hoping for Christmas, though. My daughter's getting married on Christmas day."

"This daughter?"

"No! My eldest. Laura's a bridesmaid."

"I'll find out where your mother is and I'll ring the ward and explain. Of course they'll let you in."

"Thank you," Emily said. "That's very kind of you."

Out of the Blue

Maria and Simon called in to see Laura in the middle of the night - or so it seemed to Laura who woke up as her sister kissed her cheek.

"Hi! How are you doing?" Maria stroked her cheek.

"I'm okay. What time is it?"

"It's five o'clock. Simon and I have an early flight to Canberra but I couldn't go without seeing you. We'll be back tomorrow. I'll be in constant contact with Mum and Beth and Matthew, and I'll be loving you across the distance."

"Thanks."

"Best of luck," said Simon, coming forward a little so Laura could see him better. "We'll be thinking about you and hoping for a good outcome."

"Thanks guys. You're the best! Now go on, off with you and do whatever you have to do with the bigwigs in Canberra." Maria kissed Laura again and then she and Simon were gone, leaving Laura to wonder later on, between dozing and waking, whether she had dreamt their visit. When Emily arrived later she told Laura that the lovebirds had been unable to say goodbye to Nan because she had been in pain in the night and was sleeping when they called by. They felt it would be selfish to waken her to yet more pain.

For Emily and Matt it was a busy start to the week, for they were flat out running between wards and, for Matt, there was the need to keep reporting in to the office for things that could not wait. Nan's pain was not settling as they thought it would, so the surgeon brought her treatment forward.

Later that morning, when Laura finally woke, she opened her eyes and said "Oh good! I'm still here!" Everyone laughed out loud.

"The doctor told us everything went well. He thinks the tumour was benign and he's pretty sure he will be able to give you the all clear very soon."

"Cool," Laura smiled. "I'm indestructible."

"Talking about being indestructible, the newspapers want to do a story on you. They're calling you The Hero of Hope Street," Emily said. "I've been referring them to the station because I don't know what police protocol is."

"Seriously?" Laura was genuinely astonished. "Have you spoken to them at work?"

"I've spoken to your friend Frances. She said the Super blasted your boss. Said you were a damned young idiot, to take such a risk. But technically you acted in your own time. Of course now that the press are calling you a hero, well, apparently a bit of good press has transformed his attitude. He's been on the television singing your praises so Frances thinks your job is safe."

"I should bloody well think so," said Laura. "They can't punish me for taking a stand against crime."

"They'd better not," said a voice from the doorway. "If they do, they'll have us to content with." Everyone's eyes turned towards the speaker, a young woman, who was accompanied by a middle-aged man and woman, and two rather handsome young men. Laura looked puzzled but then it dawned on her.

"You're from the service station, right?"

"Yes." The young girl smiled without entering. "I wanted to bring you these." She was holding the biggest bunch of roses Laura had ever seen.

"Come in," Emily said getting up from her chair.

"I'm really sorry you got hurt protecting me," the young girl said.

"I'd like to say I did," Laura said. "But this…" she was pointing to her bandaged head, "…had nothing to do with the blow to my head."

332

"They found a tumour when they did the X-rays." Emily explained. "If she hadn't tackled the gunman we would never have known, and it may have killed her or caused brain damage. Anyway, I'm Emily, Laura's Mum, and this is Matthew, Laura's uncle." The girl shook Emily's outstretched hand and introduced her family – her mother, father and older brothers.

"They're twins," she explained. Just then the nurse came to the door. She beckoned to Emily who excused herself. Outside Laura's room the nurse seemed grave.

"It's your mother," she said. "Her nurses have been trying to reach you and your brother."

"What for?"

"They want you to go up there straight away."

"Oh!" Emily had not yet taken in the urgency in the nurse's voice. "I'll just go and…"

"Straight away. I'll look after Laura's visitors. Get your brother and go."

"But why? What's wrong?"

"They'll tell you when you get there." Emily turned to Matt, who was close to the doorway.

"Matthew…" she pulled at his sleeve. "We're needed in Nan's ward." He looked puzzled. "Now," Emily stressed.

"I'll be back!" he said to Laura and her visitors. Then he turned his attention to Emily.

"What's up?"

"I don't know." Emily said as they hurried away from Laura's ward. "The nurse wouldn't say. I've got such a bad feeling Matthew. Something is wrong."

"Don't imagine the worst," Matthew said, calling the lift. "They probably just need us to sign something." However, when they got to the ward, the nurse took them to an empty, quiet lounge.

"Sit down," she said. "I'll get the doctor for you right away." She turned to go but Matthew caught her arm.

"Don't go. Tell us what's up."

333

"The doctor will tell you. He'll explain things so much better than me."

In the five minutes the doctor took to get to the ward, Emily and Matthew went through a hundred possible scenarios. The minute the doctor appeared striding towards them, Emily was on her feet moving swiftly towards him.

"What?" Emily said. "I can't bear it. Tell us quickly." This left the doctor no option but to get straight to the point.

"I'm sorry. I'm afraid your mother died half an hour ago. We've been trying to locate you."

"Oh no! Don't say that!" Emily whispered. "Not that."

"I'm afraid it was her heart. She had a mild heart attack, followed by a massive one a few minutes later. I'm so sorry."

"But she has cancer!"

"She was being prepped for treatment when she had the first heart attack. We did everything we could, but when the second one came, there was nothing we could do." Emily had paled. She walked the short distance back to a chair checking her mobile phone as she went.

"We thought we should switch our mobile's off in the hospital." She said, sitting down.

"I'm sorry." The doctor repeated.

"She died on her own." Emily said, utterly shocked. Matthew put his arm around his sister, and she broke down and sobbed into his chest.

"What was the time of death?" Matthew asked.

"Ten o'clock." The Doctor said.

"Around the time Laura was waking up," Emily said, still enfolded in Matthew's strong arms. She turned her head staring into the distance, to the river beyond the highway. "While Nan's life was ending, life was going on as normal. I never imagined such a thing on a beautiful morning like this."

"I want to see her," Matthew said.

"Of course. Maybe you should have a cup of tea first. I'll tell the nurse to bring you one."

"No! Thank you."

"Well take a moment to let your sister get used to the shock. If we can help in any way, the nurses are trained..."

"Of course. Thanks." Matthew watched the doctor retreat and didn't envy him his job. When he turned on his mobile phone he saw all the missed calls. He ignored them and phoned the only person he wanted to talk to at that moment.

"Renata. Can you come to the hospital? Bad news I'm afraid."

"Oh no. Poor Laura..."

"No, not Laura. Nan."

"Nan?" Renata's voice held a multitude of questions. "What do you mean?"

"There's no easy way to say this, Renata so I'm just going to say it. She died a short while ago." There was a gasp, followed by a long silence, until Renata broke it.

"I'm so sorry Matthew. I'll be right there."

"Thanks," he said gratefully.

Matthew called Beth next. She was cramming for her Exam.

"Beth, can you come to the hospital? There's good news about Laura but bad news about Nan, I'm afraid." Beth was sensitive enough to know that Matthew would never call her away from an exam unless it was something really urgent.

"Is the cancer more advanced that we thought?"

"It's not that," Matthew said. "It's... I'm afraid she's... It was a heart attack. She died about half an hour ago."

"Oh No!"

"We were with Laura. Our mobiles were off. We were only a stone's throw away and they couldn't reach us." Matthew heard a small sob and then Beth's voice came again, tight with emotion.

"Does Maria know?"

"No. I'm just about to phone her."

"I'll come straight to the hospital."

"Good. See you soon."

335

As Matthew was phoning Maria, Beth phoned Mikey. He called the office to ask for time off, and picked her up a quarter of an hour later. She was waiting for him at the kerbside.

"I'm so sorry." He wrapped her diminutive body in his strong arms and let her cry. "We'll get through it together," he promised. After a while she pulled away from him.

"I need to get to the hospital – to my family."

"Of course." Mikey gently kissed Beth's tears, and then applied himself to the task of delivering her into the heart of her family, where he knew she would find comfort.

Matthew could not break the news to Maria gently. She was in Canberra on really important business and only the truth would bring her home.

"It's Nan," Matthew said. "She had a heart attack."

"Is she okay?"

"No Maria. She didn't make it." He didn't miss the sob as Maria drew breath.

Maria and Simon were with Rick Walters when Maria took the call. She would have normally let the call go onto voicemail, but prior to ringing, Matthew had sent her a text to say he would ring again in ten minutes, and that she must pick up because it was very urgent. Maria, Simon and Rick had just been in conference with a variety of Government personnel, their aides, and ARC representatives, who had responded well to the proposals, put forward by Chadwick and Stevens, the architects appointed to do the feasibility study of the Boondall site. There were other meetings to attend, but when Rick Walters heard the sad news, he sent Maria home right away, saying he could manage with Simon, who would be home the following day, in time for the funeral. Maria did not argue. By the time she got back to her room she had already changed her flight. She threw her belongings into her travel bag ready to meet the taxi Simon had arranged for her. She arrived back in Brisbane on the six o'clock flight, and as soon as she could, flipped open her mobile.

336

"Where are you Mum?"

"I'm at the hospital with Laura."

"I'll be there in half an hour." The heat hit her when she left the airport building the temperature being way above average for the time of year. There was a long queue but the taxis were lined up in single file, and it wasn't long before she was heading straight to the Royal. By the time she arrived, Nan had been transferred to the morgue. Maria, finding Renata waiting for her outside the entrance to the hospital, threw herself into the older woman's arms and finally allowed her tears to flow freely.

"I can't believe it. I was so sure she'd be at my wedding." Maria sobbed.

"I know." Renata said simply. "I know." They sat down in the hospital foyer until Maria's tears had settled and then Renata said: "Do you want to see her? If you do I'll go with you."

"No. I've thought about it and I'd rather remember her as she was." Maria said.

"Your Mum and Beth are with Laura. Matthew's taking care of the arrangements."

"Poor Uncle Matt. He's always taking care of us. Nan was his mother. Who's going to take care of him?"

"I'll take care of him, Maria. Don't worry. Being practical is what helps him cope." Maria threw her arms around Renata, and allowed herself to sob again. When the convulsions had eased she wiped her face and said:

"I'm alright now. I'd like to see my family. Let's go to the ward."

Arrangements

Nan died on Tuesday and was cremated on Friday. The following Monday Beth offered to sort through Nan's things. Mikey, who was on a late shift, did not want to leave her alone with such a sad task, so he decided it would be a good day to fix the hole in the boat. Matthew's plans for a day on the River with Renata had not yet eventuated because of the busyness surrounding Nan's death, and Mikey had been asked to do extra shifts to cover for sick colleagues. But now work had returned to normal and he could use some of the time he had accumulated to be with Beth while, at the same time, allowing her the space to grieve.

Nan's house was empty and quiet because Emily was spending a few days at Laura's to ensure there were no repercussions from her surgery. They were finally watching Bugsy Malone.

Matthew was attending to the formalities of death, wanting to lift this burden from Emily, who had dedicated the last few months to caring for their mother. Nor did he want Maria and Simon to be burdened with it when they were already so busy.

"I appreciate your consideration, Matthew," Maria said. Maria rang her mother next. "But what about you, Mum? It must be awful for you."

"No, I'm fine." Emily asserted. "I'm handling it. Nan and I made our peace in the end. It's a comfort."

"Okay. If you are sure you don't need me."

"I don't, and you have enough to do."

Matthew called in on Emily and Laura on his way back home late that afternoon.

"Are you getting through it all?" Emily asked.

"Yes. I've done all the immediate things. Mum left a checklist, would you believe. It's from a government website and it tells you what to do when someone dies. She had everything we need to do listed – even phone numbers, so we wouldn't have to go looking for them. There's a will, Em. Did you know that?"

"No."

"I've been to Mum's solicitors. She left us the house. We'll need to decide what to do with it. Do you want to live in it?"

"No. I've got my own place."

Laura was the last of Emily's daughters to move out when she scored her first job, and Emily, now that she was earning good money, had bought a low-maintenance home in an old suburb, not far from her mother's, and near enough to the University that she could walk to work.

"I wouldn't mind living at Mum's. How would you feel about me buying you out?"

"Yes. No problem. We'd have to have it valued."

"Yes."

"You know what Matthew, I'm glad you want it because then we can still visit, and it will put you at the heart of the family where you deserve to be. I think Mum would have approved. I'm surprised, though. I thought you were happy with your own place."

"I am. But it is a nice family house." It was a surprising statement for Matthew to make and it fuelled his sister's curiosity.

"Are you thinking of getting married?"

"No. Not yet anyway. Maybe never, or maybe down the track. Just don't mention it to Renata because we haven't discussed it. I'm sure it's the last thing on her mind at the moment, and I don't want to frighten her off by rushing things. Women aren't the only ones with hopes and dreams," he added when he saw Emily's smile.

"She's lovely Matt. We all love her."

"I know. So do I."

"But I don't understand. What will you do with your place?"

"I'd like to sell it and do Nan's up. Or maybe I'll rent it out."

"When would you have time for renovations? You're already working seven days a week."

"Yes, but that's because I've been getting ready to start my own consultancy. I'm hoping, when I do, to work only a couple of days a week. The rest of the week I can spend improving Nan's house, thereby increasing its value. You know how much I like messing with wood."

"Yes," Emily agreed. "You're like Dad that way. Oh by the way, Mikey's fixing the hole in the boat today."

"I didn't know it needed repair." So followed Beth and Mikey's holey boat adventure.

"So make sure to take the life jackets with you when you go out in it with Renata."

"Actually, I was going to talk to you about that. You know how Mum and Dad loved the river? Well, we have to decide what to do with her ashes."

"And you want to scatter her ashes on the river, do you?" Matthew nodded.

"What do you think?"

"It seems like the most appropriate option."

"The trouble is we can't all get into The Duck Boat, so I was wondering if, on Sunday, you and I could take Mum's ashes up to The Venus Pool, where Mum and Dad saw the black swans. I thought it would be significant to scatter them there."

"Have you checked if it's legal?"

"Who's to know? I'm not telling anyone."

" I think it's a great idea, but what about the girls? If we do that they can't be there and I don't like the idea of leaving them on their own on the bank at such a sad time." They fell silent for a while. Finally she concluded: "You know what I think? I think Nan would have liked you and Renata to do it. I

340

think she would have liked the idea of me staying behind with my girls, waving her off."

"Are you sure?"

"Yes. I'll talk to the girls about it though. See what they think. But just be aware that the swans may not be there. Nan always thought they might have just rested there on the way elsewhere."

"It doesn't matter." Matthew said. "It was a lovely memory for her, and I always think Dad's in the river. I know he went missing in the bay, but the tide comes and goes up and down the river. Since we can't bury them together, let's at least make sure they're close to each other. I like to think maybe they'll find each other somehow. It's crazy, I know, but it's how I feel."

"You're right. I think it's a lovely idea. The girls might want to hire canoes, in which case I could travel with you and Renata. Let's see what they say. It'd be nice to think we were sending her on her way back to Dad."

Tom and Jerry

It was hard to imagine there was to be a wedding in a little over a month. The dressmaker was the first to intrude on the family's grief. She telephoned to say that the bridesmaids needed to come in for a fitting. Laura was reluctant because her hair now sported a bald spot, giving the impression that she had a bad attack of the mange.

"Nobody's going to be worried about that," said Emily.

"I will be," protested Laura. Emily thought about this for a while and then had an idea.

"If you could go any colour you wanted, what colour would you like your hair to be?"

"Purple."

"No. Being serious."

"I am being serious."

"Okay, let me put it this way. If you could go any colour you wanted, bearing in mind that you are a police officer, who has to front up to her boss, what colour would you choose?"

"I'd absolutely love to front up to the boss with purple hair," admitted Laura. "But I'd probably be penalised. Let's see... blonde." She finally concluded. "But a silvery blonde, rather than a brassy yellow one."

Emily had a colleague whose daughter was a wig maker. Somewhere between Laura and the bathroom, Emily dialled her number.

"Hi Rosy." She spoke softly. "Is there any chance you can get hold of a blonde wig for Laura."

"Long or short?"

"Better make it longish... no make it shortish..."

"Let's say shoulder length," said Rosy.

"Terrific. You can get me on my mobile. I'm staying at Laura's. Did you hear she was hurt in an armed robbery? Not badly thankfully."

"Yes. There was a photo of her in the local rag."

"Was there? I didn't know that. Which one?"

"You probably won't get it now unless you go to the library. The story's a few days old. I'll see if I've still got it and I'll drop it in later when I bring the wig."

"Thanks."

"Did you know that the story of the robbery was in the Newspaper?" Emily asked Laura.

"Yes. And my photograph."

"How did the press get a photograph?" Emily asked.

"I gave them one – well, I should say I gave Tom and Gerry one."

"Tom and Gerry?" Emily's tone had shifted from surprise, to puzzlement.

"They're Daffy's brothers." Emily continued to appear nonplussed. "The twins," Laura said as if it were obvious.

"Oh you mean the brothers of the girl whose life you saved?"

"Well, I wouldn't put it that way, but yes."

"Are they really called Tom, Gerry and Daffy?

"Mm." Laura replied.

"And are their father and mother called Mickey and Minnie?" Laura burst out laughing.

"That's funny Mum."

"It's not. The poor kids! Fancy calling their kids names like that?"

"Relax, Mum. They're just names I call them. Daffy isn't her real name. It's Belinda." Emily thought about asking what the connection between the two names was, but then decided to let it go. She was more interested in the newspaper article.

"So, where did they get a photo of you?" Laura's mobile was on the bed and she waved it in front of her mother's nose.

"Of course," Emily said. "Can I be the last person to see it?"

"I would have shown it to you if I had it, but I didn't take it. Tom took it. He's just set himself up as a freelance

343

photographer – a very cute one, in my opinion. He asked me if he could photograph me because it would really help his career if he got the only photo anyone had managed to get. He also wrote the story. As a result, the editor says that he'll keep him in mind for their overflow and employ him freelance, which is just what he wanted."

"What about the other one - Gerry. What does he do?"

"He's even more cute. He's a light bender."

"Oh yes!" Emily grunted. "Sidekick to Luke Skywalker, I suppose!"

"Ha Ha!" Laura exclaimed, sarcastically "A light bender is someone who makes bright, flashing neon signs. He says he loves it because it's very creative."

"Well, to me, it sounds like he belongs in Star Wars. Anyway, how do you know so much about these twins?"

"I don't, but I'd like to know more. I swapped emails with Daffy and the whole family now emails me, especially Gerry. When you're a legend everyone wants to know you!"

Old Bags

Mikey interrupted Beth who was sorting through Nan's stuff.

"I don't suppose you know if Nan had any old paint pots left over from when the boat was painted?"

"No. I don't. Wait a minute! Maybe there are some in the shed." Beth had been ruthlessly piling unwanted garments on Nan's bed. "I'd like to get rid of Mount Kosciusko," she said indicating the huge mound of clothes. "I'm running out of space." Pointing to a high shelf she bargained. "If you'll get that big suitcase down for me, I'll have a look for some paint for you."

"No worries," said Mikey, easily lifting the suitcase down.

"Thanks," Beth said.

"Where do you want it?"

"On the bed."

"Oh! You want it on the bed, do you," Mikey joked suggestively.

"Keep thinking about paint Cassanova!" Beth said, giving him the brush off. "I've got to get these clothes packed and into suitcases before anyone can get near the bed."

"So do you want the other suitcases too? Mikey asked.

She nodded her head as she threw pillows on the floor.

"I knew it would come to this," Mikey said, pretending to be dismal. "You'd rather…"

"Paint!" Beth interrupted, striding off along the corridor. Mikey followed her down the stairs and under the house to a place near the back door where keys hung on a brass hook. "Here it is lover boy," she said, giving him a peck. It was all the encouragement he needed. He wrapped her in his arms and she melted, for five seconds, against his naked upper torso She could feel his arousal, further south. "Later," she said teasingly, giving his crotch an unexpected poke that made him jump.

"Ouch!" he said. But she had taken off down the garden. Mikey followed on, and by the time he caught up with her she had opened the shed door and was rummaging inside. She negotiated the lawn mower that hadn't been used since Grandpa Doug had last mown the lawn, because Nan had always got someone in to do it.

"There are old paint cans along the back wall. You'll be lucky though. They've probably gone off by now." Choosing one with paint runs similar to the colour of the boat, Beth handed it back to Mikey, staying where she was in case she needed to hand him another. Mikey found a large screwdriver on the shadow wall and prized the lid open. There was a hard skin half way down the tin.

"Looks like you might be right." However he managed to pierce the skin several times with the screwdriver, the end of which was now aquamarine. "There's some left. It'll do the job. I only need a bit."

They each returned to their separate jobs, Mikey to sand and paint, and Beth to fill not one, but four suitcases. Completing this job she shut the wardrobe doors and started on the chest of drawers. She found Nan had an extraordinary amount of baggy old knickers. She allocated them to the rubbish. Bras were a different matter. They were in good condition and some of them beautiful and hardly worn. *Mum might be able to use those*, she thought looking at the labels for sizes. Opening Nan's pyjama drawer she found a stack of beautiful nightdresses. Nan had always preferred them to pyjamas. There were one or two that had been bought for Nan's birthday, a few months before. There were a few in smaller sizes than the rest, because Nan had lost weight as her disease progressed. Beth chose an aquamarine one that **she** had bought, and particularly liked, and putting it aside, decided to try it on later.

346

In the bottom drawer she found all sorts of everything, flimsy georgette scarves and the serviceable thick woolly shawls Nan wore 'to keep the life in me' in the winter, when she would often complain of 'cold in the bones'. In the same deep drawer, she uncovered a large box marked 'treasures'. She opened it briefly and saw it contained bits of old toys, baby clothes, birthday cards, and drawings. She set this aside so she could look at it when the room was less messy.

In the trunk, at the bottom of Nan's bed, that had once been used to store their fancy dress clothes, Beth found lots of handbags. There was no point in keeping them. Beth piled them up besides the suitcases. She would find a bin bag to put them in later so they would be easier to transport to the local op shop. She began to sort Nan's shoes, binding them into pairs with strong rubber bands. Some of them were almost new. *Shame* she thought. *But I don't know anyone who would wear them.* Nan had suffered with her feet and so she always bought good ones. Beth couldn't think who would want them, but nevertheless, she piled them up beside the handbags. Finally, she took the nightdress she had set apart, and tried it on.

When Mikey came in an hour or so later, he found her asleep on Nan's bed, still wearing it, and looking beautifully seductive.

"Well look at you," he said spooning himself around her. "Mind if I join you."

"It's the heat," she said. "It always makes me sleepy in the early part of the afternoon."

"You stay there and rest, then. I'll take all this stuff to the op shop if you like. Just be there when I get back, right?"

"Right!" Beth said yawning. "Did I tell you that you make me feel cherished?"

While Mikey moved the suitcases to the car, Beth drifted back to sleep. He found empty cartons downstairs and put the handbags in one, but not before going through them. In one he found $300. In another a pair of sapphire earrings, and in another some bits and pieces, including a prayer book, a rosary, a small crucifix on a cord and a larger crucifix. He quietly crept upstairs and placed these items on Nan's bedside table, throwing the shoes into another box that he also took downstairs. Slipping out quietly he loaded up the car, before letting it freewheel backwards down the sloping drive, so he would not awaken Beth.

"Thank you dear," the op shop lady said.

"Thank YOU," Mikey said. "I hope they're of some use."

"Just look at all these shoes. I'll phone the old folks home right away. They're really good leather, and they're always coming in looking for decent shoes like these. By the time they're old, most of them have got dickey feet. They'll think it's Christmas."

"Well it will be soon," Mikey said with a wave of his hand.

Mikey stole back into the house and slipped onto the bed besides Beth. He didn't wake her up. He decided to enjoy the feel of her as he fitted himself around her again. It wasn't long before he was snoring so much that he woke her up anyway. She got up, leaving him there, intending to find a book so she could read until he woke up, when she noticed the items on the bedside table. It was the wad of money that first caught her eye and she wondered where it had come from. The sapphire earrings were just studs, but Nan never bought junk jewellery. In fact she never bought jewellery full stop. They must have been a gift – maybe from Grandpa Doug.

She wondered if the rosary, and the small crucifix on a cord had belonged to Nan's life as a nun. *I wonder what this was for. It's a bit too big to wear.* She was, in fact holding the larger crucifix. She felt sad, thinking, *I'll never be able to ask Nan now*, but wondering, more optimistically, if her mother might know. She opened the prayer book and flicked through the pages. There were a few pictures of various Saints slotted between the pages, but slipped between the last page and the cover was a stiff card, rather battered at the edges where it stuck out of the prayer book because it was bigger than it. It was Red with Royal Blue rays fanning out from the left hand corner. Written on the red rays were the words:

Magical Mystery Tour Fancy Dress Party,
Thursday 23rd December
7:45pm,
Royal Lancaster Hotel Bayswater Road,
Entrance to Westbourne Suite,
Telephone 262 6786,
No admittance without this card.

Beth was still holding it a few minutes later when Mikey woke up.

"Did you put the nightdress on for me?" he asked. "You suit that colour."

"Not really," she said distractedly.

"Oh! Okay. Any chance of a cup of tea then?" he asked, deflated.

"I'll make one." She said, deep in thought before she asked. "Mikey, do you know anything about all this stuff?"

"Yes. I found them in the handbags you were throwing out."

"You're kidding!" she said.

"My police training, I suppose. Always check out handbags! We never usually find money though, because that's usually gone by the time we get them. There was three hundred dollars in one of them."

"I didn't even think to search them," Beth said. "I don't have anything valuable so I don't think about such things. I wonder if this is a real ticket to the Magical Mystery Tour Fancy Dress Party. Maybe she really did go to it."

"Don't be daft! She was a nun," Mikey said.

"Well, where did this come from if she never went?"

"I don't know. But it's not the real deal, I can tell you that."

"How?"

"Because the real deal's probably in private collections all over the world."

"You're probably right." Nevertheless Beth made up her mind to see if there were any photos of the 'real deal' on the Internet.

"I wonder… I suppose I should have checked the pockets of the clothes you took to the op shop?"

"I didn't check any pockets. I didn't even open the cases. I just left them and said we'd call back for the suitcases."

"I think I'll telephone them and ask them to check," Beth said. "I can tell them to keep the suitcases at the same time."

"Are you going to leave that nightdress on, because, if so we might be about to have our first row. It's not fair to tease."

"I'm sorry," she said going into his arms. "I was just trying to figure stuff out." A few seconds later she said: "Mikey! I thought you said you liked me in this nightdress?"

"I do!" He smiled. "But I like you even better without it."

A Box of Memories

After the fitting for the bridesmaids' dresses on Saturday, at which point Maria returned Nan's wedding outfit and picked up her wedding dress, Emily suggested that the girls go back to Nan's to pick up anything they particularly wanted. Beth had cleared out most of Nan's clothes, but there was still favourite bits and pieces, items of jewellery, photographs and bric-a-brac.

The tiny teapots, it was agreed, should stay at Nan's for when the family gathered there.

"Matthew and I don't want much," said Emily. "Just some photos and some of Dad's paintings. But we don't have to rush all the other stuff that's at Nan's. As for Nan's memorabilia, well you said you wanted it, so you can sort through it all and keep what you want. You can take the rest to the op shop. I can help with that if you need me, or with anything you are unsure of."

The girls decided to make an occasion of it by having the usual tea ceremony. Then they opened the first box. It contained souvenirs of their childhood.

"I remember making this when I was about two year's old," Laura giggled. Of course she had been much older but they were in a playful mood.

"I remember that!" said Maria. "You said it was a fairy." It was, in fact, a stick figure, made out of Paddle Pop sticks with a paper dress stuck on it and wild hair made out of wool.

"Look at this!" Beth said. "She kept my snowman." Beth, being sentimental, was touched. Maria found a picture she had drawn of a hairy-faced Nan. She was quite mortified. "Why would she keep that? I turned her into a werewolf!"

"Look at this," Laura said. "It's rude." It was a Valentine card and it said: 'To the Lovely Lady.' When you opened it up it said 'You turn me wild with excitement!' It featured a naked

351

man with a bit of string attached to his penis, in such away that when you opened the card, it stood to attention.

"Oooaah!" Laura said, just as she used to when she was a child and saw something rude. "Who do you think sent it? And why did Nan keep it?"

"If she kept a drawing of herself as a werewolf, I think she'd just about keep anything." Maria said. Beth concluded that Grandpa Doug must have sent it, but Laura disagreed.

"Grandpa Doug would never send that."

"Why not? You know how good he was at cartooning," Maria said.

"Here's another one… and another one…"

"Look at this one. It must have been Grandpa. Maybe he gave her this one the year he tiled the floor downstairs. It's the same sort of tile. What's written on it? Can you make it out? It's a bit faded and smudged. It must have been done years ago"

"I can read some of it," said Beth. It says:

Let me be your Valentile
Lay me any time you like
But don't leave me Flat
Or Walk all over me

"I can't make out the rest."

"Give it here," Laura said. She puzzled over it for a moment and then she read:

Let us lie side by side
Forever cemented
By our love
Without a
Groutch between us

They all agreed it was Grandpa Doug's silly sort of humour.

"Wouldn't you love it, though, if some man gave you something as personal or as fun as that for Valentine's Day?" Maria asked. Beth was the most surprised.

"I didn't know Grandpa Doug was sentimental. I always thought he was far too shy to be really affectionate."

"He was always very affectionate with us," Maria remembered. "Maybe it was because we were children. I bet he wasn't shy when he and Nan were on their own together."

"Obviously not," said Beth.

"I feel like we're violating their privacy," Laura's job made her consider protocols.

"No. Don't feel like that," Beth said. "Nan and Grandpa Doug are dead and these things tell us more about them. If Nan hadn't wanted people to find them she wouldn't have left them here. I think it's all very sweet."

"It's gross," said Laura.

"It certainly shows a side of them that we never knew about," Maria agreed.

"You know the thing about these Valentines is that they all have one thing in common? They are all addressed To the Lovely Lady and they are all signed Your Secret Admirer." Beth said. "It's so romantic. Imagine being married and your husband pretends to be a secret admirer just to make you feel good."

"What all these souvenirs say, though, is, no matter how well you know someone, you really don't know them completely. I mean everyone inhabits their own secret, private world, don't they?"

"Yes, and Nan's was peopled by some very unusual people." said Maria.

"Well, I don't know about that. Maybe we would all be surprised if we knew what went on in each other's mind.

"I'm not telling you what goes on in mine," said Beth. "It's X rated. Anyway, maybe people's secret worlds are what make them extraordinary."

"Well, this is all getting too deep for me," Laura got up and took her cup to the sink. "I've seen enough of Nan's private world, for one day. I'm going to walk up to the shop. Does anyone want anything?"

"Do you want me to drive you up there?" Maria asked, suddenly concerned.

"No, I'm fine. It's only a five-minute walk, and I've been cooped up far too long. It will be good to stretch my legs."

"We'll both come with you," said Beth.

"Oh for goodness sake, I'm fine," argued Laura "Please! Just let me get on with the rest of my life. Anyway, you should stay and carry on going through these things. You enjoy it more than me."

"Actually, I should be getting back. I'm snowed under," Maria said, getting up too.

"Is it all getting a bit much?" Beth asked.

"Oh no! I love it. It's just busy. I'd love to sit and go through everything, but I just can't. I hereby leave all the Beatles memorabilia to you two as I can't see myself having time for it for years."

"I don't particularly see me doing anything with it either," Laura said. "I wouldn't mind some of Nan's sixties music. At the same time, I don't want your student mates wrecking it."

"Actually, I'm going to move into Nan's room," Beth said. I've got plans for Nan's stuff. But if ever you want any of it, it's yours too. I'll sort of be the guardian of it, if that's okay. I'll look after anything that's valuable, like the Magical Mystery Tour Fancy Dress Party invitation, and George's autograph."

"Brilliant," said Maria. "Saves me worrying about it. I'll let you know when the dresses are ready."

"Bye Boo," said Beth kissing Maria's cheek. "Bye Boo Boo Boo," she said, kissing Laura.

"Bye Boo Boo," they said returning the kiss, and leaving her alone with her dreams.

354

The Venus Pool

From the cliff top overlooking the river Emily sat, gazing in awe at its glowing golden transparency. The sun was full on it but not in a sparkling way. She struggled for a word to describe it. *Glorious,* she decided at last. She had never seen the Brisbane River looking so transparently glorious.

It's the drought, she thought. *There's no silt running into it to muddy it.* It was so clear she could even see the weeds growing in the riverbed being pulled and stretched by the tidal flow and even the colours of the rocks and fish. She made up her mind to paint the scene in the days following the scattering of Nan's ashes. Down in the translucent water she would paint a form, to symbolise her mother. She would embed all her fondest memories in the painting, along with the hope that her mother would be reunited with her Dad, in peace. She sat for a few minutes trying to engrave the scene into a detailed memory. She thought about the scattering of Nan's ashes again and was glad the girls had agreed that Matthew and Renata should perform this task.

"I felt like I said goodbye to her when we were going through her belongings," Beth said.

"I don't want to say goodbye to her," Maria said. "It's too final when she's so alive in my memory."

Laura just said "It's okay with me."

Emily drove down to the boat ramp where the family had agreed to meet. She was the first to arrive, followed a minute later by Matthew and Renata.

Shortly after Maria, Simon and Laura arrived and, entrusting the urn containing Nan's ashes to Emily, Matthew and Renata began to untie the ropes that fastened The Duck Boat securely to the top of Matthew's car.

When Beth and Mikey arrived soon afterwards, Matthew said:

"You did a good job of repairing the hole in the boat, mate."

"Do you know your way to the Venus Pool, Matthew?" Emily asked.

"Good question. I couldn't find anything about it on the Internet. However, I remembered that Mum used to write about their trips on the river in outdated A4 sized diaries. I found a stash of them in a trunk under the house. Renata's got the one with The Venus Pool trip in it! She's going to guide me.

Beth's ears had pricked up at the mention of Nan's diaries and she interrupted her work of fitting the detachable seats into the boat.

"Can I have them?"

"If you want them." Frankly, Emily couldn't see what Beth would want with them.

Beth and Mikey positioned the beanbag, and stowed the life jackets.

"Have you got a picnic?" They asked.

"Of course," Renata said. "I went to a delicatessen on the way and got some lovely treats."

"Ooh! What did you get?" Beth asked.

"Smoked salmon and cream cheese focaccia. Some dates, cherries and nougat, for dessert."

"We should have got some beer," Matthew said.

"I got pomegranate juice, and lots of bottles of spring water. I thought about beer but alcohol dehydrates you."

"Nan would be proud of you. She always said you can never take enough water on the river," chuckled Beth.

Emily held the urn containing Nan's ashes until the boat was ready for launching. Then Matthew took it from her and, when Renata had finished settling herself on the beanbag, entrusted it to her. Matthew, bare-footed in the shallow water, pushed off and then leapt into the boat. Settling onto a seat in the middle of the boat, he locked the oars into the rowlocks and began to pull. The Duck Boat moved away into the

356

current where it gathered speed. It was a silent group that watched Nan take her final journey. Nan's daughter and grand daughters watched until the boat turned a bend and was lost to view and then spent a quiet, thoughtful hour together. Emily had brought flasks of boiling water and an assortment of teas. Beth had brought the tiny teapots. They clinked their cups together and sent a blessing Nan's way before going their separate ways. Beth would go home to have a break from sorting. Mikey and Laura were rostered on at work. Simon and Maria had to fly to Canberra again for a meeting the following morning. They would fly out later that day because they wanted some free time to explore Canberra – a welcome break from the long hours they had been working. Emily would go to the art shop to buy materials. She was glad that she had made the decision not to join Matthew and Renata because she knew that the new painting would put her in touch with her feelings in a way that was more significant for her. On the river Renata and Matthew made progress.

"Isn't it peaceful?" Renata said delighted by glimpses of wildlife she had not expected to see. "Do you know what that bird is?" She asked.

"A spoonbill," Matthew remembered after a moment or two of searching his memory. "It is peaceful," he agreed. "Mum and Dad used to say that they might be the only people ever to have explored the entire Brisbane River and its creeks in a rowing-boat. Mum loved the creeks best. She said they had obviously been landscaped by God, because nothing manmade could be that perfect."

The sun was warm on Renata and she was glad of the umbrella for the shade it would give her when it blazed more intensely. For now she enjoyed its warm caress. They played lizard spotting until Matthew spoke.

"Better check Mum's diary so we know what to look out for."

"You can't go wrong, Matthew," she argued. "There's only one way to go."

"I know, but read it anyway. It seems the right thing to do somehow since we are going to scatter Mum's ashes."

"Yes," Renata agreed. "It looks like she scribbled some notes while she was out on the river and then wrote it up again later, because there is a second description, and the scribbled notes are crossed out. The second account is much fuller than the first. I'll read it. Here we go."

The river is particularly beautiful today, as if it has captured the golden sun giving it a transparency that enables you to see what is normally invisible below the surface. The river has two colours - deep green in the shadows, and bright gold when the sun shines on it unhindered. There isn't a strong current and so it should be easy rowing for Doug. Up ahead I can see two high rocks. They remind me of an ancient myth about someone who had to work out a riddle while passing between rocks such as these. If you could answer the riddle correctly, your life would be spared. If you answered them wrongly you would be struck dead. Furthermore in successfully passing beyond them, you would find treasure or wisdom or whatever your heart yearned for. As we draw close, they are towering over us, and the entrance between them narrows. The river bends, so we cannot see what is ahead. Now the passage through is even narrower and overhung with trees. Branches brush against us as we slowly work our way through.

Oh but my! There is a wonderful surprise. We have come into a widening - a transformation of the river. Indeed, it is now less like a river, and more like a tranquil lake hemmed in by banks and cliffs, and hidden by trees. Afloat on its surface, so dense that we have to inch our way forward so as not to hurt them, is a flotilla of black swans. There must be a hundred or more of them. Doug has stowed his oars in order to observe the spectacle. Floating beside the swans, like tugs among ocean liners, are countless ducks and moor hens. I cannot help but feel it is a holy place – a sanctuary. We gape in wonder.

We realise we are not welcome. The swans begin to honk. This increases in volume until it is quite frightening, but it is not until they start to fly over our heads that we feel really threatened. War has been declared and the swans are bombing us.

'Let's get out of here!' We say as one. They are warning us. Their body language is hostile and I have heard tell that the beat of a swan's wings could break a neck.

My spine tingles. Hairs stand up on my skin. Sweat, more than is caused by the heat of the day, drips from my brow onto my paper. We retreat, and once through the greenery that protects their sanctuary from the world outside, the noise subsides. We are thankful to have escaped the wrath of nature.

It dawns on us that the lake of swans is not on the main drag of the river. A piece of land sticks out on the left hand side of the bank forming a small peninsula, and we rowed to the left of it instead of keeping to the right - a simple mistake if one does not know the river. We are glad of our error – to have witnessed this truly awesome spectacle.

We find our way back to the main drag and continue our journey in silence - thinking, reviewing. There are gardens overlooking the river, and we wonder if the residents can see this spectacle from their backyards.

Perhaps nobody knows about the swans. Maybe they are hidden by the overhanging trees, bordering the river, Doug suggests.

Renata closed the diary.

"Do you think the swans were migrating?" Renata asks. "I'm afraid to hope to see them in case I am disappointed."

"Maybe they stopped for a rest. Or maybe this is somewhere they settle to lay and hatch their young."

"We'll know soon enough because the great entrance rocks are ahead. I wonder whether Nan was likening them to the Oracle at Delphi when she mentions them in her diary?" Matthew turned to see them.

"Wow! It reminds me of a scene in the Lord of the Rings where the hobbits are sailing down a river."

"It's a pity you can't see where you're going when you're rowing," said Renata.

359

"Dad sometimes used to turn round and paddle as if he were in a canoe. The Duck Boat's a bit wide for that but you can do it for a short while." Matthew made the turn as he spoke. "Dad also used to say that rowing on the river is like a metaphor for life."

"How so?" Renata asked.

"Well, like life, you can't see where you're going. You can only see where you've been, so you need a good woman to guide you."

"Ah! I like that metaphor," Renata said with a smile.

"Well, here we are. I wonder if this is where your Mum and Dad found an opening into what Nan describes as the lake." The branches did indeed thin out enough to let them through, but they did not see any swans. "Nevertheless it is idyllic," Renata said, "and it guards the secret of the swans. What a beautiful place to scatter Nan's ashes. I think she would approve. Here you are, Cushla." She handed him the urn, tears springing to her eyes now that the time for goodbye had come. She had only known Nan a short time, but it was long enough for them to grow on each other.

"Thank you," Matthew said, gravely, taking the urn. He took off the lid and looked inside. Scooping up a handful of ashes he scattered them gently on the water where they floated for a while, until he ruffled the surface and they sank. Then he tipped the rest, very slowly, into the water.

"Goodbye Mum," Matthew said. "I hope you find Dad and the peace you both deserve. And I hope you see lots of friendly black swans wherever you are."

"Wouldn't it be lovely to come back here from time to time?" Renata said, as they paddled back through the sacred waters of Nan's resting place.

"I'd like that," said Matthew. "Would you like to go on further?" asked Matthew.

"I'm happy to go on, but you're the one rowing. Shall we go on for a while and then, when you feel like a break, we can stop and have some pomegranate juice and read what Nan has to say about the rest of their journey upstream?" So, later, while they ate nougat and dates, Renata read that Nan and Doug had gone upstream as far as College's Crossing.

"College's Crossing is worth seeing," said Matthew. "We used to swim there when we were kids. It's very popular."

"What are we waiting for then?" Renata opened Nan's diary again and perused it. "Mind you, it says here there's a natural barrier on the way where the water becomes too shallow to pass because of the gravel that has built up there. It says that your Dad had to haul The Duck Boat over it... and later on there's a large pipe that crosses the river. They had to lie down in the boat to go under that."

"Mmm! I suppose it all depends on how high or low the tide is, and whether there has been much rain recently."

"It never stopped Nan and your Dad though. Maybe they had such lovely experiences because they weren't daunted by the obstacles."

"The Duck Boat isn't that heavy. If I do have to haul it up onto the bank to get past the pipe, I reckon I could do it."

"Yay!" Renata packed up the picnic and soon they were away again.

Honouring Nan

Each dealt with their grief in different ways. Some of them had people to fill the void. Simon and Maria, for example, found solace in each other. It was true that Maria was devastated that Nan was not going to be at her wedding. Nevertheless the happy day came and went with joy, and there was comfort in knowing Nan no longer suffered. Maria and Simon were big-hearted people. They let go of Nan and concentrated on serving the common good. On the day of the wedding Emily walked her daughter down the aisle and said.

"Nan would have been so proud of you, Maria."

"I know," Maria said. "But now it's your turn to be proud."

As for Matthew and Renata, well they also found comfort in one another. Their life settled into comfortable togetherness and separateness, until they married five years later and Matthew's dreams were fulfilled. Matthew the mathematician now had time for making furniture. Renata, the scientist, took pleasure, in filling her free time with simple activities, which she researched extensively before taking up.

"Look," she said, one day.

"What is it?" Matthew was glad of her broaching the subject because he had been puzzled by her endeavours.

"A sock. It's knitting." Matthew smiled indulgently.

"Learning basic skills is a good thing to do." Renata enthused. "You never know when knitting might be useful. Ghandi believed in learning basic skills. He even made the fabric for his own clothes."

"Did you know that there are complex mathematics in the heel of a sock?" Matthew asked.

"Well, what constitutes complex mathematics for you, Cushla, is just common sense to me."

Laura had struck up what she insisted was just a 'friendship' with Gerry the light bender, which meant that she spent most of her free time with him and his family, who loved her, and why would they not? After all, she was their very own super-hero.

When they were together, Beth and Mikey lived in a world only lovers could inhabit, becoming more and more besotted as time passed. Beth passed her exams. She passed exams every year for many years and while she worked on her undergraduate studies, and then on her postgraduate studies, she dreamed dreams that would take years to realise.

With her family otherwise occupied, Emily felt the loss of Nan more than she could ever have imagined. Matthew and Renata were aware of this but knew it was not something they could fix.

"She'll work it through," Matt said. "She feels things more deeply than most. She just needs time."

In the lead up to the wedding, Beth had been helpful in this regard, since Emily sometimes eased her soul's pain by painting.

"I want you to consider the crypt your studio." Matthew had said. "At least until I am ready to renovate it, or until you become an established artist and have a swanky new one, whichever comes first." So the place that had once been painful to her, became a place where she felt enabled and healed.

Beth had agreed to stay at Nan's until Matt was ready to move in. Then she would move into his place. This suited Beth well because over the Christmas holiday, there was always a mass exodus from the units and houses that surrounded the University campus. It was the perfect time to surrender her share-house back to the landlord, who would fill it with next year's intake, now not far away. Matthew had agreed that just prior to the recommencement of the University year, he would be ready to move into Nan's, so any of the fellow tenants of her share-house, could move into the house he would be vacating.

"Of course they're not vandals," she assured him. "In fact most of them are quite house-proud."

"Which just leaves you, Beth. I will expect you to look after the house and not keep it like a pigsty."

"I won't. I promise." In the meantime Beth stayed at Nan's and, ever the philosopher, she would discuss, with her mother, the daily reminders of Nan that gradually sorting through her belongings brought up. For example, very soon after Nan's death, Beth found a reminder Nan had written to herself.

"Why would she write herself a note to make a Christmas cake – after all, there would be wedding cake?" Beth puzzled. In the end she asked her mother.

"I don't know. Perhaps because it would be the last one she would be able to make."

"Of course! I should have realised." A little later she said: "Let's make a Christmas cake for her then – well not exactly for her, but in her memory." Beth suggested.

"If we make a Christmas cake in her honour, we can't just make any old cake," said her mother. "You'll have to find her recipe – the one her mother handed down to her." This took Beth into other mysterious areas of Nan's life and the recipes she found conjured up Emily's childhood memories. So began an entirely new phase of story telling:

"The smells of home were strong when I was a child. I loved the mouth watering aroma of baking bread and the sweet, sticky, toffee smell of plum jam spitting into the gas flame."

"Who on earth makes their own bread?" Beth asked.

"Nan did - all the time, when I was little… in England."

"Why didn't she just buy bread?" Beth asked.

"It may surprise you to know, Beth, my dear, that sometimes, and in some countries, it's easier to stay at home and bake bread than to take kids out to the shops."

364

"Why?"

"Because people haven't always had cars, for starters." Emily heard her Mother's voice speaking through her. "Nor do they have such glorious weather as we do. In Australia, it doesn't matter if you go to the local shops practically naked, or without shoes. But in England, for example, in the winter, you have to dress kids up in warm clothes - and by that I mean waterproof suits, boots, scarves, hats, gloves. By the time you've dressed a second child, the first one's undressed again. Then you have to do it all again and, eventually, you get one child in the pram and the other sitting on it and trudge through the snow and ice, skidding all the way, wiping snotty noses, and trying to jolly whinging kids along. That's why Nan made bread. I still remember how the smell of delicious, mouth watering, baking bread used to permeate the entire house, warming it, and making it cosy on cold wintery days."

So Emily and Beth made Christmas cake, bread, and eggnog, in Nan's memory, and such discussions fed each other's need to understand, remember, accept and heal. Then each would retreat into her own private world, to use what she had learned in new ways. They both strived to reinterpret age-old issues, such as love, loss, happiness, grief, bliss and discontent. Emily produced canvas after canvas and because Beth was influential in Emily's self-discovery, she understood the depth and dimensions of her mother's art. In fact she became so passionate about her mother's talent that she helped to market her paintings. Soon Emily began to have small exhibitions that would lead her into a new future.

Introspective Beth delved into Nan's diaries. She became fascinated by the idea of internal worlds, especially her grandmother's. So it was that she was always finding new revelations, in old photos, letters, poems, scribbles, stories, and things worth noting, that Nan had left behind. The more she read what remained of Nan, the more she realised how much more there was to Nan than what was evident on the surface. Beth gathered together these precious pieces of memorabilia like pieces of a jigsaw that one day, when she put it all together, would portray the enigma of Nan. Thus, this time of grieving Nan was important to Beth's understanding of life and, therefore, to her growth. It would take many years before it would reach maturity, but in the meantime, when she and her mother were together, she would ask her endless questions.

"Do you think Nan went into the convent because she was happy? Unhappy? Do you think she might have been frigid? Was she more religious than most? Was she indoctrinated? Bullied? Loved? What made her who she was - someone that turned her back on the world and then someone who embraced it again later? What were her thought processes? Who was she at her innermost being?"

Of course Emily could not answer her daughter's many questions. But they would speculate, so bringing up more questions to add to Beth's already long list. Thus she postulated a thesis, which would later turn into a PhD. In support of her thesis, Beth would use Nan's story, embedding many philosophical theories in its pages, such as whether Nan's encounters with George Harrison and The Beatles were real? She did not attempt to define her grandmother. She would write of Nan as she had found her: grounded yet ethereal; serious yet joyful; predictable yet novel; strong yet gentle, kind yet disciplined, idealistic yet sacrilegious, practical and yet as nutty as the Christmas cake she loved to make. Beth would portray Nan as the enigma she was. She would portray her as someone to explore, rather than know.

But why write about Nan at all? Beth would ask herself frequently over the years. Who would be interested in such a woman? Finally she concluded that the answer was as enigmatic as Nan herself: Why? Nobody and everybody, of course!

"And a few million baby boomers, who still dig The Beatles," said Mikey.

366

"And those who, like me, really love a good Nun story," said Renata.

George Harrison, Beth thought, *would understand why she had written about her grandmother. His words will be the alpha and omega of my thesis, she decided, as she wrote them on the final page of her tribute to Nan.*

I asked myself
what right have I
to write this book?

It is a medium.

We either do it well
or badly.

All you can do
in the end
is to keep on doing
the best you can
for yourself

and try to keep

unattached.

George Harrison, I, Me, Mine: (1980)